THE EVIL EMPIRE OF CAL SCHANK

By Lionel A.W. Domreis

THE EVIL EMPIRE OF CAL SCHANK

By

Lionel A.W. Domreis

TIME TO RETURN TO THE 1950 S

Remember those years? The war was finally over and you were adjusting your lifestyle to peace. You weren't going to play war no more! It wasn't all that easy was it? Well, step back in time with Earnest Lange, 41st Infantry Division Veteran from Oregon, when he decides to move to Santa Barbara, but isn't sure just why. Soon he is involved with a mystery that brings in the New Chinatown Chinese Tong in Los Angeles, the Los Angeles Police Department and even the Australian Navy. The latter makes a dramatic rescue of a key witness from a South American Coastal City. There are dramatic scenes in The Los Angeles General Hospital and the Los Angeles County Courtroom. A touching love story between a Santa Barbara physician and his patient will charm you. Oh yes, the Villain is Cal Schank, who works from his luxurious Private Rail Car, 'The Schankrila.

CAST OF PRINCIPAL CHARACTERS & KEY SCENES

Cal Schank. The Villain who rules his evil empire from his private rail car. (Chapter 1)

Ruppert Snyder. His Los Angeles area Manager. (Chapter 1)

Della Robertson. A prisoner in South America. (Chapter 2)

Reginald Robertson. Her Father who fails to rescue her. (Chapter 2)

Earnest Lange. 41st Infantry Division Veteran who moves to Santa Barbara. (Chapter 3)

Bob Schank. Son and Santa Barbara Manager of Schank Investment Co. (Chapter 4)

Tony G. Newly retired Mob hit man. (Chapter 4)

Ah Wing, Delores (The Dragon Lady) Dr. Fu and Wang Sing, Tong Leader. (Chapter 9)

Maude Newberry. Penniless retired housekeeper. (Chapter 10)

Lt. Merced and Sgt. Andrew. Santa Barbara police officers. (Chapter 12)

Lt. Alex Brown, L.A. Detective and friend of the Chinese Tong. (Chapter 12)

Lode Owens, Georgia Peach from Atlanta and companion to Cal Schank. (Chapter 13)

Lexus Taylor, Attorney for Cal Schank. (Chapter 17)

Martha Schank. Cal Schank's estranged wife. Son Bob lives with her. (Chapter 18)

Dr. Emery Smith, widower and Physician for Martha Schank. (Chapter 20)

Taekwondo experts. (Chapter 22)

The surprising drama at Los Angeles General Hospital. (Chapter 24)

ISBN-10: 9780985809812

EAN-13: 0985809817

*This Novel is dedicated to my fellow Veterans
of World War II and The Korean War
who did not return.*

*MAY THEY ALWAYS BE REMEMBERED,
NEVER FORGOTTEN.*

TABLE OF CONTENTS

CHAPTER 1
CAL SCHANK

It was March 1950. Cal Schank, owner of Schank Investment Co, was seated in his Los Angeles office talking to his local manager, Ruppert Snyder. He slipped his hand inside his coat pocket taking out an envelope–and tossed it onto the desk between him and Ruppert.

"Here's a couple of pictures to add to our top secret file."

Ruppert's eyes opened just a trace wider and Schank observed a slight curve of anticipation on his lips. The envelope was sealed and he opened his desk drawer extracting a beautiful stainless steel letter opener, with which he carefully slit the envelope.

Then with a grin aimed at Schank he took out four pictures, laying them carefully before him on his desk. His eyes focused carefully on the pictures--he lifted each picture–slowly giving his full attention to whatever the pictures presented.

Finally he said, "Is that Senator Adix?"

"None other than the respected statesman in his birthday suit."

"Who did you get these from?"

"A lobbyist that had to pay a gambling debt."

"I don't know what you paid for them, **Cal, but these are dynamite!"**

"The right picture is worth a lot more than a thousand words. Worth more than gold!

"It's our Ft. Knox." Schank smiled, " Put those in our 'Rogue Vault."

Ruppert bit his tongue as he thought of the power Schank had over so many business and political leaders. He knew power corrupts. He thought of the role he was playing.

"I'm the Los Angeles Manager of the Evil Empire of Cal Schank."

Just then Ruppert's secretary rang through on the intercom, "Mr. Snyder, you told me to keep checking with the Union Station and I finally received word that 'The Lark' will be ready to depart in an hour and Mr. Schank's private rail car is being attached to The Lark right now."

"Thanks, Mildred."

Both men looked at each other and they knew it was time to go.

CHAPTER 2
DELLA ROBERTSON AND HER DAD REGINALD.

Della Robertson was once a carefree sun tanned Aussie beauty born and raised in the small northern tropical city of Rockhampton in the Province of Queensland. Now she was drugged and a prisoner in a small West coast city in South America.

The last she had seen of her father, Reginald, was when his attempt to rescue her failed. She knew he was in the hands of the military junta — unless he was already dead.

The strength and vitality of her youth kept her conscious enough to daily beg and cry for word about her father.

"As soon as he passes on I will commit suicide. I cannot go on like this, but I must wait until I know my Father's fate for certain."

She felt her world was ending-most any day would be her last.

Just as the mortally wounded soldier often would call for his Mother- Della's mind returned to those tender moments of her youth. "Daddy would be gone for months at a time. "Then he'd return to Brisbane, Sydney or Melbourne to unload cargo from his ship. He'd get leave for a few days-and I'd be Daddy's little girl again.

"**Those were precious days–now he's losing his life trying to save mine**.

"It's my fault–I never should have done what I did. My poor Mother's lost both of us.

"**It's not 'God save the Queen' anymore.** Dear God, could you somehow save my Dad's life for my Mother."

The crushing realism that her mistakes were ruining her parents lives made losing hers seem insignificant. Della fainted–there was no one in the room to help her.

Until the last three months Reginald Robertson truly exemplified the rugged Australian male. He was born 49 years ago also in Rockhampton, better known as Rocky.

It was located about half way between Brisbane and Townsville. The homes were built on stilts giving its people an outdoor basement, without walls, and level with the ground. Life was meager for it's residents. Bicycles were an acceptable way for men to travel.

The beautiful Australian coast was less than 25 miles away. The nearest tiny coastal city was Yeppoon, hardly more than a fly speck on the vast coast line. Limited development of that vast continent challenged these pioneers turning the males into rugged men fully equal to any Errol Flynn. And gave their women true grit.

Reginald shipped out as a seaman when he was 18. He married his Rockhampton girl friend on his first leave. It was urgent–she was pregnant.

He sailed on one of the thousands of small Dutch boats moving cargo and people between the hundreds of large and small islands dotting that part of the Pacific ocean.

Now, he lay bruised and beaten on the floor of a tiny jail in South America. His mind was delirious. **Nature's gracious way of turning reality into oblivion.**

CHAPTER 3
EARNEST LANGE

Earnest Lange grew up in Portland, Oregon. During his third year at the University of Oregon he was drafted. Inducted into the U.S. Army June 25, 1941.

He had scarcely finished basic training in the desert at Camp Roberts, California when Pearl Harbor turned life into World War II.

After basic training he was tossed into the 41st Infantry Division which received the dubious distinction of being the first Infantry Division to be sent overseas.

It was a strange coincidence General Douglas MacArthur escaped from the Philippines the same day major units of the 41st left for the Pacific.

When MacArthur said, "I will return," as he looked at the 41st Division and the other few forces sent for him to command it looked impossible. Japanese forces were quickly taking island after island.

This March 1950 Lange was seated in the living room of Alise Merchant in Oregon City, Oregon located about 15 miles from Portland.

"Alise, it's time for me to take off. Got to get some sleep so I can start for Santa Barbara early tomorrow morning."

"So much has happened since we met a year ago. Now, with my folks almost killed in a car accident I had to move in to take care of them. It doesn't seem fair–not for my folks or myself. How about you? How do you really feel about all of this?"

"Alise, my dear, you brought the first real female companionship into my life I have ever enjoyed. Maybe I'm running from my wife who deserted me while I was overseas–**maybe I'm just running because I don't know any better.**"

"**No, Lange,** you had me read the life of Sir Arthur Conan Doyle, who wrote the Sherlock Holmes stories. You aren't running–you are going to Santa Barbara for a purpose. **For some unknown reason you are needed there more than you are needed here.**"

"You're a sweet lady, Alise–I wish I had your faith and your wisdom."

"Quit picking on yourself Lange — I'll always love you–even though I am much older than you are. You don't have to marry someone to love and respect them. You'll do great in Santa Barbara–I'm going to pray for you each day you are gone."

Lange and Alise embraced–and she walked him to his small blue coupe parked outside her folk's home. There were tears in their eyes as they parted.

Lange left Portland by 7 A.M. the next morning. He didn't make it quite to Sacramento the first night. He had driven in the dark long enough and his eyes, mind and physical weariness told him he had to stop driving and get some rest.

He was again on the road early the next morning. As he went through the town of Salinas he counted the number of heads of lettuce trucks dropped and the number was sizable.

He knew he was less than 100 miles from Camp Roberts, where he was in the last group of recruits to complete training before Pearl Harbor. As he passed through the small community of King City he thought of that summer of 1941 and the 115 degree temperatures. "I thought it was misery, but I never knew true misery until we hit the New Guinea jungle."

Lange paused at the Camp Roberts gate and realized there were too many memories inside to cope with right then–so he drove on slowly looking at the rows of barracks easily visible from the highway. "I got $21.00 a month, less $6.60 for Insurance for a net of $14..40. "Then I went overseas at $30.00 a month, plus $6.00 overseas pay, less $6.60 insurance for a net of $29.40. **And if you died overseas during the month you never got full pay for the month.** You only got paid through the day you died."

Then he tried to laugh as he grimly thought of the $1.00 per month Camp Roberts laundry charge he saved by going overseas wearing the same filthy clothes day and night.

He continued South and passed through San Miguel, with the old Mission right on the Hiway-then through Paso Robles, San Louis Obispo and Santa Maria. He had a quick late dinner at Anderson's Inn at Buellton, including some of their famous Split Pea Soup.

He was now a mere 50 miles from Santa Barbara–yes it was 'D" day in a different way. He asked himself for the thousandth time, **"Why am I doing this?"**

Within 90 minutes he had pulled off 101 into Goleta and taken Hollister Avenue which turned into upper State Street in Santa Barbara. On that road he found Bam's Auto Court where he rented a tiny cottage which barely had room for a bed, tiny kitchen and bath.

Lange took one suitcase inside, took a shower and virtually collapsed onto the bed. It was December 1944 when Lange after almost 3 years in the 41st Infantry Division in the South Pacific had returned and been assigned to the Redistribution at Santa Barbara.

When his ship arrived in San Francisco there was no greeting from either the Military or any public thanks. The soldiers were given a paper bag with two baloney sandwiches which most men in disgust fed to the sea gulls. After reaching Camp Stoneman he called his wife.

She said, "I won't be down to see you. I am in love with someone else."

His first Christmas Eve was spent sitting in a coffee shop drinking coffee by himself. Still the city was a magnificent place to arrive at after life in the jungle where hepatitis, jungle rot, dysentery, malaria, dengue fever and the Japanese were the daily bill of fare. In her own special way Santa Barbara was perhaps like a beautiful irresistible lady one could never forget.

CHAPTER 4
CAL SCHANK & RUPPERT SNYDER
GO TO SANTA BARBARA

Cal Schank and Ruppert Snyder sat in the back seat of the company 1948 Lincoln Continental V-12, one of the first true luxury automobiles built after the war. The Company chauffeur drove as close to the entrance of the Union Station as permitted.

He jumped out and opened the door on the side Schank was sitting. Ruppert exited on the same side. Schank carried a gold trimmed black leather briefcase.

The Chauffeur doubled as a bodyguard for Ruppert. He was as nimble as might be expected for an ex-prize fighter. His broken nose and battered ears illustrated the beating that body appendages take in the ring. He quickly opened the trunk of the Lincoln and took out a large Samsonite two suiter belonging to Ruppert.

Several porters were hoping to be the first one to grab the luggage.

Schank and Ruppert strode through the Union Station with a self assurance that was not shown by the other arrivals. They exited the building leading onto the train tracks without offering any tickets to the ticket checkers. Instead they received a hearty, "Good afternoon, Gentlemen," and this was followed by a salute from the gate attendant.

The train was centered just outside the station making minimum walking distance for it's passengers. The two men strode like Sea Captains to the end of the train. Attached to the Lark, the classy overnight Southern Pacific between Los Angeles and the San Francisco Bay area, was a private railway car.

The name Schankrila was etched in gold letters, a high class version of vanity plates.

Those private mansions on wheels had every bit the class of a multimillion dollar yacht. Their versatility far exceeded their water bound luxury counterparts. Not only was seasickness eliminated, but they were impervious to weather conditions. When ice and snow, winds and rain pouring in sheets closed the highways and airports the trains could still move. .

On the outside, a private railway car was sixty feet of steel, built by Pullman, American Car and Foundry and others. **The interiors were virtually carved from rare woods, and decorated with the finest furniture, drapes and linens.**

Private bedrooms, parlors with pianos, complete kitchens and observation platforms scarcely touch on the costly ornate interiors. Suffice it to say money was no object.

On board ladies dressed in their finest gowns. It was the top of the ladder and the ultimate travel style for business and society–an ego trip beyond compare.

Schank and Ruppert were both agile and didn't need the step stool to board. In 15 minutes the train would pull out, but the Schankrila would only go approximately 100 miles north to Santa Barbara, the first of very few stops the fast Lark made.

Santa Barbara was a legendary beautiful Coastal City. Until the end of World War II it was claimed every big name in American Industry and Society owned an estate in adjacent Montecito.

Schank's visit to Santa Barbara this day in March 1950 was forced. Schank had received his original financing from a Chicago mob family. That was 25 years ago. Recently he had been informed that Tony G., the top hit man for that family, was retiring with a new wife and moving from Chicago to Santa Barbara. That shocked and dismayed Schank as he knew retirement was uncharacteristic of powerful men.

Then Schank received word that Tony wanted an immediate meeting with him. Schank's son Bob ran his Santa Barbara operation putting Tony in Bob's backyard. **Schank knew there would be hell to pay** and expected Tony to muscle in and disrupt Bob's operation.

As the train got under way, Wan, the Chinese Steward appeared and both men ordered some Pacific Northwest smoked salmon and bottles of Schlitz. Schank said to Sammy, his bodyguard, "Take a few winks of shut eye so you will be wide awake this evening."

As soon as the salmon and beer arrived Schank turned to Ruppert, "I'm so damn mad at Tony G. demanding this meeting I've been tempted to tell him to go to hell."

Ruppert responded with, "Cal, I'm sure you have got yourself prepared for this meeting. Why don't we change the subject."

"O.K. Ruppert. Tell me a little about the deal you will be working with this evening."

"Just the usual stuff, Cal. I'm meeting Mavis Scott at the Mar Monte. She has been talking to an old guy by the name of Potter. One of those old Seniors in Montecito. He has some stock in an old corporation and Mavis has been trying to get it off his hands for as cheap as possible."

"So why didn't she?"

"Well, you know how that goes. She sold the old bird on the idea that she is just a poor working gal and is doing him a favor. He's a little smarter than she suspected and he said he will go for the deal if her boss gives his signature on the deal–and he wants to meet the boss."

Schank laughed. "She is a nice kid–you're kind of sweet on her yourself. Maybe you just dreamed all this up so you could spend a couple of days with Mavis away from the office?"

"Now why would I ever think of something like that?"

"You know we men all have that same affliction–it's called women. We want to love them and leave them, but it's easier said than done."

"You having more trouble with Lorie Owens?"

"When haven't I had trouble with her? I've got to get rid of her."

"That's a subject I'd better stay off, Cal."

"Tonight I have to concentrate on Tony G. while you go off frolicking with that cute Mavis Scott. Wish we could change places for the next couple of days."

"I didn't know you liked Mavis."

"I've got eyes haven't I?"

"You and everyone else. She sure is a nice kid."

Schank turned in his swivel chair to watch the scenery hoping he could relax a little.. By the time the Schankrila reached Ventura for the run virtually along the edge of the beautiful blue Pacific his apprehension and anger were fighting for first place.

They passed through Carpinteria, the foothills of Montecito and into the City of Santa Barbara. It was dark as the train pulled into the small Spanish style station.

Bob was nervously waiting for his Dad. He didn't dare be a minute late. He was driving a 1947 Cadillac 62 series. His Dad had purchased it new in Los Angeles and given it to him as a gift. Schank got off his private car as soon as the train stopped to unload and load the few passengers and detach his private rail car. Santa Barbara was such a small city it merited a stop because it's residents had the money to travel extensively, and had influence.

Schank had already given instructions. Ruppert was to stay on board until the private car was detached from the Lark, which was headed for Oakland. He would also remain on board until Lorie's food had been delivered to her room.

Then Sammy could eat and the Chinese cook and steward, Choy and Wan, would eat whenever they felt like it. Schank's instructions to Sammy were loud and clear, "No one else except Ruppert would be leaving the rail car tonight."

Schank and his son Bob drove the short distance to Bob's office.

For Ruppert it was only a half dozen blocks walk from the train station to the Mar Monte. The walk was mostly on Cabrillo Blvd. The wide palm tree lined street bore the name of the Spanish Explorer who came into the Santa Barbara channel in 1842.

His name was Juan Rodriguez Cabrillo. Not until 1919 did the City of Santa Barbara take it upon themselves to recognize the explorer who sailed for Spain by naming the street for him and installing a bronze plaque.

That walk was an adventure in itself. Walking from the train station directly to Cabrillo you first were thrilled by the moorage of hundreds of boats of all sizes. Next came Stearns Wharf jutting some distance into the Pacific. The wide spacious boulevard was further enhanced by the well kept green grass, the palm trees, the sandy beach.

All bordering the beautiful Pacific that had lured mankind since Cabrillo's discovery.

Ruppert Snyder knew nothing in Los Angeles compared to that walk. So it was that after carefully stepping from the Schankrila **he set off briskly for Cabrillo Blvd.** and the Mar Monte Hotel. The latter was set on the north side of Cabrillo Blvd.

As Ruppert cut across the tracks from the rail station a nondescript looking vehicle was parked nearby. Under it's hood was an engine tuned to perfection. At any speed it hardly made a sound. The driver turned on the engine and car moved to where Ruppert was headed. The car stayed sufficiently behind Ruppert until the driver and the man beside him noticed two men step out of the shadows. **Each man gripped one of Ruppert's arms.** That was the signal they were waiting for.

One man had stuffed a gag into Ruppert's mouth. The other slipped his hand inside Ruppert's coat removing the snub nosed .38 caliber revolver from the holster under his left armpit. Ruppert's arms were twisted behind him and handcuffs snapped on them.

At the moment the car arrived the man seated beside the driver stepped outside, opened the back door of the car and quickly moved into the rear of the car.

The two men who had accosted Ruppert moved swiftly. They threw Ruppert into the back seat. The man already in the back seat instantly checked the handcuffs and the gag in Ruppert's mouth. One of the two men stepped into the back seat.

The other shut the back door, moved swiftly into the front seat and the car moved ahead just as he closed the front door quickly. **None of the men said a word.**

The car moved up Cabrillo Blvd. and then turned away. It crossed Hiway 101 and turned up Sycamore Canyon Rd. After turning off Sycamore it continued finally turning into a secluded lane. Barely visible tall walls, an iron gate and the shadows of an unlighted estate.

The front seat passenger got out, inserted a key, and the gate opened quickly and silently. Seeing the gate move brought a smile to the driver, but his lips remained sealed.

They loved that gate. It was a special love that men had for mechanical things.

The car moved through the gate and it closed automatically. The man outside stood observing it. He checked that it was locked. Only then did he get back inside the car.

Many years ago the estate had hosted fine dinners, with lovely, exquisitely dressed ladies and men in tuxedoes. It had known the smiles and laughter of children. Tonight it was dark and foreboding. The shrubbery had purposely not been trimmed for several years.

The outlines of the buildings could now be seen. The vehicle moved slowly and almost silently to what appeared to be a garage or large shed. One of the men opened one set of doors. The car moved inside.

A dark sack was placed over Ruppert's head and he was pulled from the car.

Ruppert's heart was beating wildly. He felt certain his death was only moments away.

His hands and feet were then bound together. "They are going to kill me someplace else. Maybe I'll be tossed over a cliff into the ocean."

Then the men were lifting him up slightly, moving him a short distance and he was lowered and moved a little. Then he heard the trunk lid slam. His heart beat even faster.

He heard the motor start–and the doors of the car slam. The car did not back up. It moved forward slowly. "I've been moved from one car to another," he knew, as his mind raced as madly as his heart. He felt like the condemned man just before his execution.

Maybe someone had prepared a nice cement burial spot for me. Perhaps under the driveway of a new house being built where I might be discovered 200 years from now.

As the car moved he could tell most of the turns were to the left. Shortly the turns and twisting seemed to stop. It seemed to him they were moving much faster and the road was smoother. He said to himself, "We are going South on Hiway 101. "

His mind went to the many times he had driven that road South on 101. Where would be a good place to dispose of him. These men had been smooth! They knew exactly what they were doing. **"I'm on my way out of this world.** Better that I don't know how or how soon."

CHAPTER 5
THE SCHANKS VISIT WITH TONY G. AND TILLIE

Many of the owners of private rail cars were industrialists who fought their way up the ladder of business and politics. Most had an underlying toughness that enabled them to push their way through the murky waters of the ordinary.

Many had struck gold or silver–others were barons of steel, timber, shipping and general industry. A few like the Vanderbilts were part of financial dynasties.

None were any tougher than Cal Schank. His 5'10" frame looked as solid as the steel forge he was working at when others were still in high school. Now in his mid 50's his scalp was still well represented with hair. Time had changed it's color from very dark to gray. Only too often an executive crossed the line and became a dictator. **Schank had crossed it.**

His face was swarthy. His lips had a belligerence which matched his eyes. His head was large and set on powerful shoulders. The rest of his body carried the same lines.

His weight topped 200 pounds. His hands were rough and large. He could have been a lineman had he gone to high school. Instead he had enrolled in the school of hard knocks early.

Tonight as he and Bob pulled into the parking lot a green Packard was waiting. One man stepped outside and with an intimidating tone said, **"Tony is in the car. Get in!"**

Schank wasn't used to this kind of treatment. His eyes connected with Tony's face seeing it's usual smirk. Schank and Bob stepped into the rear compartment of the Packard and were greeted with, "Great to see ya, Cal. Going to be great to work wid ya. So this is the kid. Pleased to meetcha, Bob."

Schank extended his hand saying, "Hello."

Bob repeated his Dad's obvious reluctant greeting.

The driver and Tony's guard sat in front. The Packard left the small business district and soon was winding it's way up the beautiful hills of Montecito. The dense foliage had been carefully planted to obscure the magnificent ocean view estates from anyone driving by..

The high walls and wrought iron gates were so formidable one would not have found it strange if armed guards stood solemnly at attention alongside the entrances.

Tony rattled on as they drove. **"You've come a long ways, Schank,** since Grandpa loaned you the money to get started."

Schank sensed that Tony was in one of those moods to tell and not listen and he was grateful not to be asked questions and have his son, Bob, see him squirm. But he knew before that green Packard took him back to Bob's parking lot there would be hell to pay.

They were greeted by Tillie, Tony's buxom, blond, former show girl wife. She played the gracious hostess well. She greeted them cordially and was solicitous as to their health.

Bob thought to himself, "No matter how nice she is I've never seen Dad so uncomfortable and worried."

Tillie insisted on a guided tour and mid-way through it Tony looked at Schank and blurted out, "Don't ya have a palace like this in Montecito?"

Schank replied, "Yes and no. You know my wife and I have been separated for five years and she lives there."

Tony continued with, "Where ya live, Bob?"

Bob had been told to say absolutely nothing and Schank stepped in with, "Bob lives with his Mother and looks after things."

Tony's wife enthusiastically chanted, "That's so nice, Bob. Tony and I would like to have you and your Mother over for dinner soon."

Bob's mind squirmed in desperation, "What do I answer to that?"

Again his Dad intervened, "Tillie, that is very gracious of you. We do believe its best not to be too social with our business associates."

"Oh that's not right, Cal. We're all family you know. Tony and I are both kind of lonely with our family and friends still in Chicago."

Tony's wife joined them for dinner and fortunately for the Schanks Tillie and Tony both rattled on during the entire dinner. With dinner over the Schanks thanked Tillie and Tony for the fine dinner. Then Tony a trace of dignity in his voice and bearing said,

"Cal and Bob, let's us retire to my study."

Schank thought, "There is nothing retiring about this bird."

Tony lost no time in getting down to business. He reaffirmed in non-parlor talk how he had become bored with not doing anything. His wife, who had pushed him to retire and buy the estate, was happy, but Tony was not.

Then Tony leaned back in his chair and put his feet on the massive, expensive and imposing dark mahogany desk.

"Youse a real operator. Before Grandpa died he told Dad you was doing real good and you'd come up with something big. Grandpa didn't say much more about your operation. "We knows youse is a high class loan shark and youse buy into anything where you can make fast bucks, **but that ain't all youse is doing is it, Cal?"**

"Your Grandpa and Dad have left me alone. Why do you want to get involved in my business?"

"Hey pal, I just want to help. My old man told me it was time for me to get out of my old racket. He told me to look into what you are doing an' kinda keep track on yah."

"I'll be in Chicago in the next month. Tell your Dad I'd like to discuss things with him as he's the top man."

"I guess that's legit, Cal. I'll tell the old man you'll be calling him for a meeting. I want to work wid ya, Cal. I knows I kin help ya."

As Bob continued to look at his Dad he realized Schank was not the top dog at this meeting. **His Dad looked more like the Dogface chronicled in Bill Mauldin's drawings than the formidable Schank.**

CHAPTER 6
THE SCHANKS RETURN TO BOB'S OFFICE.

Tony's men drove Schank and his son, Bob, back to the Schank Investment Company office. Schank said to Bob, "Let's go into your office and talk a little about your operation."

Bob was unlocking the door when he heard the phone ring. As Bob hurried and got the phone he listened for a moment and then turned to his Dad.

Schank was laughing. "You want some privacy, Bob? Some gal chasing you?"

"No! It's a lady, but it's for you, Dad."

Taken aback a little Schank responded, "For me? Did she give her name?"

"Yes, Mavis Scott."

"O.K. I'll take it Bob. Hello, Mavis, what can I do for you?"

An obviously agitated voice said, "Let me talk to Ruppert."

"He's not here, Mavis. We left the Schankrila before he did."

"I know the train was late. What time do you guess he left for the Mar Monte where I was supposed to meet him for dinner?"

"Several hours ago for sure. You mean you haven't seen him this evening?"

"He surely called you, didn't he?"

"I haven't had any conversation from him since the middle of the afternoon. I called him to make certain he was coming up and he said the train was delayed for perhaps an hour.

"I checked with the Santa Barbara station and they said the train came in and your private car was detached. I apologize for being so curt, Mr. Schank. I just figured – well, you know–I guess I thought maybe you told him to come with you."

Then Mavis continued with, "Did he bring a girl friend up with him on the trip and have to stash her in some other hotel? You know how he gets around."

Cal knew Ruppert wasn't any worse than he was. "No, Mavis he didn't have anyone with him and told me he was going directly to the Mar Monte to have dinner with you. You know it's only a few blocks and he wanted to walk those half dozen blocks to get some of the travel out of his bones. **Are you calling from your room?**"

"Yes. I rented two adjacent rooms. The door is open between them."

"Mavis, you know we don't call the Police, but I'm going to have Bob make a call or two. Maybe he got hit by a car or fell and is injured. Give me your room and phone number.. Bob or I will call you back in fifteen minutes. **Meanwhile say nothing to anyone!**"

Bob made several calls. The police said there were no accidents or ambulance calls in the past hour. Schank had poured himself a drink and had drained his glass. He kept voicing tough guy expletives which did nothing to reduce the intensity of his concern.

"Dad, was Ruppert on anyone's list that you know of?"

"I can think of several guys we have stepped on pretty hard, but no one in particular. **And why would they grab him in Santa Barbara?** Los Angeles would make more sense. Right now I am wondering if you and I need any protection. Is it possible that someone grabbed Ruppert **and we are next tonight?**"

With those words Bob's face paled. "Do you really mean that, Dad?"

"Right now I'm thinking this office is a lonesome spot to be. I'd rather be at the Mar Monte. We need to add some muscle. Call The Shadow. Let me talk to him."

The Shadow was in and Schank was terse with him.

"Grab all the firepower you have and get over to Bob's office in five minutes."

"What's happened? I'm not a gunman for hire you know."

"Ruppert is missing. He was supposed to meet Mavis at the Mar Monte. He never showed. Don't waste time asking me questions. Just get over here fast."

Bob called Mavis and said they would be there in a few minutes. They had no news. The Shadow was there in ten minutes. He lived in a small nondescript apartment less than a mile away. Schank decided they would take both cars, but he would ride with the Shadow. They were on their way to the Mar Monte Hotel.

CHAPTER 7
MAVIS SCOTT

Mavis was beside herself with fear and anxiety. "I've come a long ways, but what am I mixed up in now? Has Ruppert been snatched and done away with?"

She was raised in the small northern California town of Redding. Small towns had a habit of giving kids a special freshness and excitement you didn't get in a crammed apartment where your only playground was concrete.

Redding was also a genuine outdoors town. Sunshine, snow, hunting, fishing, boating, you name it. Redding had it. Beautiful Mount Shasta and the beautiful lakes created by the melting snow. Redding was also a lumbering town with lots of timber and lumber mills.

Living an outdoor life was good for her face, figure and vitality. Her medium height was trim and her pretty face was further enhanced by long hair with a reddish tint made more attractive with it's natural curl. **She was a saucy, peppy, cute gal everyone liked.**

She acted in every play she could in grade school and high school. Everyone, but her boy friend, who worked in a service station, said she was a natural actress. Upon graduation from high school she took off for Hollywood.

After her few dollars were gone for living expenses she took a job as a waitress. She found out how much more cocktail waitresses were making so she changed to that work.

All this was occurring at the end of the War. **She enjoyed all the soldiers and sailors at the U.S.O.** She used to say, "I'm not a movie star, but the servicemen treat me like one!"

Mavis practiced her acting on everyone. It seemed to work for everyone except a genuine film scout. Los Angeles had more than it's share of smooth operators who claimed they had connections to the top of the film world.

When the war ended some of the rougher crowd at a couple lounges got ideas about her. She took a few wrong steps with the wrong people and had a couple of hard falls.

By the time she fully realized she was running in the wrong circles she was in too deep to get out. Those people were both insistent and threatening.

Ruppert took a shine to her and one day she found she was indirectly involved with him. That was her "D day". Her disaster day. She knew Ruppert was skating on thin ice and she was one of his skating partners. Ruppert was a "hard ball" and the longer you were associated with him the less likely he would accept "no" from you. You were his slave!

She was realizing Ruppert had been stepping on a lot of toes and it was beginning to be **difficult to figure how many of his friends weren't really his enemies.**

When Bob, Cal Schank and The Shadow arrived at the Mar Monte Bob called Mavis from the lobby and they went up to her room. Mavis said, "Still no word from Ruppert."

"The room isn't registered to Ruppert?" asked Schank.

"No, both rooms are registered to me. Ruppert was that way. He never wanted his name to be on any hotel register. Didn't want to leave any trail."

"So if he never shows up no one will be the wiser," commented Cal Schank.

"I guess that's the way it is."

"Mavis, Ruppert briefed me on what he was up here for. I want you to promise me that is confidential."

"Hey, in our business the leaky faucet leaves a trail. I'm like the three monkeys. I hear no evil, see no evil and say nothing. That way I can't be quoted."

"O.K. Mavis, that's what I wanted to hear."

"We're sure a gloomy and apprehensive foursome. Let me add a little humor. During the war, at the U.S.O. I danced a few dances with a Marine on leave from Camp Pendleton. He told me his boot camp non-com told him, 'Keep your mouth shut and your bowels open.'

"I told Ruppert that was my motto. He said everyone would live longer if they followed that. I was never sure if that was a threat."

Bob laughed and said, "That's the same kind of advice my Dad gives me."

That even brought a half smile to the very unsettled Schank. He said to himself, "No doubt about it. Mavis knows the right answers. Ruppert always did say Mavis was one in a million in that regard."

Just then there was a knock on her door and all three men jumped up from where they were sitting. "Relax guys! I'm starved and ordered myself some dinner."

Schank quickly replied, "We'll all go in the next room and lock the door. Let us know when the room steward is gone. I've got a phone call to make anyhow."

A few minutes later Mavis opened her side of the adjoining door and knocked. "It was my dinner. The steward is gone and my outside door is locked."

Schank replied, "Finish your dinner and keep your door locked. Don't call the room steward to pick up your tray. We'll try to come to some conclusions meanwhile."

Schank went to the phone and made a call to Los Angeles. When it was answered he said, **"I want to talk to Travis."**

"In case he is not in who shall I tell him is calling?"

"If he is out you tell me where he is, or else you won't have a job after 30 minutes."

"Just hold please."

Schank was on hold for several minutes and finally an irritated gruff voice came on the line. "I'm here, who is calling?"

"Don't ask any questions. Just listen. Ruppert came up with me and walked from the station. It's about six blocks and three hours later and he hasn't arrived at the Mar Monte yet."

"I'll be damned. He might stand up some other babe, but not Mavis. He'd do most anything for her including cut my throat."

"Quite your bitching. Just get your driver and his most reliable pal. Load them in your LaSalle special, along with plenty of ammunition and get here as fast as you can.

"Don't change clothes. Don't eat. Don't even go to the bathroom. Just get here fast. The Mar Monte Hotel. And damn it, don't tell anyone where you are going. Not even your men."

"I hear you and I'm on my way."

"Don't keep me waiting. I'm in an ugly mood."

With that out of the way Schank yelled at The Shadow, "Get Mavis in here."

When Mavis entered Schank said to The Shadow, "Go into Mavis's room. Stay alert. I want to talk to her privately."

With the door shut and Mavis seated Schank started in. "We're going to be leaving in the morning. I want you to stay in your room the rest of the night and check out in the morning. **"Bob will line up a couple of rooms for Travis.** I'll stay with Travis. The Shadow will stay in this room. Rap on his door if you have a question. You pay for these two rooms in the morning. If the room clerk questions you just say Bob and some of his friends used it."

"I'll do just as you say."

" Don't I recall you grew up in Redding?"

"Yes, I did."

"Contact the man you and Ruppert were to meet in Montecito. Tell him you have to return to your home town for a few days and your boss didn't make it this trip.

"Then go to Redding! Stay there and on the third day call Bob. If you have to leave a message use the name Susie and give the number backwards.

Then Schank opened his billfold and took out a thousand dollar bill and two one hundred dollar bills. He handed them to Mavis.

Mavis said, "Thank you, Mr. Schank."

She observed his face. She had never seen it look so strained. **She wondered if all the Napoleons looked like that when their Waterloos appeared on their horizons.**

Schank and Travis and his two men left in the LaSalle at sunrise. His son, Bob, and The Shadow went ahead of them to the train station where the Schankrila was expecting to be connected to the early morning Lark headed back to Los Angeles. Bob informed Sammy, the bodyguard, the train was to return to LA on schedule, but without Schank.

No other information was relayed to Sammy. The Shadow was instructed to be Bob's bodyguard for the next couple of days until Schank personally instructed him otherwise.

CHAPTER 8
SCHANK RETURNS TO LOS ANGELES WITHOUT RUPPERT

A half hour after daylight, Schank, Travis and his two men turned onto Hiway 101 at State Street. Fifteen minutes later their bulletproof LaSalle was passing through the tiny coastal city of Carpinteria. From Carpinteria 101 ran close to the ocean for the next 30 miles and when it reached Ventura they turned inland to Los Angeles headed for Schank's LA office.

Schank and Travis were in the back seat. The early morning sun sparkling on the blue Pacific failed to bring any cheer to the gloom surrounding them.

Each had known fear, but this time it was on a much higher level. One of them was missing. Finally Schank broke the silence. **"I guess I always expected someone to hit one of us. I think if we sit back and don't panic someone is going to contact us."**

"Got any strong feelings?"

"Not anything I'm sure of. Still evaluating."

"You sure took me by surprise with that call. I think I'm getting too old to be running around late at night."

"That's not what you tell your girl friends is it?"

"I used to think I had the world by the tail owning a couple of night clubs with a bevy of luscious gals to choose from. Ever since I met Mavis Scott I wished I could junk it all and settle down with her. But that damn Ruppert wouldn't let me get close to her."

"So maybe you got rid of him."

"There have been a couple of times I wished he would just disappear. Say now, maybe I will have a chance at Mavis. Where is she going?"

"That's my business. That subject is closed–understand?"

"I could tell you were pleased he disappeared. Believe me if someone has grabbed him we've got big problems. If someone wants to take over my operation you'll be out, too."

Soon they were entering the mainstream of morning traffic in Los Angeles. Cars and trucks going a minimum of seventy miles an hour on five and six lanes of traffic. Ramps off and on. Vehicles dodging in and out like swarms of racing ants.

The night air had cleared only a little of yesterdays smog. Soon the morning bedlam of cars and trucks would bring it back.

The surrounding hills made Los Angeles like a giant cup of coffee filled with carbon monoxide instead of caffeine and motorists whose nerves were frazzled.

As they neared Ruppert's office Schank broke the silence again, "I feel like the Captain of a ship caught in a sudden storm. My ship has been breached by a gigantic wave."

"Almost sounds like you have a premonition of disaster. That's a hot topic for discussion. For me good common sense is best, which is also giving me bad vibes."

"We're in it too deep to get out. If we did we'd be like Tony G. and want to get back into action again."

Soon they were entering the Los Angeles office of Schank Investment Co. The office secretary was very surprised to see them. "Where is Ruppert?" she immediately asked.

"Ruppert has some other business to take care of. I'll be here for a couple of days and take care of things while Ruppert is gone," came Schank's reply in a tone that also said, "Subject is closed."

The coils of the Los Angeles Octopus of Schank Enterprises was a writhing body of activity. It was easy for Ruppert to start a project and hard for him to successfully follow through. Schank knew things were out of control.

Too many irons in the fire. Too many holes in the dike for the fingers of one man to plug. Schank had correctly concluded Ruppert had to be replaced. Now someone else had taken Ruppert and what had they done to him? Was Schank next?

Schank continued with, "Where's Ruppert's schedule for the day?"

"I have a list of things that we need to do. I make it daily on my own. But Ruppert never follows it."

Mildred handed Schank 3 pages.

"What the hell! Three pages of pressing matters. Mildred, just tell me what is the most urgent!"

"Mr. Schank, we're hopping around trying to keep from being burned. It's perhaps just my intuition, but we are getting pretty far out on a limb with the Chinese–they want a meeting with you–**if you don't mind my saying so I think it should be soon."**

Just then the switchboard transferred a call to Ruppert's office. Mildred took the phone,

looked at Schank and said, **"It's Wang Sing, the head of the biggest Chinese Tong in Los Angeles,** will you take it?"

"Damned if I do. Damned if I don't. Guess the fat is really in the fire. I'll take the call."

CHAPTER 9
AH WING, DELORES AND DR. FU.

Ah Wing was a Chinese leader, diminutive in size, but well known for his intelligence, compassion and ability to bring opposing factions together. Born in China he became a cook's helper on a tramp freighter, sailing from one port to another around the world.

Lange had met him first about 20 years ago. Under most unusual circumstances.

When Lange was in the third grade, in 1930, he worked his way down N.E. Broadway and Sandy Blvd. to the Portland waterfront selling the Saturday Evening Post. It was a thrill for him to walk up a ship's gangplank and sell the Post. He would fantasize he was going to sail away as a cabin boy, **and see the world.**

Ah Wing was then a full fledged cook having mastered the art remarkably well. Next on his agenda was to learn to read English. His first Post purchase was from Lange, the young lad who was so obviously awed to be on a tramp freighter.

When the war started Dec. 7, 1941, Ah Wing's ship had the dubious distinction of being one of the first to be torpedoed. He was rescued only to be sunk again. Rescued once more he was grateful his company had run out of ships to be sunk. His ability to read and speak English, as well as Chinese found him a job as an interpreter.

After the war he became a Chinese diplomat and philosopher without compare. When questioned by a stranger he would humbly remark, "Cook has to deal with all kinds of crazy stomachs. Make one excellent diplomat." How he renewed his friendship with Lange was in true Sir Arthur Conan approved fashion.[1]

Delores Lee was Ah Wing's secretary and confidant. She had a remarkable likeness to what some claimed to be the Dragon Lady. She was very beautiful and born in China.

Her husband lost his life as a Chinese Infantryman fighting the Japanese.

Last year, when she met Lange for the first time, she confided in him that she saw the same haunted look in Lange's eyes she remembered her husband had.

That was when he received a few days medical leave. She felt drawn to Lange in such an intense manner that it challenged her composure at first. **At times, when she looked at Lange, it was almost as if her husband had returned to her — as Lange.**

To Lange she was a miracle of charm and beauty. Someone he was in awe of and yet he knew she was unobtainable for him and they could never fully mesh.

She knew it was up to her to clear the decks. She told him one evening, in the tiny apartment she used when she visited the Portland Chinese Tong headquarters, "It's not to be, Lange. There exists an eternal flame between you and me. I am grateful for that. We cannot fan it beyond what it is as I am Chinese and must serve my people as an assistant to Ah Wing."

Then she would stare at him–her eyes riveted to his. Neither dared say a word more.

Dr. Fu was a tall impressive Chinese. His appearance and actions made one think of the literary character Dr. Fu Man Chu, also chronicled in the Saturday Evening Post. A man of few words who was called in only when the most serious decisions had to be made.

After Lange had helped solve a major world wide mystery last year Dr. Fu had said to Lange, "Without question young man, you were Chinese in your prior life."

Lange replied, "Would you tell Delores that?"

The tall Dr. Fu paused for several moments before he slowly replied, "I have been responsible for the lives of many in my time. I have also gambled at high stakes with leaders of the world. What is between you and Delores is what you Americans call in the sports world, 'Out of bounds,' but let me say in the strictness of confidence if Delores were my daughter and you asked for my permission to marry her I would say yes."

With that Dr. Fu had extended his hand to Lange. After shaking hands he had bowed, turned, and walked away. **All three Chinese were headquartered in San Francisco.**

CHAPTER 10
MAUDE MAYBERRY.

Maude Mayberry was one of millions of immigrants who came to the United States a half century earlier to seek a better life with high hopes and tears in their eyes they entered the New York Harbor. The Statute of Liberty was their symbol of hope.

It didn't guarantee anything. The immigrants met with a wide variety of successes and failures. Some started as peddlers pushing junk carts in New York and became financiers of world renown such as the Rothchilds.

Maude was only six when her parents left a small hamlet outside of London, England. They knew remaining there would leave them in their lowly servant status the rest of their lives. In America they heard of the sunshine of the West Coast and the beauty of California. Santa Barbara, in particular, fascinated them. Without funds for housing they became servants on a large Montecito estate, her Mum as a domestic, and her Dad as a gardener.

The weather, the sea and the beautiful flowers and clean air made them feel they had made the right step. Maude was doing cleaning chores when she was only seven. **In the 1930's live in domestics were making as little as $10.00 a month.**

After many decades working her Mum had several severe bouts of undiagnosed illness. "Just me old age dragging me body down." Then she would occasionally say, 'Me thinks my time may be coming."

Her Dad was over 70 when news came his only brother had died in London and left them slightly over one thousand pounds. "It was an act of providence," her Dad said.

Her Mum's remarks were, "Fancy us folks being heirs to more than a stray dog or cat."

The inheritance made it possible for them to buy a small duplex on Bath Street and have a little cash to live on. Maude occupied one half and her Mum and Dad the other. Each had one small bedroom. Soon they ran out of money and needed to borrow money to live on. With no income to show they could make monthly payments they could not borrow through legitimate channels. **In desperation they turned to Schank Investment Co.** There they signed for a balloon payment in five years with exorbitant interest. Mum died and Dad lingered for a few more years and passed on. Now the entire balance was due in less than six months or Maude would lose the duplex.

She came home one afternoon and found her apartment had been ransacked.

CHAPTER 11
LANGE GETS LOCATED

The morning after arriving in Santa Barbara Lange bought a copy of the News-Press hoping he could turn to the classified and find a job and a low cost rental. No jobs, so he drove to their office just off State Street and placed a job wanted ad.

From there he tried a couple of rental ads, but both were unsatisfactory. He knew there were areas like lower Bath Street with small older homes. The beach was just a few blocks away. (To my readers that did not know the city in 1950 let me say the underpasses and freeway did not exist and the area was forty-five years newer and well maintained.)

It was just noon, and to save money he decided to buy some bread and cheese, some oranges and a pint of milk. He parked near a small Mom and Pop corner grocery store on Bath Street. He thought to himself that it slightly resembled the corner grocery store at N.E. 28th and Halsey street in Portland where he had started working in the sixth grade.

He remembered the name, Irvine & Farrens.

That was the fall of 1932. Folks would come in, stand around the pot bellied wood stove and discuss the terribly depression. Most drivers still had Ford Model T's.

So today in Santa Barbara Lange thought, "I may pay a little bit more than at a larger store, but these Mom and Pop stores know what's going in the neighborhood."

After he paid for the purchase he asked the pleasant grocer and his wife, "Do you know of any small rentals in the area?"

"Mrs. Mayberry just down the street may have a rental. She only comes in every few days. Poor lady doesn't have much money to live on and her renter just left."

The grocer's wife added, "Maybe I shouldn't tell you, but the rental will need a lot of work. Maude hasn't any money to fix it up. All the problems she has had with her folks being sick and dying, and them always being out of money is making her hallucinate. **She called the police the other day** claiming someone broke into her side of the duplex."

"What did they take?" asked Lange wondering about the neighborhood.

"That's what makes it so strange. Maude claims someone went through everything in her apartment and only took a note her Dad had written to her. Claims it didn't say anything. What's very strange is any thief could tell she has nothing! So why break into her place? She is as poor as the proverbial Church mouse!

"Thanks for the information folks, I have some experience at working on houses. Maybe I could come to her rescue."

"You'll get your reward in heaven, young man. Maude needs help. We work night and day in this small store or we'd pitch in and help."

Lange went to his car and ate his lunch quickly. Then he walked to the address given him. Maude was in and was in a dither. "My bloody renter left me-owing me rent, too. Be glad to show you the place, lad. You look like a honest young man."

"Thank you, I'd like to see it."

Lange liked the location. It was only a couple of blocks from State Street and not far from the beach. He expected it to be run down–and it was. "Looks like it really needs some painting."

Maude was almost in tears as she replied, "Lad, I know you're right, but I don't have any money. I'm too old to do the work and ain't got no money to buy paint. You paint it and I'll only charge ye $35.00 a month for the first four months."

Lange knew that was no bargain, but it was obvious this old lady was desperate. He knew his Dad, whose occupation was working over houses, would have likely done the work and not charged her a dime. That thought stuck in his craw and the only way he could live with himself now was to say, "Mrs. Mayberry, if you want to go ahead on that basis I will give you a check, start the work tomorrow and move in as quickly as I can."

"Could you pay me in cash? I never had me no checking account and know nothin' 'bout cashing checks. I worked all me life as a housekeeper on an estate. I got me $10.00 per month in cash. Spent it so fast I never needed no bank."

Lange's quick mind immediately went to his Mother's church friend who had lived an identical life. Another little English lady, with a limp. Jennie was her name. Never married. Always a live in housekeeper. Never made more than $10.00 per month.

Lange said to himself, "Now here is one reason I was supposed to come to Santa Barbara. My Mother won't miss me quite as much when she hears about this."

Four days later he moved in making certain he didn't back into wet paint. **Two days after that he saw a newspaper ad that seemed very interesting.**

"Business Manager with accounting and sales experience needed."

"That would be right down my alley. And look at that address, on lower State Street. I'm on my way to check that out."

When he saw the small size of the business he was disappointed. He nevertheless went in the door and the boss was in. Mr. Parks was in a rush, but took time to see him. "Let me quickly tell you my needs. First I have the Bank of America on my back. My business is growing by leaps and bounds and I don't know beans about accounting.

"I need a big loan. The bank wants facts and wants me to have an accountant who knows what he is doing. Secondly, we build Service Stations mostly for the Seaside Oil Co. "Third, we sell automotive equipment such as Grayco Lubricating Equipment and Weaver Twin Post Hoists. I'm too small to hire someone for each job–it's kind of embarrassing to say I want a business manager, accountant and salesman all in one man."

Lange looked at Mr. Parks, realizing this enthusiastic man wanted a lot. "I graduated with a full B.B.A. degree in Business Administration from the University of Oregon. Also, took four years of accounting through Advanced Cost Accounting.

"Second, I know some about construction work. Worked my way through college doing it. I even built two homes after I got out of school. **As to automotive equipment I know next to nothing.**"

"The first two are our most important. You probably know one end of a wrench from the other, and if you don't know we can label them."

Then Mr. Parks laughed and Lange laughed even though he didn't think it was so funny. Then Parks said, "I just have some plain vanilla application forms from the stationery store. I'm very interested in you. Could you please fill one out and let me take it home and I'll give you my decision in the morning."

That was fine, and by 9 A.M. the next morning Lange was working.[2]

CHAPTER 12
LANGE BECOMES VERY CURIOUS

Lange found the accounting part of his job duck soup. Getting a system established for record keeping and accounting was simple for him. Learning about the construction of service stations wasn't tough either. Learning about automotive equipment was another story.. Then he was asked to assist his boss demonstrate a new field–undercoating a car.

It was a dirty messy job — it was awful.

On the California Coast rust came with the weather and the cars were not undercoated. So equipment firms were sold on the idea coastal car owners would jump at the chance.

First the car was raised up on a Weaver Twin Post Hoist. This hoist did not rest the car on heavy rails, which would block the application of the material. As the demonstrator stood under the car the material was supposed to spray evenly and give the car a heavy undercoat.

The manufacturers of the material had failed to provide a proper nozzle.

The asbestos fibers which were supposed to add volume to the material continually clogged the nozzle. Then you would open the nozzle further and the material would come out in clumps. At times more material was getting on the demonstrator and the floor than on the car. It was an embarrassing and unsatisfactory.

His boss remained optimistic they would get the nozzle to work right.

As he watched his boss struggle with the nozzle, Lange's mind wandered to Maude's break-in. One day he called the Santa Barbara Police and left a message for Lt. Merced,

"I have returned to Santa Barbara and rent the other side of Maude Mayberry's little duplex. Could I talk to you for a few minutes when you are not busy?"

Lange placed the call from work, and it wasn't 30 minutes later when he had a call from Lt. Merced. "Welcome back to Santa Barbara. What brings you back? Are you working?"

"Thank you for the welcome. Yes, I am working as a combination business manager, accountant and salesman for the Automotive Equipment company in the same block as Seaside Oil Co. As to why I returned that would take a little time and I'm not certain I really know."

"I'm off duty at 5:30. Can you stop by for a few minutes?"

"You bet. I have a question to ask you also. About Maude's break-in."

"Sgt. Andrew knows more about that than I do. Maybe he can be around at 5:30. Can't promise it, however."

At 5:25 Lange was at the police station and Lt. Merced was ready to see him. They exchanged greetings and Merced said, "You had a question about Maude's break-in?"

"Of course I am curious what you think. Also, living next door I wonder if I should be alert for anymore break-ins."

The Lieutenant nodded toward Sgt. Andrew who said, "It could be either way. Her imagination or she might of had something of value at one time. Ordinarily we don't want private citizens to mess into police matters."

Sgt. Andrew continued with, "Perhaps she is just hallucinating, and you living next door to her might be able to ease her apprehension. On the other hand maybe there is something in her past she has forgotten about.

"Some of these old folks have some pretty valuable stuff they have forgotten about. And mark my word, Lange, some

46

of that stuff is going to get a lot more valuable making for more break-ins and more police headaches."

Lt. Merced chimed in with, "I'll go along with Sgt. Andrew and don't get to bugging us about it-we are busy–damn busy. Lange, we haven't the time to spend with every little old lady or man that thinks someone has entered their home. You wouldn't believe the calls we get."

Lange laughed. "Thanks, and by the way how is the officer who befriended me in those dark days when I first returned from the South Pacific?"

"Oh, you mean Lt. Alex Brown?"

Lange nodded.

"He unofficially is still the liaison between the Los Angeles Police Department and ours.

Maybe once a month he comes up on Friday and stays at the Californian Hotel.

"On his own time Saturday he fishes from Stearns Wharf, where he met you. I talk to him often. **Shall I tell him you are back in town?"**

"Please do. Maybe I will drop him a short note."

Lange got in his blue coupe and headed for his dinky duplex apt. He laughed to himself as he thought of how life was always one mystery after another. **He had only recently reread the story about Sam Spade and the Maltese Falcon** and his mind took a spin back over the story. As he cooked himself the usual meal, mixed vegetables and fish.

He pondered the question over and over again, "Could an old lady like Maude have come into a valuable possession that could be painted over to hide it's value, as in the case of the Maltese Falcon?"

His mind continued asking questions. "Could it be a valuable painting, maybe even covered with another painting. No, it isn't it as Maude didn't have any painting stolen."

As he tried to concentrate on the newspaper he ate two oatmeal cookies and drank two cups of coffee. He felt the urge to go next door, talk to Maude and see what he might learn.

She was home when he knocked and invited him in. He informed her his curiosity had driven him to see the two officers.

Maude was obviously heartened. "We old folks feel as if nobody cares about us. What did ye learn?"

"Sorry to say, not much. They suggested I talk to you about your possessions and maybe go over some of the things you and your folks had at one time. Did you dispose of–I mean get rid of things when you moved here?"

"I'm not thinking we did. We never had much of anything. I'll try to think real hard."

For the next two evenings Lange used all his spare time to cover things with Maude. Each time he returned to his tiny apartment he was distressed how little enjoyment life had given Maude. No opportunities except a menial job. Never made more than $10.00 per month.

It was a disappointment to both that Maude could not think of anything valuable. There were no vases or figurines that could be valuable nor were there any pictures except some prints that likely sold for one dollar or less.

A few inexpensively mounted family pictures. No oil paintings, watercolors or pencil sketches by some famous painter. None by any painter or artist.

Lange thought about how hard he also was working in the third grade. Then a night shift standing on the corner of N.E. 33rd and Broadway selling newspapers and magazines until 9 P.M. "I'm not giving up, Maude–and I don't want you to either. Just keep on thinking about everything. Who knows what will pop up?"

That night, after returning to his tiny apartment he said to himself, "Tonight I'm going to bed and dream of something pleasant. Like I was married to Delores Lee, the Dragon Lady. Like the song says, they can't stop you from dreaming."

So with that optimism Lange went to bed. He did dream of Delores. He dreamed she had agreed to marry him. He was so thrilled that Delores was going to be his wife.

They were to be wed in San Francisco. The Minister arrived. Everyone was there including his old accounting buddy from the University of Oregon, Charlie Sing.

Finally a messenger arrived with a grim note. "Delores had changed her mind." The wedding was called off. **In his turmoil Lange woke from his dream.**

He thought to himself, "Perhaps that was my past nixing my present. I was dreaming about when my girl friend cried and cried when our 41st Infantry Division was put on a three hour alert to go overseas."

"Please, let's get married so I'll have someone to wait for."

Lange knew he was the one that should not have shown up for that wedding.

The next morning he was realizing perhaps he ought to seriously try to find some young lady who was delicious enough to take some of the flavor of Delores out of his mind. The office secretary, Jean, was rather a nice gal.

He knew that was supposed to be a no-no. Don't date anyone in the office. On the other hand, sometimes opportunity does knock under unusual circumstances.

That evening, after finishing dinner he decided to walk up Cabrillo Blvd. past the Mar Monte all the way to the Biltmore Hotel. His mind went to the Chumesh Indians who used to farm and live where Santa Barbara was now. **Then Cabrillo arrived from Spain.**

In time the Chumesh were overwhelmed by the invaders. Then we go overseas and fight other nations. **Now we maybe break into little old ladies homes and steal from them.**

His mind went briefly to some of the Native American Indians in his 41st Infantry Division. He had grown up living on Wasco Street and the streets on either side were Clackamas and Multnomah. All three were named after Oregon Indian tribes, but he had never really had contact with American Indians before being drafted and assigned to the 41st Infantry Division.

He was surprised there were American Indian scouts in the division.

The Indian name that fascinated him most was, "John Rides the Horse." John actually had to sign his name in full in order to draw his pay. Pay days didn't come often overseas. Lange wondered what John might be doing right now–as he thought he realized he didn't know if John had survived.

Then he tried to laugh as he asked himself again, "I don't even know what I am doing here myself. **Wonder how much of my life I am going to spend at the crossroads–never knowing which bridges to cross and which bridges to burn?"**

CHAPTER 13
LORIE OWENS, GEORGIA PEACH
FROM ATLANTA.

She first saw the light of day in a small rural town about fifty miles from Atlanta. Kind of like River Hill. She was a beautiful child with blonde hair with a tinge of red and enough tendency to curl that nature would keep her hair beautiful forever.

Her facial features were perfect with eyes you could not miss.

Her lips seemed to tempt. Her nose had a slight tilt that completed the picture of a pert and happy, pleasant young lady. Her Dad was in the Merchant Marine and Lorie and her Mom lived in a small apartment over the neighborhood grocery story. Her Mom worked there and Lorie started helping at an early age.

Work and her genes gave Lorie a lithe, truly feminine figure that made men stop and other women sigh with envy. She learned to speak well at an early age and would mimic the grocery customers. Lorie's Southern accent would have charmed Scrooge himself. Her smile, soft voice and the way she pronounced words was awesome.

Her Dad survived one ship sinking not long after Pearl Harbor. His skills were desperately needed as the Liberty ships began pouring out of the Portland, Oregon shipyards. He did not survive his second sinking.

For Lorie and her Mother the impossible had occurred. Her Mother tried to put it into perspective by saying, "Lorie, dear, war is like a reverse roulette wheel. If you are in the wrong place at the wrong time you become a casualty. It must be so much harder on the men than on ourselves as they fight to survive."

Mrs. Owens didn't expect Lorie to understand as Mrs. Owens didn't really understand it herself. **When Lorie graduated from high school they moved to Atlanta, Georgia.**

Lorie had great rapport with the wholesale grocery salesmen and they found a job for her and her Mother in Atlanta. That proved to be easy, with so many men in the service. A few years later her Mom came down with breast cancer and Lorie quit her job to take care of her Mother.

Then her Mother died and Lorie was very despondent over the loss of both of her parents. The soldiers were returning and good job openings were fewer.

She dressed herself up and started going to hotel lounges to dance. There was one she particularly liked because it was frequented by well dressed businessmen eager to wine and dine a pretty girl. It was there she met Schank and he pressured her to travel with him.

She knew it was wrong, but one day she agreed to take a trip from Atlanta to Chicago with Schank. Her Mother had a sister there. Schank promised her a private bedroom, but it had a continental bathroom shared by his bedroom–giving her virtually no privacy.

Then she agreed to take a second trip. Then a third. He was still solicitous and romantic, but insisted on romance on his terms. Soon she was his regular companion. Within months those nagging fears in the background of her mind became reality.

She begged him to just break up the agreement and let her go. In a drunken stupor he slapped her around and threatened to kill her–told her he would be the one to decide where she

52

could go and when. **Then he locked her in her room for a week.** The room had a tiny hooded privacy cupboard door, waist high.

It's purpose was the ultimate in privacy where breakfast, or any meal or snack, could be delivered to the occupant without the steward being able to view the occupants of the room. The occupant pulled down on the hood, giving the food deliverer a small counter to lay the food tray on. Move the hood back closed the doorway, and the food was now available to the occupant.

Lorie found Schank increasingly brutal and herself more often locked in her bedroom. One day she said to the steward, "Oh, I'm desperate. Please find help for me."

"I understand, Missy. I try to help!"

Occasionally there would be short periods of time when Schank would show a little remorse and promise things would be different and permit Lorie to accompany him.

His bodyguard Sammy was always along and she was warned any attempt leave him would be met with the most dire consequences–**he threatened her with death!**

When Ruppert disappeared the Schankrila returned to Los Angeles without Schank. Wan, the Chinese steward, and Choy, the Chinese cook, rattled to each other in Chinese like two magpies on a talking marathon. Choy, the most talkative of the two, became very annoyed. "Soon we run out of food. Maybe we all eat rice?"

Wan countered with, "I can stand the rice–but this like being locked up in cage. Sammy refuse to let us off car. We sit here do nothin'. Lorie locked in her room. I notice even Sammy not too happy–**something very strange going on!**"

"What strange thing you think happen, Honorable Wan?"

And so it went. The same old questions without any good answer. With Lorie Owens locked in her room Sammy started to annoy the two Chinese. Finally one day Choy responded with, **"Sammy, soon we run out of food. My ancestors very good cannibals.**

Wonder what kind of steaks and stew we can make out of you? Maybe soon time to return to culture of my ancestors. "

Sammy would laugh and move away. He was a little punchy from his prize fighting days, when he seldom won any fights, and the little Chinese cook did intimidate him especially when he shook his meat cleaver at him. .

The inactivity caused Sammy to sleep a lot and grow lax. On several occasions he permitted Wan to take Lorie's meal to her small food access door.

On a couple of occasions Wan delivered a meal to Lorie when Sammy was asleep. Each time he would say, "Missy Lorie, open hood half way–I talk to you for second or two."

Wan's eyes would switch from Lorie to down the hallway where he could see the outline of Sammy. The third night since the Schankrila had returned to Los Angeles without Schank such an occasion for privacy came up. He spoke quickly to Lorie, **"Missy Lorie, I get message during night from Chinese who speak through cook's outside ventilator. Schank is daily at Ruppert's office-no sign of Ruppert."**

"So that's why we are alone. Wonder what happened to Ruppert?"

"Rumor is he disappear-no one know where."

"I don't think he would run out on Schank!"

"I do not know. We have plan for maybe you escape."

"Oh, Wan, don't tease me! Is there really a chance?"

"Life never certain Missy. Schank must attend meeting at New Chinatown Tong. Wang Sing will request you accompany Schank. Don't pick fight with Schank–be cordial. Maybe he bring you. If he ask you if you know Delores Lee be sure you answer, 'Think one time in ladies rest room-you know how ladies wait in line there and talk.'"

"Oh, I will, I will, Wan! Oh ,Wan, I am desperate. Please help me."

"Time I go now, Missy. Please memorize what I just say. Maybe we have no more chance to talk."

With those last words Wan pushed the hood closing the door and he quickly and silently shuffled back down the hall. He noticed Sammy's eyes were firmly closed and his body jerking a little. To himself Wan thought, Maybe he back in ring fighting. He likely have many dreams of what Americans call 'Good old days.'

That night again at precisely 1 A.M. came a muffled voice through the ventilator in the tiny galley. The voice showed great relief that Wan had gotten the message through to Lorie and concluded with, "I come back each night if more news. Wang Sing must play Schank like big fish he is. Give little more line-pull line in when able."

As Wan decided it was time to knock it off and get some sleep Choy exclaimed, "Maybe we big detectives like Charlie Chan."

"O.K. Charlie–get some sleep–maybe time you shut up."

A rather disconsolate Choy climbed up to his tiny upper bunk. "Maybe you get to fix your own breakfast, Wan."

CHAPTER 14
NEW CHINATOWN, LOS ANGELES

The Chinese established a much admired and loved community in San Francisco which tourists flocked to. When New Chinatown in Los Angeles opened somewhere around 1930, it became instantly popular. Oriental stores and wonderful food brought folks from miles around. The giant shrimp were unbelievable..

Los Angeles, with vast agricultural areas such as Orange County, was different and not easy to centralize a Chinese Community. On the other side of the coin was the fact that the larger geographical area of Los Angeles offered the Chinese the opportunity to spread their business activity to a much greater extent.

As an example, San Francisco, Portland and Seattle didn't have the oil wells that Los Angeles had. The Chinese, like everyone else, liked the idea of an oil well pump going up and down, 24 hours a day bringing in liquid gold.

Many a young Chinese laughed and said, "My fortune cookie says, 'Get oil wells working 24 hours a day. Forget about making chicken almond chow mein, shrimp egg roll and barbecued pork. Let us skip 20 hours a day in hot kitchen. **Let oil wells do the work. Chinese go out to Malibu and surf."**

Even Frank Sinatra would have replied to that, "You've come a long way baby."

There was citrus gold that gushed from a squeezed orange, lemon or grapefruit. Raising the old Chinese staple rice was another golden opportunity. Rice grew well in California. The Chinese were proud of their internal system of discipline and it was on that note that Ah Wing, his secretary, Delores, and Dr. Fu were visiting Los Angeles.

The Tong leader in Los Angeles was Wang Sing. He possessed the objectivity and push that the youth seemed to demand, along with the reverence the old understood and hoped would continue.

Trying to mesh the present without losing the wisdom of the past created many problems. This included handling real property such as land and buildings. **On top of this came the operation of businesses such as New Chinatown.**

Wang Sing put it well when he said, "Early history of Chinese in America most often involved menial tasks such as building rail lines. Now we are full citizens both legally and in the operation of our own businesses."

Ah Wing would claim his humble abilities were limited to within the Chinese Community itself, not outside business matters. He was so very proud of their business accomplishments he would listen intently to the smallest details. Likewise his old Chinese bones tingled when he was told of the leadership both in business and education the younger Chinese were achieving.

This trip to Los Angeles found Ah Wing burdened with apprehension and fear. He had undertaken a task that would unburden a debt he felt he owed. Delores Lee, his aide and confidant, could sense the pressure he felt.

"Dr.Fu is in charge. He will not let you down!"

"I know, **but it involves The Evil Empire of Cal Schank. I sense much danger!**"

"As you often tell us, **'Problems create opportunity.'** Chance for much good."

"Yes, Delores, I let myself fall into same trap of despair I caution my countrymen to avoid like proverbial poison. I bow humbly to you for your more intelligent advice."

"As you know very well when my husband is killed despair takes firm grip on me."

CHAPTER 15
DINNER IN NEW CHINATOWN.

**It was exactly five days since Schank had been struggling
with the disappearance of Ruppert Snyder** and trying to decide
how soon he should bring in a replacement for Ruppert. The
secretary said, "Mr. Wang Sing desires to speak to Mr. Schank."

"Hello, Wang Sing."

"Hello, Mr. Schank, maybe not most important matter to big
executive like you, but we must talk to you about Newsmith Oil
Field. Certain Chinese heirs have stock and we understand your
firm is trying to acquire them. Some question as to method you
use."

"What do you mean by that?"

"Very difficult to talk over phone. Would like to meet at
dinner tonight at 7 P.M. at Pagoda in new Chinatown."

Schank immediately recalled the words of Mildred that
Ruppert had serious conflicts with the Chinese. "O.K.," "I'm very
busy, but if it is important I will have dinner with you."

"Thank you very much. We have minor request to add.
**Delores will be at the dinner and she requests you bring Lorie
Owens."**

Schank replied, "The request is very unusual."

"Perhaps Delores just pick up Lorie Owens and two ladies
have lunch together today."

Schank was almost panicked by the thought of the Chinese going out to his private rail car and finding Lorie locked up. "O.K., I'll bring Lorie to dinner."

"This is your promise, for sure, Mr. Schank?"

Schank's anger rose. He didn't like to be pushed. Suddenly the realization came to his mind that Wang Sing had made no mention of Ruppert. **He thought to himself it's almost like those damn Chinese know he's missing.**

" I give you my word."

"Cook is preparing special dinner. See you tonight. Thanking you very much."

I will never understand them. They always have an afterthought, change times or want to include someone else. I'm going to put the pressure on them tonight.

Schank turned to Mildred, "Get me Sammy on the short wave."

"Sammy, this is Schank. I'm at Ruppert's office. You having any problems?"

"None, Boss," came the short reply.

"Sammy, I'm going to have dinner this evening with Wang Sing at New Chinatown. They insist I bring Lorie. You bring her to the parking lot of the Pagoda at 7 P.M. sharp. Travis will bring me in the LaSalle. Then you can take off for an hour and eat dinner. Be back at 8 P. M. and wait for me. Do you understand for certain?"

"Yes, Boss. I know exactly what I'm to do. Wan and Choy are chomping at the bit and maybe going a little stir crazy. We need fresh supplies!"

"O.K. Let them go for the night and tell them to be back in the morning with some fresh supplies. That makes sense."

Travis was getting very tired running shotgun for Schank. The disappearance of Ruppert without any clue made him agreeable to accept the assignment. **He also knew that once Schank made up his mind he might as well accept.**

It was after 6 P.M. and he and Schank were seated next to each other in the back seat of Travis's luxurious LaSalle limousine. It was a fortress on wheels with a special sixteen cylinder engine. Between its gleaming black exterior and its blue tapestry interior was a layer of bulletproof sheet steel. It's one inch thick glass windows would stop police grade ammunition. **The apprehension visible on Schank's face was one sign his gut was tied in knots.** He thought to himself, "Whoever knocked off Ruppert is laughing at me hoping I'm sweating blood."

Schank kept trying to get his mind off Ruppert. He said to Travis, "The Chinese once met Lorie and I guess they like her."

Travis did not reply and Schank continued, "I figured I might as well agree. I can never talk those Chinese into any of my requests. Once they don't answer your question you might as well go in another direction. They act like they never heard the question. Sometimes they bow, and show no expression. I know damn well they are playing games. It infuriates me."

Travis came back with, "Don't sweat it Schank. It's just their way of doing business. They have a thousand years experience in handling problems. At least you know they aren't going to budge. You know, Schank, I want everyone to do it my way and don't argue with me. You're that way too."

To himself Travis grimly thought, "I'd sure rather deal with the Chinese than with Schank."

"Travis, how long have you dealt with the Chinese?"

"I went to school in Anaheim with Chinese. Their Grandparents laid a lot of the railroad track in LA. many years ago. They were treated miserably. Beaten, robbed, you name it. You got to hand it to them. They rose above all that. Now they are powerful, excellent business people. And damn hard working! You don't find them on welfare. Don't cross them is my advice. If they like Lorie that will help the meeting."

"That really bothers me. I was planning to get rid of her very soon. Haven't quite got the details worked out. Delores Lee is in town. She sure is a dead ringer for the Dragon Lady. Apparently she is the right arm of Ah Wing. Maybe they got to talking in the ladies rest room. **Women make all kinds of friends while they are waiting in line. It's kind of crazy. They are always saying "Oh, I met the nicest lady in the rest room."**

"You never let Lorie Owens out of your sight. That's probably the only place she got to talk to another woman.

"You know I try not to ask questions. Naturally, I am sure as hell curious what you and Ruppert were tangling with the Chinese over this time."

"I'll give you some of the scoop, but, Travis you know me. Let a word of this out and I will raise hell with you."

Travis tried to laugh a little, but there was always something very strange about Schank. Travis could not put his finger on it. Now, for the first time, Schank had an aura of desperation about him. He seemed just as mean. Travis said no more and for a time there was an eerie silence. **Travis was deep in hock to Schank.** Eight years ago he had borrowed the money from Schank to buy his first strip joint in Hollywood.

The guy that owned it decided to go into the Navy. Later Travis borrowed more from Schank to buy another. **Like being in debt to the company store.** You never get caught up. Travis paid Schank by skimming. Schank didn't want checks and didn't give receipts.

Finally Schank broke the silence with, "One of the things we play around with is oil wells. Always figured I'd get 25, then go for another 25."

Curiosity got the better of Travis and he said, "How many do you own now?"

Schank's failure to reply showed Travis the Chinese weren't the only ones that ducked a question.

Schank continued with, "They pump oil 24 hours a day. They are like a slot machine that never stops paying. There are some hot rumors of a new find. I'll tell you in strict confidence. It's in the Newsmith area. Would you believe the damn luck. Some Chinese also own some stock in that corporation. I almost had controlling interest.

"**When I get voting control we sell out to one of my private corporations.**"

"For something like ten cents on the dollar leaving original stockholders with not even a pot to sit on?" asked Travis.

"That's my business. Anyhow we've done it a dozen times. Got it down to an exact science. Yeh, I like the oil business. Like it more each day."

"So what do the Chinese think about all of this?"

"That's why we're having this meeting. They don't want to sell out. There is still some stock missing. Ruppert had been working on that angle. **If we get it before the Chinese we will have control."**

Hearing those words Travis interrupted raising his voice and shouting, "I just told you to play square with the Chinese! What's one more oil well if you're not around to collect the oil."

Schank quickly replied, "Why didn't you tell Ruppert that?"

"Hell, I've warned Ruppert a dozen times about deals he's not handling right. He comes in to my main club and brags. He never pays any attention to what I say and never pays the check or leaves a tip for the waitress.

"Oh yes, he tries to pick up any girl he takes a fancy to even though she has a boy friend. **Don't let me forget, he's always telling me how to run my business."**

Schank did not reply. He just kept thinking. His mind and his stomach were churning in unison. He could not get his mind off Ruppert. Schank was realizing he should have picked someone like Travis to deal with the Chinese instead of Ruppert. "Travis you seem to know more than I realized. Could the Chinese have had anything to do with the abduction of Ruppert?"

Travis then turned in his seat. This was sure a different Schank. **He was actually asking a question.** Travis changed his voice to a kinder level with, "If they did, you will never know. You know the difference between the Chinese and you, Schank?"

Schank did not answer. "There are a lot more Chinese than you, Schank."

A week ago Travis would have never dared talk man to man with Schank. Things were different now. Desperation and uncertainty had torn down the impregnable barrier that previously existed between the two men. Travis now had real reason to be concerned. If the house of Schank came crashing down, so would Travis's ready source of emergency cash.

Travis with a most serious note in his voice said, **"Have you ever met or heard of a Dr. Fu?"**

Schank thought for a few moments and replied, "Maybe I have. Refresh my memory."

Travis came back with, "He's tall, quiet, but very imposing in appearance. He is rumored to descend from a long line of brilliant Chinese physicians. It is claimed that he can look at a person and read their mind.

"Like a combination of Sherlock Holmes and Dr. Fu Man Chu. He is held in awe and respect by everyone who knows of him whether Chinese or not. He makes the final decisions when major actions are being considered."

"What do you mean Travis? He's their terminator?"

"Something like that. I've only heard rumors. I don't ask the Chinese questions."

A worried Schank queried, "So what do they do when they hit a guy?"

"One strong rumor is they ship the guy to Panama. Don't ask me what happens to him in Panama. The story is Dr. Fu insists on meeting the person first before agreeing to the hit. If you meet him tonight my guess is you may be in big trouble."

Those words shocked Schank and the throbbing in his head became more intense. **"So Ruppert might be in the hold of some junk freighter on his way to Panama?"**

"Could be. **Remember you can't outrun the Chinese. They are all over the world."**

Schank was listening intently. "How come you know so damn much?"

"Two of my best high school buddies, in Anaheim, were Chinese. We keep in touch. They are great guys and I respect them. One teaches math in College. The other is a CPA. When they have male guests from out of town they take them out to dinner or a dinner show. "Often they want to see more bright lights. They bring them out to my number one place, the one I hang out at. So the gals on stage strip down to their waist and bounce around a little. **You know they don't show any more than the gals on the beach at Malibu.**

"There is never any hanky panky with them. I never let them pay. When I go to new Chinatown I mention their names and I never get a bill for dinner. Bartering is centuries old. By the way **did you ever stop in to see my old pal Jack Ruby in Dallas?"**

"I did once. He sent word he needed $50,000."

"Did you loan it to him?"

"I did and he paid it back in six months. He wouldn't tell me what he wanted it for." Just then the limousine entered New Chinatown and soon the three story Tong headquarters was visible. Next to it was the beautiful Chinese Pagoda Restaurant. Both were ornate structures with intricately designed roofs. In typical Chinese fashion the corners of the roof were turned up to turn away the evil spirits.

They immediately spotted the car with Sammy and Lorie. Both cars moved as close to the entrance as possible. Sammy escorted Lorie to the door. When Schank reached her he took a firm grip on her arm.

Lorie was thrilled to be in civilization, but as Schank grasped her arm his firm grip and presence made her whole body shiver. She had an overpowering feeling that tonight was her last chance for freedom. She thought to herself if I don't get away tonight my life isn't going to be worth a plugged nickel. **It's like living with a knife over your head held by a thread.**

The moment they stepped inside the door they were met by a Chinese who bowed to them and said in excellent English, "Good evening, Miss Owens and Mr. Schank. Please follow me."

They passed the entrance to the main dining room and entered another door. They were in an alcove off the main dining room. Schank had expected the room would be entirely private. A large dining table was set up in the alcove at which no one was seated. Then a side door opened and four Chinese stepped through the doorway.

First was the beautiful Delores Lee. Ordinarily Schank's mind would wonder how he could he get close to that gorgeous creature. Tonight, instead of excitement he felt chills go up and down his spine. He thought she looks like she could walk right up to a man and cut out his heart. What kind of a woman really lurks beneath that shimmering silk gown?

Without exception when Delores appeared, be it male or female, **everyone's gaze was drawn to her like a magnet.** Her perfect complexion, her beautifully coiffured hair, her graceful arms, long thin fingers with unbelievably long nails.

"She looks different tonight–like the rumored genuine Dragon lady!"

He thought, "She seems capable of pulling the mask from a man's face and tearing his chest open leaving his throbbing heart unprotected. Was she about to push him off a cliff? It wouldn't be like Moriarity and Sherlock Holmes."

He knew if he was going to join Ruppert that Delores would go unscathed. She would just take a short look at him as he fell from his castle and turn that beautiful body of hers around moving on to her next conquest.

Following closely behind Delores were three Chinese men. Schank recognized the first as Ah Wing, venerable Chinese Leader and philosopher. Next was Wang Sing, Tong leader and Chinese powerhouse. The adrenaline surged in Schank's veins as he saw the third Chinese man for the first time ever. **He was very tall, well over six feet, with a singular air of authority. His face showed no emotion.**

When the Chinese delegation reached Lorie and Schank. Delores extended her hand to Lorie, but not to Schank. **Delores said, "We have special guest tonight, Doctor Fu."**

At that moment Schank felt the kiss of death embracing him. The unexpected appearance of Dr. Fu overwhelmed Schank. He felt as if a giant fire breathing dragon had entered the room. Its writhing body had suddenly confronted him. Its hot breath would soon overpower him.

None of the Chinese leaders bowed. Schank noticed this breach of Oriental custom. "Let us be seated," Wang Sing said gravely.

With that he moved to the alcove and indicated a seat to Schank. "Please be seated here."

Wang Sing's voice was devoid of any inflection indicating his state of mind.

Wang Sing took the seat to the right of Schank and Doctor Fu where the table curved. There he could look directly at Schank who could not return the gaze without moving his head. Ah Wing sat to the left of Schank Schank's apprehension commanded him to be very alert.

His mind was observing everything much as a rat frantically watching which way the cat is going to pounce. For the first time in over twenty years Schank was scared. He noticed, with dismay, Delores and Lorie were seated together at the far end of the table. **"If Lorie decides to make a break for it there is nothing I can do,"** Schank thought and his anger rose.

Chinese men, in business suits, took the remaining seats at the table. Wang Sing introduced them. In a few cases he stated their position in the Chinese hierarchy.

Schank's attention was drawn to the two women. He saw Delores lean close to Lorie and whisper. He wished he could hear what they were saying. Lorie was aware that Schank was staring at her. She tried to concentrate on Delores' hushed words.

"You do not leave with Schank tonight. Your freedom has arrived."

It was as if God had opened the gates of Heaven to her. The words were so surprising Lorie almost gave herself away. She was barely cool enough to keep her emotions hidden.

"During the dinner I will slip into your hand a small shaker. Sprinkle it heavily on a portion of your dinner. Slip the shaker back to me. Eat that portion immediately! It will make you so ill you will want to throw up. Tell me when you feel that way.

"Follow my directions only. Trust me completely! Do not become confused. All of this has been carefully planned. Do not despair! Do not be frightened! Is this very clear, my dear?"

The low, but strong voice of Delores, and the last two words, 'my dear,' cast the matter in stone in Lorie's shaking body and mind. **She whispered, "I will trust you. Being sick at my stomach will be nothing compared to the hell I've been through.**

"I will be so grateful — I'll owe you my life."

Delores knew much more about Schank than Lorie Owens knew! The Chinese cook and steward on board Schank's private rail car had been planted there by Wang Sing. Now, those two small Chinese were in the kitchen of the Pagoda thrilled that Lorie was about get away from Schank. They had removed their few belongings from the Schankrila.

No Chinese would ever serve again for Schank in any capacity. Schank had crossed the Chinese line in the sand.

Chinese waiters set out mouth-watering platters of authentic Chinese fare prepared for discriminating palates, not the mouths of tourists. As Schank bit into an unbelievably large shrimp, he wondered if he was like a condemned man, eating a delicious meal before the trap door in his gallows opened.

The uncertainty and intense gloom that engulfed Schank was in stark contrast to the sudden rays of freedom warming Lorie's heart. The terror of her life with Schank might be over this evening. "Oh, I hope this isn't a dream. **Please, please, may it come true," she prayed.**

It was all she could do to keep her emotions in check and not burst out crying. The dying infantryman will often call to his mother in his agony. Lorie's thoughts went to her deceased mother. She slipped her hand onto Delores lap and Delores grasped it saying,

"Steady, Lorie, breathe slowly and deeply. There are four LA policeman at a nearby table. Don't look for them! Just know those four are here to protect you."

The food was helping Schank regain some of his composure. His eyes continued to rove as he built a mental picture of the room and the people in it. Suddenly his chopsticks stopped in mid-stroke. He was looking at a table of four men who didn't look like tourists or salesmen.

He continued to gaze at them, then turned to Wang Sing with, **"Those four men look more like cops than tourists."**

Wang's impassive mask broke into the very slightest smile. "Very observant. They are officers of the Los Angeles Police Department. You are much like Sherlock Holmes himself. We Chinese big Sir Arthur Conan Doyle fans. Also big fans of Charlie Chan. **Maybe police following one of us. What do you think?"**

Schank tried vainly to return a smile and show he was not ill at ease. To himself he thought, "That's a crock. Does everyone know what happened to Ruppert except me? Is the word out I am going to be hit so the cops are here to protect New China Town?"

The Chinese gourmet food had been relaxing Schank. Now the slight increase in his composure fled. His gaze moved over the dining room as he asked himself, **"Just where are my big time enemies? Are some of them seated in this room tonight?"**

Travis' driver didn't turn the limo's engine off after Schank got out to enter the Pagoda. His driver had turned the car around and headed for the nearby restaurant owned by the math professor and CPA. Their taste buds opened into full bloom once they had gotten rid of Schank. They were high on giant shrimp, shu duck and chow mein with cashews, but were ready to spring for any new entree the Chinese might offer them.

"Hey, there's a speed limit!" Travis was pounding on the limo's dividing glass. "I'm buying dinner, but you pay for any tickets. And remember this is my limo and not that pile of junk you drive."

The driver turned to the bodyguard, riding shotgun, "Driving this buggy for a living sure keeps me humble when I drive my old rattle-trap home."

Travis was starting to relax for the first time in days.

With Schank gone he had his own palace on wheels, but Schank had the big one, the sixty foot all steel private rail car.

He spoke into the intercom, "Hell, I'm as impatient as you to start eating that food. Guess I'm getting old. It's better than dancing girls. And causes a lot less trouble. The Chinese know the right business to be in."

Sammy, Schank's driver, also had to be back in an hour. He had to race five miles to get to his favorite bar to get together with his brother, Al, and a bunch of his pals. It wasn't often he got time off in Los Angeles and he could hardly wait to sink his teeth into a thick roast beef sandwich on San Francisco sourdough and wash it down with a cold brew.

And see if he could pick up any rumors about Ruppert's strange disappearance.

He took a few chances, burned a little rubber, but he made it there in five minutes and jumped right out and walked as quickly as his broken down former boxer body could. **He was excited! At the last minute he had called his brother, Al, who had been his trainer 25 years ago. He sure hoped Al would be there.**

"Those were the days when we worked out in that old gym on Tenth Avenue in Chicago. Al would always tell me I was the greatest. I knew I wasn't, but Al kept me going, until I had that fight with Wicked Willie.

" Oh, what the hell, I ride in a private rail car, eat three squares a day and ain't sleeping in no flop house. Sure my old lady left me long ago, but she was a nag. I was damn glad to see her go."

Then the flash back that always haunted him. "Maybe Al can tell me where my daughter is now? I always loved that kid! I know she once loved me—when she was a kid."

Sammy was so hyped up, so intent on a few minutes of friendship away from Schank, **that he never noticed the car following his erratic driving.** The moment Sammy stepped inside the bar that car pulled alongside his car. Two men got out and one stayed inside.

The two men quickly jimmied the trunk of the car Sammy had been driving. **Then they opened the trunk of their car and transferred a large sack to Sammy's trunk.**

They closed the trunk carefully and drove across the street to wait for Sammy to come out. The men had been through a lot together. Their friendship and dependence on each other went back many years to when they were infantry men in New Guinea.

Now again they were very alert. Generally not talkative one broke the silence. "The monkey is off our back. We did it. It sure wasn't tough like being a dog face in the jungle. **"Those crazy night attacks by the Japs still give me nightmares.** My wife wonders if I will ever shake them."

"We're still in the jungle, buddy. It's going to get worse, not better."

"Remember how Tokyo Rose would call us the 41st Division Butchers. Claimed we carved them up. We never took prisoners, not after the first one suckered us."

The third one said, "We learned the hard way. I can still see that first Jap who held up his hands. Louie thought the Jap behind him was raising his hands, but he threw a grenade. Louie–my sister and he were engaged."

" That was our password to fire," the driver recalled, "Here's one from Louie. Lucky the Japs couldn't pronounce the letter L."

They all fell silent remembering the white crosses left in clearings in the tall kunai grass in the Jungle. **When each man went down a little of their soul was buried with him.**

Even back in the U.S. they weren't certain how much of them was still back overseas. **It had taken years to get that thousand mile long island back from the Japs.**

Surely the brave efforts of the thousands they left behind should not be in vain. That was why they reluctantly accepted this dangerous mission.

One of them said, "It used to be a big deal when a few mobsters in Chicago shot each other. St. Valentine's Day

Massacre, what was that, six guys? How about 10,000 casualties suffered by the 32nd Infantry Division in 30 days at Buna.

"Believe me, my crystal ball says before we reach retirement kids in Los Angeles will be killing six people a day."

"You're nuts," another said, "Kids aren't going to get violent. You just live in a bum neighborhood. Kids will turn around now that their fathers are looking after them."

Each of them had been watching a third car. Their 'point' man was inside.

Their conversation was cut short when Sammy came out and headed back to the Pagoda. The two cars followed. They knew where Sammy was going.

Sammy was happy. Al had shown up and it was like old times. Sammy wanted to quit right then and stay at the bar. "Didn't realize how much I've been missing." It was only Sammy's brother, Al, who convinced him to hang in there.

"Schank's looked after you." Al reminded him. "Hang in there, do what he says. Let's think about it in a couple of weeks. Your daughter is coming out to visit us. I won't say nothing about maybe you'll be there. Let's surprise her."

"That'll be great, Al. You're the greatest brother any guy ever had."

Sammy's car pulled into the Pagoda parking lot and he leaned back in his seat. The roast beef was the best and the two bottles of beer were taking over. Then he remembered, they never discussed Ruppert. He said to himself, "Guess I took too many punches in my time.

"Why do I keep thinking it's time for me to quit?"

Just then Travis' limousine approached the Pagoda parking lot.

Two of the Tong's lookouts saw Sammy return. One quickly entered the Pagoda and handed a slip of paper to a waiter who immediately delivered it to Delores. Delores read it, then slipped a small vial into **Lorie's hand. Lorie's body tensed and she almost went into shock as her hand grasped it.**

She sprinkled one section of her food with the powder and slipped the vial back to Delores. Lorie quickly ate the sprinkled portion and had scarcely finished when her throat and chest began to burn. The pain became so intense her stomach contracted in spasms as it churned in violent protest. **Quickly she put her hand over her mouth as her body started to eject it's violent intruder.**

Delores stood up saying quietly, "Lorie is ill. I will take her to the ladies' rest room."

Delores had spoken so softly Schank did not hear the words although he had been carefully watching Lorie never letting her out of his vision. Schank said, "Why is Lorie Owens leaving?"

Even though he knew the answer very well Wang Sing replied, "I will inquire."

Wang Sing then spoke Chinese to some of the adjoining men and soon there was the unmistakable sing song of many Chinese all speaking at once. Finally Wang Sing looked at Schank saying, **"It appears Lorie is sick. She looked quite pale when she arrived."**

Wang Sing was known for his dexterity in mixing American slang and Chinese. Also on occasion he could be too honest, flinging reality in the face of someone he did not respect.

So on this occasion he continued with, "Yes, she did look very pale. What were you doing with her? Locking her in her room and not letting her get outside?"

Wang Sing's eyes stared at Schank as he spoke those words. Those words hit Schank in the pit of his stomach as he realized how right Travis was. "You should never underestimate the Chinese."

Then Wang Sing poured it on with, "You fail to learn American phrase. 'Maybe fool most of people most of time, but not fool all the people all of the time.'"

Schank bristled, losing his cool as his fist hit the table in frustration, "So that's it, you set me up! Well that's what you think. Lorie is my business, not yours!"

With those words he shoved back his chair and stood up and pushed himself away from the table and headed in the direction that Lorie Owens had gone with Delores.

At that moment the normally not talkative Dr. Fu looked at Wang Sing and said, "You describe Schank to me so very well. **Only person he fool is himself. Too much power for small brain to handle.**"

Schank moved quickly around the corner of the table and then down the side of it. He was not careful as he walked and brushed against several of the men who were still seated. Schank was making a spectacle of himself!. Except for Delores and Lorie, who had already left the room, the rest of the diners were still seated as if nothing had happened. Obviously Schank was in hot pursuit of Lorie.

As he reached the farthest end of the table, and was about to step into the main dining room, he suddenly found himself confronted by a man. The man stepped in front of Schank as if he was challenging him. This man had been seated at the nearest table with three other men. The other three remained seated.

The man challenging him was over six feet tall and broad of shoulder with a square jaw. He appeared to be about 40. He might be a match for Schank and then again he might not.

Schank gave him a sudden firm shove and the man staggered from the strength of Schank's right arm. The other three men leaped from their chairs and a scuffle ensued, but it was short lived. One Chinese stepped from another table and gave Schank a karate chop that took the wind out of his sail.

Schank was handcuffed, stood up and marched from the dining room into the adjoining hallway. He protested loudly and one of the police officers said mockingly, **"First you make one dumb mistake, you attack a police officer. Then you make three more dumb mistakes. You attack three more police officers."**

Schank quickly responded with, "You never identified yourselves!"

Lt. Alex Brown, the recipient of the first blow, took over and said, **"I have a warrant for your arrest."**

Schank immediately said, "What are the charges?"

Lt. Brown replied, **"You are charged with kidnapping and interstate prostitution.** You have the right to remain silent and you have the right to call your attorney. Those words are not required, but we at LAPD are ahead of the legal game."

Schank replied, 'I know all that. Let me call my attorney!"

Lt. Brown replied, "You can do that as soon as we book you. First, we have additional police business to accomplish. **Right now we have more arrests to make."**

With those words and with one officer holding onto each arm of Schank, the five men moved through the side exit of the Pagoda and into the parking lot. The first thing Schank saw was two police cars. Schank looked for Sammy's car and saw an officer standing alongside.

Sammy was still inside. Then everyone heard the siren. It's sound became louder and louder as the ambulance pulled to a stop in front of the Pagoda. The attendants jumped out, pulled out the stretcher and swiftly moved through the front door of the Pagoda.

Lt. Brown said to himself, "I wonder what has gone wrong. At best this is not the kind of publicity the Chinese want."

Lt. Brown asked his three fellow policemen to hold down the fort and he would step inside and see if his help might be needed. Lt. Brown knew where the rest rooms were and he headed that way. **After several minutes the stretcher came out of the ladies' rest room with Lorie on it and Delores following it.**

Delores paused for a moment and whispered to Lt. Brown, "Lorie Owens is so weak she is barely conscious. Schank did this to her. **She is one lucky lady she was with friends when she collapsed.** Chinese Doctor is coming in moment. He will go to hospital with us."

Lt. Brown stood aside and watched Lorie Owens being taken to the ambulance. Then he sprinted to the parking lot and instructed one of the police cars to accompany the ambulance and called for a back up replacement. Lt. Brown watched the doors of the ambulance shut, the sirens turned on and the ambulance was on it's way.

Lt. Brown paid particular note that the Chinese Doctor had stepped into the Ambulance. **Obviously Lorie was in a lot more serious shape than anyone had suspected.**

The departure of Lorie in the ambulance came in full sight of Schank and **the true evil of his mind came to the front as he said to himself,** "Too bad she didn't collapse on one of our long trips out of town. Now I'm in the soup for kidnapping her, interstate prostitution and maybe even attempting to kill her.

"And then they claim I attacked four police officers. As soon as my attorney gets here all these phony charges will be dropped."

Lt. Brown now approached Sammy's car, "Sammy, I have a warrant for your arrest for kidnapping and interstate commerce You have the right to remain silent and the right to an attorney."

Sammy saw his boss, Schank, was already in custody and he said in a polite manner, "I understand." **Right now Sammy felt his world collapse** as he recalled less than 30 minutes ago he had the overwhelming feeling he should quit Schank immediately. His brother Al had talked him out of it. No, he couldn't blame it on good old Al.

Lt. Brown surprised both Sammy and Schank by saying, "Impound this car, but meanwhile open the trunk to make certain there isn't something in it that is evidence."

Sammy was bewildered and looked at Schank who said, **"Sammy, give them the keys. They are going to open it anyway. There is nothing in it!"**

Meanwhile the first of the news media had arrived having picked up news of the ambulance from the police scanner. Flash bulbs were popping and movie film was being run through the latest in cameras.

A camera man moved to the back of the car adjusting his focus as he waited for the opening of the trunk, saying to another reporter, "Five bucks there isn't anything in it."

The reporter said, "I'll take that bet just for the hell of it!"

One officer took Sammy's keys and found the right key. The lock sprung open and the officer lifted the lid. Inside they saw a huge sack. One of the policeman saw it and shoved it a little.

Then he turned to Lt. Alex Brown saying, **"My God, it almost feels like a body."**

With those words, the powerful and formerly indomitable Schank came as close to fainting as any tough guy ever comes. Simple Sammy was likewise shocked. He vainly tried to step forward, but was immediately restrained by the police.

Lt. Brown yelled, "Everyone back. At least 10 feet back. No one comes close. "

Then he yelled at the eager cameramen and reporters, "Anyone crossing this line is to be clubbed first and then arrested for interfering with the law. And this particularly applies to newspaper people and cameras. No exception! Does everyone understand this?"

The newspaper people knew that if he was a 2nd Lt. in the Los Angeles Police Force he had at least 20 years experience.

The sound of his voice made everyone back off. The excitement was at a fever pitch. Everyone was straining. What was in that huge sack?

Lt. Brown commanded, "Sergeant Smitty, open the sack."

Sgt. Smitty stepped forward. Taking his knife from it's holster he carefully felt for a clear place in the sack and made a small incision. As he widened the incision he looked inside. He said, "It's a large person with pants."

Lt. Brown said forcefully, "Is the person alive?"

Sgt. Smitty gingerly slipped his hand inside the sack and felt considerable warmth. "Lt. Brown, I think so. It's almost hot in that sack."

"Open the sack more, "commanded Brown.

"Holler to them. Ask them if they are alive," continued Brown.

Sgt. Smitty did as instructed and felt a groan inside and a little movement of the body.

Brown was bending over and hearing the groan said, "Get the sack open."

Slowly and carefully Sgt. Smitty used his sharp knife. He and Brown could see it was a man in the fetal position securely trussed, blindfolded and gagged. As they endeavored to take off the restraints they saw it was a very professional job. They knew his mouth would be extremely sore from the tape so they gently opened it enough to let him speak. "Who are you?" commanded Lt. Brown.

Ruppert Snyder felt like the infantryman who was unconscious when the battle ended and has just come to, bewildered and not believing he was still alive.

He answered with, "My name is Ruppert Snyder."

As soon as Ruppert was completely freed of his bonds Lt. Brown took another paper from his pocket and said, **"I have a warrant for your arrest."**

Ruppert was shocked, but being alive and in police custody was better than where he had expected to end up, very dead. "What am I charged with?"

Lt. Brown turned to the paper in his hand and said, "The same as your boss has just been charged, **"Kidnapping and interstate prostitution."**

"You have just found me so how can I be charged with kidnapping?"

"You will be taken before a magistrate and you and your attorney can make your case."

The newsmen were overjoyed with what was happening. They thrived on the misfortune of others. They knew the scene would now move to police headquarters so they scattered to the nearby phone booths. If you had been using the phone they gladly would have given you ten bucks to turn the line over to them.

This was spectacular! Ruppert Snyder was claiming he had been kidnapped. No word of that had hit the press. Now he is found trussed and gagged in a gunny sack inside a locked trunk. Boy what headlines this was going to make. The headline would be a grabber. **KIDNAPPED MAN ARRESTED FOR KIDNAPPING**

Well, that was the newspaper business and would be worth an extra edition. The news boys and the public would love it. An ambulance was called for Ruppert and two police officers accompanied him. **One group of tourists remarked to**

a nearby Chinese, "If you have entertainment like this every night we will come more often."

The Chinese got the last word in saying, "We don't shoot this movie on a regular basis."

CHAPTER 16
SCHANK GOES FROM STEEL RAIL
CAR TO STEEL CELL

Cal Schank and Sammy were taken directly to Police Headquarters. As soon as they got in the police car Schank yelled at Sammy, "I've got a hell of a lot of questions to ask you, but don't say a word until my lawyer, Lexus Taylor. talks to you."

"I understand, Boss. Don't worry, I won't say a word. I don't know nuthin' bout nuthin'."

There was absolute silence on the way to the station, but both men were doing a lot of thinking. Sammy was totally stressed out as he asked himself again and again, why didn't I stay at the bar. Secondly, he didn't even know Ruppert was missing. How did he get into the trunk?

Schank was almost as confused as Sammy. Things were happening so fast and none of them made sense. Ruppert's disappearance and his reappearance. Just what was behind all of this? Some relief entered Schank's mind because no one had killed Ruppert and Ruppert would stand up for him.

Then his thoughts went to Lorie he almost mumbled out loud, "She slipped from my grasp. I waited too long to get rid of her. I didn't give those Chinese enough credit!"

Upon arrival at the police station Schank was given the opportunity to call his attorney Lexus Taylor. Lexus was, of course, not at his office in the evening and Schank yelled at the answering services operator, "I'm his best client and I'm at the main police precinct. I don't care what the expense is. Get word to him. Send private messengers to all the places he might be. Just get him down here."

With no lawyer in sight the officers went ahead and booked Schank and Sammy and locked them up.

There was the usual shortage of jail space, but they did some shuffling and put both men in the same cell.

As Schank's power increased over the years his patience went down in proportion. **As he paced back and forth in his cell his anger was boiling.** He yelled and swore at Sammy, Lorie, the Chinese and even Ruppert. And he cussed his attorney for not being available.

When Lexus finally arrived he took one look at Schank and knew he'd need a gross of kid gloves to handle that raving maniac. Lexus saw it was no use to engage Schank in any conversation. So he just kept repeating, **"The charges under the Lindbergh kidnapping laws prevent bail.** The charges under the Mann Act for interstate prostitution are just more wood on the fire."

"If you can't get me out I'll get another attorney," Schank shouted at Lexus.

"You're out of your mind and if I stay around you any more this evening I'll lose mine too. I've got plenty of thinking to do and both of us better get some rest. Tomorrow can't be any worse than today."

"Go ahead and go to that ritzy condo you have while I rot in this cell. **By tomorrow you damn better have some good ideas."**

"I'm not going to talk to you until you settle down. Besides that I am tired and I need to think. Neither of you should answer any questions. I'll come by in the morning, but not until I have reviewed the charges and consulted with a couple of my associates."

Lexus turned to the door and shouted, "All through for the time being."

The guard appeared immediately and **as Lexus left. the very silent and downcast Sammy put out his hand to Lexus saying, "Do your best for the boss."**

Schank ignored Sammy's remark. With Lexus gone Schank resumed pacing back and forth, ranting and raving, then yelled at Sammy, "I will fight this down to the last notch. I am not guilty of kidnapping."

Sammy could not help himself, "Boss, you don't have to worry nuthin' about me. I ain't going to say a word. But you know you kept Lorie locked in her room."

The gravity of his situation had just been explained very simply by the punchy Sammy. Schank thought to himself, "Even a dumb jury, with people on it like Sammy could convict me."

Sammy, not used to saying the prayers his Mother had taught him as a kid, was at this moment of despair thinking of his deceased Mother. "Mom, if I ever get out of this I promise I will never get tangled up with a Schank again. I need your help, Mom."

Schank continued his fury of words and Sammy spoke up again, "Let's us take it easy."

Those words from a servant were the last straw. **Schank slapped Sammy on the side of his head, with his powerful right hand.** Sammy staggered hitting his head on a metal bed support rod. He tried to remain standing holding onto the rod, but was too dazed. He fell, but managed to reach the lower bunk. His body reached the bed, his legs didn't.

Schank paid no attention to Sammy and continued to pace back and forth, shouting obscenities. A half hour later Sammy seemed to gain enough strength to pull the rest of his body onto the bunk. There he lay with all of his clothes on.

On his hourly check of the cells the guard observed Sammy had apparently decided to get some rest. The guard said,

"Sammy has gotten smart and gone to bed. Why don't you shut up and crawl into that upper bunk."

Schank never replied. He thought Sammy was sound asleep so he sat down in one of the two chairs.

He continued to swear and make threats. An hour later the guard again passed the cell. This time the guard said nothing.

CHAPTER 17
LORIE OWENS FILES CHARGES.

After an hour of examinations conducted by the Chinese Doctor and a staff physician their diagnosis of Lorie was inconclusive. Delores had brought the vial containing the Chinese herbs Lorie had taken with food. The hospital laboratory easily recognized it as a mild emetic that should not cause any side effects. After the hospital medical team heard of her confinement on the Schankrila they were very concerned.

Any thing from a complete nervous breakdown, a pending heart attack or an attack of hiatus hernia could be contributing illnesses. Even her blood count was far below normal. For certain she must be carefully monitored and be given fluids for at least 24 hours.

Very reluctantly the Doctors agreed to let her be interviewed by a female deputy district attorney, Sally Smith, who had the reputation of being a caring officer of the law. She promised to ask her questions without any pressure or intimidation.

Sally was extremely bright and cheerful and most often very successful in obtaining information She knew she had to put Lorie at ease in order to gain her confidence and obtain information that would later hold up in court. A court reporter accompanied Sally.

The answers Lorie gave were simple. **"Yes, she had been detained against her will and she had requested many times to be permitted to leave.** She had been taken over many state lines against her will. She had been forced to submit sexually to Schank and when she refused he often slapped her and raped her."

Delores held Lorie's hand as she related these terrifying experiences. Lorie felt a great strength coming to her from Delores as Schank's brutal treatment was being recorded. Lorie knew Delores had saved her life. Yes, Lorie would file charges and would sign them as soon as they were typed up.

With Lorie Owen's signature, the deputy District Attorney, Sally Smith, put out her hand and said, "Lorie, here are my day and night numbers. Call me anytime. You have done the right thing by signing these charges. **Too many men just use us as they see fit.** Kidnapping is kidnapping and rape is rape. Both are felonies!" .

As Sally had departed the hospital room she said to herself, "As they say, this is going to make the cheese a lot more binding. We'll hold back on the rape charges for a few days and then amend the indictment. What a dirty rat Schank is. **My brother lost a leg in the War. I'm serving in the war to make America a decent place to live in by helping society get rid of scum like Schank."**

She was rushed by police car to Headquarters to file the affidavit in support of the charges. The District Attorney had concluded the case was too big for him to sleep through so he was there when Sally arrived.

"You did your usual great job, Sally. This is an outrage! It's brutality of a most felonious nature."

"This is what our job is all about. This is what the citizens of LA county pay us for."

"I like modest people. As long as they do the job well. Thanks, Sally."

There were many other wheels turning. Dozens of steps the general public would never dream about. The Justice Department, Treasury, FBI and even the Internal Revenue Dept.

were all interested in Schank and had to be notified and brought up to date.

Action on their part would include court orders to close Schank's dozen or so offices. All office records would be impounded and twenty four hour guards posted at each office.

No one ran an operation like this without skimming. Al Capone had a lot of followers.

CHAPTER 18
BOB SCHANK AND HIS MOTHER MARTHA

Back in Santa Barbara Schank's son, Bob, still had the Shadow accompanying him. When he tried to explain this to his Mother she had gone through the roof. Bob couldn't tell his Mother about Ruppert and made up a story that someone had tried to rob him. Like a typical mother, who knew her son well, she knew she wasn't hearing the truth.

Reluctantly she permitted the Shadow to stay in one of the small guest cottages on the estate.

With Bob alone in the house with her except for two servants and the gardener, she quizzed Bob, but his mouth was as tight as the proverbial clam. **In frustration and desperation she repeated what she had told him many times.**

"Please Bob, get out of this business with your Dad. I can live with my sister in Anaheim. You're welcome to live with us. Let's do it now before something serious happens!"

"Thanks, Mother, for the offer. You know, I am really going to give it some serious thought. For right now I need to go to bed and get some rest. Goodnight, mother."

Bob hugged his mother that evening, something which he didn't do very often. She watched Bob trudge upstairs to his bedroom in the east wing of the estate. Just watching him struck terror in her heart. **"Please, God, help Bob and help me."**

As Bob reached the top of the stairs he turned east to the luxurious private suite he slept in. It had it's own private sitting room, small library, bath complete with shower and separate tub. A small private kitchen with automatic coffee maker, dishes, sink, stove, refrigerator and pantry which his Mother watched over and always had stocked with Bob's favorite snacks.

A wine and liquor cabinet was in the sitting room as well as a tiny bar in one corner. The piece de resistance was the luxurious bedroom. The cherry furniture was large and the wall paneling was in matching cherry.

A large walk in closet held an assortment of clothes that Bob could not wear out if he had lived to be two hundred years old. Bob liked to have his friends see the suite he lived in.

It impressed everyone, but in those Montecito hills his suite would not come close to equaling the grandeur and exquisiteness of what hundreds of women called their bedroom suite. One woman boasted, "She had 35 coffee tables on approval before she found one she felt suited her decor. "

However few equaled the fabulous rooms in the William Randolph Hearst estate at San Simeon. There a whole room might be purchased overseas, disassembled and reassembled at San Simeon.

Bob was a well built six foot young man. He had strong features he obviously inherited from his powerfully built Father. His hair was dark with some wave to it. His eyes were dark and had kind of a furtive look. His Mother knew that also came from his Father.

She watched Bob's figure turn at the top of the stairs, and disappear toward his suite. She then walked slowly to her favorite chair. **"I might as well sit here. I can't go to sleep."**

Martha, long before her life became lonely, had become a great fan of Sherlock Holmes and her library included all of his stories, as well as all of his historical novels.

When Sir Arthur Conan Doyle gave up writing his Sherlock Holmes mysteries to devote all of his time to writing historical novels, his world wide mystery readers were devastated. They felt his greatest writings were about Sherlock Holmes.

. Holmes leading critic of this writing change was his own mother, who was very dear to Doyle. Finally, after such a worldwide clamor, with his dear mother topping the list of those demanding more of Sherlock, he was forced to bring back Holmes.

In the last decade of Doyle's life he lectured all over the word on instinct, perception and what some might term clairvoyance. He stressed that God remained omnipotent, above all.

Martha attended one of Doyle's lectures and was particularly struck by his belief in premonitions and glimpses into the future. "Right now I feel there is an aura of disaster encircling this family. I feel a giant crevice is opening and Bob and his dad are falling into it.**"Whether you call it women's intuition or believe Doyle's lectures** I feel a sinister evil coming into play. Our lifestyle is shaking and the devil is going to have his day. I'm not a drinking lady, but right now I'm going to pour myself a glass of French grape.

"If it's so good for French digestion maybe it will be good for my woozy stomach and headache. I'll also have some toast with sliced avocado and tomato on it.

"I'll have salt on it whether it's good for me or not. I'm worried and frustrated."

As she went about fixing herself a light late snack her past flashed before her. She felt like the woman about to be publicly condemned. She thought about how she had been an art major in college and a junior weekend prom queen.

She never felt she was glamorous, but she was pretty. Her Dad was in management and her Mother a housewife. **It was an accident that she met Schank A bad accident.**

He was selling steel calling on her father when she dropped by to get a ride home with Dad. Schank had pursued her after that meeting. Her Dad had serious qualms. Her Mother envisioned Schank would go a long way.

And he had. success after success. When he bought the Schankrila he was seldom home and now it had been five years since she had seen him. **He had obviously tired of her.**

Her attorney had advised her to hang in there. So that was what she had been doing. She took her wine and toast to the coffee table beside her chair. The wine put her to sleep. **She missed the ten o'clock news and when she woke at 11:30 she went right to bed.**

CHAPTER 19
THE NEWS BREAKS.

The news media had called out all stops and were working feverishly to be first with the most facts. It did not reach major news stations until after midnight. In Santa Barbara anything close to home could not be broadcast until it was carefully verified.

The Associated Press release received by the Santa Barbara News-Press said:

HEAD OF SCHANK INVESTMENTS ARRESTED FOR KIDNAPPING AND INTERSTATE PROSTITUTION. HEAD OF HIS LOS ANGELES OPERATIONS WAS FOUND TRUSSED IN SCHANK'S CAR. CLAIMED HE WAS KIDNAPPED IN SANTA BARBARA, BUT WAS ARRESTED WITH SCHANK ON THE SAME CHARGES.

Soon after the Santa Barbara Police Dept. heard the news flash their telephone lines heated up as if a 5.0 earthquake had struck the city. Reporters converged on the police department. **Local radio stations felt they could not delay beyond the 7 A.M. news.**

The police chief was sleeping soundly when he was called with the news. He immediately grabbed the telephone by his bed and called Los Angeles demanding to be placed in contact with Lt. Alex Brown, their direct liaison. "I'm at my home right now and here is the number. As soon as I get dressed I'll be at my office.

"Tell him this is the first news we've had of any kidnapping in Santa Barbara. Why hasn't someone called us? Its damn embarrassing! We've got the radio and the press on our backs to say nothing about the townspeople. We should have been called right away."

With that he slammed down his phone, yelled at his wife and got dressed quickly. Ten minutes later he was at his office where he found Lt. Merced, Sgt. Smitty and half a dozen others had beat him by a few minutes. Just then the phone rang.

It was Lt. Brown from the LAPD. **"What the hell kind of a liaison man are you Brown," yelled the chief.**

"Now calm down. A cable with all the details is being typed up right now. You'll have it in ten minutes. The fact that Ruppert Snyder was kidnapped last night, most likely in your city, is not important because he has been found in Los Angeles.

"He's alive and in fairly good condition. So don't sweat that out now. Start doing some detective work. Was Ruppert on the Schankrila? Was he meeting anyone in SB?

"Check the hotels. Talk with every taxi operator in town."

"I know all that! I used to be a detective. What's worrying me is what do we say to the reporters?"

"Now that's where you get to use your charming personality and finesse."

"I don't like that crack, Alex! You know damn well the spot I am in."

"You're the chief. I am only a 2nd Lt." Lt. Brown chuckled as he teased the chief.

Finally the Chief grinned as he noticed the others in his office were amused.

"Just get enough bodies on the job so the clues don't get cold! The FBI, Treasury and Internal Revenue have issued orders to close, lock and guard all of Schank's offices. Our wire will include that authorization. Get a search warrant issued."

"Are you bucking for 1st Lieutenant?"

. **"That's a joke, I hope. It took me 20 years to make second Louie.** I'm just bucking to hold onto my job."

Both men laughed ending the conversation on a friendly basis. The chief turned to the men in his office and said, **"Men, here are my orders!"**

CHAPTER 20
MARTHA SCHANK.

The two sleeping pills she had taken were enough to let Martha sleep a little. Her clock radio was set at it's usual five minutes to seven. She liked to start her days listening to the news at seven. The announcer began with his usual enthusiastic, "Good morning, seven o'clock news listeners. Here is a big story from Associated Press.

" AP reports there may have been a kidnapping in Santa Barbara the night before last. The startling story is that the alleged kidnap victim, Ruppert Snyder, was found by the Los Angeles police in a gunny sack in the trunk of his boss's car.

"Ruppert and his boss, Cal Schank, owner of Schank Investment Company, have both been arrested for kidnapping and interstate prostitution."

Hearing those words Martha screamed, " I knew it! I knew something sinister of earthquake proportions was happening. Oh, what will happen to Bob and to all of us?"

The announcer continued with, "Ruppert Snyder is claiming a kidnapped man cannot be arrested for kidnapping and this strange story is attracting national attention! Hold on folks, here is another hot news item coming in on the AP teletype. Let's take a station break, folks, while I study it."

Martha jumped out of bed without putting on a gown over her shimmering silk nightie and ran to the bottom of the stairs and screamed "Bob, turn on the news. Bob get up right now." Bob had the seven A.M. news on and was sitting up almost paralyzed with fear. He was saying things like, "Ruppert Snyder is expendable, but my Dad–arrested!"

Getting no reply from Bob caused Martha to go up the stairs more rapidly than she had ever climbed them. She saw Bob sitting up and they both heard the announcer, "I'm back with the latest. Los Angeles police have just revealed that Schank's guard, Sammy, who was sharing a cell with Schank, was found dead this morning."

Martha collapsed on Bob's bed and he cradled her head in his arms. She was sobbing so hard her whole body was shaking and Bob feared she might be having a complete breakdown. He moved her body to a comfortable position on his bed laying her head carefully on his pillow. **Then he called her Doctor's home. A servant answered and Bob yelled, "This is Bob Schank. Mother has collapsed."**

In a moment Dr. Smith was on the line. " I've just been listening to the news. I'm shaken up myself. Tell me your Mother's condition."

Bob described it briefly. "Take her pulse, Bob."

"It's just under 100. A little irregular and she seems to be stirring."

"Her sedative pills are in a blue bottle. Double check the prescription date. It should be 1950."

Bob found them in the medicine cabinet. "I've got them!"

"The usual dose is one every six hours. Give her two right now. Don't move her. I'll be over within 30 minutes. I don't expect her to pass out again, but if she does call an ambulance. I think my office should find a nurse to spend the next eight hours with your Mother.

"She needs to be checked–help her get dressed–help her to her bathroom. Any objection to getting a nurse?"

"Absolutely not, Doctor. By the way all of this is driving me up against the wall. Can I take a couple of the pills in the blue bottle?'

"I think you're going to need something stronger than that. I'll give you a prescription when I come out."

Bob's phone rang, "The Doctor must have forgot something." he thought to himself.

It was Eileen, Bob's secretary, "Bob, I have been trying to reach you, but your line has been busy. I just heard the awful news over the radio."

"Mother fainted and I have been talking to her Doctor. Yes, the world is crashing for the Schanks."

"Did you hear the part about your office being locked up?"

"Just part of it. Mother was screaming and then she fainted."

"This would be tough on any woman. Your Mother is so nice. Can I help?"

"Thanks, Eileen, now cover the rest of the news please."

"The newsman said guards have been sent to all Schanks offices in the United States and that all records are impounded."

"Things are going to be rough, Eileen. Rougher than you can imagine."

"I have often worried, Bob. I regretted business became Evil at times."

"Eileen, I'm here in the room with my Mother waiting for the Doctor to show up. Maybe I'll call you later. Right now I have my hands full."

"I'm sure you do, Bob. Good luck and good-bye for now."

Bob started for his bathroom and his phone rang again. "I'll bet it's the newspaper or some reporter," he grumbled as he picked up the phone.

"Is this Bob Schank."

"Yes, it is. Who is calling?"

"Detective Lt. Merced, Santa Barbara Police Department," came the crisp forceful voice.

"Yes, Lieutenant, go ahead."

"Mr. Schank, did you hear the news report either last night or this morning?"

"Just this morning. My Mother fainted and I apparently didn't hear all of it."

"Your office is sealed off. We have posted a guard because of orders we have received from certain government agencies. **We are inclined to believe you may have a lot of information including the alleged kidnapping you failed to notify us about.** We would rather talk to you first without arresting you. You are ordered not to leave town.

"**Get medical help for your Mother and be at our offices by 9 A.M.**"

"I can make that. Mother's Doctor is due in less than 30 minutes. I am not dressed and would like to get a little food in my stomach to settle it."

"We'll expect you then."

As he hung up the phone Bob muttered to himself, "If I had only listened to my Mother. She may not know a darn thing about business. Her wisdom is only exceeded by her sweetness. "She told me a hundred times to get out of Dad's business and go out and get a job on my own. Not to be a slave to Dad. Was she ever right!"

Bob looked at the worry and sorrow in his Mother's eyes. "I've failed you, Mother," he said as he took her hand. Her natural beauty was now hidden behind her pale face and frightened eyes. She looked so helpless and fragile.

"**I'll do what I can for you, Bob. You know that. I've always prayed for you every day. Guess my prayers were not strong enough.**"

"I was too headstrong. Maybe Dad was too powerful and I was a weakling."

"Have you done anything you could go to jail for?"

Bob started to answer, then he stammered and became silent. The silence was making his Mother cry again. "**Mother, I can't undo what I have already done.**"

Suddenly all Bob could think of was money. He'd been paying all his personal bills as well as the estate expense from the company account. He knew it was illegal.

His Dad told him everyone else was doing it. Right now Bob realized if the government attached the business account he would soon run out of funds. He'd better cash a check for five or ten thousand and be a few minutes late for his appointment with Merced.

When Dr. Smith arrived and completed his examination of Martha they moved her downstairs to a sunny dining nook off the kitchen. Dr. Smith told the cook what to fix and soon all three of them were having breakfast. They picked at their food. Smith said, "I tell all my patients to eat a hearty breakfast no matter how they feel and I'm not setting a good example. **Let's eat something. It's bound to be a long day."**

Dr. Smith's wife had died a number of years ago and he never told anyone he had a crush on Martha. It was something that he didn't quite understand.

Upon his becoming a widower it seemed the frequency of his examinations of widows went up four or five times. His office nurse finally made up a chart and teased him each Monday morning as to how the week would go. **Those with the nicest figures were always finding aches and pains that required them to undress for examination.**

What the good Doctor didn't tell his nurse was some of the truly obscene circumstances he was often confronted with. Finally one day his nurse said privately to him, in an accent that she obviously had taken care to practice, **"In the immortal words of Winston Churchill,** never in the history of Montecito have so many wealthy widows chased one lone widower as much as in the case of Dr. Smith vs. the widows of Montecito."

Then with an impish impudent look on her face she said, **"Oh, Dr. Smith, I have this pain just below my navel. Maybe you could stop by my apartment this evening. I'd like to show it to you."**

There were more than a few times, on a house call, that Dr. Smith had his hands full. The temptation of a hot blooded romance seemed to be always there. None of his other patients seemed to compare to Martha. Even though she had lived by herself for many years he knew she was still a married woman and that meant hands off to the very ethical Dr. Smith.

This morning as he left she put her arms around him for the first time ever.

He could not resist holding her tighter than a conventional hug. He had to bite his tongue to keep from saying, "Martha I love you so much. I want to take care of you forever." Instead he said, "Martha, you'll be all right. When I'm through with my patients today I'll stop by. **If you like I'll have dinner with you and make certain you eat.**"

"Oh, would you, Dr. Smith? I feel like I'm having a nervous breakdown."

Just then the gardener called, "I'm going to open the gate for a nurse Edwards. Is that all right."

"O.K.," said Bob, who had taken the call.

Minutes later Dr. Smith was giving instructions to the nurse and asked her to stay until he arrived at the end of the day to get her report and to check Mrs. Schank.

As Dr. Smith went out the door Bob Schank wondered for the first time about Dr. Smith and his Mother. Did the good Doctor have a special feeling for his Mother? Bob found himself saying to himself, **"I sure hope that is the case. Dad has been rotten to her."**

As Dr. Smith drove out the gate of Schank estate he began talking to himself. His first words were, "I've got to keep from making a fool of myself. Now that I have put my arms around her I feel like I can't hold back any longer. Yes, I have it bad! I find Martha irresistible."

As he drove he continued to ponder that question. Of recent years he had gone to bed at night thinking about her. And often during the night he dreamed they were together.

As he stopped his car in his parking spot he leaned back saying to himself, "Doctor, heal thyself! But how?"

His nurse saw the tall thin Doctor with his wire spectacles walk in the office that morning and suddenly a thought flashed into her perceptive mind, **"This man feels deeply about Mrs. Schank. He looks so forlorn."**

His hair, even though he was just over 50, was almost white. It had gotten so much whiter as his wife had become ill. He was a precise and dedicated Doctor, but right now he looked as if the last bit of zip had exited his life. He looks five years older than when he left his office last night.

In sympathy she said, "Shall I call a Doctor for you."

"You are very perceptive, Alice. I wish I could confide in someone, but like Harry Truman, whom I used to hate until I finally realized what a great man he really was said, 'The buck stops with me.' **I feel so sorry for Martha!**

"She has had all that money can buy, but that is all she has had. No life of her own. And now this. I wish I could help her. **Somehow I must help her."**

Alice did not reply. She said to herself "If I had to bet my life right now I'd bet he's in love with her. So that's why he's still single. **He had to go and fall for a married woman."**

The Shadow had hardly slept and had the radio on all night hoping the music would lull him to sleep. **When he heard the 7 A.M. news he hoped he was having a nightmare.** Ruppert and Schank arrested? How did Ruppert get in the trunk of Schank's car?

He pulled himself upright in bed and slapped his face to make certain he was not asleep and dreaming. . He knew where he was and he realized his main client was in big trouble. There might be no more pay checks from Schank. His mind went to the many jobs he had done for Bob Schank and his dad in Santa Barbara. In addition he had gone out of town for several. He asked himself, **"Should I make a break for it and get out of town?"**

He wanted to go the main house and talk to Bob, but he had seen two cars enter.

He didn't know they were the Doctor and a nurse. Within the hour Bob knocked on his door and discussed matters with him very briefly. Bob instructed him to go back to his apartment and wait for a call from him.

Maybe he should stop at the grocery store and lay in a couple of days supply of food..

Bob Schank was waiting at the bank when it opened at nine. He quickly stepped to a teller and presented a check to himself for $10,000.00.

"Just a moment Mr. Schank," I have to have checks of this size signed by a bank officer. She stepped away form the counter and a few moments later said, "The manager would like to discuss this with you in private."

She led Bob to the manager's office and he was asked to be seated. The manager said in an apologetic tone of voice, "I have no idea why, but I have been advised to put a stop payment on any withdrawals from your company account. You haven't been using your personal account for several years and I believe there still is a few thousand in it.

"Also, your Mother has a personal account and there is about $3,000 in it."

"That is a break. Thank you."

Bob knew he was now late for his appointment with Lt. Merced so he left right away. It was only a few blocks from the State Street bank location to the police station.

Bob Schank was seated in the Chief's office along with Lt. Merced and Sgt. Smitty. Lt. Merced started the ball rolling with, **"Tell us in exact detail all your activities the night before last.**

"I don't think I should say anything until I have talked to my attorney."

"Are you saying you won't?" asked the chief.

"I guess that is my decision."

"Lock him up, Sgt. Smitty."

"What are the charges," demanded Bob Schank.

"Suspicion of being an accessory to your father, for starters. **Sgt. Smitty, look up all the dirt we have on Schank Investment Co and Bob Schank personally.** Didn't we have a complaint from a couple of young ladies. Didn't one accuse you of rape?

"Take him out of my sight now before I give him a working over that I will regret later. You hid behind your Dad for years. Now you're both in the can and it's been long overdue. Throw the book at him."

Bob started to comment, but the chief interrupted with, "Take him away now!"

As soon as Schank and Smitty were out the door Lt. Merced looked at the chief saying, "Is there something personal between you two?"

"I have a personal dislike for his kind. They have foreclosed on several really poor folks. They hold high interest rate mortgages on several others that are about to lose their property. They are like a small Mafia. I can hardly wait to get into their records. I'll bet we'll be shocked."

Lt. Merced came back with, "How about The Shadow and his records. I think we better pick him up on some charge before he destroys them."

"Yes, pick him up right now if he isn't already on his way out of town."

CHAPTER 21
DELORES CALLS LANGE.

That morning, in the hospital Lorie Owens was being checked by several Doctors and going through a number of additional tests. Lorie cried whenever Delores left the room.

Lorie was heavily sedated much of the time and Delores was finding this intense isolation difficult to endure. She missed the comradeship at the Tong.

Right then Delores wished she could see Lange. I must call him! He's only 100 miles away. Delores had previously told Lorie about Lange. Lorie Owens, with a note of sadness in her voice and in her expression had answered, "I hear about so many nice people. What a shame I ran into a bummer like Schank."

"Even among Chinese we have what you Americans call 'Bad Apples.'"

"He is much more than a rotten apple. He is cruel and unscrupulous."

"Too much power ruins many a person. Turns them into a dictator. Samurai warriors not always kind and gentle. Most American Chinese are dedicated to being good citizens.". .

Delores opened her purse and took out Lange's number. She placed the call and asked for Lange. Jean the office secretary replied, "I believe he is in and not on the telephone."

With a smile on her face Delores said, "Please tell him the Dragon Lady is calling him from Los Angeles."

That was a shock to Jean. She had wondered why Lange didn't seem to have any kind of a girl friend. And now some tease from Los Angles was calling herself The Dragon Lady. The door to Lange's small office was open. "The Dragon Lady from Los Angeles is calling you," Jean almost whispered, afraid to say it out loud it sounded so preposterous.

"Maybe this isn't a tease? Maybe its bad news for poor Lange? Did he have a problem with a Chinese lady and did her wrong? And the Dragon Lady is after him now?

"Maybe it wasn't his fault? **Oh I hope he isn't in trouble. I was about to encourage him to take me out on date.** Even though I know office romances are frowned on as they are fraught with danger for both parties."

"Is it really you?" The obvious happiness in his voice was picked up by Delores.

Delores laughed and said, "What do you Americans say? 'I put you on spot with office secretary' by saying Dragon Lady."

"Now that you mention it I think I may take some ribbing. They don't see any evidence of a girl friend so now you become the mystery woman in my life."

"Life is a mystery, Lange, isn't it?"

"It sure is, but you are always in my dreams. Like to graduate from them to reality. By the way were you anywhere near the big pinch last night?"

"Very close. I will tell you more later. Can you come down to Los Angeles? I am helping Lorie Owens."

"You don't mean the lady that caused Schank to be arrested?"

"Yes, I am at Los Angeles General Hospital with Lorie Owens. Maybe we could only have lunch together."

"Maybe I'll put a ladder up to your hospital room and carry you away."

"You mean elope? Maybe if I drink enough of my special tea I will have strength to elope with you. Think Ah Wing might not be too surprised."

"It will only take me 10 minutes to buy a ladder and I'm on my way."

"Tomorrow is Saturday, can you visit me then without ladder, around noon? You have an aunt and uncle in Anaheim. Can you stay with them?"

"I'm sure I can get Saturday off. Let me write down the phone number and address of the hospital. "

After Lange read the numbers back for verification Delores said, "Thank you, Lange. I must get back to Lorie. Hold off on ladder for now."

"Keep thinking about it, Delores. I can buy a ladder in Los Angeles. Can also borrow one from my Aunt and Uncle."

"Good-bye for now, Lange. Should time come for you and I, no ladder will be needed." She spoke those words softly and with obvious sincerely. **Lange would never forget them.** He sat in his small office, in the kind of romantic daze that only too often comes to men and women. In his frustration he mumbled to himself.

"Maybe life is like being in a puppet show. Or like war where a bullet misses one man and kills another. I'd drive a hundred miles any day to see her."

Just then Lange's boss stepped into his tiny room saying, "Jean said you just received a call from the Dragon Lady. **I thought that was just literary fiction.** You didn't list her as a reference. Come to think about it you look a little dazed. Perhaps I said the wrong thing."

"I guess I am. Delores is a Chinese Lady. The right arm of a West Coast Chinese Leader by the name of Ah Wing. I met him first maybe 19 years ago. Delores reminds me of the Dragon Lady in the old Saturday Evening Post stories. She called me from the hospital where she is attending Lorie Owens, the young lady Schank is alleged to have kidnapped."

"I can see why you look surprised. I had no idea you had high ranking Chinese friends."

"Delores has asked me to come to Los Angeles General Hospital tomorrow noon and have lunch with her."

"You've been working Saturday's here and it's time you took one off."

That evening Lange was busy packing a few things and checking his car. He also called his Aunt and Uncle in Anaheim asking them if he had to stay over would they want him to stay with them. They were delighted.

Then Lange knew he must tell his landlady he would be gone. He knocked on her door and she invited him in. She let him know she was doing a lot of worrying. He searched for the right words finally saying, **"The Schanks are going to be in such hot water they aren't going to foreclose on you or anyone else for awhile."**

"Thank you, lad, I been telling me lady friends you are like the son I never had."

CHAPTER 22
TONG HEADQUARTERS, NEW CHINA TOWN.

Back at the #1 Tong Headquarters in New Chinatown Ah Wing did not sleep well. He had a nightmare in which his Secretary Delores Lee was killed while trying to defend Lorie Owens . In the nightmare Lorie Owens was also killed.

Ah Wing had a private breakfast in Wang Sing's apartment. Ah Wing expressed his fears. Wang Sing replied, "What Americans call 'gut feeling' is not to be ignored. I am not acquainted with security force on duty at the hospital. If Lorie Owens is put out of the way Ruppert would not testify against Schank. Whole case against Schank may fall into Pacific Ocean like rumor has it giant earthquake may do to LA."

Ah Wing nodded and said, "Much wisdom come from your lips."

"What suggestions do you have, Honorable Ah Wing?"

"I have many ideas perhaps. All depend on resources of Chinese Community and willingness to commit such resources."

Just then there were several knocks on the door.

Wang rose and said, "Excuse me. I go to door."

The person at the door handed Wang a note. He read it, bowed, and shut the door. He handed Ah Wing the note. It said,

"Schank's body guard was placed in error in Schank's cell overnight. This morning he was found dead."

Wang Sing spoke rapidly, "No time to delay. Must take important steps now. Delores Lee and Lorie Owens must receive more protection than just a guard outside the hospital door.

Sing's mind had several plans running through it. Now he knew he must use the plan that would be foolproof even in case of sudden surprise. He replied to Ah Wing, **"We have very skilled black belt Chinese. Also school for several years on Taekwondo. All students in advanced class can break at least 50 boards in 25 seconds."**

Ah Wing replied, "You have great number of such people?"

Wang Sing replied, "At least 20. This includes women. We assign Chinese couple to sit outside of Hospital Room and one female inside hospital room. We must explain to them the serious possibility that gunfire might render their Taekwondo useless. They are all fast like lightening in the sky. They can act while gunman is still drawing gun if they are close enough. **One board per half second is very fast. Do you not agree, Honorable Ah Wing?"**

"Oh, to be young again and able to move swiftly.. I agree. Could we act on this now?"

Wang Sing replied quickly, "You agree. This is way to go?"

"Maybe two more guards just inside hospital entrance. Watch from waiting room."

"Yes, Ah Wing. Also excellent training session. Our people will be anxious to help."

"Must also protect Delores Lee," replied Ah Wing with great concern in his voice.

"I understand and share your great concern. Delores must not be harmed."

"Chinese very fortunate you survive sinking of China Queen by Japanese submarine during the war. You help many Chinese to survive since."

With those words the necessary wheels were set in motion immediately. Subordinates were chosen and the chain of command was established quickly. The centuries of Chinese wisdom was not like Pearl Harbor and many other American failures. On the other hand the Chinese had made their share of mistakes over the centuries.

Chinese with advanced Taekwondo training would team up to guard the hospital room. Two posing as a couple would be seated on one side of the door. The Los Angeles Police Department guard would be seated on the other. One Chinese would be in the room with Delores and Lorie Owens. **Two additional Taekwondo experts would be in the lobby. One seated and one moving around.**

Meanwhile they would rush one expert Taekwondo couple to the hospital room door right now and call Lt. Brown. He was the kind of a detective they expected no problems with.

Lt. Brown was himself a 5th degree black belt holder. He said it had saved his life on two occasions and had prevented severe personal injury to himself on too many occasions to even try to count. They had thought of making Lt. Alex Brown, while he was still just Sergeant Alex Brown, an honorary member of the Chinese Community.

When the Chinese couple arrived Lt. Brown was there. He was very pleased. He had not slept well last night. He knew the lives of Lorie and Delores were in extreme danger!

The very intelligent Delores Lee breathed a sigh of relief. **She knew anyone seeking to do away with Lorie Owens would also take her life without a moments hesitation.**

CHAPTER 23
A CONTRACT ON LORIE OWENS.

In the morning Schank looked at Sammy and wondered why he hadn't moved. He yelled at Sammy and still no response. A few minutes later he looked at Sammy and thought, "He's out like a light."

Schank had seen many a person knocked out, but Sammy looked glassy eyed. He reached for Sammy's wrist to check his pulse. **He found none.** His mind went back to the hard slap he had given Sammy. "They can't hang me for slapping a guy! I'll tell them he went berserk and took a punch at my and I just slapped him. O.K., that's it!"

Schank called the guard as he thought, "This could be a big break for me."

The Coroner found two big bruises on Sammy, but Schank would not answer any questions and called for his Attorney.

After consultation with Schank, his attorney Lexus Taylor issued a statement.

"The two men argued. Sammy, who had been at one time been a semi-professional boxer, swung at Schank. Schank ducked and in self defense slapped Sammy. Sammy's death had to be occasioned by something other than one hard slap from Schank."

Sammy's body was brought into the Coroner's lab and carefully checked. The Coroner issued a statement to the police which was not released to the public. The Coroner's statement said, "Sammy has been slapped hard and his head hit a metal object. A blood vessel broke in his brain. This could have been caused by a weakness from a prior boxing injury."

The press were doing their job when they reported:

KEY WITNESS AGAINST SCHANK DIES IN CELL.

Why were both men in the same cell?

Schank and Taylor knew that Sammy would have cracked when the case went to trial. Now they had a chance. Ruppert would not testify against Schank. That only left Lorie Owens all alone in her charges against Schank and Ruppert.

Schank looked at Lexus. "Get the best. Get Tony G. out of retirement if necessary."

"How much shall we offer for a contract?"

"A million. It's clear sailing with her out of the way."

Lexus looked at Schank. "I don't like to do it, but we're forced into it."

CHAPTER 24
LANGE ARRIVES AT L.A. GENERAL.

Bad timing almost costs him his life.
Lange left Santa Barbara Saturday morning right after breakfast so he would have plenty of time to get to L.A. General by 11:30.

Within 20 minutes he would pass through the tiny city of Carpinteria as he headed for Ventura. Hiway 101 would virtually hug the beach for the next 30 miles..

Whether you served in the Pacific and drove on the West coast or served in Europe and now were driving on the East coast the result was the same. Your thoughts went to the other side of the ocean and the men you left there. Part of you would also remain there forever. **Life magazine published the dramatic picture of the first Americans killed in the war as they lay dead on the beach at Buna, Papua, New Guinea.** Their bodies sprawled as they fell. The picture was awesome and terrifying.

It was as if the waves were softly and gently caressing their bodies as they lay, never to rise again by their own power. Their boyish laughter would never ring again. It had been spent forever by the bullets, bombs or grenades that downed them. **No chance to ever again shake hands with them, and smile!**

It was as if nature, who had delivered them into this world perhaps 20 years earlier, wanted to wash them gently now, as she reclaimed them forever. To never return them to their Mothers and Fathers, their brothers and sisters, their wives and girl friends.

Lange felt tears trickle down his cheek. He knew only too well that was the way war was. It was a matter of timing. If you were in the wrong place at the wrong time that was it. Now as his car reached Ventura, with Port Hueneme and Oxnard nearby, highway 101 turned away from the coast and headed toward Los Angeles. He thought to himself about the subject of timing and that if he wasn't observant and careful he might become a casualty of the seventy mile per hour freeway traffic.

The hundreds of entrances and exits from the freeway system seemed to throw cars into and out of the system with abandon. "Can it get any worse?" he wondered that sunny April Saturday morning.

But it did get worse. He made two wrong turn-offs. "Got to concentrate on this crazy road system or I'll be late."

Finally, he pulled into the parking lot. He noticed several police cars and several policemen seemed to be standing around outside. Before getting out he ran a comb through his hair, tried to adjust his tie, then realized a bathroom stop would satisfy an urgency.

He entered the lobby and told the receptionist he was to see Delores Lee. She didn't seem like she wanted to follow through, but finally called the room and Lange talked to Delores. The receptionist asked for identification and then gave Lange the room number and the directions.

He then explained to her he had just driven down from Santa Barbara and would like to use the rest room first. She gave him directions.

As Lange entered the rest room he noticed two men dressed as Doctors were just exiting two of the stalls. He said to himself, "That's kind of strange for Doctors to use the public rest rooms. Wouldn't they have one for medical personnel?"

Then he noticed they did not wash their hands. "Now that's very strange," thought the very detailed and observant Lange.

As the two doctors went out the door he got a very strong whiff of cologne. For Lange it was like he was once again in an infantry division in the Jungles of New Guinea. His sixth sense told him something was wrong. Doctors washed their hands and didn't smell so strong of cologne. "Wonder what that smell would do to a patient with respiratory problems?"

That thought did it. He stopped and did not use the rest room facilities. Instead he went out the rest room door and looked for the two Doctors. He noticed they were just stepping into an elevator. He walked to the elevator door and watched the needle stop at four.

"That's the same floor Delores is on. Oh well, I'll tease her and ask her if a couple of doctors with dirty hands and an overdose of cologne tried to get a date with her. That's it. Those birds with medical degrees are running me big competition."

Lange headed back toward the rest room muttering, "Oh well, better to have loved and lost than never to have loved at all. **Anyhow, my biggest competition is all those single Chinese men."**

As he finished using the bathroom he soaped his hands and washed them with hot water.

Once in the hall he said to himself, "I'll take the stairs. I need the exercise. "

Meanwhile the two doctors in question had moved swiftly from the elevator to room 418. "If they don't let us in without argument we'll take the guard and I'll then go in the room and take out Lorie. You watch the oriental couple waiting outside."

They advanced authoritatively to the guard saying, "Doctors Able and Sentana to treat the patient."

The guard replied, "Sorry, Doctors. I have strict orders to not admit anyone unless they are with a certain doctor or nurse."

Immediately one of the men took a snub nosed 38 from his pocket and pressed it against the gut of the guard saying, "You have orders now."

The two Chinese were on full alert. Like infantrymen waiting for a sneak attack. This was it! The Chinese man yelled to divert attention, but at the same instant his right hand slammed the right arm of the man holding the revolver.

The force was so strong it broke the man's wrist and the gun fell harmlessly to his side. **The gunman screamed in pain, but six more blows struck the gunman and he collapsed in a heap, not even a moan coming from his throat.**

Meanwhile the Chinese lady had struck the second man with her first blow only half a second after her partners first blow. Her first blow was a paralyzing hack to the back of his neck with her left hand. Almost simultaneously her right hand struck him on his neck just under his chin.

She struck again with two more blows with her left hand and two more with her right hand. He collapsed on top of the man who had held the gun.

The two Chinese then studied the two fallen men. They each reached down and felt the pulse of the fallen men. There was no pulse. Each stood erect, then bowed to each other, then gave the victory signal of the Taekwondo warrior.

The guard was in double shock as he looked at the two Chinese bowing to each other and at the gunmen on the floor in Doctor's uniforms. His eyes quickly looked for the revolver that had been in his gut just seconds earlier. Seeing it on the floor and the two assailants lying motionless on the floor was unbelievable.

The guard screamed into his walkie talkie, "Red alert. Room 418. Two assailants down."

The guard's heart was pounding so hard it seemed to be trying to push through his chest and his hands were shaking so much he felt embarrassed and hoped the Chinese did not notice. Then he exclaimed, "I'll thank you until my dying day, which was almost today! How did you do it?

The two Chinese bowed humbly and said, "We tap them in right places."

Then the Chinese man turned to the lady and said, "You very magnificent! No wonder you best student in Taekwondo class. Great honor to work with you."

The Chinese lady then bowed to the Chinese man and complimented him.

Just then Lange entered the hall and was aghast. He stopped, unnerved at the obvious fight that had just taken place. His quick mind told him, "Time to stay out of the way. I might have messed up the whole deal. I knew there was something screwy about the men in Doctor's uniforms. I'm sure reinforcements are on the way."

The guard in the lobby and the guard outside the hospital left their posts like they had just heard the firing gun for a hundred yard dash. The lobby guard yelled to the receptionist, **"Red alert, red alert! Room 418. Alert everyone! Everyone stays where they are!"**

The Chinese couple in the lobby said to each other, "We stay here and offer backup."

The first guard took an open elevator. The second guard took the stairs two at a time. This was police work at it's finest and most dangerous, like the infantryman who had just leaped from a landing craft. The adrenaline surged in their veins.

The lobby guard taking the elevator yelled, "This damn elevator needs a passing gear." He would have been panic-stricken with the delay, but he had heard the words 'assailants down.'

He hoped that was correct. He jumped from the elevator when the door opened on the 4th floor. His gun was in his hand, poised to fire as he headed for 418. He expected bedlam.

Instead he saw two small Chinese and one very pale guard standing with his gun drawn. . What looked like two Doctors were crumpled on the floor. "My God!" he said to himself, **"Phony Doctors, why isn't someone handcuffing them?"**

The guard yelled, "We're safe. These two Chinese did all the work and saved our lives. I just saw the most amazing demonstration of Taekwondo. I thought it was Korean, but if the Chinese can adapt it to the lawlessness of Los Angeles who cares."

The Chinese man bowed as he said, "We just graduate from class. This our first opportunity to practice. **Lady is best student in class. I almost fail the class. That is why best student get put with me. Maybe to protect me, too."**

The lobby guard immediately dropped to the floor and reached for the wrist of one man trying to find a pulse. He looked up and said, "No pulse! He is dead!"

By then the other guard had reached room 418. He watched as the lobby guard took the arm of the second man and tried to find a pulse. He looked up again saying, "No pulse either."

Then in utter astonishment he repeated himself, "These two men are both dead!"

Then the door guard bowed to the Chinese as they had bowed to him saying, "Lucky day for State of California. Two less thugs. It'll be a lot cheaper to bury them than to house them and give them a trial with appeal after appeal!"

Then he said, "Guess we call the coroner now."

Just then Lange decided to turn back, but his movement was noticed and one of the lobby guards yelled, "Halt."

Then he approached Lange with his revolver aimed at him. "Identify yourself."

Lange realized the predicament the officer was in and he politely replied, "I was on my way up to see Delores, the Chinese lady in the room with Lorie. I went in the rest room and two Doctors came out of the stalls. I thought that was very strange. I decided to follow them, but they had taken the elevator. I went back into the bathroom, then came up.

"Sounds like a good story, but we need proof. "

"If you feel more comfortable you may handcuff me, Officer. You may also go in the room and ask Delores to come out and identify me."

"Long as you don't mind I will just handcuff you. I'm doing that with your permission you understand."

"Sure, go ahead. It'll be a new experience for me. First and last, I hope."

The officer snapped on the cuffs and marched Lange to the door of room 418. One guard stepped inside and asked if Delores would care to identify Earnest Lange. They had him in handcuffs outside.

Delores was horrified and speechless as she stepped outside the room. The officer closed the door. Then she saw Lange, "Oh Lange, you might have been killed!"

Lange smiled as he said, "Boy, if I had brought a ladder I would have really been in trouble."

One guard said, " What are you talking about– bringing a ladder?"

"Officer, that is just a private joke between Lange and myself. Lange is my good friend and his friendship with Ah Wing goes back almost 20 years. I had just spoken to him and he was on his way up to see me. You can remove the handcuffs and I guarantee him to be no threat to any of us."

The two Chinese bowed saying in unison, "Any friend of Ah Wing is our good friend, too. Very happy to meet you."

The guard unlocked the handcuffs and Lange once again explained to the entire group how he had first observed the phony doctors. Delores said very solemnly, "Except for Ah Wing's concern we might all be dead including you, Lange."

Lange knew a little humor might be appropriate so he said, "Maybe I need to go to the bathroom again."

Everyone laughed, but not very loudly. Delores said with a smile on her face, "Come in and use ours. Let me introduce you to Lorie Owens first. I think it best that we hold back and not tell her what happened."

Then one of the guards said, "Suppose instead of Lange it had been one of their backups with a Russian AK-47. Taekwondo from a distance of 50 feet would not do much good. Let's make an emergency call for reinforcements."

They placed their walkie-talkies to their lips and demanded more help. Help was promised including Lt. Alex Brown. The door guard opened the door of room 418 just enough for Delores and Lange to slip inside, **as they wondered who would arrive first. More gunmen or more Los Angeles police.**

Lorie Owens was asleep and Delores said, "Poor gal, she might have awakened just long enough to die. **She has had enough terror. Even Dr. Fu will be shocked."**

Delores and Lange spoke quietly so as to not wake Lorie Owens, as they briefed the inside guards. The inside Chinese guard remarked, "Wish I could have helped. I need practice."

The inside police guard looked at the inside Chinese saying, "Your two countrymen saved our lives and we thank you."

The inside Chinese Guard bowed and with a twinkle in his eyes replied, " Hope your life worth saving."

Lange laughed and said, "I have a Chinese friend in Portland, Oregon, that has a sense of humor just like him. His name is Charlie Sing."

The inside Chinese guard replied, "Charlie is cousin of mine. I learn all my bad habits from him."

There was silence as the gravity of their situation was taking hold. Lange broke it by saying, "I thought when I left the South Pacific as a dog face in an infantry division that the war was over. I guess war is around every corner."

"I know just how you feel, Lange," added the LA policeman. I was in the Marines and fought on Guadacanal. I sure felt lucky to make it back, but in this job I never know if tomorrow is going to be my last day. For sure today could have been. Then he paused — and said no more suddenly realizing there was still another 12 hours left in the day.

The voice level was higher than usual and the voices woke Lorie. She asked, "What's going on? I guess I am so heavily sedated that I have been asleep for some time, haven't I?"

Just then there was a knock on the door and Lt. Brown entered. Delores bowed and said to Lorie, "This is Lt. Alex Brown of the Los Angeles police department. He is here checking on things. **And this is my friend I told you about, Earnest Lange, who prefers to just be called Lange."**

Lorie looked at the pleasant young man and her still groggy mind tried to recall what Delores had said about Lange. Her graciousness came up with the right words, "I have been looking forward to meeting you. Any friend of Delores is for sure a good friend of mine."

"And I feel the same in reverse. You must be a very nice lady, Lorie."

At that comment Lorie burst into tears taking Lange by surprise. Delores patted her hand and said, "Lorie has been through a lot in the past few months and having friends to look after her and say kind words is touching her heart very deeply. **Those were tears of joy, not of sorrow Lange."**

"They sure were," Lorie said between sobs.

Lt. Brown knew it was time for him to leave so he commented, "Things look secure. I want the two guards to remain in the room. Have your lunch and just relax. Don't be concerned about any noise outside. I'll take my old fishing buddy Lange with me. I'll have lunch with him and then perhaps he can come back upstairs for a short visit."

Delores' quick mind did a recall, "I remember Lange told me how you met. Wasn't it on Stearns Wharf in Santa Barbara? You were fishing. Weren't you a Sergeant then?"

"I had been one for a long time. Lange was in uniform and had just returned from the South Pacific. He was very sick and very sad. As sad as any of the Sad Sack cartoons during the War."

Delores looked at Lange with a special smile of understanding and affection.

Outside the room Brown said, "We've got reinforcements coming, but we don't know how many reinforcements the other side has."

The hospital administrator was outside making certain the Coroner did not waste a second. Finally the Coroner gave the O.K. to move the bodies and a cleaning crew was standing by for a rush cleaning job. Lt. Brown asked the Coroner, "Any comments?"

"They died in seconds from the hemorrhaging caused by the severe blows. The Chinese couple have filled me in on what they did and it checks out 100%. I've been in this business 20 years and have never seen this before."

"Honorable Coroner, we have just finished class. We just graduate."

"What do you mean by that remark? You planning to go about knocking off all the bad guys in Los Angeles with this technique?"

"They have my permission, Coroner," laughed Lt. Alex Brown.

The hospital administrator added. "If there had been a gun fight we would have had bullet holes and blood all over the place."

"Taekwondo not bloody like bullets. Chinese are very neat."

As the administrator was prepared to leave he knew he had been edgy and wanted his last words to have a little sense of humor. So he bowed to the Chinese and pretended to speak as a Chinese saying, "Much obliged. Next time we want someone killed in hospital we call and ask for you. You are fast and neat. Almost sanitary."

Not to be outdone the Chinese bowed and in their very best English said, "We enjoyed doing business with you and appreciate your recommendation."

Lt. Brown said to Lange, "Let's take the stairs for exercise. I will request Lorie and Delores be moved to the Tong headquarters this afternoon. This is like a place under siege. We don't have the manpower nor can the hospital be turned into a fort and still function."

They entered the cafeteria and picked up a tray and silverware. Each took a ham sandwich, a small salad and coffee. Lt. Brown insisted on paying even though Lange protested.

Then Lt. Brown asked, **"Lange, Do you have something going with Delores Lee?"**

"I was in grade school when I sold Ah Wing his first Saturday Evening Post. He was a cook on The China Queen. My folks were also immigrants and I guess Ah Wing and I both learned to read well by reading the Post.

"I loved those stories on Alexander Botts and the Earthworm Tractor Co and of course, all the stories about the Dragon Lady and Dr. Fu Man Chu. Any Chinese stories including Charlie Chan."

"Lange, you didn't answer my question."

"Back in basic training in the field artillery at Camp Roberts in the summer of 1941 we had a surprise visit from Rita

Hayworth. She was wearing that slinky black sort of negligee and all us men thought she was the most glamorous lady we had ever seen.

"Maybe it's us men. Rita was a pin-up in tents and mess halls everywhere. So maybe The Dragon Lady was a pin up from my youth."

"You know Lange, I'm a trained detective. I ask you a question and you don't answer it. **Were your folks part Chinese the way you duck my questions?"**

"Because I don't know the answer. At times I feel Delores likes me very much. But there is a fence between us. She is Chinese and I am not. You tell her you think I am part Chinese and see if that helps. She devotes her life to Ah Wing and helping the Chinese he helps.

"Before you put me in a bare room and have a bright light over my head, and don't even give me a drink of water to cool my thirst I'll answer your question.

"I do have a special deep feeling for her. Maybe like Rita Hayworth, glamour does attract us. I don't think it will ever go any further than that."

"You know, Lange, I'm older than you by about 15 years. But we share that great disappointment in life that is perhaps hardest to bear. My wife left me for a businessman. Your wife left you when you were in the South Pacific for a guy that didn't have to go to war.

"I look around at the single women and don't know if I want to go through that again. **Maybe we both look at someone we can't reach because that is safe and we won't get hurt again?"**

"Thanks Lt. Brown. Now bring me up to date on Schank."

Just then there was a call on the loudspeaker. "Lt. Brown to the office, please."

"Now what's gone wrong? Go ahead and eat your sandwich. Come to think of it I'll take mine with me. It may be the only time I'll have to eat. I'll leave the coffee."

Lt. Brown found a phone and it was the chief himself. "O.K. Brown, give it to me quick. **The press is driving me nuts. So is**

the Mayor, the City Council and any moment I expect a call from the Governor's office.

"Oh, oh, hold on. My deputy tells me the hospital administrator is on the phone."

"I'm back. He's demanding we get Lorie and the police out of the hospital. Claims Lorie is well enough to move."

"That takes away all our options. Get the armored ambulance over here and ten squad cars to run shotgun. Let's move her. We can never secure this place in a million years. A couple of gun men dressed like doctors almost got her. We can't frisk everyone. doctor and nurse."

"They will be there in 30 minutes Lt. Brown. Hold the fort until then."

Lt. Brown headed back to the Cafeteria saying, "I could sure use a cup of coffee and I'll tell Lange I'll see him later."

Lange was pleased to see Brown return so soon and remained silent until Brown said, **"Don't repeat this, but the arrangements are made for Lorie and Delores to leave. This place is too hot to cover."**

"Won't it be kind of scary moving them? The assailants must have had a couple of others outside. What are they up to?"

"Exactly what is worrying me. I can't take a chance. Do we make an end run, go through the middle and just how much force is waiting to tackle us?"

"Sounds just like what the infantry goes through."

"The police force is the infantry. It's no football game with the game lasting just a couple of hours and the brutality is then over."

'I had hoped for perhaps lunch with Delores or least a private visit with her."

"Not here, Lange! You'll have to talk to the Chinese about visiting her at the Tong."

"My God, Lt. Brown, I don't think I like this town any more! Maybe I shouldn't go visit my Aunt and Uncle in Anaheim. Just go back to Santa Barbara."

"Lange, I am certain Delores is going to be here for at least the preliminary hearing for Schank. If it isn't urgent to see your Aunt and Uncle **I suggest you go back to Delores' room with me for a few moments and then go back to Santa Barbara.**

"One of these days I'll be up there and we'll go fishing again. Things are too messed up here for visiting now–**this is life and death stuff, Lange!**

"**There is big time money out there–and a contract on Lorie Owens!**"

"O.K., Lt. Brown. I'll take your advice. I'll call my Aunt and Uncle and then head back to Santa Barbara."

CHAPTER 25
THE TONG IN NEW CHINATOWN.

Ah Wing and Wang Sing, the Tong Leader, were conversing. A loud rapid knock was heard and Wang Sing spoke in Chinese, "Come in."

The entering Chinese said, **"They are both safe in the Tong. The armored ambulance was blown up.** Driver of ambulance only occupant. He is dead."

Ah Wing asked with a tremor in his voice, "And the others?"

"At the last minute Lt. Alex Brown took Delores and Lorie in separate police cars dressed as policewomen. They were not with the ambulance. There were other injuries in the convoy. Lt. Brown's separate convoy arrived without a scratch."

"What happened to the attackers?"

"Two were killed and the third has survived. Word out is he will never sleep until he confesses. He will have two guards in the room with him 24 hours a day."

"Thank you," Wang Sing said as he nodded. The messenger left quickly.

Ah Wing seemed to be struggling for words. It was obvious the kindly older Chinese was having trouble controlling his emotions. Wang Sing understood.

He bowed to Ah Wing saying, "May I help you to your room?"

There was no reply from Ah Wing, just a slight nod of his head.

Wang Sing helped Ah Wing to his feet and to his room.

CHAPTER 26
LT. BROWN ASSAILS THE ASSAILANT.

After delivering Lorie Owens and Delores safely to the Tong headquarters Lt. Alex Brown was about to depart when he received word of the attack on the armored ambulance, **the death of the driver** and the injury to several policemen in the convoy riding shotgun.

Lt. Brown was incensed. He said to Dr. Fu, who brought him the news, " You can count on the full resources of the Los Angeles police department on this. **I must reach the chief immediately."**

"Dr. Fu replied, "We have a small private room you can use."

Lt. Brown said, "Thanks and just give me a few minutes to talk to the chief alone. I would like to make some remarks privately which perhaps you should not hear."

"I understand very well, Lieutenant. While you are making those remarks I will be making some remarks to certain Chinese here that likewise I would not want you to hear."

"Touché," thought Brown. "I'd sure like to hear them, but as a police officer I am better off not knowing what the Chinese will do."

Upon entering the small room Brown called the chief who said, "The roof fell on us again. You were right again by sending the ambulance as a decoy. Are you trying to get my job?"

"Chief, some day I'd like to be a Captain. More for my Dad's sake who retired from the force as a Sergeant. Beyond that keep me off the promotion list."

Then the chief related what he had learned from several of the survivors, who were now sitting in the conference room with him. "Wish you were in this room right now with us, but I have the feeling you need to stay at the Tong and coordinate with us here. Keep the officers and cars you have and you be the judge how you deploy them. We will send relief in a few hours. **What do you think the Chinese are going to do?"**

"The Chinese are cautious. They will put out feelers about hit artists and they will get lots of information, which they may share none of with us. Meanwhile, Chief, the Chinese will count on you to short cut the process by keeping the surviving assailant under 24 hour interrogation until he cracks."

"If we don't get the right answers from him soon we may call you in, Brown."

"You put me in a room alone with him. Give me a half hour."

"What you'll do is against the law, Brown."

"They killed a police officer driving a police ambulance. Chief, just put me in the interrogation room with him, if he doesn't crack in the next couple of hours."

"You have my word on it, Lt. Brown."

Ah Wing was still trying to shake himself out of his gloom when Wang Sing said, "You have yet to meet Lorie Owens, yet have done much for her. It is time to meet her and discuss her father."

Ah Wing realized he was so shaken by the frightening events of the day he had not done what he had long dreamed about– meeting someone from his rescuer's family. "Let us check with the Doctor. "

Wang Sing was back in a few minutes with the Chinese Doctor who wavered at first, but recognized matters of such serious nature must not be delayed.

"She is much younger and stronger than you, **Ah Wing. Let us see Lorie now."**

The three Chinese walked slowly to Lorie's room, knowing it was time for the past to be revealed. Delores was also there. After the greetings and introductions a very nervous Ah Wing spoke. "Your father and I worked on the same ship, The China Queen. Did you receive news about your father during or after the war?

"Yes, I did. Mom and I knew he survived one ship sinking, but not the second."

"You and your Mother suffered so much!

"I would not want to be the first to bring you such news. Your father saved my life. I was a cook on the China Queen."

"Oh, I remember when Dad sent us letters from the Queen, as he called her. Apparently you both survived that sinking."

"Your father was on deck watch and I was bringing him a sandwich. It was a long watch and I knew he was hungry. Truth is he and I very good friends. I sneak him a sandwich. I make it when no one is looking.

"I just hand him sandwich and Japanese torpedo hit just aft of mid-ship. If either of us had been off duty, and below deck in our quarters, it is doubtful we would have survived. We were both thrown off the deck into the water. I could not swim."

"Dad was an excellent swimmer. He taught Mom and me how to swim well."

"Your father saw me floundering and yelled, 'Hang on, Ah Wing. I'm coming to get you."

Suddenly Ah Wing could not say another word. Tears came to his eyes. The Doctor said, "Lorie, when a man or woman goes through this they are haunted by nightmares for as much as 30 or 40 years. The terror repeats itself thousands of times in their dreams. They wake up at night screaming the same words, because it is happening to them all over again."

Lorie had begun to cry herself, but she regained enough composure to say, "I've had a hundred nightmares about my Dad so I understand. First hand experiences, during wartime, must be so terrible. I wonder how the service people were able to continue fighting."

"You sound like your father. He was very considerate. I will continue," said Ah Wing. "Lorie your father swam to me and pulled me to some cabin wreckage. He pushed me on some boards and an American destroyer saved us within a few hours. I was severely injured and still limp and have some pain. I'm grateful to be able to get around.

"Your father was very patriotic and hired on as crewman on a Liberty ship. I was not an American citizen. I am proud to say I am now American citizen. Your father's Liberty ship was torpedoed. Almost everyone went down with the ship. **I tried to locate your mother. Never successful as so many with same last name as yours.**

"When Chinese cook and steward on Schankrila mention Owens we double check and much surprised to find you are his daughter. I knew I must help you! Old Chinese tradition we owe our life to person that save ours. That is reason we work hard to save your life."

Lorie Owens was still crying, but managed to say, **"Now you saved my life so you have paid your debt to my father.** If Dad could only know what you have done for me."

"Perhaps he had a hand in it. Many things do not happen by accident. Sir Arthur Conan Doyle, writer of Sherlock Holmes stories, have definite opinions on that," replied Ah Wing.

Lorie continued with, " After Pearl Harbor Mom and I became so frightened. We got word he survived the sinking of the China Queen. **When he wrote he was going to ship out again Mom had a premonition we would never see him again."**

The Doctor entered the conversation with, "Perhaps that is enough discussion for each of you. I observe you are both under severe strain, but pain is only too often the price we pay for living. **Delores' husband was also killed fighting the Japanese.**

"I was a Doctor with a Chinese unit. In 1940 I was too severely injured to go back so I got to live. I never forget each day to bow and honor those that did not return."

Looking at Lorie, he continued, "Each day I now also remember your father. Best you both wait until tomorrow to visit more."

As the men left the room Lorie and Delores held each other's hands.

Lorie was very shaken and overwhelmed from speaking to someone who had shared her Dad's life. Delores, whose composure usually hid her innermost thoughts, felt a terrible sadness as she relived the war again, which also took her husband's life.

Ah Wing returned to his room to lie down and rest. His mind returned to the war in the spring of 1942. The seas were a little rough that day and he was walking carefully across the deck to Zac's duty station. Then the loud explosion as the ship shook from the torpedo blast. His body flew through the air as if a tornado had lifted him sending him hurdling through space. His breath was squeezed from his body as he lapsed into unconsciousness.

He woke up under water, fighting, struggling. That movement was enough to bring him to the surface. Then he was gripped with the realization he could not swim. Then he heard a voice. It was Zac calling to him. **He would never forget that moment, that voice and those words, "Hang on, Ah Wing, I'm coming to get you."**

Lt. Brown was pacing back and forth in his tiny room in the Tong. Finally he called police headquarters. "Getting anywhere?" he asked.

The Sergeant he spoke to replied, "Not a word. He's afraid to talk. Hold on, the Chief heard you are calling and says for you to come in."

The traffic was heavy, but he made record time. He used his siren to go through several signals. When he got there the

Sergeant handed him a folder. "We took his fingerprints and we got lucky. We know who he is."

"Do you know who he's working for?"

"We weren't that lucky."

Brown scanned the contents of the folder then strode to the interrogation room and entered it with the adrenaline surging in his veins. "O.K., you guys clear out. I'll handle Stebbins by myself. **Maybe you'll just need the coroner when I am through with him.**"

"O.K., you rat. Time to rat on your dead buddies and whoever hired you."

"I was just the driver. Didn't want to be, but they forced me to go with them."

"Who made you?"

"Always had a poor memory. Maybe I can think of their names later."

"You've been in the rackets since they kicked you out of high school. Robbery, extortion, carrying a concealed weapon; you've done them all. Then you got greedy for the big bucks and hired out as a hit man. How could you be so dumb to take a job to hit a friend of the Chinese?"

"Friend of the Chinese? I didn't know nuthin' about that. I want a mouthpiece. What youse is saying is just like Greek to me."

Brown exploded, "Stand up, Stebbins!"

Brown slapped him so hard on his left cheek Stebbins spun almost completely around. Brown held up both fists, "You have three seconds to start talking!"

"O.K., you win. I'll talk, but you've got to protect me."

Brown laughed, "Protect you!. Here's the kind of protection you are going to get."

Brown hit Stebbins with two quick very hard blows. Stebbins staggered and hit the floor clutching his face and stomach where the two punches had landed.

Stebbins lay on the floor groaning and Brown stood there watching him. Finally Brown said, "You coward. Stand up and fight like a man with your fists or if you've had enough I'll call in the steno and we'll take your complete confession."

Stebbins realized the other hit men were all dead and his only hope was to cooperate and confess. He replied to Brown, "O.K., I'm ready to talk!"

The intercom had been on the entire time. Brown said, "Bring in the steno."

"No first aid kit? You are tough, Lieutenant?"

Once Stebbins started talking he spilled everything. As soon as the major points had been covered the Chief hurriedly left the room. He had work to do and it was all related to what he had just learned from Stebbins.

CHAPTER 27
LT. BROWN RETURNS TO THE TONG.

It was now way past the dinner hour, but Brown was anxious to get back to the Tong and confer with Dr. Fu. He was suddenly very hungry.

At the Pagoda he asked for the chow mein they were featuring. As the waitress took his order he declined the tea, saying, "I'm going to have a bottle of beer with my dinner."

He was thirsty and his tongue felt dry. His nerves were frazzled and he knew he had broken the law by hitting Stebbins. "Maybe the beer will relax me. I sure need it. This Saturday I was scheduled to be off. I was going to go wharf fishing for Bonito.

"Instead, four deaths and a half dozen injuries in one day. This is like real war. So now that I'm a 2nd Louie it's like my Dad told me:

"You know what a promotion is? You get a new badge, and maybe 15% increase in pay. Then you're expected to handle 50% more problems. So you lose 35%."

When he had finished eating he asked the waiter for his check.

"No check today, Lt. Brown."

Brown knew no amount of insistence would make any difference and anyhow the waiter had left so he had no one to argue with. In a few minutes another Chinese appeared and bowed. "Please follow me."

Soon he was back in the Tong and was ushered into a room where Wang Sing and Dr. Fu were seated. After the usual formalities of greeting each other Dr. Fu came to the point, **"Did you interrogate the assailant?"**

"Yes, and we were lucky. We got a supposed full confession from him. At least we got a number of names and a story. We are now thoroughly checking it out. "

"Can you share those names with us?"

"I can give you the names we have. You'll get more as soon as we get them."

Wang Sing said, "Thank you."

Dr. Fu's expression did not change as he said, "Maybe with those names we run you a race. See who can figure out the others first."

"We'd like your help. Here are the names Stebbins gave us."

Brown knew the Chinese would never rest until they knew all the answers.

CHAPTER 28
BACK TO SANTA BARBARA

Having spent only a few minutes with Delores Lee.
The weather was warm and the smog was not only visible overhead, but was down to the sidewalks. It irritated Lange's eyes and he could feel it all the way into his sinuses. **He wove through a myriad of roads, freeways, underpasses and overpasses before he reached the San Fernando Valley. The song about it would remain forever etched in his mind.**

Many of the replacements in his Infantry Division from Southern California made it their theme song. Just like those from San Francisco talked about leaving their heart there.

As he thought about Delores his mind bounced back and forth thinking it was nice to see her, but why was fate against them?

He had a friend who used to say at times she was out of sorts. **"I think that is where I am right now."**

He didn't pay any attention to a small sign pointing off the hiway.

It said, "Foundry-Machine Shop."

It was now owned by four former infantrymen from his division. They had played a big part in the drama that had engulfed him.

Would they ever meet again?

143

After another half hour of deep thought and almost careless driving on Hiway 101 he began to feel very tired. He hoped a couple cups of coffee would permit him to continue driving. As he was passing through Ventura he stopped at a small cafe. Lange took a seat, put one elbow on the counter with his chin resting on his hand. When the waitress appeared he said, **"Just coffee please. Straight and strong!"**

"I can tell. You are a little tired and need to stay awake."

"Is it that obvious?"

"We waitresses do look at the way a person walks in! If they sit upright and don't put their elbows on the table. You flunked both tests."

"You're a regular Sherlock Holmes. Maybe you ought to be a sales person."

"What do you mean 'ought to'? We are salespeople! Our cook makes the best fried chicken your mouth will ever get the chance to taste. While you're having your coffee think about it. I can have the cook fix it up for a take-out. You can have it for dinner."

She served him the coffee, winked at him and moved on to the next customer. When she came back to check on his coffee she said, **"You remind me of my brother.**

"He was in the Service. When he got home he found his girl friend had gotten married. He has kind of the same look in his eyes that you do!"

Then she dashed off again to serve another customer. "My God," he said to himself, "Is she clairvoyant? If she's a witch she's a pretty one."

He turned slightly to watch her. She had a lithe figure, trim, but in a sense athletic. Her hair was blonde and her face was tanned. She wasn't beautiful. She was spirited with a happy smile. **"What is there about men like myself? Why are we so easy to read?"**

He reflected for awhile concluding with, "I guess it's a defensive ability women have to learn. There are a lot of lying guys out there. Or is it just intuition?"

She was back soon with, "Last chance to order the chicken! I checked with the cook and he has some he could have ready for you in five minutes."

"Tell him I'll take it, and by the way how is your brother doing now?"

"Just a second, let me turn in the order — — oh yes, my brother, well, you know I really don't know how to answer that. He's living in Goleta and he is kind of working at establishing a business of his own. He worked for a company in Los Angeles and complained about the rat race there."

"Sounds like he made a wise choice."

"Where do you live? "

"In Oregon most of my life. I just came back to Santa Barbara where I am living now."

"What do you do?"

"I'm a strange combination-business manager, chief accountant and salesman.

"We sell automotive equipment. My name is Earnest Lange."

"I think your Mother looked in your face and decided there was just one name for you."

"Are you a witch? That's exactly what happened. My Mother was going to name me after a famous English actor, but she took one look at me and said, 'He's Earnest.' Please call me Lange. I hate the name Earnest. No friend of mine calls me that."

She laughed and said, "I am a witch and my name is Sally Stevens. My brother's name is Sid. Would you believe he is an itinerant office machine repairman?"

"I do declare!"

"Why don't you look him up and if you care to, get my address from him and then write me and tell me what he does. My brother is one of those guys that thinks communication means never explain anything **and never say more than 24 words in any one day."**

"I do declare," Lange replied.

"Say, you may be as bad as my brother. You've said three words and repeated them twice. As for that phony North Carolina accent where did you pick that up?"

Lange laughed, replying, "I picked that up from John Wayne."

"You know, maybe your Mother did pick the wrong name for you."

"My infantry division was all originally from the Northwest–Oregon, Washington, Idaho and Montana. When the casualties started our replacements came from California and the entire rest of the United States. We couldn't believe how some of them talked. **We had guys from Brooklyn that wanted to be cowboys, just like the song.**

"Two of my best pals were Jewish kids. I learned a lot from them! The guys from Chicago were something else. Now that I'm virtually all by myself I don't miss the war, but I miss the guys. So decided to go around and use a few of their phrases."

"I take back my insult. There's the bell. Your chicken is ready."

Sally put out her hand saying, "I bet you do miss them. You know, now maybe I know why my brother is the way he is. He was on a baby flat-top. They called them Kaiser-Coffins. It was sunk by the Japs in the battle of Leyte-Gulf. Only a third of the men survived. Look up my brother, please, he needs some companionship. **Tell him Mom and Sally miss him.**"

Lange picked up the chicken, paid the check, and left. As he got in his car he thought, "She doesn't have an engagement ring or wedding ring, but Ventura is a long ways away. **If this scene was being played in Santa Barbara I'd sure like to see her again.**"

Soon Lange had passed through Carpinteria and a dozen miles later was passing along the base of Montecito. His mind went back to his second year in college when he read, 'Hearst, Lord of San Simeon,' the fascinating tale of the newspaper

146

tycoon that built the most fabulous estate in the entire United States. **Lange thought to himself,**

"None of the estates in Montecito come close to the one built by Hearst, but in comparison to my tiny duplex apartment I'm living in absolutely 'nothing.' Like the music, 'It's almost a shanty in old shanty town,' but it sure beats the New Guinea jungles."

Before he could mentally discourse further it was time to turn off 101 and make his way to Bath Street. He put the dinner in the refrigerator, set his alarm for 6 P.M., slipped off his shoes, lay down on the small sofa. In seconds he was asleep.

He was warming the chicken in his oven when the his doorbell rang. He knew it would be Maude. **He invited her in and the same sadness gripped his mind as he looked at her wrinkled face and the battered condition of her clothes.**

"She has likely mended them dozens of times. If only I could help her."

"Come in and sit down, Maude, I've been thinking about you."

"You have a kind heart, Lad, may the Gods of Goodness always be with ye."

"Maude, I still have some Sherry left. May I pour you a small glass?"

He noticed her hesitate, "I insist, Maude! I can't drink alone."

"My dear Dad would say, "Go ahead, Maude."

Lange poured a small glass for both of them and handed one to Maude. "Here's to your good health and a little wealth along with it."

She raised her glass, Lange noticing the eagerness as her lips touched the glass and the liquid reached her tongue. It seemed like she was reveling with happiness at the first taste. **"Even a wee drop is like medicine to me old body,"** she said as she held firmly to the glass.

Just then the timer rang and Lange dashed for the oven. He took out the food and moved it to the table. He had put two plates on the table saying, "Maude, I bought some fried chicken in Ventura. Please have at least a taste of it and tell me what you think of it."

Maude protested, but soon was seated and it was obvious she was relishing the taste of the warmed up chicken. They each had another glass of Sherry and Lange wondered if he should help her back to her front door. With dinner over he asked, "Maude, any more thoughts about anything else that might be missing from your apartment?"

"Lad, I think about it all me wakin' time. I don't have much to do except me weekly meeting with me Old Housekeeper's Society. Me wonders why we call it a society? Only society we ever saw were the estate owners we worked for. Now we have that fancy name."

Lange thought, "They even have a Humane Society for dogs and cats. **People like Maude worked all their lives, but never got far off the floors they scrubbed."**

"Better I am getting back to me own place, Lad. I'll bloody well keep thinking about the thieves that broke in. Never heard no other word from Sgt. Andrew."

Lange made certain that Maude reached her front door without stumbling and bid her goodnight. As she closed and locked her front door she moved her body to the rocking chair she sat in a lot and looked at the picture of her parents.

"What's to become of me, Mum and Dad? I don't know what to do."

Lange's thoughts of poor old Maude's predicament were equally somber as he went about putting things away. He made coffee and wished his mind could escape from his concerns about little old English ladies.

He used to worry a lot about his Mom's friend. Now there were two. Lange was just starting a cup of coffee when his phone rang, **"Is this you, Lange? Sgt. Andrew here"**

"Yes, it's me. I'm a little tired. You must be working late."

"I'm on the late shift tonight. I just talked to Lt. Alex Brown. He called from his apartment in Alhambra. That guy must work 24 hours a day."

"It's a rotten place for a policeman. They never fold up the streets at night."

"That's why you couldn't pay me enough to work that City. In the past week the Santa Barbara police are having the same problem.

Lt. Brown tells me you almost got yourself bumped off. Don't you know better than to use the rest room when a couple of hit men are switching into Doctor's clothes?"

"Please don't remind me of it. "

"Lt. Brown asked me to call you and make certain you got back O.K. How's that for service. And it just happens that Lt. Merced and I want to talk to you Monday at 11 A.M..

"Fine with me if my boss says I can have the time off."

"Try to make it Lange. Forget about my kidding. You were alert enough to spot them as phonies."

Then he laughed and added, "I gave Lt. Brown a bad time, too. Asked him why he didn't have the rest rooms covered. Enough of that, see you Monday."

Lange said to himself, "Tired as I am its Saturday night I'm going to take a walk up Cabrillo Boulevard and see some folks strolling along leisurely. Then I'll walk out on Stearns Wharf and wonder when I might have a girl friend and the money to enjoy an evening dinner at The Harbor restaurant."

As he walked he thought of his first Christmas back in the States after almost three years overseas in an Infantry Division. That was December 1944. His wife had told him she was in love with someone else. The morning of December 24th he took the bus to Los Angeles and stayed at the YMCA. He spent Christmas Eve at the counter of a coffee shop drinking coffee. The radio was on a 24 hour news station.

The announcer was telling everyone to stay home. The hospitals were full. There were already 25 people killed in drunk driving accidents and 300 injured. The next day he took the bus back to Santa Barbara where he was helping process soldiers just back from overseas.

"So why am I back in Santa Barbara now?"

CHAPTER 29
SCHANK MEETS WITH HIS ATTORNEY.

Now it was Sunday morning and Lexus's phone rang. It was one of the jailers, who identified himself as Ray, "Mr. Taylor, your client is asking for you."

"Who are you trying to kid?"

The jailer laughed. "Not you for sure, Mr. Taylor. It's just my Sunday demeanor."

"You go to—.you know, maybe I should appreciate a little civility. O.K., tell Schank I'm going out for a decent breakfast and will be down to see him when I feel like it."

Then Lexus laughed, "Ray, try that Sunday demeanor on him."

The jailer did not reply except to hang up.

Lexus took a quick shower, put on some casual clothes, went out the door of his exclusive Condo, in the Beverly Hills-Wiltshire District. The Sunday newspaper was outside his door and he picked it up immediately focusing on the headlines.

SECOND ATTEMPT TO KILL STAR PROSECUTION WITNESS FAILS.

Rumored that witness is now safe in Chinese Tong Headquarters.

The article then went on to detail the amazing killing of the two assailants at the hospital by two Chinese with super skills in Korean Taekwondo. The story gave no explanation as to how Lorie Owens escaped when the ambulance was blown up.

The police declined to discuss the matter. It went on to say there was a rumor that a female Chinese with a remarkable likeness to The Dragon Lady was with Lorie Owens.

The writer inferred that if Schank had called for the hit he had crossed 'The Chinese Line in the Sand' and the equivalent of a Holy War was being ignited.

As he entered his car in the underground parking lot Lexus Taylor was a worried man. He read the entire article before starting his car and then said to himself, **"If those damn fools had got her we would have been home free."**

When Lexus arrived at the jail Schank was furious. Lexus leaned forward and whispered "It's just her word against ours. Ruppert supports you. I have talked to him two times. He knows you wouldn't be stupid enough to carry him alive in the trunk of your car."

"I just can't figure out who did it. Who grabbed Ruppert and two days later put him in my trunk. It's crazy. Someone has been doing some mighty deep planning. Did you get the full details of the snatch from Ruppert?"

"I got Ruppert's story. He had just left your private rail car and as he reached Cabrillo Blvd. he was grabbed, gagged, handcuffed, a hood was placed over his head. He said whoever did it were sure professional. He was tossed in a car, driven some place.

"Then taken South and placed under guard. No one ever talked to him. He never saw the face of anyone or heard anyone speak."

"So he could never recognize a face or a voice?"

"That's right. Those guys were good."

"Any word on the hit men?"

"They are dead. Didn't you hear the rest of the story?"

"The guards took out my radio. Did something else happen?"

"If just the first two men had been killed that would have been bad enough. Some of their buddies tried again. This time attacking the police ambulance that was taking Lorie away from the hospital. **We know that two more of them got killed and one captured alive.**

"Even the newsmen don't seem to know anything. The police have put a lid on things.".

Schank was shocked as listened to Lexus. "How could they be that stupid?"

"How did you get so dumb as to hold onto Lorie Owens."

"She knew too much. Where is she now?"

"My guess is that she is holed up in the Chinese Tong in New Chinatown. That's off limits. Even the police don't mess with the Tong."

Schank came back with, "I should have let Lorie Owens go. I should have paid her off, and hoped she would keep quiet. I was afraid she would blackmail me."

Taylor just nodded and said nothing. **He knew the problem with Schank was the universal problem with dictatorial people. They thought they were invincible!**

Lexus sort of relished the publicity for now he was as famous as any Hollywood Star. Just then the guard approached the table. bench. "Time is up."

As Lexus exited the front door of the heavily guarded jail he was met by a reporter and a photographer. The camera of the photographer flashed and the reporter eagerly asked, "Are you going to win this case, Mr. Taylor?"

Lexus knew he was on the stage right now even though the preliminary hearing had not been held. He drew his body up straight and turned his lips into a smile. He thought it bad luck to brag he was going to win. He also knew he dare not turn the public against him.

Taylor looked the reporter in the eye, "I believe in justice. Come to the trial."

Lexus Taylor strode toward his car. The smile on his face did not go away.

CHAPTER 30
SOUTH AMERICA

The Chinese are everywhere.
As the days progressed Ah Wing and Wang Sing were overwhelmed by the hornet's nest of emergencies. They were extremely worried. **With Sammy dead the entire case seemed to rest solely on the testimony of Lorie Owens.**

Wang Sing had put the matter in perspective by saying, "Chinese accused of trying to 'save face.' Everyone likes to save face. Chinese civilization has been doing it longer. **No stone will be left unturned until we resolve this matter!**

"Our Chinese network will be put on full alert. Time to test it again anyhow. Dr. Fu has been granted full permission."

Dr. Fu possessed not only fantastic intelligence, but had the rare talent of being detailed and systematic in the carrying out of all details. It was this latter which enabled him to have the complete trust of not only his own race, but of virtually everyone that came in contact with him.

He and his subordinates began the tedious job of crossing every bridge they could think of to find out who the assassins were, **and also where else Schank's tentacles might have reached. Their secret coded messages even reached South America.**

For centuries the Chinese had been content to operate in waters near mainland China. As the Spanish, the Dutch, the English and Americans traders came to them with their furs and other valuables to trade for spices, gold and silver the Chinese had moved into other parts of the world, even to South America.

Dr. Fu's coded messages spread thousands of miles. One had reached a small coastal city in South America. A few days later Q. Song, the local Tong leader, received an air mail packet with written details about Schank. The small town newspaper did not have affiliations such as United Press. Their news reached them at the pace of the Pony express. That city was normal to the extent that military power dominated. Those without it accomplished little or nothing at all. Rumors about new prisoners and escaped prisoners were spoken in secret and in hushed tones. **Treatment in the local jail and prison was known to be brutal and savage with more deaths than survivors.**

The brothel had a radio and there had been a news flash about Schank. Della heard one of the girls talking about it. She pondered it almost every waking moment wondering if that might mean some hope for her. She could only conclude, "There is no way I can get word to the Los Angeles police."

Uppermost in her mind was, "Is my father dead, or is there any hope he might still be alive?" She knew it was hopeless for both of them. Her physical condition took a turn for the worse and she became incoherent and appeared to be in some form of dementia.

The cook tried to help her and settle her down. One day the cook made an offhand remark to the Chinese grocery delivery boy, "Do you have an herb that might help Eloise? She throws up anything I fix for her. It's almost insulting."

The Chinese boy replied, "What idea you have cause this?"

The cook laughed and said, "Makes me think of old joke, 'Not Chinaman's chance of finding out something.'"

"Never hear such thing! You sure that is Chinese? We alla time get blame. No one else to blame, they blame Chinese."

Suddenly the Chinese delivery boy thought of the inquiry of his Tong leader.

"I check to see what herbs maybe suitable. Is not Eloise an Australian girl?"

"I'm not supposed to discuss anyone with you, but yes, she and her father who was recaptured with her are Australian. He is in jail, unless he's dead. She is likely in shock. Claims her real name is Della, but the Madam makes us call her Eloise."

"Cookie, my lips are sealed. I search for herb that might help her."

"OK. Chin. I never told you anything. Just that Eloise's stomach is upset. Something to at least help her keep her food down."

Chin went to his store and directly into the back room. He moved some boxes and then slipped behind a curtain. Chin opened a locked door, went through it locking it behind him. He found the small flashlight that was attached to a wall and he scurried down the steps and down the passageway, which seemed to have a turn off every few yards.

Finding the right passageway was a confusing maze, but not to Chin.

He had practiced many times by closing his eyes, and counting his steps. He didn't need the flashlight. Hands along wall, turn right, go past two passageways, turn left, pass two passageways, then make a left.

The Chinese Underground was a series of tunnels that branched out in as many directions as the size of the Chinese Community. There was always the rumor that they were established first to Shanghai drunken sailors for various ship owners.

Their real purpose was to permit easy movement at any time of day or night, avoiding the scrutiny of the non-Chinese in the Community, some of who did not like the idea of the Chinese bustling around.

Factually there was a further magnificent use for the underground, avoidance of the outside weather conditions, as well as being invisible to the outside world.

Chin pulled the signal device by an iron gate, making certain of the timing, and it was swiftly opened. He expressed his need to meet with Song, the Tong leader. His urgency was obvious and his wish was immediately granted.

Song listened to Chin, "Chin, you are wise to bring this information to me quickly. Much like looking for needle in haystack, but I detect a similarity that we must immediately pursue. Schank is arrested for kidnapping, but details from Dr. Fu are that he planned to get rid of Lorie Owens. Is it possible he is has gotten rid of other ladies? Yes, very possible!"

The Chinese had learned many centuries before what the Americans had failed to learn in World War II, costing thousands of lives that need not have been lost. From Pearl Harbor, Dec 7, 1941 to the Battle of the Bulge, in December 1944.

American intelligence was coming to individual conclusions instead of passing on details to the top military leadership. Even a Chinese peasant knew one bee might indicate a nearby swarm and not dismiss the slightest detail.

Song's mind was moving as fast as an abacus operated by a Chinese mathematician. "Who could I get to talk to Della to see if there is a connection?" Then he recalled the name Eloise. She was a beautiful Australian lady whose Father had twice tried to rescue her. Was he alive? Song knew he had no answer to that question."

Then an answer came to him. "Take first things first. Dr. Fu has high level connections with the Australians. This is information Dr. Fu can use as he sees fit."

In the case of intelligence via public transmission facilities the Chinese had learned to not send direct. Instead do a loop around the block, like a person that might be tailed. The cables went to other designated cities, with a code as to the final address.

A steady stream of cables between any two cities might alert local powers. Information was bought and sold in many foreign localities. The Chinese had their under ground maze, but their above ground grape vine was equal or better.

"Chin, I write a short cable in our code now! **You wait very few minutes and you take it to cable office."** The cable read:
YOUNG AUSTRALIAN LADY DELLA STOP PRISONER LOCAL BROTHEL. STOP. FATHER WAS IN LOCAL PRISON STOP HIS RESCUE ATTEMPT FAILED. STOP. MILITARY JUNTA IN POWER STOP.

Upon receipt of the cable Dr. Fu immediately met with Ah Wing, Delores and Wang Sing. Dr. Fu's manner revealed the urgency he felt. His eyes seemed to fix on all three at once. "We must talk with Lorie Owens. Always small chance we help someone."

"Most certainly, Dr. Fu," was the quick response from all three.

"Thank you, Delores, please go to Lorie's room now. If she is asleep we must try to waken her. I see great danger and opportunity if there is a connection."

As they looked at the stately Dr. Fu they felt his great power flow to them. Delores immediately left the room and Lorie was semi-awake. She said, "I try to force myself to stay awake during the day. Otherwise I don't sleep at night. It is so peaceful here and I feel secure. But deep down I worry about the future. Do I have any?"

"My dear, you must relax. Your future is assured."

Lorie had finally been informed of the first attempt on her life, but not of the second and the Chinese felt no useful purpose would be served by telling her at this time.

Dr. Fu was invited into the room and after inquiring as to the state of her health he said, "Does the name Della mean anything to you?"

Lorie immediately answered, "Do I recall a Della? I sure do!"

"Under what circumstances do you recall the name Della?"

"Several times Schank called me Della, which led me to believe at one time she lived with him as I did on the Schankrila."

"Do you have any idea when that was?"

"No, I don't. At first I used to tease Schank that he had so many girls he couldn't remember our names. That was just at first. Then when our romance started its downward spiral he told me to 'shut up.' He had his mind on more important things than a name."

"So you would guess that she was maybe with him for some time and that she could have immediately preceded you. Would that make it perhaps a year ago or more?"

"If I had to guess I would say that."

"Now, the important question. What happened to her?"

"That is exactly the question I asked Schank. I asked him that every time he used her name instead of mine. He would get increasingly angry as I asked him that question.

"I became more and more curious. As our romance faltered I became more interested in finding out. **I figured I might share the same fate as she did.** As things got worse my mind really dwelt on that subject. **What happened to Della?"**

"Very logical," replied Dr. Fu. "Why don't you try to relax and think if Schank ever indicated in any way where she might have gone."

Lorie leaned back, but continued to focus on Dr. Fu. as she tried to recall. Finally she said, "Dr. Fu, I can't think of anything more."

Dr. Fu kept looking at Lorie and Delores knew he was endeavoring to hypnotize her without revealing that fact to her. Dr. Fu snapped his fingers and said,

"You are completely relaxed Lorie. Just think of your association with Schank. Tell me again the times he called you Della and tell me your response."

Lorie's eyes seemed to glaze. She was obviously thinking hard. "I remember the first time. We were having dinner at the beautiful Palace Hotel in San Francisco. We stayed there for several days. Our suite of rooms made me feel like a queen.

"The dining room with the glittering chandeliers was awesome. I was raised in a rinky dinky town fifty miles outside Atlanta, Georgia. When I moved to Atlanta I saw fashion and style for the first in my life. I met Schank in the lounge of a lovely hotel there."

Dr. Fu realized Lorie was going back too far for the time being. So he interrupted saying, "Let us go back to the Palace Hotel in San Francisco."

"Oh yes, we were seated in the dining room. We had ordered dinner and having a glass of wine. Schank looked at me and said, **'You look so beautiful tonight, Della.'** It just ruined my evening. I asked him who Della was. 'Oh, she's a lady I met once.'

" I kept after him that evening and for the next couple of days. All to no avail."

"Did you ever get any response from him as to where she was, or to where she had gone? Tell me about the next occasion he called you Della."

"That happened on several occasions. Each time I bugged him to tell me about her. Did he like me better? I tried to trick him and spent much time concocting devious ways to bring up the subject in an innocent fashion.

"I'd have been better off if I shut up. Maybe it was a way to vent my anger.

"Wait a minute! One day we were fighting verbally on that subject and Ruppert was on board the Schankrila. I accused Schank of still seeing her. I asked Ruppert if she lived in San Francisco. I'm trying to recall — — What did Ruppert say?"

Dr. Fu nodded his head to Delores, the Dragon Lady, whom he had trained in hypnosis to the point he had told her, "You are now better than your teacher."

Delores immediately recognized she was to take over. She spoke softly, but firmly to Lorie, "Take your time, my dear. We are in no hurry. Everything is peaceful. You are with friends who are going to take care of you. You will remember very shortly what Ruppert said to you, won't you, Lorie?"

"Yes, I will, Delores. I will remember for you. You are so kind to me."

Lorie said nothing as her mind struggled to remember. Then she started to talk very slowly. "I remember — - Ruppert said,

'Oh, hell, Lorie–quite your bitching—and worrying about Della. Schank isn't playing around with her.

"She's probably out of the country. Who knows where. Maybe she went back to Australia or went to South America. Get off the subject— — and stay off it.'"

"**I asked Ruppert if she was Australian and he said she was. So I figured she went back to Australia.**"

"**Did Schank know Ruppert said something to you about Della?**"

"**Let me think. No, because Ruppert came back to me later and said,** 'He was just lipping off. He didn't know where Della was, but for certain Schank was not in contact with her.' **Funny thing though. Several times later he still called me Della.**"

Dr. Fu stood up, moved quietly to Delores and whispered in her ear, "Please continue. I must take action immediately! Situation is very dangerous for Della. Maybe too late to save her father. **We must save Della as witness for trial of Schank.** Maybe even for preliminary hearing. I go now. Take all the time necessary with Lorie."

Dr. Fu moved quickly to where Ah Wing and Wang Sing were waiting. The emotion showed on his face as he said, "**Please call Emergency Council meeting now!**

Dr. Fu was still standing, but he stopped talking. **It was almost as if he was receiving some type of extra-sensory message.** They had seen that in the Doctor's face before. "**I sense extreme danger. Must deal with this matter decisively now!**"

I will send cable to South America and call Panama if Council approves.

"**May have found most vital witness and save lives of two people.**"

Dr. Fu seldom showed this much emotion and Wing and Sing left the room immediately. Dr. Fu's mind was made up. He would write the cable giving the orders, but the Emergency Council must review it. His brilliant mind knew he was training the younger Chinese to act with care and with cooperation of the leaders. He sat at his desk as he wrote.

AUSTRALIAN LADY DELLA LIKELY VITAL WITNESS STOP

MUST BE KEPT ALIVE AT ALL COST STOP PAY HIGH RANSOM

FOR HER AND FATHER STOP CONTACTING PANAMA TO HELP

STOP. SEND MORE DETAILS MILITARY JUNTA STOP HIGHEST

PRIORITY STOP DIRECT CONTACT DR. FU ONLY. STOP.

The Chinese Tong Emergency Council met quickly not changing a word in the cable. Full speed ahead was agreed upon. **The cable was on it's way when Dr. Fu placed a direct call to Panama.** He talked to the Tong leader there explaining the need for immediate action.

It was agreed one C-47 would be placed on emergency standby. A minimum of twelve rangers would be needed and a back-up C-47 was vital.

The Tong leader would call every twelve hours to give Dr. Fu his personal report. Dr. Fu asked that the Ranger leader be included in the calls.

As Dr. Fu concluded the call the Emergency Council continued it's meeting. The concern showed strongly on the face of Dr. Fu.

As the council moved to adjourn for the night Dr. Fu was solemn. "When the need for action presents itself we must act. **This plan is fraught with danger! Let us ask our honorable ancestors for their help!"**

CHAPTER 31
MARTHA SCHANK AND DR. EMERY SMITH.

The flower of true love unfolds. .

With the press of his other patients, his affection for Martha and his knowledge that human emotions gyrate and teeter-totter Dr. Smith was uncertain where Martha's mind was. He kept asking himself, "Is she about to have a nervous breakdown from her years of strain?

"Life is like an old, dirty, dusty road, full of continual bumps caused by those you associate with and then there are the pot holes that come when you don't expect them. Their depth is unknown until you sink into them. "

Martha's thoughts were similar except she was experiencing them. She had watched the turmoil and mental fatigue in her son's face on a daily basis. She would say to herself, "I can read Bob like a book, up to the wall that hides his actual business activity with his Father which he has done to spare my feelings. Instead it works the reverse. My imagination creates such terrible pictures."

Now that her son was locked up, and the extent of the charges against him not known, her worst fears had become reality. Dr. Smith had correctly placed her under 24 hour nurse's care at her home, not wanting her to be hospitalized and subject to the curiosity of the staff and the press. **He knew that could be the final blow to cause her to break down.**

Dr. Smith desperately wanted to tell Martha, "I have been in love with you for years. Will you file for divorce and I promise to marry you. Don't worry about losing everything, I will take care of you forever and ever. So help me God!"

As he shaved that morning he looked at himself in the mirror and the first thing he said was, "No guts! You operate on someone taking their life in your hands and you haven't got the nerve to tell a beautiful lady you love her. Why I'm no better than John Alden."

By the time he finished breakfast he thought of a step he could take which might give him enough of a kick in the pants to get things started. He called his attorney from his home and left a message with his answering service.

The answering service called attorney Jason Meldrum at home. He immediately called Dr. Smith, who was still at his house. "Hello, Emery, it's Jason, how are you?"

"Hello Jason, and thanks for calling me at home. Can I talk with you on the basis of client privilege so it's strictly confidential?"

"You sure can. Go ahead, Emery!"

"Would you believe it involves a female?"

"Hell, Emery, Now I've heard it all. I thought you had your prostate removed, or something like that. I never knew you were dating. Did you get yourself into big trouble?" He was laughing hard. Jason wasn't playing the role an attorney does who listens to his client. Instead he was playing the part of a golf buddy, and they were playing golf at the Montecito Country Club, where they regularly ribbed Dr. Smith, without mercy, over the fact that he was a real nice, single high class physician without a girl friend.

"You'd like nothing better than to know I was in a jam with some woman and needed an attorney."

"Well, Emery, you'd sure take a pasting at our Saturday morning golf game."

"Wait until I get you on the operating table one of these days. I'll shut you up for good. Matter of fact, the others included. I'll leave all my tools in you and sew you up."

"Okay, Emery, you win! What can I do?"

"It's about time you asked. I hope you aren't billing me for the time you spent teasing me. You aren't going to leak a word of this to anyone. Not your wife, and particularly not our golf foursome."

"It'll be tough, Emery, but you have my word."

So in the next five minutes Dr. Smith raised the question of Martha initiating divorce proceedings against Schank. The attorney concluded with, "As you are my client and Martha is your patient it might be better if I do not render an opinion on that for Martha. "Off the record, however, this may be exactly the correct time for her to file proceedings. This will alert the authorities to their marital status. His wrongdoing will affect her ownership rights and he may also be liable for mishandling her property rights."

"Splendid. I will talk to her tonight and try to get her agreement, Meanwhile, please pick the very best attorney to handle it. I will guarantee payment."

"You will! The Hippocratic oath you took at Medical School doesn't extend to this extra-curricular activity does it? Is it possible that you're in love with Martha?"

"You attorneys are pretty clever. We Doctors know when to keep our mouth shut."

"I understand, Emery. Behind the joking no one wishes you more happiness than I do. I'll give this my special attention. I think I already know who will do the job right!"

For the first time in a long time Dr. Smith whistled as he got ready to drive to his office. As he started his car's engine he felt a surge of resolve permeate his body, almost like he'd prescribed a new medicine for himself and it was finally giving him some relief. As his car passed the Santa Barbara Mission on his way to his office, he proclaimed to himself, "I'll call up Martha and give some excuse for coming over this evening. First, I will tell her I love her. Then, I'll change the subject and tell her about talking to my attorney. I know I want to marry her!"

"It won't be John Alden and Priscilla tonight. It will be Dr. Emery Smith and Martha."

The rest of the morning his step was lighter and he felt ten years younger.

After he returned to his office, from having a quick lunch with a surgeon associate, he received word the early evening nurse assigned to Martha had a very sick child she must take care of. Dr. Smith thought to himself, "Is it possible my luck is on a roll? I'll tell Martha I'll pinch hit for the evening nurse and I'll cook dinner in the bargain."

A half hour later, from his private office, he called Martha. She was delighted. "Oh, Dr. Smith, I can't imagine you would take off your entire evening to look after me and even cook dinner for me. **I am going to accept quickly, right now, before you change your mind.** That will be so lovely and I thank you so much."

"It'll be my pleasure. I must get back to work now. See you about six P.M."

"Good-bye for now, Emery."

The rest of the afternoon Dr. Smith felt like the young man who has suddenly gotten a date with a girl he admired for years and never had the nerve to ask. When he told his office nurse he was going to leave at 5 P.M. as he had an early appointment she said, "I hope it's monkey business. If it is, you are about two or three years late in goofing off."

It took Dr. Smith less than ten minutes to drive home from his office. He didn't live in Montecito, but had a spacious home on the ridge behind and above the old Mission.

His living room and dining room had a direct view of the Pacific Ocean. A spacious deck, the full width of the house, led from those two rooms for outdoor dining and viewing, the kind of living which made Santa Barbara the envy of so many cities.

He knew he would forever miss the beautiful lady who had been his wife since his internship many years ago. Since her death he had counseled many a patient to proceed with their lives, but he failed to convince himself. He had met Martha at a charity benefit. Martha had called him as a patient when her Internist retired.

Something happened when Martha came for her first visit to him. When he closed the door to begin his consultation with her he **actually thought he heard his deceased wife saying, "Here she is, Emery."**

Or was it just the overpowering aura that was Martha, which made him feel, "Here she is, Emery."

Whatever it was, he would always remember he was rattled. In fact, so much he felt like a new intern making hospital rounds for the first time with an M.D. Her papers and patient chart had previously been sent to his office and he had looked at them briefly. As he talked to Martha he was almost afraid to touch her.

She had some aches and pains, and had a small surgery that needed to be checked periodically. A couple of times he almost felt his hand shaking. When he completed the examination he said, "Martha, I believe you are doing fine. I'd like to be your regular internist. Don't hesitate to call me at any time."

What he had wanted to say was, "Please, Martha, may I be your internist forever. No charge whatsoever. Call me even if you have only a headache."

As he stepped out of his shower this evening he felt a few pangs of guilt. He was in the house he had shared for so many years with his wife. They had no children, due to medical problems they discovered soon after they were married. Without the distraction of children they become very close and completely devoted to each other.

As their friends' children grew and the problems of raising them at times became overwhelming, they accepted what fate had decreed and found special joy in each other.

Their outside social activity was taken care of by the multitude of activities continuously going on and which his earnings as a Physician enabled them to participate in.

Cultural opportunities abounded in Santa Barbara, including memberships in Historical Societies as well as the Arts. Membership in the Coral Casino Beach and Cabana Club, right on the beach and across from the beautiful Biltmore Hotel.

Membership in the Montecito Country Club where the championship course was situated high enough for the golfers to be awe struck with the view of the Pacific.

The view from the club dining and social facilities provided the same enchantment. The ocean breezes brought cool evenings on even the hottest day.

Martha had taken a shower early and spent considerable time trying to decide what to wear. She said to herself, "I have been in shock, but tonight I am going to try to put it all behind me, if only for a few hours. I'll dress as if this is a special date."

She laughed at herself for the first time since Schank had been arrested.

"What do I have that will make me look the youngest possible?"

Then she became a little self conscious.

"Should I let a little extra amount of my figure show? I know they say, 'Dress like a million dollars and you may really feel that way.' I sure need a mental boost!"

Martha slipped in an out of half a dozen outfits before she settled on a light blue silk dress that fit rather tightly on her hips. It was cut low enough to show some curve and the promise a classic bosom was being hidden. She was still a fairly trim, early fifties lady with traces of gray in the dark hair she refused to color.

At 5'6", her 130 pounds were enough to give her curves in the right places. She was gracious and charming, but most of that was wasted on her female bridge partners two afternoons a week. The estate had a full time gardener. However, Martha spent much time in the yard planting flowers and doing minor trimming herself.

Tonight she opened the door personally for Dr. Smith and as soon as she shut it looked at him saying, "Thank you so much for coming."

Then with a sense of embarrassment she said, "I'm so happy to see you I almost feel like hugging you."

With those words Dr. Smith extended his arms and moved toward her. Martha realized she was the instigator. As she moved toward the Doctor suddenly all her bottled up emotions overcame her and she threw her arms around his neck and clung to him.

For the moment the suddenness of it almost frightened them. Then without releasing their arms they looked at each other and their lips came together.

Now he could scarcely control himself. His strong arms gripped Martha more firmly. This time they kissed almost passionately. For a few seconds Martha was afraid and then Emery said, "Martha, I love you!"

She became slightly dizzy and he realized the power of the emotions that were surging through her so he broke the embrace. He firmly grasped her hand and led her to the seclusion of a small den. They sat together on a small sofa. With his arm around her she snuggled against his shoulder.

"Martha, when you came to me first as a patient I felt something that I had only felt toward my wife, who had died the year before. I thought about you often and in less than a year wondered if I was in love with you. I knew you were married so I could not say anything. **Martha, I now know for certain I am in love with you!"**

"Oh Emery, you have taken me by complete surprise. I am so flattered that you have thought seriously about me for so long. Why, I am just overwhelmed! May I just sit here for a few minutes without speaking?

"Could you maybe pinch me to make certain this isn't just a dream."

"Where would you like me to pinch you?"

"I'd settle for another kiss Emery!"

It was a long kiss and this time Martha let herself enjoy the emotions that were surging through her body. She thought to herself it's been so many years. I feel like a teen-ager right now.

"Emery, I know you are the nicest man I have ever met. I am sure of that. If I were single I'm sure I would be thrilled to say I love you. To be honest with you, Emery, my dear wonderful man, I've been alone so long I'm not certain what love is."

Then she paused and Dr. Smith could tell she was struggling for the right words.

"It's O.K. Martha darling, I'm not rushing you. I understand."

Martha moved forward and looked at the kindly Doctor. As her eyes searched his her tears began to flow. <u>"Emery, I could be happy with someone that could continue to love me—forever!</u> As you know, I haven't even seen my husband for over five years."

Emery looked at her saying, <u>"Martha, you have covered the subject so much better than my just saying I love you. What really matters is can two people be truly happy with each other forever? It isn't enough to say 'I love you.'"</u>

"Thank you so much, Emery. That's the way I know it must be."

At that moment Emery and Martha knew it was time for a breather. He squeezed Martha's hand and said, "Shall we cook dinner together?"

"I wouldn't have it any other way."

"Shall we have some wine, Martha?"

"Yes, and may I go off the pills you prescribed for me? I'm so happy."

"It would be just as well to skip them for the evening. If we keep going like this we both might have to take some blood pressure pills."

By the time they sat down to eat the steak Dr. Smith had brought from his freezer, along with some vegetables and a fresh garden salad, they were on their second glass of wine. They ate leisurely as they looked at each other in a mature, yet very loving way. Each was ecstatic they had vaulted above the multiple petty disasters of life and were spending some hours of genuine happiness, a romantic and thrilling evening.

When dinner was finished Martha said, "Shall we walk around the garden and help our digestion a little? Would the wonderful Doctor Smith prescribe that?"

"I prescribe we should spend a lot of time together."

So they walked and talked. They returned to put the dishes in the dishwasher and once again sat together on the sofa. Dr. Smith placed his right arm around Martha's shoulder, and she leaned back feeling secure in his arms.

They relaxed saying little. Dr. Smith broke the silence. "The reason I was so outspoken is I talked with my attorney this morning."

Then Dr. Smith related the conversation with his attorney concluding with, "It's, of course, up to you, Martha. "

Things were happening so fast Martha couldn't answer right away. Finally she said, "I do realize that with my husband's arrest I should make a decision. Stand by him or not. "For five years now he hasn't even cared to tell me where he is. Bob has been looking after my personal affairs, but he is in jail also.

"Emery, I would like to meet with an attorney to discuss the timeliness of this."

"I'll locate one for you and you can go from there."

Martha knew it was time to change the subject and she was the hostess. "Let me put some records on. I haven't danced in years. Do you dance, Emery?"

"Let's try it."

As they danced on the tile floor of the den they felt as if they were floating on the soft white clouds that ringed the city that

173

evening. Only too soon a call came from the gate. The night nurse had arrived. She did not know the Doctor was taking the place of the regular nurse and at first was shocked saying, "Has Martha taken a turn for the worse?"

Dr. Smith smiled and explained the absence of the other nurse. He could scarcely contain himself from saying more.

Instead he said, "Now that you are here I'm going to take off and get some sleep."

Martha had entered the room and said, "I'll walk the Doctor to his car. I'm feeling fine. Nothing to worry about."

The nurse looked at Martha and wanted to say, "You are absolutely beaming with happiness and look like you have never had a sick a day in your entire life."

She also wanted to say, "Looks like the Doctor's house call is just what you needed."

Nurses observe a lot and are tempted to acknowledge that no one fools them too often, but know the Physician-patient relationship is not one to intrude on.

Martha paused to look at the stars before she re-entered her home. "I feel like the sailor whose ship has been tossed and turned by a violent storm. After virtually giving up ever surviving, he finally sights land ahead."

CHAPTER 32
BACK TO WORK FOR LANGE.

Lange is caught in the middle again.
Monday morning Lange showed up at work at 7:30 A.M.
His boss was already there and said, "My wife and I are both
mystery fans and from the news reports we have been getting
you are sort of leading a double life. My wife is intrigued with
the fact you know Delores Lee. My wife would like to invite you
over for dinner but I knew she would just quiz you."

"Mr. Parks, maybe the Chinese can figure out how to spray
that undercoating on."

Mr. Parks laughed as he thought of Lange's frustrations with
the equipment.

Lange continued with, "I got here early partly because the
Santa Barbara police want me to come to their headquarters at
11 A.M. this morning. They didn't say why, but I'm sure they
just want to hear what I know."

"I'll bet they do! Why the whole town is in an uproar!
Imagine a kidnapping right down on Cabrillo Boulevard. Go
ahead and meet with the police."

"Thanks and I'll work as late tonight as necessary to make
up for time lost."

"I'm not worried–you're putting in lots of extra time. You
are conscientious."

When Jean, the office gal, got to work at 8 A.M. she looked in Lange's office and said, "That Dragon Lady friend of yours gets around doesn't she?"

Then to show her female claws a little she added, "You didn't spend much time with her did you?"

Lange thought of telling Jean to 'Go stuff it', but he knew that would be very tactless. So he kind of bit back by saying, "You're right."

As Jean went back to her work station she thought to herself, **"Each day he becomes more interesting, but I can't compete with an exotic Chinese lady."**

As the morning progressed Jean got her spirits up to, "Well, I'm here and she isn't."

Then her mind reminded her that she lived with her Mother who had managed to chase off a couple of guys. "My Mother thinks I should be taking care of her–not get serious with a guy, but I'm ready for the right guy! **Looks like Lange needs a local female good friend."**

Lange had hoped to hear from the Bank of America Friday as to what stage the company loan papers had reached. The business was growing well. So it needed cash to pay for equipment and money to operate in the time lag until accounts receivable were collected. Lange had just completed a detailed financial statement as requested by the Bank. They had already told him things looked good. As to the financial statement his boss was not entirely pleased **as some of Mr. Parks' own estimates of assets had failed to be accurate.**

The bank had pointed out that was exactly the reason they wanted the work done by an accountant with credentials. Service stations under construction involved cost accounting. Lange recalled that under the renowned Professor Stillman, Advanced Cost Accounting did not seem overly difficult.

At 11 A.M. Lange was at police headquarters. His boss had informed him that ever since he was a kid, he had always wanted to be a private detective and as long as Lange performed his responsibilities well it was all right for him to work with the police. His boss added, "I kind of envy you, Lange."

Lt. Merced and Sgt. Andrew wanted complete details about the assassins. After fifteen minutes on that subject Andrew changed the subject to the alleged Maude Mayberry break-in.

"I've been checking any and all break-ins in the past year. Partly because we've curious, but mostly because the City Fathers and the public are driving us nuts. You can't believe the phone calls we are getting. They all want to know what the hell is going on in this town." He added, "Guess they are concerned that we might turn into another Chicago."

Lt. Merced took over with, "Does The Shadow mean anything to you?"

"You mean like me and my shadow?"

"Now don't be a smart alec. The Shadow is a one man private eye. Really he is the biggest snoop in town. Nothing high class-mostly just a dirt digger."

"A real fun kind of a guy."

"Among his clients are The Schank Investment Co. We have him locked up as well as Bob Schank, who is Cal Schank's son and runs a small branch office here."

"Amazing! Now the ball game is for real."

"I couldn't get a word out of Bob, but the Shadow, one Manny Jones, the last name of which is not legit, decided to talk. And he admitted to being the lookout for the break-in of Maude's duplex. Claims the actual break in was done by a babe from L.A.. We're inclined to think that's the truth."

"So what did they actually steal from Maude?"

"There's where the whole damn thing falls apart. Manny claims he has no idea. I'm inclined to think he might be telling the truth–then the next minute I know he is lying. You know, this isn't an easy business, Lange."

"Is that the end of our visit? I have lots of work I can do back at my office."

"No, that's not the end of our talk. There is an undercover agent who allegedly was the guy Ruppert Snyder came up to

Santa Barbara to see. A Mavis Scott tried to get next to this man, but he demanded to see the boss.

"The undercover agent wants to meet you."

"Now who's kidding who? This must be a joke!" exclaimed Lange.

"No, I'm giving it to you straight up!"

"How will I get in touch with him?"

"He will contact you."

"Maybe it's time for me to pack my bags and go back to Portland. I'm just a small town kid."

"Hell, you've been in an infantry division overseas, graduated from College. Now it's time for you to tackle the world."

"I don't want to play war no more! Remember that song? I used to sing it in Church."

"We have one more deal to talk to you about."

"Do you have any Tums?"

"Come on, Lange, quit trying to be funny. We have a deal for you!"

"How much do I get-how much vacation pay, retirement, etc."

"If you are going to be that way the interview is over."

"I'll try hard to be nice for a few more minutes. Keep in mind I went down to Los Angeles to have lunch with a friend and almost got killed. My friend almost got killed twice."

"You mean Delores Lee, The Dragon Lady, is your friend?"

"I had hoped to go to L.A. and elope with her. That's beside the point. Go ahead and spring whatever you planned to."

"Very interesting, Lange, you got friends where we ain't got no friends. Only Lt. Brown has friends like that–and Brown really likes you. Yes, very interesting!"

"Now will you treat me with a little respect?"

"Maybe. Anyhow-like I said we have Manny locked up. Maybe you'd like to take over his business. You could upgrade it into a high class private eye deal. With your business background and all these old folks in Montecito with the big bucks, who knows what it might lead to. Think of the classy people you will meet."

"Are you talking about me opening an escort service or being a Private Eye? I'm thinking of the Rupperts and Schanks and the assassins. Every day I was overseas in an infantry division was one too many!

"I will not take a job that involves running around carrying a gun, crawling over fences at night and dodging bullets. I was in the army once. Once was enough!"

"So you almost got bumped off going into a hospital rest room. You going to sit around all your life and let all the good guys do the work?"

"This must be a nightmare. Who would want to be a private eye? Sorry, men, time for me to vacate your premises and go back to pushing my pencil."

Lange stood up–then he added, "I can't even find a girl friend. Thanks, anyway."

As soon as Lange left Sgt. Andrew looked at Merced. "I told you so!"

Merced looked at the Sergeant and replied, **"Get lost."**

That afternoon Lange said to the office secretary," Jean, have you ever heard of a guy by the name of Sid Stevens? An itinerant office machine repairman."

"Sure, he comes around here once in awhile. He'll repair your old clunker, or take it in on one that he's already worked on. Matter of fact, he does what most office machine people try to do. They take in your old one, loan you another and hope you become addicted to the new one, and then they sock it to you."

"What kind of a guy is he?"

"Let's see, you know, he's all right. Sort of mild mannered like you. Seems to know his stuff like you."

"Wonder if he could get those nozzles to work on that undercoating equipment?"

"Good thinking, you know you should mention that to Mr. Parks. Now why are you asking about him?"

"I met his sister in a restaurant in Ventura."

"Do we have love in bloom?"

"If she lived in town instead of 35 or 40 miles away I'd try to get a date with her."

"It's about time. You've been here several weeks and I was beginning to think you were a hermit and never looked at a girl."

"My past experience might indicate just looking is the way to go."

As Jean walked away she said to herself, "Looks like his door is wide open."

That evening, after fixing dinner, Lange took a walk. His route was simple. First the train station and the Moreton Bay Fig Tree, both of which were only a couple of blocks away.It was claimed that the Fig Tree was the largest of its kind in the nation. Planted in Santa Barbara in 1877 it was claimed 10,000 people could stand in its shade at noon.

Then to Cabrillo Blvd. and the Yacht Club and out onto the public portion which housed the commercial fishing facilities. Then up Cabrillo to Stearns Wharf. Then out to the end of the Wharf, and again up Cabrillo past where his old Army barracks were.

Then past the Mar Monte Hotel, behind which he had worked out of a Quonset hut processing other returned soldiers.. Then all the way to the Biltmore and the Coral Casino and thence back to Bath Street.

If he still needed more exercise a walk up State Street to the Fox Theater would suffice.

He had scarcely returned to his tiny apartment when the phone range. It was Lt. Brown of the LAPD calling from his apartment.

He laughed and said, "Understand you didn't kick up your heels when Lt. Merced propositioned you. I don't blame you."

Then he continued with, "You know, Lange, it is such a rat race in L.A. in another few years I wouldn't mind retiring and running a small detective agency in Santa Barbara."

After several minutes of conversation Lt. Brown concluded with, "Santa Barbara is a very unique place. With all those bucks, held by so few, there are a lot of crooks frothing at the mouth to pick their fat pocketbooks. I've got more than a few ideas I could discuss with you, but right now is not the time.

"By the way I am authorized to tell you confidentially the name of the guy that is going to contact you. This is top secret!"

"O.K., Alex, but why the secret?"

"He's been a secret treasury agent for 40 years. He's looked over a dozen replacements and never found one."

"My God, I can't believe it! Is this world full of so many crooks that everyone is out trying to hire me to help stem the tide?"

"Sorry, my good friend, that's the way the ball is bouncing right now. Skip the P.I. deal until we can sit down personally and talk about it. Look out for assassins in the bathroom."

"Did you get a bad time over that?"

"Did I? I caught holy hell on that, only the guys that gave me a bad time weren't very holy. Sometimes I wonder how some of these crazy expressions we use come into being.

"Right now I have to help the District Attorney get ready for the preliminary hearing. Then you and I can do some wharf fishing off Stearns Wharf. O.K.?"

"O.K. I'll follow through, but I am shocked there is so much evil in our great nation."

Lt. Brown didn't have the right reply to that on his fingertips. Finally he said, **"You know Lange, the evil Empire of Cal Schank has lots of company.** Here are my phone numbers again. You can call anytime! Sorry to be so blunt."

CHAPTER 33
DELORES CALLS LANGE.

A very timely call.

Time was moving swiftly — as it always seemed to do when matters were pressing.

Delores Lee, the gorgeous Chinese lady with many similarities to the legendary Dragon Lady was in the small, but exotically furnished room the Chinese Tong had furnished her.

She had little time to relax since she had arrived in Los Angeles. The events of recent had been so terrifying it took all the courage and stamina she could muster. She was privy to all the plans to rescue Della Robertson who was being held in a brothel in South America.

As Delores reviewed the contemplated rescue, which was being planned by a special group of elite rangers in Panama, her heart was filled with extreme fear. Something seemed to be telling her that the task was too difficult. Her fear was fueled by the concern she saw in the face of Dr. Fu, who with the Chinese Council must make the final decision.

He had received word the small South American City where Della was held was in firm control of a ruthless and extremely powerful Military Junta. To send the Rangers from Panama might be sending them to certain death.

Her heart was burdened and the special herb tea, that normally would relax her, seemed to have no effect. She said to herself, "I must do something to take my mind away from this. **"Dr. Fu is considering all the factors and will not make a rescue attempt that is doomed to failure."**

Her thoughts moved to Lange and her heart seemed to lighten. "It's been over a week since he drove down to see me. I must call him to inform him of my sorrow in not being able to see him privately. Yes, I'll call him right now."

In her small case she found his number and dialed him. It was 10 P.M. Thursday, April 20th, when she made the call and he was home. "I am so pleased to find you in, my good friend Lange. How are you?"

"With your call I am suddenly transformed from my lonely status to one of happiness."

"Maybe you are part Chinese. That statement sounds like it has a Chinese lilt to it."

"All sales management books say, 'We must alter our conversation and action to fit the situation. If you are talking to a San Francisco banker, who talks slowly and is very formal, you do likewise.' When I talk to Chinese I feel a special kinship and I guess I do talk differently."

"The man who wrote that book stole the idea from the Chinese. We have known that for a thousand years. Lange, I had been hoping to invite you down very soon, but we have too many problems to cope with. Not much time for visiting."

"Delores, I know you well enough to wonder if some new fear or problem has come into your mind. Is there anything I can do to help?"

"We do have a matter I cannot speak of. There is great distance involved!"

"Delores, I doubt that I could be of any help, but if you could give me a clue maybe I can toss out an idea."

"Suppose a special need came up to rescue two people in another country which was in absolute control by a strong Military Junta."

"Now there's a tough one! **There are a lot of story book novels** where one man beats off twenty guards, slips through windows, over fences and gets away with it. When I got into an infantry division, and was sent overseas we learned the tough way, the deadly way. **Don't send a boy to do a man's job. Don't make a landing with only five percent of the force needed. Against a Military Junta you will need a Commando force of great strength.**"

"**That is exactly our concern, but where do you get such a force?**"

"You need a military force to safely combat another military force."

"You think like I do. You recall we discussed my husband's death as a Chinese infantryman. I learn much from him when he would get a few days leave, after leaving the hospital, each time he was wounded. Sorry to bother you. Did not mean to give you more worries. You have a new job. Enough to worry about."

"**Hold on, Delores. I want to ask you one question. What nationality are the folks you need to rescue?**"

"Interesting question. I tell you in most absolute confidence. You promise?"

"I sure do. You know my lips are sealed. I have enough military and legal background to know an idle lip can sink the ship."

"Now you're stealing another old Chinese saying. My question is, if it involved rescuing an Australian girl in a small port city in South America how would you go about it? Your infantry division was involved with the Aussie's in New Guinea so you know a lot about them."

"Yes, I do. I have 100% respect for them. Let me think for a moment. You know April 25th is ANZAC Day for both Australia and New Zealand. It is their Memorial Day. **"Almost 3,000 men were lost by those two nations in scaling virtually impossible cliffs in Europe in World War I.** I can't recall the names of the cliffs.

"Delores, those Aussies are rough and rugged fighting men. You know, the Aussies love a good fight. They would go any place to rescue an Aussie gal."

"I know much about the rugged Australian soldiers. It would take months to get together a force together. No, Lange, we don't have much time. How would they get into the city along with all the necessary guns and ammunition to accomplish this?"

"You mention it is a coastal city. I have an idea, Delores. How do you say in Chinese, 'Kill two birds with one stone?"

Delores rattled off a half dozen Chinese words. Lange replied, "Ich verstest nicht."

Delores laughed, "I know those German words well, but you don't know what I said in Chinese. O.K., Lange, how do we — -" and then she rattled off the Chinese words again.

"You use the Australian Navy. Find the nearest Aussie Naval vessel in the general area. Have them pull into the port claiming they have severe engine problems. Then because the men want to celebrate ANZAC Day have them stage a big parade and get into the city that way. Then attack the necessary building and rescue the lady. As far as I am concerned there is some Errol Flynn in every Aussie male."

"The Australian Navy-very interesting–like a giant dragon coming to their rescue. **Let me just pause and think for a moment, Lange."**

Soon she continued with, "Lange, I ask you to please stay near your phone and I must make no more comments. Your idea offers great strength. I go directly to Dr. Fu and inform him of our conversation."

Lange sat back and his active mind expanded on his sudden suggestion.

Scarcely a half hour later Lange's phone rang again. It was Dr. Fu who spoke. "Lange, I am most intrigued by the cleverness of your idea. Often fate steps in when help is greatly needed. Please elaborate."

"The Aussie ship would come into the harbor presumably for engine repairs. The men would request permission to celebrate ANZAC Day with their usual parade.

"They will come ashore carrying some arms for the parade. Automatic weapons can be broken down so they are not obvious. Maybe carry some in drums.

"Once they are ready I would say forget about the parade. Just have them go into action. They will be so mad they will totally wreck the building and hunt down the perpetrators of the abduction of the lady. The Aussies are very spirited and patriotic!

"They would take this as a personal challenge and it would give their entire Nation another meaning for ANZAC Day. I'd like to be there to see them in action once again."

"Lange, the psychology of motivation is at the root of all great accomplishments. If we can get it put into action."

"Where are the folks?"

"The daughter is in a brothel. The father was in jail. He tried to rescue his daughter and he may be already dead."

"Those Aussies will go for the rescue. Every man on the vessel will volunteer. They will rescue both of them and create so much damage that South Americans will think twice before mistreating another Aussie.

"They can take them both on board the Aussie vessel immediately. Once they are on board they can leave the port city safely. What a way to celebrate ANZAC Day."

"Lange, your enthusiasm and your idea of using adequate forces has made this a most important call. I will present this to our Chinese council immediately and I recognize your plan is more powerful. That is if the Australian Navy would go for it.

"Our plans to rescue them with a small commando force flown into the city is too fraught with danger. I, too, have some experience dealing with Aussie soldiers and civilians and I concur with your knowledge of their ruggedness."

"I am sure the Aussies will say this is going to be a bloody good show."

"Yes, that is the way it should be. Help from their own countrymen and not bring the Chinese into the picture at all. Yes, logic suggests using your plan," said Dr. Fu as he thanked

Lange and closed the conversation with a promise of silence from Lange.

Delores and half a dozen other Chinese were in the room as Dr. Fu made the call.

Ah Wing and one of the young elite Chinese council were listening in on other phones.

All were seized with the drama of the situation. The coincidence of the timing with ANZAC Day was remarkable, but as Dr. Fu said, "My experience with Aussies is that they are proud and true to their country and ANZAC Day 365 days a year. "

Luck seemed to be with the Chinese. Australian Naval headquarters confirmed there was a Australian light cruiser within 300 miles of the port and it had been scheduled to observe ANZAC Day only 100 miles south of the port where Della and her father were imprisoned.

When the Captain of the Cruiser heard a crooked American might be responsible for her being placed in a brothel, and her testimony might clinch the case against the unscrupulous procurer he said, "Mates, you can count on our giving them bloody hell and we'll get our lady out safely. We might burn down the town, but we'll get her out!"

"You'll save the Chinese section of town won't you?"

"You have my promise on that."

Dr. Fu informed the Aussie Captain an emergency squad was being sent to the port from Panama and they would be in immediate contact with the Tong leader, Q. Song.

The Captain ended the conversation with, "I will be in contact with you soon, but one way or another we are going to head for that port and give it an all out go, Matey."

Dr. Fu had been called many things in his life, but never 'Matey,' by an Aussie. He did not mind in the least.

A call was immediately placed to Panama and the emergency squad leader's response was one of enthusiasm and gratitude. He said, **"Those Aussie are as tough as they make**

them. This is going to be a military experience none of us will ever forget.

"Hell, we'll march in the next ANZAC celebration they have, if they will let us. My men are going to be eager for this one.

"We were the scared dozen before this call. If the planes only last for one way we can go back on the Cruiser. It will be great to work with the Aussies."

After Dr. Fu told the Chinese how relieved the Commandos were they cheered, clapped their hands and were also very relieved.

Ah Wing said, "As Doyle lectured all over the world much that occurs is put into motion by powers beyond us. So strange my friendship with Lange starts when he is ten years old. Now 21 years later, his war experiences bring us help we need."

"Dr Fu's stern face relaxed a little as he said, "I am going to rest easier tonight. I now go to my room. First, I give thanks to our ancestors.

"Suggest we all get the first few hours of real rest we have had in several days. By tomorrow we will be hearing more from the Australians."

CHAPTER 34
ABOARD AN AUSTRALIAN LIGHT CRUISER

It's let's go mates.

The Australian male was a rugged fighting man during war time. In peace time when men worked away from the cities, fighting was a way to relieve boredom. Serving in the military on the cramped quarters of a Naval vessel the men craved excitement. The Captain called his officers together to give them the word they had been assigned a most important and very unusual rescue mission.

Each officer briefed the men that served under him. The officers could not contain their enthusiasm. When the news reached the men every single man volunteered to serve.

Excitement on board reached a fever pitch within 24 hours. To rescue a fair Aussie damsel in distress and her Aussie father electrified everyone on board. The comments of just one sailor was typical. "Even the diesel engines are sounding like they have a purpose now."

Not every man on board had spent his entire military time on board ship. The war had matched and mixed many a soul just as it had taken many a lad and lass to the great beyond as they valiantly dedicated their lives to Australia.

Two men, Jerry O'Leary, and Joseph Michael, were typical of the veterans still serving in peace time. They had both

The Evil Empire Of Cal Schank

entered the service before Pearl Harbor. Part of their training and encampment was near the little town of Seymour, Camp Seymour to be exact, about 60 miles from the large Aussie City of Melbourne in the Province of New South Wales.

Overseas in North Africa they lost many mates in the battle against General Rommel, the German Desert Fox, as well as from the lack of water, sand storms and the deadly heat.

Jerry and Joe each had been wounded many times as they continually risked their lives. Part of combat was rescuing wounded mates under fire. They were closer than most brothers would ever be.

After the war, they worked in the north on cattle ranches then hacked away at cutting sugar cane on plantations. They concluded they were very tired of sand and dirt and wanted to be around water as well as see the rest of the world.

They considered going back into the military. They decided even a cramped bed on board ship was still a bed, not a luxury a foot soldier could carry around in a pack on his back. It wasn't easy to get in the Aussie Navy, but their prior service bravery opened doors for them and they were finally accepted.

Jerry and Joe thrived as Navy men. The men they served with knew they were heroes, but at times weren't quite certain that all the tales Jerry and Joe passed out were authentic. **They were partial to Melbourne Bitter Ale and never left Australia without an illegal supply.**

Often after a few rounds they forgot that military rules had to be tight on board ship and frequently were the subject of disciplinary measures, reluctantly charged against them, but seldom enforced. The Captain of the Aussie Cruiser, was a war hero himself and he used to say to the officers under him, "I'll be damned if I know why I tolerate Jerry and Joe."

His executive officer knew the Captain tolerated them because deep down in his heart he kind of envied them.

"Sure, you have the prestige and the pay to go with it, but deep down in your heart you admire them for what they are, a couple of bloody great Aussies.

"They buried hundreds of their buddies fighting Rommel in the desert. So now and then, with a few beers, they crack up a little. **They deserve it for the nightmares they have to bear the rest of their lives."**

So it was when the Captain said, "Give the job to the desert rats," it was always with a note of admiration and respect in his voice. The Officers and Chiefs took to planning the mission with a vigor the Captain had not seen since war time.

His executive officer responded with, "Captain, this is war."

They knew they would be planning, adding, amending and striving for new ideas right up to they moment they landed. They moved all the men into squads of varying sizes. It was realized that the rescue attempts for Della and Reginald were the most vital and **would need two squad leaders who were utterly fearless, but most of all would not panic under fire.**

There were only two men's names spoken. They did flip a coin, however, heads was Della and tails was her father. Jerry came up heads and so it would be his squad that would rescue Della. It would be Joe's squad that would rescue her father, and hopefully he was still alive and could be moved.

Jerry and Joe were called into the small staff conference room. They saluted and were told to sit down. They had tried to adapt a polished military bearing, **but usually failed to hide all their irreverence toward military rules and regulations.**

The executive officer quickly reviewed the plan saying, "This is just for starters. We will be working on this night and day until our feet hit dry land. **What do you think about it? Jerry, you answer first."**

Jerry and Joe both felt the adrenaline rising. It was obvious to them that the two most dangerous jobs were going to be the squads rescuing the two Australians. Jerry took one look at Joe. Joe nodded. Jerry spoke, "Me and Joe just volunteered to be the two squad leaders to rescue Della and Reg. Please don't give the job to anyone else. We'll do our damnest to be better sailors afterwards. Just don't give the job to anyone else," **he pleaded.** The Captain looked at the two men, then looked at the executive officer and the others assembled in the staff room and he said,

"These two men have just volunteered. Are there any other nominations?"

No one said a word. The Captain said, "Don't hold back. Are there any other nominations?"

Still no word from anyone else.

The Captain said, "No question these will be the two most important squad leaders in the rescue. I think we better take a vote. All in favor raise your hands. Keep them up I want to count and make certain every officer here is voting."

The Captain stood up and carefully looked the room over. Then he looked at Jerry and Joe, **"The desert rats have it unanimously. Let's everyone give one loud cheer for them."**

Jerry and Joe stood up and saluted. The executive officer looked at the Captain and said, "You know Captain, I think those birds finally gave a regulation salute."

The Captain winked at the executive officer, something he seldom ever did. Then he said, "O.K., Jerry and Joe, let's sit down and really start in earnest on this rescue. Build into the plan our headquarters are notifying the Military Junta today that our engines need emergency repairs and we must put in port on April 25th.

"That being ANZAC Day we wish to first have a small parade and get rid of some of our sea legs. If they turn us down we have to have an alternative plan as well. One way or another we are going to put into that port on April 25th. And the rescue is going to take place on that day.

"There may be two C-47's come in from Panama with a dozen rangers to help us, but you know how that goes. **Make our plans to do this alone if necessary!**

"This is the most unusual assignment this vessel has ever received. We are expected to do a bloody good job, men. Now, let's get to work."

By midnight they had a first draft of the plan. Much work would go on while the plan was being checked and rechecked and amended. Sub-plans included the actual weapons that would be used. How the automatic weapons and light machine guns would be broken down and carried.

Important, but not minor, was the fact they would be supposedly going on shore to conduct a parade and they must not attract any suspicion which might blow the rescue.

Built-in was the one thing they didn't like to discuss. That was the subject of casualties. They had to be prepared with medics to patch up any of their wounded and men to carry them back to the ship. **The ship's doctor would stay on board.**

In spite of the fact there was always the grim side of war, the excitement on board never diminished. **Men** who were not assigned to the major fighting squads were begging to be included and **were offering to trade up to six months pay for the opportunity.**

Almost 24 hours later as the vessel was heading for the South America port and the Captain was eating lunch in the officer's mess, he whispered to his executive officer.

"I know it has seemed kind of strange to you officers that I haven't kicked Jerry and Joe off this ship. I have even told my wife on several occasions I didn't quite understand why I hadn't court martialed them.

"My dear wife would look at me and say, 'You know we women are often teased because we come up with that excuse 'Women's intuition.' You men call it 'A gut feeling.' Whatever you call it, there is an aura that surrounds a good person. One that leads them to do things they are not always certain they know why they are doing them.

"'For some reason you're keeping Jerry and Joe on board. Don't fight it. There's a reason! Be it no more than they have earned some special consideration. **God let them live through the war. Who are you to cut them down to size now?'"**

The Captain recalled how he never knew how to handle his wife on that subject. He spent so much time at sea that time with his wife was very precious. So he'd shift the conversation to something else. He said no more as he continued with his lunch.

The executive officer said it for him, "You and your wife were both right. Yes, even I wondered at times about your tolerance. I knew the men revered them. In fact, I was jealous at times, they respected Jerry and Joe more than me., but now we all have the answer, we need them now! What's your wife going to say about Jerry and Joe now?"

"She's one smart lady. She won't say a thing. That's one agreement we made before we got married. No one throws things back at the other. No 'I told you so's.' I told my wife that would sink our ship of marriage, and she agreed."

"You are a wise man. It's hard to run a ship through a storm when things are stormy at home."

Coded cables were being sent from Aussie Naval Headquarters and with each cable the fever pitch increased among the officers and men on the cruiser. Each new concern was met equally by the dedication of the entire crew. On this forthcoming ANZAC Day their skill, determination and bravery must rise to the highest Australian military standards.

They knew only too well.
THEY MUST NOT DESECRATE ANZAC DAY WITH FAILURE !

CHAPTER 35
LEXUS TAYLOR AND SCHANK

His private rail car remained unoccupied.
Due to sheer exhaustion Schank was finally able to sleep in
his small, virtually bare cell. A toilet, small wash basin and a
double decked cot bore no resemblance to the lavish furnishings
of his private rail car. The three meals a day delivered to him
through the bars of his cell were a drastic departure from his
own private cook and steward.

There was no stock of liquor and wine and no freezer with
the best steaks.

No longer was he staying in the best hotels. The Muelbach
in Kansas City, The Waldorf Astoria in New York, The Mark
Hopkins in San Francisco were, but a few. He had a favorite
in every major city. In Los Angeles he particularly like the
Ambassador. At times he went to it's night club, the Coconut
Grove.

Los Angeles, like New York, was a sea of pleasure spots
whose only limitations were time to explore them and money to
pay the enormous tabs.

The glitter of Hollywood's movie studios, Grauman's
Chinese Theater, the unlimited supply of entertainment on
Wiltshire Boulevard and restaurant row on La Cienaga Blvd.

It was afternoon and Lexus was meeting with Ruppert Snyder giving him the news they were working on the final date for Schank's preliminary hearing. The District Attorney felt the case was much stronger against Schank. **If they could nail him by getting the judge to rule he should stand trial, then would worry about Ruppert later.**

The D.A. had not made a decision whether to add charges against Schank for the attempted murder of Lorie Owens while she was in the hospital. "They might hold the charges back, get the trial set on the original charges and then add the additional charges," Lexus reported to Ruppert.

Ruppert took this as good news for the moment. He had convinced himself he had the odds in his favor. He said to Lexus, "I have no idea who kidnapped me, but it appears like they might of done me a favor. Have you and Schank come up with any ideas?"

"No ideas worth discussing. Got to see Schank now. You know why I came to see you first. Have to build up a little ammunition as all Schank does is rant and rave until I can't stand it any more and leave."

Lexus left Ruppert's cell and moved on to Schank's. The latter was his usual arrogant and disagreeable self. Schank fumed, sputtered, swore, and demanded Lexus account for the time he was spending on his defense.

Lexus was finding his fuse getting as short as Schank's. Just before he left he shouted at Schank, **"We're going to do this my way. I'm the attorney, not you !"**

As the jailer let Lexus out of the cell it was all he could do to contain himself and not make a remark. He would report to the District Attorney all he observed.

CHAPTER 36
LANGE MEETS WITH
MR. STANFORD POTTER AND WIFE.

Lange was sleeping in fits and starts. He thought to himself. I need some fun! A girl friend instead of all these problems. Now what does Potter want to see me about? What kind of a guy is he really? I'll call Lt. Brown and see if he'll tell me more.

So Lange called Lt. Brown in Los Angeles asking, **"Has Potter lived in the Santa Barbara area for a long time?"**

"Lange, why do you ask?"

"I happened to recall my Uncle in Anaheim has been there a long time and is in the Orange County Historical Register."

"So you wonder if you might look up Potter. That's a darn good idea, Lange. You'll need his first name. **It's Stanford and, yes, he has lived there a long time.**"

Lange went to the Santa Barbara library. There he was, Stanford Potter. He was rather a distinguished guy. Served in World War I in an artillery battery. No, not in Harry Truman's company. Gassed in the war and slightly injured by a shell fragment from a German 75 mm. Had become prominent in the processing of tree grown agriculture.

As the crops adjusted from nuts to citrus he was in the vanguard of the visionaries coming up with new ideas that kept the area abreast of the times.

Then Lange noticed a reference to the Biltmore Hotel, one of the three hotels the returning soldiers from overseas got to stay in for seven days.

Lange looked for more information on the Biltmore where he had spent his seven days. **Just 23 months after it's gala opening Black Friday, October 1929,** had occurred. Fortunes were lost overnight as the terrible depression turned into a virtual grim reaper. It brought desperation to millions, and even death.

Virtually everyone was affected. Many former rich and famous found themselves on skid row, in the company of those they had shunned and ignored before.

Many fine hotels closed, but the Biltmore remained open. In 1932 The Biltmore Beach Club was opened and eight new cottages were added. Dinner served in the breathtaking La Marina dining room cost as little two dollars.

It was operating at a loss and on November 13, 1936, only nine years after it was built, it was sold at Sheriff's auction at the country courthouse for a top bid of $476,000. [3]

Lange was totally captivated with the article as he and his Dad in the late 1930's worked on foreclosed houses taken back by various financial institutions such as Portland Trust and Savings Bank, Home Owners Loan Corporation and Metropolitan Life.

Lt. Merced was extremely curious about the call Lange was to receive from an unnamed source. Finally he called Lange, "Did you get that confidential call?"

"Not yet. Having any fun these days Lt. Merced?"

"We're on the hot seat in this town now. Boy, am I catching hell and so is the chief. Yesterday a Limo pulled up to our front door and a chauffeur helped a little old lady from Montecito up the stairs. **Imagine that, Lange! They are walking in the front** door now to complain. Arriving in their big cars and their chauffeurs."

Lange laughed even though he knew it was not desired. "What did she say?"

"I'll tell you what she said! She said, 'I do declare, Lt. Merced, this town is going to hell.'"

"What did you reply?"

"I looked her right in the eye and said, 'My dear lady, I do declare you are right!'"

"What did she reply to that?"

"She smiled and looked at me and said, 'You know, Lt. Merced, I think I like you.'" "Those kind of folks know their way around. I'm almost 31. By the time I'm 75 maybe I will finally know what's going on in the world. **What kind of a racket did her family have to make their money? That always interests me.**"

"She's a canning heiress," replied Lt. Merced.

"You mean as in masonry jars? Maybe the Kerr Estate?"

"No, canned food. Not Heinz, but one of their big competitors. It's the chief's policy not to give out any names."

Mr. Stanford Potter called Lange. Lange was out, but returned the call shortly and Potter asked if 5 P.M. this same evening at Lange's office would be O.K. Lange agreed and after they hung up he thought to himself. **Potter is cagey.** He wants to be in the position that if he takes one look at me and wants to run he will only have to walk out the door of our office.

Promptly at 5 P.M. Mr. and Mrs. Potter walked in the office.

Lange introduced the Potters to Jean and she left for home exiting with, "Good Evening, and nice to have met you, Mr. and Mrs. Potter."

Lange invited them into his modest cell size office. They were older than he had expected. Their skin was no longer smooth, the hair on their heads was mostly gray and there were bags under their eyes. They hadn't stood straight and tall for years, and as they sat down each grasped the arm of the chair as they moved rather slowly into it.

Both looked directly at him. Lange realized he was being confronted by four eyes that were strong and forceful and whose ages were near four score and ten. He was relieved that after their searching eyes had confronted him a smile appeared on the lips of each. It was almost as if they were telling him they liked him.

Mr. Potter spoke first. "It's always nice to view a small business. I had a small business once. That was many years ago. When it got big I wished it was still small. **Tell me, Lange, why you have returned to Santa Barbara?"**

"I keep asking myself that question. I know I have to work. I seem to run into funny situations which make me wonder why I came back."

Mrs. Potter interrupted with, "We've all been through that. You look level headed."

Then Potter spoke, "I heard from Lt. Brown about your narrow escape the Saturday before last. Also got word you have a neighbor, Maude Mayberry, that is about to lose her duplex to Schank Investment Co."

"You know a lot about me."

"A little about you. A lot about Schank Investment Co," replied Mr. Potter.

"You do! Any suggestions?"

"Well, perhaps I do, but right now their office is closed. Let's put that aside for the time being. My wife and I have reservations for dinner at the Harbor Restaurant on the Wharf. We'd like you to be our guest. We have dinner there a couple times a month. I was told Herbert Marshall, the big time movie star, will be having dinner near our table."

Lange quickly thought to himself, "From what I read Potter has the bucks to pay for my dinner and I sure want to get him to help Maude if he can."

To the Potters he replied, "That sure would be a treat. I'm happy to accept."

"Excellent. Let's be on our way!"

Lange could tell the Potters knew the menu backward and forward. They both ordered shark. Sharks and the South Pacific were not a pleasant memory to Lange.

He settled for roast beef and wondered if they were going to give him the third degree. Finally he realized they were waiting for him.

"My folks moved from Orange County back to Portland in 1925 just after the big earthquake. We went through Santa Barbara and my Dad said there wasn't a chimney left standing. I've always been curious to learn more. Were you living here at the time? "

"We were both here and remember it so well. The damage was terrible! The historic Santa Barbara Mission and the beautiful Arlington Hotel were illustrations of the cultural and the business losses."

Mr. Potter continued, "There were many interesting side incidents to the terrible destruction created by the '25 earthquake. For instance, Carpinteria is about 13 miles away. **One man hitched his wagon with his horses and drove from Carp to upper State and took several loads of the Arlington's doors.**

"One would never guess he was going to use them to build a beach hotel. Not only using the doors inside, but also for exterior siding. Believe he called it the Near Beach Hotel as it was a couple of blocks from the beach.[4] I'm glad the history of the city interests you. If you live in a place you must study it's history. If you don't love it enough to do so you're living in the wrong city."

"It will always be special to me as this was my first home back in the U.S. after almost three years overseas. My wife had deserted me for someone else and I used to walk up and down the beach a true sad sack.

"I was discharged at Hoff General Hospital in Santa Barbara with some disability. I went overseas a healthy 175 pounds and left the jungle at about 110 pounds."

Mr. Potter smiled, "I remember it so well. It was completed in April 1941 Hoff was one of those things the military did in advance. There were 33 ward-type buildings, 25 by 150 feet. A total of 100 buildings with a floor area of over 330,000 square feet. **Like a good and bad story. It sure was needed."**

Mrs. Potter spoke next, "So this was your first home overseas. I hope we citizens of Santa Barbara treated you right!"

"Yes, and perhaps that is why I have returned. I learned what a fine city this is."

Mr. Potter spoke, "If my wife and I leave now we can get home before dark. I prefer to drive in daylight. I will call you again. We both have enjoyed meeting you."

"Thank you for the fine dinner and it was a pleasure to meet you both."

On the way home Mrs. Potter spoke some of the few words she had said all evening. "Well, Stanford, what do you think?"

Potter answered, "Kind of a funny thing. I got his name from two reliable sources."

"Who were those, Stanford?"

"The Chinese put his name in the hopper. They seldom make a mistake. The other was a Lt. Alex Brown, highly respected with the LAPD. I'm telling you too much already."

"No, you're not. Time is overdue for your replacement."

" I haven't been able to find someone I trusted, who has the mental savvy to grasp the smallest details and work them through. There is no margin for error in our work."

"I understand. Reliability has gone out of style and real ability never was in style."

"This is only the spring of 1950. I don't like what I see on the horizon–10, 20 and 30 years down the road. Lange is 31. The next 40 years will be a lot tougher than it's been for me."

"I know you're right. I don't like to think about it."

The next day for Lange was the usual mish mash, phone calls, billing, letters to answer. The bank had not called. Finally the boss could not stand it any longer. He said, "I think I will call them personally."

He placed the call. The other line rang. It was the bank. The loan had been approved. Mr. and Mrs. Parks can come in and sign the papers.

Mr. Parks extended his right hand to Lange. "We did it! I hired the right man!"

"Now we can get the show on the road.

"We've got to get that undercoating machine to function right. We've got some equipment coming in next week that runs hot oil through an engine. Clears out the deposits and raises the compression ratio back to normal."

Lange didn't say anything, **but he groaned and thought, "** I guess progress demands experimentation. I suppose I'm one of these guys that wouldn't have believed Orville and Wilbur Wright, or Edison and Alexander Graham Bell. Maybe I am old fashioned."

It was Friday evening and Lange had just finished his fish, mixed vegetable and oatmeal cookies and coffee dinner. "I'm going to sit back in this old broken down recliner and try to relax."

He was asleep in five minutes. Soon his phone rang. "Lt. Merced here."

"Yes, Lieutenant. I had just fallen asleep."

"Sorry to interrupt, but this is important. I just heard from Lt. Brown and two treasury agents are going through Bob Schank's files at 10 A.M. tomorrow morning. Brown insisted you be there. I don't know what goes with you, but you are requested. **Shall I pick you up as Sgt. Andrew and I are both going to be there?"**

"Will you turn on your siren?"

"I thought you were half asleep. **Don't be so smart with me!** Anyhow, that's not all. Brown said for you to get a Power of Attorney from Maude. That will be your excuse for being there."

"I'll take my trusty #5, Remington portable typewriter and type up a reasonable facsimile and head next door to Maude's. By the way, I planned to be at my office at 8 A.M. Saturday morning so could you pick me up there?"

"Guess I have to whether I like to or not. Have you given any more thought to taking over from The Shadow?"

"Oh, I think about it. How lucky I'm not a private eye."

It didn't take Lange long to type, in duplicate, a document authorizing him to act in her behalf. Then Lange took the agreement next door. Maude was so pleased to see him and invited him in.

Lange tried his best to explain what Power of Attorney meant, but was sure she did not understand. Finally she shrugged her shoulders and said, "For sure, lad, it makes me heart beat better to know the police have not forgot about me."

Back in his own small apartment Lange was surprised he was so excited. He said to himself, "I have another idea, even if we find nothing."

He was at his office at 8 A.M. His boss was there and he told his boss in confidence the police would pick him a little before ten.

His boss replied, "I knew a few minutes after I met you that you had a lot on the ball. I never dreamed you'd have so many balls coming at you at the same time."

"I really liked softball and baseball as a kid. All of us kids dreamed we would be in the major leagues some day. Then came the Infantry. That was a league I was lucky to survive. I guess just trying to live is a league with problems I never imagined."

CHAPTER 37
SCHANK'S OFFICE, SANTA BARBARA

At 9:45 Saturday morning Sgt. Andrew entered Lange's office saying it was time to go. In the police car Lange saw not only Lt. Merced, but two other men. He was introduced to two United States Treasury agents by first names only, Hank and Harry. Lange thought to himself I'll bet those names are as fictitious as some of the counterfeit bills they chase after.

The guard outside Schank's office recognized Merced and Andrew who didn't bother to introduce the other three. The keys had been obtained by court order from the office secretary, Eileen. Just then she arrived. Merced thanked her for coming, then said, "Show me everything related to The Shadow.

"First, give these two government men an overview of your filing system so they can decide where they want to start. Do you understand my request?"

"Yes, sir," was her short answer, but to herself she thought of the pending disaster to the company. **Why it's just like taking off all your clothes in public.**

Eileen was a gal in her mid-thirties. Dark hair, dark eyes, pleasant slightly rounded face to match her slightly rounded figure. At 5'6" her 140 pounds were well contoured. She wore a pastel print cotton dress.

Lange thought to himself, "These two officers and the Treasury Agents do this as an everyday job. I've gotten, with almost a five year absence in-between to serve in the Army, a full B.B. A. in Business Administration. But I never got to see the real dirt in the secret files of an unscrupulous businessman. **Boy, this is going to be an education worth moving to Santa Barbara."**

As those thoughts and many others ran through his mind he felt his whole body tense. Once again he felt as alert as he had to be in the jungle. Only this time the bullets were aimed at the enemy. This time he could just stand and watch them fly.

Then he almost became hyper as his mind strained with the hope that even a small clue might be found as to why poor old penniless Maude Mayberry had her small apartment ransacked.

Merced was the first to hit pay dirt. The files involving The Shadow were all contained in one single file drawer. "My God, look at these pictures."

Lange and the treasury agents moved to the file where Merced and Andrew were.

Lt. Merced said, "Make certain Eileen is in the other room."

When that was checked he said, "Lange, I suppose officially we cannot let you look at these, but if you swear you never saw them — —."

"My lips are sealed forever."

"They damn well better be. Here are two typical pictures of what are in this file. One is just generally incriminating. It shows a man known to the general public playing a little cozy with a female who is likely not his wife. In the second picture they are without clothes. The man is obviously a damn fool to be playing around, but invading his privacy is in my book a most serious offense."

Lange was carefully observing the agents as they searched, made notes, but mostly talked into recorders they had with them. **He said to himself, "Surely we men overseas were not fighting to protect this kind of scum."**

Lange became increasingly fascinated as he observed the agents. They obviously had done this hundreds of times. Finally the Agents asked Sgt. Andrew if he could get some lunch sent in to them as it was so much quicker. **Lange was feeling very useless,** but at lunch time he asked, "I sure hope you find a file on Maude Mayberry."

"We're looking, Lange. Lt. Brown made a special request for you on that one."

Lange said to himself, "That Lt. Brown doesn't miss anything. Except, of course, to check the rest room for assailants."

When they got into the Real Property Loan files they checked more closely. After a half hour Hank said in a loud voice–obviously agitated, "Why there must be several hundred loans–all at illegal interest rates. It appears the majority of the properties were foreclosed by Schank Investment Co. Those that did manage to pay off paid horrendous fees. This place must be kept guarded 24 hours a day. This evidence is dynamite!"

Lange was chomping at the bit saying, "Could you skip ahead and look for Mayberry?"

One of the agents thumbed ahead and found it. He glanced at it quickly, then passed it to Lange. **"That poor old lady is going to lose her house in less than six months and look at that interest rate."**

"She lives next door to me; she was a housekeeper all her life. Never made more than $10.00 a month, plus room and board."

"Even the Army pays better than that," said one of the agents. He then turned to Merced and said, "You guys probably make more than that, too."

Merced didn't take too kindly to the remark. Then the agent said, "I've got an idea. Talk to you later about it."

The agents rushed through the other files, making notes and dictating their findings. They had said there was no need to look at every file. They would have all the files picked up Monday morning and scrutinized carefully at the nearest Treasury office.

There remained one other storage cabinet. It looked more like a safe. For certain it appeared formidable. Agent Hank called in the office secretary and asked her to open it. **"I don't have a key to that," answered Eileen.**

"There is a penalty for lying to the U.S. Government. I am going to rephrase my question. Do you know how to get into that safe? If you do I request that you find the key and open it immediately!"

Then the agent dictated the time of day, the circumstances, her name, and his request. The police officers watched her face. Lt. Merced spoke, "I can see it in your expression. You know where there is a key. Let's get it. You are holding up four officers of the law, plus the agent of Maude Mayberry."

She looked as if she was going to faint. She grasped one file drawer handle as she steadied herself. She said not a word as she went to her own desk drawer. She opened the bottom right drawer, reached far in the back of it and pulled out an old beat up make-up case. Her hands were shaking so much she could hardly open it.

Things were jumbled inside and there were several keys. She picked out one and handed it to the agent who had requested it. Then she continued to remain seated at her desk. Lange said to himself, "She looks like she is drained and doesn't have the strength to get up. There must be a real skeleton in that safe."

Agent Hank became a little apprehensive as he watched her face. He handed the key back to her saying, **"You open it. We're all going to stand back in case there is some kind of a trigger in it."**

"You don't have to worry about that. I'll open it."

As the door swung open Hank spoke. "You take the contents out one at a time. Stack them on this desk and explain one at time what they are and what is inside."

"We have three cash boxes. I only have a key to two of them."

They found one box which had smaller bills up to $100.00 denominations. The second box had an assortment including $1,000 bills. Agent Harry quickly picked the lock on the third and found it had 'Pay to bearer' C.D.'s. in denominations of $10,000 each.

Agent Harry placed all three boxes side by side opened. From the same case his lock picking tools came from he took a camera. He carefully focused and took two pictures.

Then Hank ordered Eileen to take out another box. Each time he scrutinized the box, set it open on the desk, made no comment and asked for the next box.

Lange said to himself, "I think he's getting a little tired and realizes the afternoon is almost over."

Lange was looking hard at the interior of the big safe and it seemed like there were perhaps only two more boxes left. He watched the secretary take out the next to last box. It was as if she was being forced to, which was the case. Her hands were shaking violently as she handed it to Harry.

He stepped back at least ten feet and everyone else followed suit. "You open it, Eileen."

"It's locked. I'm not supposed to know what is in it, but I accidentally observed it. I'm sure it won't blow up anyone, but the Schanks."

She seemed to become very sad as Hank took the box and picked the lock. Harry opened the lid and both agents studied the contents. The office secretary swayed a little and went back to her chair.

Suddenly Hank said, "Bonsai!"

The police officers moved toward the box. It was now sitting on the desk. The agent had put on gloves as he handled the items. "What do you make of this, Lt. Merced?"

"I'll be damned. Stock certificates, and what is that?"

"It's forgery equipment. Miss, bring out that other box."

"I don't feel well at all, sir. It's pretty heavy. I promise you there is nothing in it to harm you. It's the rest of the forgery equipment and several printing plates. As I said, I only saw that stuff once and that was by accident. I had nothing to do with it. I'm glad you found it. Really I am. **I knew it was evil. I've been scared to know about it."**

All five men were standing as agent Harry brought out the box and opened it. Printing plates. **Merced groaned, "So now we have a forgery ring operating under our nose in Santa**

Barbara. Those little old ladies in Montecito are going to crucify us."

Hank said, "First, we are going to take a complete set of pictures. Second, Merced we are going to have you take this to the police headquarters and guard it with your life. "This is too hot to leave here. Can't take any chance with arson. We don't know who Eileen is going to talk to after she leaves here. Eileen, I am going to dictate to my recorder my demand you tell no one until we give you written permission."

"I promise. The Schanks never knew I saw it. Bob momentarily stepped out of his office, I went in there accidentally and came out fast. Bob asked me if I was in his office and I lied and said no."

Lange looked at the first agent and said, "I'm acting as Maude Mayberry's agent. **She had her place burglarized and only found a letter from her father missing."**

"Maybe to get a signature for forgery purposes. An old trick. If you can't find what you want print up another one and forge the signature. Let's take a look."

The agent rifled through various papers in the second box muttering various names and finally he said, "Bonsai, maybe this is it. Here's a letter from Mr. Mayberry to his loving daughter Maude."

"My God, those dirty rats. I hope they all fry in hell!" Lange yelled out loud.

Lt. Merced laughed, "Maybe now you'll consider becoming a private eye. Kind of fun to see you really mad. We have to deal with these kind of people all the time. Just like you had to deal with the enemy overseas. Our war against criminals goes on every day and never ends. **You served five years. We go for 30 years."**

The agent was continuing to look and for the third time that afternoon he said, "Bonsai." Then with his gloved hands he held up a stock certificate, "T & S Telephone Co., ten shares — common stock — par value $1.00. The certificate had been made out to a Johathan Smith and endorsed to Archibald Mayberry. The date on that was December 22, 1929, two months after the stock market crash. Then there is a second signature transferring the stock to Cal Schank. It is dated November 30, 1930.

Lange looked at the agent saying, "I never heard of T & S Telephone Co."

"Frankly neither have I. But I'll make a bet with you I am sure of winning."

First, he turned to the office secretary and said, "Miss, I request the local Police take you into custody for further questioning by Treasury. I'll bet the local Police have more than a few questions they will ask you. **You knew about a lot and said nothing."**

As soon as she was out of the room he turned to Lange saying, "To answer your question more fully if this stock was found in an old trunk, someplace in an attic, you might bet it is worthless. When you find someone is making up old certificates, and stealing letters in order to get a signature to forge, that's another ball game.

"You know damn well it's worth a bundle. How much that is I can't guess. It won't take long to trace it. As it was once a telephone company there is a good chance, and I say that with the usual reservations, that it was bought out by a larger phone company and could even be a part of the Bell system today."

"Wow," was Lange's comment. Then he suddenly felt a few tears come to eyes for Maude's sake. He said to himself, "There are so many little old people who are really poverty stricken. If only a few can get a break. It sure looks like Maude may be one."

Hank continued with, "Go to your client and neighbor, Maude, and try to gently pull out the information from her. **Might be a very interesting story behind this, Lange,** and you know we agents need some success stories to keep us motivated. **We have families, too, and they like to hear good news."**

Merced and Andrews said, "So Maude was not hallucinating. Her place was really broken into and she knew damn well all that was taken was a letter from her Dad. The thought never entered my mind it might be used for a forgery. 'Course I'll never admit that to anyone else, but the chief."

Hank chimed in with, "Let's knock it off, men. Harry and I will be here Monday morning at 9 A.M. I'll sign for all of this stuff. Meanwhile I'll make certain SBPD gets a cable of authorization."

It took another half hour for the pictures to be taken. Hank asked that all the contents of the big safe be taken to the police headquarters. He said, **"$ 10,000 Certificates of Deposit, Payable to Bearer shouldn't be floating around by themselves."**

"And Lt. Merced, please make certain this place stays guarded. I suggest you even alert the fire department there are special things of value here. In case of fire direct lots of water to this suite of offices."

Lange thought to himself these agents are really thorough.

With the office secure and the secretary in the back seat, the police car with Merced and Andrew took off.

The agents were staying at the Californian Hotel where Lt. Brown of LAPD always stayed. The Schank office was only two blocks east of State Street, and less than ten blocks from the Californian, which in turn was near the beach.

As they walked away from the building Hank, obviously the Agent in charge, knew that he had been asked to look Lange over as a possible recruit for Treasury. He knew Lange had three prior recommendations. If Hank approved him Lange would be recruited.

So Hank said, "Lange, lets have a cup of coffee, a bottle of beer, or whatever. I need a sandwich to go with it. The government will pay for it if it's not over our per diem. "

Each ordered a roast beef sandwich. They were hungry and didn't talk much. Lange had a hundred thoughts running through his mind. Suddenly he said, **"You do have a fascinating job!"**

"Do you mean that seriously?"

"Maybe. For a serious answer I have to think a little more."

"We're always curious what people think. Tell me a little about yourself."

"Only on the basis that you tell me about yourself, too."

"O.K., it's a deal."

So the three men got much better acquainted in the next hour. They then walked down State St. to the Californian Hotel. As they parted Hank said, "Do you have a big date tonight, Lange?"

"I guess I do. I hope it's with a little old lady by the name of Maude. I'll see what she can remember."

Agent Harry, who hadn't said much spoke, "You have my best wishes on this one, Lange. My Dad was an agent. **Dad said, 'I live for the good. Try to forget the bad.'"**

CHAPTER 38
LANGE BRINGS THE NEWS TO MAUDE.

It was only a short distance to Bath Street. He could hardly wait to talk to Maude. He expected her to be home as she didn't have any funds to go anyplace. He went to his small apartment and took off his tie and suit coat. Then grabbed a sleeveless sweater, his portable typewriter and part of a bottle of Sherry he had left.

When she answered her door he said, "Maude, we found your Dad's letter that was stolen. I need to talk to you for perhaps an hour. Would it be convenient now or would you prefer another time?"

That message almost caused the poor old lady to faint. For certain she was very bewildered. Finally she answered, "Come in, Lad. Guess I never expected to hear about that letter again and **my old legs aren't so steady anymore. They have done their share of house work in their day.**"

"I've brought some Sherry so maybe we can relax."

Her face brightened. Each time he entered her apartment he felt an overwhelming sense of sorrow for Maude.

After the Sherry was poured Lange said, "I want to give you the story and ask you some questions. Can we keep this discussion confidential between you and me?"

"It'll be mighty hard for me not to tell some of my lady friends when we old time housekeepers meet once a week."

"I understand. But you'll try, won't you?"

"For you I will be tryin me best, Lad."

"O.K., Maude, here's how we found the letter."

He covered the matter slowly, and concluded with, "We think the letter was needed to forge your Dad's signature to some document, likely a share of T & S. Telephone Company stock."

"I'm knowin' for sure, Lad, Dad never had no money to buy stock. Evenings we'd sit in the kitchen. We had no parlor to sit in, ye know. We would have tea and maybe scones. Dad, he loved cinnamon rolls. Maybe Dad knew about things like stocks, but if he did he never talked 'bout it. We wuz always talking about money, mind ye.

"We wuz working for the Smiths. They had a big estate in Montecito. **Mr. Smith wuz talking about buying a Rolls Royce.**

"Dad was so excited. He wuz hoping real hard Mr. Smith would get one. Dad would say over and over, 'It would bring part of England's finest to the estate. We'd get to see it every day. Maybe get to help wipe it down sometimes after it was driven. Even Mum would like to do that!' Yes, it was a thrill to just talk about it.

"Dad never owned a car of his own, ye know. Never had no driving permit."

"So you worked for a Mr. Smith. What was his first name?"

"His first name was Jonathan."

"Johathan Smith," Lange said out loud as he could not contain his excitement.

"Do you remember when you worked for Johathan Smith?"

"I'm not remembering the years so well, but I do remember the terrible things that happened. They were bloody awful."

"Take your time, Maude. Tell me a little about the bad things that happened."

"I'm remembering it all started with something called Black Friday. It wasn't Friday the 13th. So's I know there is worse days than Friday the 13th."

"Are you talking about the stock market crash? That Black Friday was October 29, 1929. Could that be the time you are thinking of?"

"I'm remembering it was all about the stock market. Still don't understand what stock is. Mrs. Smith tried to explain it to me, but I don't think the poor lady knew much about it either."

"Do you remember the start of the depression?"

"Sure as I know the Queen of England and all her family I know the depression! That was it! That was when Black Friday struck us all like the very devil it was. Yes, Lad, that was when it all started. It sure was black on that day. Sure and every day after that was black, not just Friday. Black for Mum and Dad and me too for almost two years.

"Maude, I don't like to bring up the unpleasant past. Could you tell me more about what happened to the Smiths after Black Friday?"

"Me old mind is bad, 'tis true, but I could fill your ear for hours about the misery those folks went through. Ye understand, Lad, after Black Friday there was no more talk about getting the 1930 Rolls Royce."

"1930, you do remember the year. When did you quit working for the Smiths?"

"I remember that well, Lad. It was two Christmases after that 'Black Friday.' You know Lad, It was too much for me to understand what they meant by all that. Mr. Smith seemed to go out of his mind right after that Friday.

"He got worse and worse and Mrs. Smith was real worried. Mrs. Smith cried and many a time I heard her say, 'How can it be, our stock is almost worthless? Our money is gone! I don't really know why you can be rich one Friday and then you are ruined.'"

"What happened to Mr. Smith?"

"He had a heart attack. Mrs. Smith thought maybe he tried to commit suicide. He went downhill and 'twas very sad, mind ye, what was happening at the estate. Soon the grocery store wasn't delivering all the groceries Mum was ordering. Mum was the cook."Mrs. Smith kept paying us, but right after the second Christmas, yes, it was in January, Mr. Smith had another heart attack and he died. **Right after the funeral Mrs. Smith told Dad and Mum that she didn't know anything about**

money. Mr. Smith had always handled that. The bank had told her she didn't have any more money."

"You mean like a checking or savings account. There were no funds left."

"Lad, I'm not even knowing what all you mean by 'funds'. Mrs. Smith said she didn't have any more money. It was terrible to just look at her and hear her cry. 'Mr. Smith took care of our money, I don't know what to do.'

"She had loved Mr. Smith and could not get along by herself. She told us she would move to San Diego and live with her sister. We could stay there until the bank foreclosed, but there was no money for electricity or gas. **And no more money to pay us.**

"We had an outside well, so we had water. There was wood enough we could cook on the little wood trash burner. It was winter so there wasn't anything growin' in the garden. There was some canned food left. It was six months before we got another job.

"The bank told us to leave and Dad said no. The bank officer said he understood. We lived in the loft above the garage. Mr. Smith's two Packards had been sold to pay bills."

"I remember those days, Maude. My Dad couldn't make the house payments either. He didn't have any stock. He was a skilled carpenter and couldn't find any work.

"The Vice-President at Portland Trust and Savings Bank told my Dad if he could pay the $25.00 per month interest he would not foreclose. I'll never forget how worried my Mother and Dad were. I was ten at the time. I sold newspapers and magazines until 9 P.M. "Bought bread that broke when it came out of the oven at Davidson and Betsy Ross Bakeries for one cent a loaf from my earnings. I did everything I could do to help.

"I suspect that my Dad never paid the $25.00 per month, and the man at the bank just kept looking the other way. My folks had four boys. **I remember one Christmas my Dad got a job selling Christmas tree wreaths. All he made all week was seventy five cents.** He sold three and made a quarter for each sale."

"Lad, I was much older than you during those days. I can tell you were old enough to understand. Now I'm where the Smith's were. I don't have any money and in a few months I am going to lose this duplex. I worry so much because I saw the Smiths lose their place. **It is all due soon and I barely have enough money to pay me electricity and gas.**

"Yes, me Black Friday is around the corner looking at me real hard. I'm scared, Lad. Then they steal me letter from my Dad. He never wrote much. Now, do I understand it is the same Schank that is going to foreclose on me that stole my letter?"

Maude began to cry and Lange said to himself, "I made her think of Black Friday and now she finds a parallel to her own desperate situation. She deserves a break and I sure hope one has suddenly come out of the woodwork."

Maude didn't seem to be gaining control over her emotions. Lange realized that it is not unnatural for a person to share their emotions. He thought, "It's kind of like getting up on your little soap box **and telling the world, 'Heh, you're always beating on me.'**

"She doesn't 'Protest Too Much.' Everyone needs someone to listen to their tears."

Lange also knew that whatever he said had to be reduced to rather simple terms.

"Maude, I know this is tough on you, but I think things might work out better than you expect. Now I need to ask you to tell me of anything you observed that might involve a stock certificate. It would be a piece of paper. Perhaps about the size of my typewriter paper. Here is one."

Maude looked at the sheet, then continued, "There were pieces of paper thrown, even some dishes and vases. Mr. Smith went bloody crazy after that Friday. He kept making phone calls, staring at the newspaper and he started drinkin' something terrible. We wuz all worried. He had been a fine man we was believin.' **Twas hard for all of us, but Dad, Mum and me knew the devil had entered the house.**"

"Tell me about some of his anger."

" When he broke a cup or a dish we would be called to pick up. The place was never neat and tidy anymore."

"Can you give me an example?"

"I remember one day just before Christmas the first year. I wuz pickin up a lot of pieces of paper and asked him if I should throw them out. **He said, "Yes Maude, and don't you ever buy any stock. He had said that to me before.**

"I replied again, 'Mr. Smith, I don't know what stock is, but I will for sure remember not to buy any.'"

"What did he say?"

"He grabbed the papers out of my hand. He looked through them. Then he sat down and signed one. He said, 'Keep this one, Maude. It's a telephone stock. Maybe it'll come back'–you know Lad– I'm not sure what he said. He would mumble and shout. I do recall I was to give it to my Dad and someday he'd give my Dad an envelope to mail it in."

"Did he say anything about registering it in your Dad's name or in yours?"

"I don't recall, Lad. Things became more bloody awful each day."

"I think your Dad, or Mr. Smith mailed it in to T & S Telephone Co. With all the turmoil and financial disaster in the business world who knows what happened. I am going to guess the signed certificate got to the telephone company office and was registered in your Dad's name. Maybe they did or didn't mail your Dad a new stock certificate. Maybe they didn't have money coming in to handle the paperwork.

"Schank was involved in cheating heirs or anyone else he could cheat. He must have found out it was valuable. **I believe he had your apartment ransacked with two objectives.** Find the stock certificate and or something with your Dad's signature. Then forge a transfer of the certificate to him, and back date it to 1930."

"I guess I still don't understand."

"Maybe they tried in later years to notify your Dad. You folks did not have a telephone number, you worked for someone else so you didn't pay utilities, so you could not be located. T & S must have been taken over by someone. Likely for their franchise rights. "Maude, that means they had the rights for telephone service in a certain area. There was likely new stock issued and it could be worth a good sum of money today. On the other hand your Dad knew the Smith family went broke and likely figured what he mailed in was worthless.

"As a matter of fact, if Smith addressed the envelope your Dad wouldn't even know the location of the firm and would have absolutely no way to know it had any value."

"Lad, you might as well be talkin' Greek to me. I don't understand stock, or what do you call it, 'regis-tour-ing?' I'm not knowin' if my Dad understood what stock was."

Maude paused and seemed even more bewildered. Suddenly her eyes seemed to light up as she looked at Lange.

"Are ye raising a spark of hope in this old lady? That old piece of paper Mr. Smith told me to give to Dad might be worth some money? Would it be worth one hundred dollars? Oh I could sure use some money."

"What would you buy?"

"If I had a hundred maybe I'd buy myself a new dress and some food.. I haven't had me a new dress for at least ten years. No, I couldn't do that. I need a pair of shoes more. Yes, I'd get me a good pair of shoes. **I bin' putting cardboard inside these to cover the holes in the soles. Maybe my bunions wouldn't fit into a new pair?"**

Lange looked at the old lady and felt his mind torn by his own emotions. His anger toward Schank surged and his sorrow for Maude's status in life made him feel like crying.

He thought of how Maude and her parents must have felt so many years ago when they entered New York harbor. There was the Statute of Liberty to greet them! And here was poor Maude today. She was entitled to "Life, Liberty and the Pursuit of Happiness."

That's what the Declaration of Independence said. What Maude and her parents got was something else.

Just then Lange thought he heard someone walking up the short walk and then he could faintly hear his doorbell ring.

"Maude, excuse me for a minute. Maybe it's the paper boy coming to collect. I don't know anyone else who might be calling on me."

As he moved quickly out the door to his place he noticed two men. "Who goes there?"

It was Hank and Harry. "Hello, Lange, we were out walking and decided to drop by and see what kind of an exclusive neighborhood you lived in. We checked with the clerk at the hotel and he said you didn't live far. This is a modest few blocks of homes. One would never know it was so close to the beach."

"I've been talking to Maude. She kind of broke down. Would you like to meet her?"

"Yes, we have a little news and would like to meet the lady."

As the agents entered they got a first hand view of why their job was so important. Maude's tiny apartment was a worn down version of vintage 1910.

She was ill at ease and unsure of herself. There was a half glass of Sherry left. Lange poured it for her and raised his empty glass saying, "Here's a toast, Maude, to better days."

After Maude had a sip Lange briefly outlined to the agents what he had learned from Maude. Hank replied, "That sounds pretty positive to me. I had to briefly touch base with my supervisor and let him know we were going to make a pick-up Monday morning.

"I asked him about T & S. He knew about them. They almost went belly up for lack of funds. People couldn't pay their phone bills, had their lines disconnected and so forth. They did hold a valuable franchise and were taken over by another company, then others and now they are a part of the Bell System."

Lange's eyes lit up like the proverbial Christmas tree, "So what's the bottom line?"

"You sound like the accountant. We don't have a bottom line yet, but that news will come in early Monday as the franchise area was rural Eastern time zone.

"They promised to call by 9 A.M. Monday. That's noon their time. Biggest point, of course, is what kind of a list do they have for lost stockholders and what have ten shares in 1929 become worth twenty one years later."

Maude looked at Hank and the eagerness in her voice was obvious, **"Might it be worth $100.00? I sure could use $100.00."**

"Maude, I can't even tell if your Dad is registered as the legal owner. Let's hope he is. Should he be I know it will be worth much more than $100.00. We are going to push off now and we hope to know more Monday."

Lange walked to the door with them and followed them out. It wasn't more than ten feet from the steps to the sidewalk. "Hank, do you have any idea?"

"At least $10,000. Maybe a lot more. Let me give you another idea. This could be worth a lot. Write up a satisfaction of mortgage and try to barter that for canceling the breaking and entering charge. The forgery charge will stand, but we at Treasury will inform our pals at the IRS to let the mortgage cancellation stand.

"We'll say the circumstances were extenuating or some kind of wordage that no one will want to waste their time trying to figure out. **We can't correct all the world's evils, but it's time someone plays Robin Hood for Maude."**

"You guys are all right! I'll go to work on that right away. Now I know for sure why I came back here."

"Keep helping folks like Maude. There's a lot like her that need help! We know."

Lange walked back into Maude's apartment. She said, "I'm sure hoping they find me dear old Dad's name in the right place. Me still don't understand all this, but I sure could use even $50.00. **Poor Mr. & Mrs. Smith. Wonder where Mrs. Smith is now?"**

CHAPTER 39
LOOSE ENDS

Doctor Emery Smith was spending the evening with Martha again. Emery had just said to Martha, "You were so beautiful before. Now you have added a youthful sparkle that makes you positively devastating!"

Just then the phone rang. It was Lt. Merced. He asked if she was alone and she said Dr. Smith had dinner with her and was still there.

"May I speak to him, please?"

"Dr. Smith, this is Lt. Merced. I don't wish to worry you needlessly, but we have reason to feel Mrs. Schank shouldn't be without a guard."

At first Dr. Smith was too shocked to reply. Then he said, "Anything to guard her safety is what we need to do. What do you suggest?"

"I think we must move her now. Let me get a squad car out there and tell her to not start packing anything until the officer gets there in case someone is casing the place. Tell her to start thinking of what she wants to take with her for a few days. Then pack when the officer is waiting in her living room."

At the Tong headquarters in New Chinatown, Los Angeles, there had been a series of meetings all day long. Leads had come in. They had been weighed carefully. After a special two hour session in the evening Dr. Fu stood up and said, "Has the security council made a decision?"

"Yes, Dr. Fu, we have. I believe you will agree with our conclusion. The assassins were following orders from Tony G. **He has caused the death of many people and it is time to eliminate him completely.**"

"Your decision is wise. I give you my approval and support. Do it with extreme care. Do you recommend the same men that handled the Ruppert Snyder job?"

"Yes."

"I agree with that decision also. It would be most interesting to meet them, but I know that can never be."

Dr. Fu paused and reflected. Then he spoke. "Oh, to be young and vigorous again."

Tony G. was seated in the men's poker room in his Montecito estate. He had declined to go to the theater with his wife. **She had said to him, "Tony, you ain't got no class. We** move to this estate to be cultured. All you want to do is the same old thing. Play poker with your bodyguards."

The game went on until after midnight. His wife had come home an hour earlier. Tony had been winning as usual. Finally he said, "O.K. boys, let's knock it off for 'dis evening."

One of his men said, "Thanks for the game, boss. Ya know it gets kind of lonely here. You miss the games we used to have in Chicago? We used to have two tables Saturday nights. And some of those gals we had serve us the drinks. Don't ya miss dose gals?"

"Yah, you can tell I misses dem all. Me old lady made me move here. It's too quiet here."

"We lost your brother, too!"

"Don't remind me of that. I'se tryin to forget it. Never will, I guess."

As Tony G. went upstairs, and his men moved to their special guard quarters adjacent to the lower level he said to himself, "I keep thinkin' Chicago is safer than Montecito. Doesn't make no sense.

"I kind of have one of those premo–what is–nitions. That last job–I had no idea the Dragon Lady was with the dame we were to hit. **Maybe I'd better figure out a way to let the Chinese know we won't pick on them again. Yeh, maybe I better do that."**

FROM SOUTH AMERICA TO PAPUA, NEW GUINEA

CHAPTER 40
ANZAC DAY

On board the Australian Light Cruiser.
Today was Monday, April 24th. The time zone on the West
Coast of South America was the same as New York. A little
fishing vessel was far out to sea when it sighted the Aussie Light
Cruiser. The fishing boat had rigged a cloth signal to its mast
and its radio merely stated its position. It headed in the general
direction of the Aussie vessel which after receiving the signal
launched the Captain's gig and approached the small craft.

They seemed to just pass each other slowly. Actually,
they slowed sufficiently for Q. Song, the local Tong leader,
to scramble aboard the Captain's gig with the help of two
powerful Aussie sailors. The gig then made a circle as if they
were just checking the fishing vessel and turned back to their
own ship.

Meanwhile the engine room crew on the destroyer had been
following instructions and the engine actually sounded as if it
had serious trouble. One of the old time salts joked, **"Isn't this
a bloody joke. Engine trouble is something we catch bloody
hell over and now we're called on to pretend the engines are
having fits."**

They were all in high spirits. Q. Song immediately met
with all the men the mess hall would hold. Squad leaders

Jerry O'Leary and Joseph Michael were introduced as was the Captain and the executive officer. Q.Song briefed everyone. He had brought several maps he had painstakingly marked.

The squad leaders quickly ran through their plans. Q. Song followed them intently and made suggestions based on the distances they would have to cover. Q. Song was overtaken with the spirit of everyone from the Captain on down. He commented, "It will be a long day before Australians are mistreated this way again in South America."

"You can believe that," came the dedicated voices from the men.

Q. Song briefed them protocol would require at least the executive officer of the ship to meet with the Military Leader and the Mayor of the City. He was uncertain as to the reaction of the Military Leaders. Was there a chance they might release Della and her Father? The right show of force might do it.

On the other hand they must prepare for violence in case it came. It was explained to Q. Song that Jerry would rescue Della and Joe would attack the jail, if necessary, to rescue her Father. Q. Song warned them to prepare for the worst and hope for the best.Ahead they could make out the outline of the shore. They were still several hours from actually docking. All hands were served early dinner and the Chaplain held a special service broadcasting it over the P.A. system. Even the most irreverent and non-religious came up with at least a silent prayer for success.

One Aussie bloke was heard to mutter, "If God wasn't a fair God he would have sent most of us to Davy Jones locker years ago for all the bloody awful language we use. He knows our hearts are right and that's all that counts. He knows living the military life on a small boat is often hell. So he grants us the right to not use the King's English."

Than another old sailor was heard to add, "At least I hopes that's the way it is."

The local officials were always out to make an extra buck. Instead of foisting just one pilot off on the Captain both a pilot and his assistant came on board to provide the navigation for the vessel to pass the right distance from the various buoys. It was a rip-off, but that was the way it was. That point had been argued before and more than likely the only question was when the assistant would need an assistant so they could charge for three.

By the time they were docked and secure the sun had set. It was just as well as ANZAC Day wasn't until tomorrow. The usual number of local people came down to watch the arrival and to try to hawk various souvenirs to the sailors. A watch was set up on the dock, but the men on duty were not to fraternize with the locals.

Representation from the Mayor's office came to pay their respect to the Captain and discuss the time they would leave the ship the next day for the ANZAC parade.

The men on board tried to rest, but they were keyed up enough to explode with any provocation. Q. Song, the Captain and the squad leaders Jerry and Joe went over and over the details. **Every man on board knew the exact role he was to play.**

Q.Song would slip off the ship, somehow, during the night and meet with the men who had flown from Panama in the C-47. That old plane had its military history, making regular flights through the pass in the Owen Stanley Range in New Guinea, between Port Moresby and the airstrip at Doboduro. The latter not far from Buna and Oro Bay, on the South East Coast.

Unless you had served in New Guinea during those critical World War II days the significance would be lost. Just as it is virtually impossible for the millions of other men and women to describe their part in any war. One can't describe in a few sentences what you lived through for years. Not knowing how many minutes more you would live.

Those C-47's had been the workhorse of World War II. The first flying models had been built before the war, in nine months. The airlines had been calling for tri-motors and this two motored plane had to prove that two was equal to three. None other than the celebrated Lindbergh, first solo pilot ever to cross the Atlantic from New York to Paris, went up on the test flight.

He then ordered, "Cut one of the engines." The plane flew on with one engine out. Lindbergh gave the O.K. and the millions of military whose lives during the war depended on the C-47 would attest to it's special place in aviation history.

The C-47's brought in from Port Moresby to the forward dense jungle of Doboduro, men, materials, food and evacuated wounded Aussies and Americans. The pilots had to cope with severe downdrafts in the pass created by the 12,000 feet height of the Owen Stanley Range. Loaded with 50 gallon drums of high test aviation gas made a perilous journey through the pass. The fighter planes and everyone else had to have the gas.

More than a few C-47's were lost that way. Hundreds of thousands of paratroopers will never forget their fear and trembling as they jumped into combat from a C-47. Often it was at night with its accompanying terror.

The planes carried no armament themselves and were virtual sitting ducks for a Zero, Messerschmitt fighter, and heavy ground fire.[5]

Q. Song slipped off the ship at midnight from the side of the ship opposite the dock. An incident was created on the dock to divert attention. It was easy to accomplish. He found three of the Rangers from the C-47 waiting at the Tong Headquarters. Sixteen had arrived and the rest were awaiting further instructions and guarding the C-47.

They were speechless with relief the Aussie Light Cruiser was in port.

They now figured their casualty rate might be low instead of maybe 100%.

The Aussie Navy weren't just reinforcements. They were a shipload of strong men. Q. Song went over the details of rescue plans and they fitted the men from the C-47 from Panama into the overall operation. The Rangers from Panama knew the power in that small port city was held by the Military Junta. **The rescue might be possible now.**

As the morning light began filtering across the sky every man on board the Cruiser was wide awake. It was like the thousands of "D days" that millions of Soldiers, Marines, Navy, Air Force and Merchant Marine sailors had experienced. The Cruiser had many veterans of World War II on board. For them they were again back at battle stations.

They once again they felt that emotional surge to uphold their Nation's honor for today, April 25th, was ANZAC Day. Memorial Day for Australia and New Zealand.

In those two countries most of the population would turn out to celebrate and honor the fallen. Not like the few that showed for Memorial Day in the United States. The Aussie spirit still had a pioneer flavor and determination.

Two Aussies unlawfully held far away from home and friends. Held under the most unreasonable circumstances and submitted to torture and terror.

This morning the rescue plans were again meticulously scrutinized and memorized. What might they be forgetting? The most pressing questions were what to expect? Like ANZAC Day, 35 years earlier, no one can estimate the death or the casualties. Just like "D" days had been all over the world.

Then it became time to leave the ship. Time to act! Time to be brave! Time to die?

At 10 A.M. the men began to leave their ship moving quickly to the adjoining dock and then onto land itself. Now they were committed. As the men marched from the docks toward the main business section hundreds of the villagers were lining the street. Word had spread and virtually all the population had turned out to view them parade. Joe's men were in the lead.

Q. Song, the Tong leader, had briefed them that Della's hoped for rescue point was beyond where the Military Junta leaders were waiting. The jail, where it was hoped her father was still alive, was located very close to the military headquarters.

The ship's Captain remained on board along with a back up party and a minimum complement sufficient to man the ship in case it was necessary to leave Port in a hurry. As the ship's executive officer entered the military headquarters every man went on maximum alert. Now the show down would start.

The Rangers, with the necessary linguistic skills to converse with the Junta leaders, were in the lead. They were personally greeted by the Military General and ushered into his immense luxurious quarters.

They sat down after greetings and best wishes were completed. The General asked, "Is the Australian Navy ready to start their parade and how much time will be needed?"

The Ranger leader turned to the Aussie executive officer and explained the question.

The executive officer replied, "Not a great deal of time. We would prefer to march just a short distance and then perform our ceremony."

"Very well, at what time would you like to start?"

"Tell him we can start almost immediately, but first he must release, in good condition, the two Australian citizens being held without reason. Australians can't parade in a city with Aussie prisoners watching us from behind bars."

There was a look of utter surprise on the faces of the Military Junta. Finally the Commandant spoke indifferently. "They are no longer here. It was all a big mistake. They are on their way back. They left yesterday."

The executive officer looked directly at the General. "That is excellent. Please tell us where they are right now so we can offer our assistance to them."

The Ranger leader translated the message. The Junta General came back quickly with," That won't be necessary as they are in good hands."

Then the discussion heated up. Their words having to be translated two ways caused the Cruiser Executive Officer to say sternly, "General, let us change the subject for the moment and discuss why they were captives here. "

"I have no time for such trivialities. I care not to reply to that."

"I must insist, General."

"Our interview is at an end unless you have other matters more important to discuss."

The executive officer rose from his chair and walked from the room and outside the building. As he stepped outside he raised his right hand and **made a smart salute to the men and said in a loud voice, "ANZAC"** The tone of his voice was strangely similar to one heard from the Japanese during the war when they shouted "Bonsai."

In seconds the Rangers from Panama had put together a light .30 caliber machine gun and dashed into the General's quarters. It was done so quickly not a shot was fired. Other Rangers went to the rear of the building with their fire power.

Jerry's men moved on a fast run to rescue Della and Joe's men moved the short distance to the prison where they hoped they would find Della's Dad. The 16 Rangers had by pre-arrangement split into 4 squads. One remained with the C-47 and the pilot, co-pilot and radio operator. Four went with Jerry, four with Joe and four remained at the Junta Headquarters.

The Prison was reached first and the Junta chief jailer had not arrived at work as yet. His guards were bewildered and confused as they faced a wall of Navy and Ranger uniforms with machine guns and automatic weapons. Joe yelled, with a Ranger interpreting, "You have only sixty seconds to surrender, or these machine guns start firing. Drop your guns and raise your arms!"

The guards were stunned as they faced the overwhelming force whose guns were trained on them. They dropped their weapons and raised their arms. Five men directed their weapons toward the guards while the rest confronted and disarmed the guards inside. "Where is the Australian prisoner?" one of the Rangers demanded.

A frightened guard replied, "Follow me."

They found Reginald Robertson in a filthy cell. Joe spoke to him gently and got no answer. Joe spoke, "He seems to be unconscious! Look at the marks on his body! He's been through hell!"

It was obvious he was barely alive. Two medics and a medical supply man had accompanied the squad. They had brought a collapsible stretcher and it was ready in 60 seconds. Reginald was carefully and tenderly placed on it and the two medics examined him carefully hoping he had not gone into cardiac arrest just when he was finally being rescued.

They almost panicked as they checked his pulse and blood pressure. They said to Joe, "Bad. Very bad! Only hope is to get him on board immediately. We take a chance in moving him, but at least we have a fine Doctor on board plus an intern in training.

"We have sterile conditions and medicines. He's about as dead as they come and still not buried."

Joe replied instantly, "Let's get the bloody hell out of here, mates."

With those words from Joe the men moved quickly. An advance party with two machine guns at the head, and the rear guard with the third. Automatic weapons protected their flanks. The Rangers and the men moved quickly to the ship.

Inside the General's Junta headquarters the Rangers and the Navy men held the General hostage. He tried to use the telephone, but one Ranger had already yanked the wire from the wall. He smiled very slightly as the General realized the line was dead. One machine gun was aimed directly at the General.

The Ranger said, "General, we either all live or you die first. What you have failed to realize is nations like Australia are so much larger than your two bit operation. If a single one of our men dies or is injured today you will die. You have my word on that."

The General's words came so rapidly the Rangers understood virtually none of what he was saying. He was livid with anger. He was not used to having his power challenged. With the machine gun within 20 feet of him, and aimed directly at him, he knew he was licked. Then a question came to his mind. "You men are from Panama. Who sent you?"

"General, consider us insignificant. Your problem is with the Australians. You are in big trouble with them."

The General shouted, "I demand to know who sent you. "

"General, it doesn't matter who sent us. This is ANZAC Day, a day you will long remember, if you live long."

Deep down in his irreverent double dealing treacherous heart the General knew the score. He had fun while it lasted. He knew he had just had his deck of cards taken away from him forever. His dealing days were over.

He sat down, looked at the Rangers and said, "I've made a decision. I've made my mistakes. Take what you want and be gone from this city."

"We want our countryman and lady. Do you still claim they are not in this city?"

"I was trying to hustle you out of town. Here we live a different life style. Life is cheap. Often I wish I had been raised in a more democratic civilization. Yes, we have the Australian woman and man. I think you already know where they are."

"Yes, our men are already on their way. If they are in good condition we may release you. If they are not we will not release you."

While a dozen of Jerry's men surrounded the brothel the second dozen poured into the large Spanish style balconied structure, after breaking down the locked door. The men inside were immediately met by the Madam who yelled and screamed. Her words came out of her mouth like a hurricane and she pointed to the door obviously demanding they leave. **Jerry grabbed her by both of her arms and yelled, "Where is the Australian girl named Della?"**

The Madam knew enough English to yell back, "Get out!"

Jerry's answer was to release one of her arms and with his free hand he firmly grasped her hair, "You heard the question. I'll give you 30 more seconds to answer."

"Let loose of me."

Jerry yelled to the other men, "Fan out and search the rooms!"

Then he slapped her across her mouth and holding firmly onto her hair he moved her toward the hall. With the noise inside and the dozen men outside many of the women rushed from their rooms to see what the noise and turmoil was.

One of them recognized immediately this might be an opportunity for her to gain freedom, she yelled, "Who are you looking for?"

Jerry yelled, "Della, the Aussie girl. We are here to rescue her and someone here better lead us to her quick."

The women were mostly English speaking and the one who had just spoken said, **"I'll tell you. I'm English. Oh, please, would you rescue me, too?"**

"We'll see. Lead us to Della!" came Jerry's command.

"Follow me. Just up two flights of stairs. Second door on the left."

Jerry passed the Madam to a second man yelling, "Hold onto her. Don't let her get away."

Then Jerry bounded up the stairs like the infantryman he once was in North Africa who was advancing with split second timing. He took two stairs at a time. Reached the first landing. Had to take a 180 degree turn and reached the second landing all in less than 60 seconds. He tried the knob on the second door on the left. It turned.

He opened the door. There was a beautiful Aussie gal. Her face was lined with the pain, anguish and terror she had been undergoing. "Are you Della?" was Jerry's brief question.

"I am, who are you?"

"We're Australian Navy, we're here to rescue you."

"Oh, thank you! Oh, thank you! But, my Father, he is in prison! Please, can you rescue him, too?"

"A second squad has hit the prison by now. He should be rescued already. Let's go, take nothing, unless you have something special, like something of your Father's."

"I have nothing here I would ever want around me again. Nothing to remind me of this horrible place. I'm ready!"

Joe yelled, "Surround her, men. Della let's move it. There should be a vehicle waiting for us. Get in it and lay on the floor."

"Are you going to take me?" cried the informer gal.

"You bet, men take her, too."

By the time the men had descended the two floors to the lobby the brothel was a bedlam of shouting women.

All, except the madam, were screaming the same message. "Oh, please take us, too!"

One of the Rangers snapped, "As soon as the two gals are safe on board ship, we'll take the rest of you women and the Madam with us to the C-47."

The women screamed with delight and joy. One of them moved away saying, "I'll just pack a few things."

The Ranger replied, "There'll be no room for luggage. Stay if you like."

She stopped in her tracks, and turned saying, "I need new clothes anyhow."

One Ranger looked at the Madam who had just said, "Don't take me. I won't go."

He laughed and said, "You'll go part of the way, but maybe not all the way."

"What do you mean by that?"

"Maybe we'll drop you and the General off in mid-flight. The door opens real easy on a C-47."

Just then a runner dashed in the front door and seeing Jerry he shouted, "Reginald is on the ship. Almost dead, but the Doc is doing his best."

Della burst into tears again and said, "Thank God. I can at least put my arms around Dad and tell him how he saved my life. He told me that was all he wanted to do. Get me free again and keep my Mother from dying of grief."

Another of the men ran in from outside. "The vehicle is here."

He didn't say more as he knew Jerry would make the decision when to move. Jerry said, "Have them back the vehicle as close to the front door as possible. **Let's not take any chance of a sniper."**

They moved toward the front door and before exiting two men gave the two women their helmets. Half the men formed a tight semi-circle and the women crouched as they left the brothel and quickly dashed into the armored vehicle.

One machine gunner sat on the hood and several men, with Russian designed AK-47's were on the running boards of the vehicle. The vehicle moved at moderate speed toward the ship so it could decisively move in any direction in case of an ambush.

Inside the Rangers announced, "First we wait for word that Della is safe on board ship. Then we wait for the General. He will have an AK-47 trained on him. **Any rescue attempt, kill him immediately! That will make the rest of them stop and think!"**

The vehicle with Della was nearing the Aussie ship without being challenged. Some of the guards ran alongside the slow moving car. Combat men often wondered in retrospect how they obtained the physical stamina and endurance when the chips were really down. The Aussie men, and even their women, had a natural toughness and ability to take on a challenge that made them unequaled. They were a perfect example of the respected phrase, 'When the going gets tough the tough really get going.'

Right now things were moving with precision and almost ease. They were all hyped up and ready for anything, however. The vehicle with the two women and Jerry drove right onto the dock.

The semi-circle of protection was reversed this time and the gangplank was slanted down to a lower deck to minimize exposure. With a protective shield of men two deep, Della and her friend were on board in less than 60 seconds. **Then she exclaimed, "Oh, thank you, oh thank you! Please may I see my father?"**

Wild horses could not have prevented her and shortly she was ushered into the small operating room on the vessel. **Her father lay back motionless on the operating table.**

The Doctor and the intern were each holding one of his arms. "He must be alive or you wouldn't be holding onto him!"

"Yes, young lady."

The Doctor extended the hand he was holding to Della and said, "Take his hand and let him know you are here. I have given him some sedation, but I held back until you got here. His knowing you are safe will give him a greater boost than any medication I can find on board this ship."

"Dad, I'm here you are safe. Can you hear me?"

No response was visible from the motionless man.

"Reginald, I am an Australian Navy Doctor. You are safe on board an Australian Cruiser. Your daughter, Della, is holding your hand. Please squeeze it if you understand she is here. Remember you're a tough Aussie Merchant Marine Officer. The men on this ship just put on a bloody good show rescuing you from prison and your daughter as well."

Della cried, "Doctor, I felt a slight pressure from Dad's hand. Oh, I felt it again. He must be so weak. He's trying. Oh, Dad, keep trying, stay alive for all of us. We need you."

The Doctor spoke again, softly, but firmly, "Reginald, squeeze your daughter's hand if you understand that she is here and safe."

"I can feel a tiny amount of pressure again, Doctor. He must be terribly weak. He was such a strong muscular man. He must be terribly hurt to be so weak." Della began to cry and sob.

"Della, you stay with him and the intern. I am going to look through my medical supplies and check every item I have to make certain I have not failed to think of something I perhaps haven't used for some time. Meanwhile keep talking to your Father. Tell him that he is on a Aussie Light Cruiser and that all the men did this voluntarily and they are counting on him to hang in there."

"Oh, I will, Doctor, I will, I will. Oh, thank you!"

Matters were going smoothly at the Military Junta headquarters. The Ranger leader said, "Take the General outside to the front of the building, and keep him covered. Do the same at the rear of the building with his Chief of Staff.

"Round up transportation and move them first to the brothel. From there we will move to the airport with the General and his Chief with an AK pointed at their heads."

As they left the General's headquarters a half dozen grenades made mincemeat of his beautifully furnished headquarters. Using the General's Staff car they moved swiftly toward the brothel to pick up the rest of the convoy.

The men remaining at the brothel were relieved to see two Military Junta vehicles and one truck with Navy and Rangers on board. The women were loaded into the truck and one vehicle. Then Jerry's number two man fired one shot. A military signal for all clear.

Three men inside tipped over cans of gasoline they had located, ran out the front door tossing in a couple of grenades to detonate the gas and make certain the brothel would go up in flames.

They reached the airport without incident and wished they had two C-47's, but maintenance wasn't complete on the other. Now it was imperative to destroy any planes that might pursue them. Three fighter planes and ten other planes were on the strip. **Machine gun fire and grenades turned them quickly into raging infernos.**

The airport employees had been herded into one building, and relieved of their weapons. Now the Rangers re-entered each building shooting at anything that looked like it might be military. Several buildings with ammunition and weapons inside were quickly set on fire, hoping the ammunition would detonate after their C-47 was gone.

The disposition of the General and his chief of staff was the most difficult decision. The Australians did not want to create an international incident by taking them on board their vessel. Finally it came down to either leaving him there or taking him to Panama in the C-47. **The vote went in favor of Panama.**

Before he was put on board the pilot looked the Junta Generals in the eye and said, "I am the Captain of this plane. Anyone who creates the slightest disturbance on this plane will be thrown out without a parachute. Many a prisoner has been thrown out of a C-47. You can add your name to the list. And, quite frankly, I would prefer that you not even be on board this plane. **Have I made myself clear?"**

The General and his chief of staff saw the firmly set jaw of a grim faced tough pilot who had just told them the rules of the game. They saw the same kind of a piercing look they had given to many of their subordinates.

The General replied, "Captain, we recognize your right to fly unhampered by us. We will not disturb you or any of the passengers."

The Captain thought to himself, "This plane is going to be overloaded. **I wonder if the Rangers will toss them overboard?** I'll alert my co-pilot and radio operator."

As the plane was loading, four Rangers stayed on the ground to guard the runway. The plane used to mud and metal strips in the jungle taxied easily on the paved runway. The pilot gunned the two engines, headed down the runway and lifted off smoothly.

The four Rangers on the air strip spread out in maximum alert. They watched it disappear into a bank of clouds.

In the air, with cloud cover three Rangers opened the door. Swiftly six Rangers ejected the two Generals into the atmosphere and grabbed the screaming Madam.

They held her upright making certain she saw the General and his chief of staff fall. Then four Rangers each took a hand or foot and swung her back and forth. She screamed, **"I'll pay you anything you want. Just don't throw me overboard."**

The lead Ranger yelled, "1,2,3, and away." The Madam was gone.

There was a loud cheer from the passengers inside. The four Rangers bowed to the small audience and closed the C-47 door.

The lead Ranger said, "You will be interrogated when you arrive. You know there was a scuffle on board the plane. Somehow the door opened. You did not see anyone go out the door. Each of you just happened to be looking the other way.

"Remember the seats face the front of the plane. Like they say, 'Keep it simple.' Don't explain. You just didn't see anything. We rescued you. We saved your lives."

The Pilot knew when the doors had been opened and finally closed. Now they were able to relax as the imbalance was corrected and the overall weight lessened.

With the C-47 safely hidden in the clouds, the Rangers on the ground took the General's car and sped for the ship. They made it without incident.

They were greeted with joy by the crew as they reached the gangplank.

The squad that had rescued Reginald had likewise left a half dozen Navy men behind. They had gone through the cells looking for other English speaking prisoners. They found none, but were in a reprisal mood. They decided to release all the prisoners. Then locked up the guards in a couple of cells and demolished all the other wooden structures.

The Chinese grocery store was only a couple of blocks from the dock. By pre-arrangement Joe and Jerry were to meet Q. Song there when the rescue was completed. Q. Song was waiting at the store in a back room. **He had a much better understanding of English than ability to speak it.**

Joe and Jerry gave him a quick run down and Q. Song was elated. "So very happy to get rid of terrible Military Junta."

Jerry asked, "Are you afraid of any acts of reprisal against you or any other Chinese?"

"That is big question. Hope very much replacement military regime will be much better. Maybe only for few years, but Chinese learn to take one year at a time. This is most exciting time for Chinese in this small city as life was fast becoming intolerable.

"You Aussies made most honorable parade this city has ever seen. Much better than Chinese New Years parade. You rid city of many dangerous dragons. Chinese never forget this day, ANZAC Day. You once again offer your lives for your citizens."

Then the venerable old Chinese stood up. Instead of bowing in typical Chinese fashion **Q. Song pulled his short body up straight and gave an almost snappy salute.**

Jerry and Joe pulled themselves up straight and returned it.

Later in private they agreed there are times when a salute to the dead almost overcomes one's emotions. There are times when you must salute someone you don't respect. **But of all our salutes we will never forget will be this one. One Chinese Tong leader and two Aussies.** May God be with him and protect him and give him a long happy life.

With the return of Jerry and Joe all hands were ready to shove off. The Captain knew the harbor was so small a pilot was not needed, but he realized that decision was not his to make. So he acquiesced again to taking the pilot and one assistant on board as they pulled up anchor and headed for the open sea. This time the motors sounded perfect.

When they were beyond the channel hazards the Pilots Tender was waiting. The Chief pilot said, "Cap-i-tan, Your motors sound much better now."

The Captain hesitated. He didn't care to reply, but knew it would not be wise to ignore the question. He choose his words carefully and spoke slowly. "Some of the motors in your city were also running rough. I hope we have helped them."

The pilot looked at the Captain and smiled. "Yes, Senor Capitan. You helped. We thank you."

As soon as the pilots were off the ship the Captain passed the command to the executive officer and checked the directions and instructions to sail for a port with major hospital facilities.

Then the Captain picked up the phone to the ship's loud speaker system and said in a strong voice, "Now hear this all hands. This is the Captain. My congratulations for a job well done. For a bunch of bloody swabs I thought for a few days I had the King's personal marines under me. **This is the finest ANZAC Day I have ever spent in my entire sea career, as well as my life.**

"I will request special commendation for all of you, but you know how that goes. I don't run the bloody Navy so what you get and what you deserve is not always the same. I am very proud of all of you. **All Australia will be very proud of you!**

"O.K. It's back to work you go. Minimum duty for everyone for the rest of the day. Special dinner rations for all. "

And then the Captain startled them all with the words, **"Put Waltzing Matilda on the loudspeaker."**

The Captain with great relief in his heart went below deck to check on his three civilian passengers. He found that Reginald was holding his own and his daughter was still holding his hand and stroking his brow. She said, "I'm praying as hard as I can that he is going to survive. I am so grateful and I hope you can get word to my Mom."

Meanwhile Della had been talking virtually non-stop to her Dad telling him again and again that they were both safe. They were in the Doctor's quarters on board the Cruiser. As Della continued to talk she occasionally would feel a slight pressure from his hand as he valiantly endeavored to get up enough energy to signal her that he heard her. She would gently touch his brow with her other hand and continued to talk and cry.

The intern said to himself, "If that doesn't give this guy the will to live there isn't any medicine in the world that will."

At times like this the Doctors were like an infantryman in combat. They recognized the importance of their role, but despaired at the odds against survival. **They realized death had a firmer grasp on Reginald than they did.**

The Doctor's brother had been a British bomber pilot flying raids over Germany. He told how both the RAF and the American bomber pilots flying B-17's and B-24's were suffering casualties as high as 30% per mission.

With 30 missions needed to get off the line the odds were so high that none would last beyond four missions unless the strange hand of fate intervened.

So it had to be with Reginald. How he had survived so far was almost beyond comprehension. **Now it was up to the two medical men and Della to bring his almost lifeless body back from the brink.**

CHAPTER 41
AH WING CALLS LANGE.

The Captain suddenly realized he had not notified anyone officially the rescue was complete and successful. He knew the C-47 Pilot would have been in radio contact. The news had been relayed on a confidential basis in code and the official news would not be sent out until after the plane had landed safely in Panama.

A coded message had reached all the way from Q. Song to New Chinatown in Los Angeles and Ah Wing was so pleased he had Delores place a call to Lange's office. He was out, but returned the call shortly. Ah Wing said, "Everything is still confidential, but it appears your plan has worked. Very strange how your going to the Pacific during war time and your Infantry Division fighting alongside the Aussies gave you this idea.

"Like Sir Arthur Conan Doyle declared there are many things going on that are beyond our imagination. **Next word you hear will be over the radio or newspapers. You must promise to not connect Chinese with this."**

"I promise again. You have my word. I would like to ask a few more questions, but may I call Delores after the news is out and raise them then?"

"As soon as news is out we may have additional matters to discuss with you. Think about you come down for Schank's preliminary. We arrange for seat for you provided no one knows it came through us."

"Oh, I would like that. I really would. Thank you so much, Ah Wing."

"For old friend like you, Lange, we always do our best. Delores will call you at proper time."

With the phone connection broken, Lange was so excited he found it difficult to go back to work. He sat back in his chair and thought, "I will likely never know the real intricacy of the Chinese underground. It has been established over centuries.

"I designed and installed business systems for a number of large firms in Portland, such as the world famous Jantzen Knitting Mills. The intricacy of the Chinese lines of communication are a thousand times more complicated."[6]

Jean, the office girl said, "Was that the beautiful Chinese Lady you are madly in love with? Maybe I better find a girl friend for you."

"It was her boss. Better be nice to me, or I'll have the Chinese underground pick you up and no one will ever hear from you again."

"Oh, yes, sir. Yes, sir! I am frightened to death. I don't want the fangs of the Dragon Lady ripping me apart."

With that remark Jean quickly turned around and left Lange's office. She said to herself, "You know Jean, this is Priscilla and John Alden in reverse. Lange has only worked here about a month and I'd like to get him to ask me out on a date. I'm sure the boss wouldn't like it."

She thought about it a little more and said to herself, " I'd like his arms around me. I'd like him to tell me I was attractive and interesting. I guess that's what every girl needs, to be admired. So we look around for the right clothes and the right colors. The men they just put on a suit and a tie and that's it."

Jean looked at her watch. It was three minutes after 5. Lange was still there and she knew he likely would stay for another half hour. The boss had not returned. **Suddenly she felt reckless, almost a little giddy.** She closed her desk and the files, turned off the light in the office where she worked and started out the back door.

Then she turned around and walked back into Lange's office, looked him in the eye and said, "Neither of us seems to be dating these days. If you have a lonesome evening and want company you could call me."

She handed him a small slip of paper, "Here's my phone number."

Then she threw caution to the wind, walked over to the side of his desk, leaned down and kissed him lightly on the cheek. **"Am I your first Santa Barbara kiss?"**

Meanwhile she had returned to the front of his desk and was looking directly at him. Lange paused as if he was seriously contemplating the question, "I guess you are."

"What do you say?"

"Oh, I guess I forgot my manners, Thank you."

"That's better." She laughed in a pleasant fashion.

Then she noticed she had left fresh lipstick on his cheek. "Oh, Oh, I guess I am just not accustomed to kissing in the office. I left a give away clue for the boss. Oh, my God, I think that's him coming in!"

She grabbed a tissue from her purse and quickly wiped the lipstick off. Then she turned and quickly left Lange's office and said, "Goodnight."

Lange watched Jean rush out of his tiny office. She was of medium height, maybe 5′5. That made her over six inches shorter than he was. She had the blonde hair and a nice tan that seemed to go with Southern California. Her weight was around 110 pounds with a reasonable amount of curves, but not buxom.

When she smiled her eyes lit up giving her face a special attractiveness. Most of the time she played the part of the efficient office girl and her demeanor didn't wear any invitational badge.

She had once made some reference to living with her Mother and no mention was made of a Father. **Lange took it for granted that she had parental responsibilities, always a limitation on outside activities.**

This evening as he watched her exit his fancy moved into a state of contemplation. Perhaps this was one of those things that fate had in mind for him. He said to himself, "I read once that you should at least test the waters before you decide not to swim.

"Right now it sounds like she doesn't have a boyfriend. Maybe I'd better call her tonight so she doesn't have to wonder if she did the wrong thing. I'll ask her for a date this weekend. Yes, that's what I'll do."

During dinner he thought of the past couple of days. Monday morning, Hank the Treasury Agent, and his assistant had picked up the counterfeiting equipment, the cash and miscellaneous other data. Internal Revenue Department had picked up additional files.

Mid-morning today Hank had called saying, "The preliminary news about T & S Telephone Co. had been so amazing I knew I must double check it before releasing any preliminary findings. I'm still wary. However, if anyone had actually owned ten shares of T & S in 1929 and had retained ownership it would be worth a small fortune today."

That was the nearest that Lange could get Hank to commit as to value. Hank continued with, "You're still going to have to hold back and say nothing to Maude except, of course, we are checking. It's not an easy matter to go back 20 years.

"After being bought out it was combined, bought out again, merged and now is part of the Bell System. We don't even know if anyone can ever locate the original stockholder register. We have an agent going through Schank Investment in Los Angeles and we believe that is where we will find the link that will bind the cheese.

"Lange, if you ever want to have a job that deals in the bizarre, consider joining Treasury. With your education and military preference you could get in. Now is the time to do it! These crooks must stay up all night trying to figure out ways to beat the Senior Citizens, as well as anyone else."

CHAPTER 42
LANGE CALLS JEAN.

With dinner over that evening Lange couldn't get up enough nerve to call Jean. He knew he had to contact Maude. **"Oh, there's my door bell. It must be Maude."**

"I'm so sorry to trouble you, Lad. Is there any good news, or is the news bad and you're afraid to tell me?"

"No, Maude, I was just going to take a walk and was going to stop in to see you. I have heard from Agent Hank. The news is still very good."

"What does that mean, Lad?"

"It means that T & S Telephone is now part of the huge Bell System. Takes time to go back 20 years and find old stock transfers.

"Schank had to be fairly certain it was valuable, or else he wouldn't be breaking into your place and forging your Dad's signature. Who knows, he likely did the same thing to a dozen other folks in Los Angeles."

"Take your walk, Lad. I won't bother ye more this evening. Can I ask each day?"

"Sure, Maude. I promise to give you a report each day. Either news or no news."

Lange could tell Maude's emotions were so strung out she was beside herself. He said, "Maude, on the way home I bought you a small present. Don't drink it all at once."

He went to his refrigerator, took out the bottle of Sherry he had purchased, put it in a paper bag, returned to Maude and said, "I'll carry it to your door, here it is."

They walked the few feet to her door. She unlocked her door, he handed her the bag. She looked inside, then she looked at Lange. "Lad, me-thinks you're getting to know me well. I don't go to no Doctor as I have no money to pay. This will be good medicine for my nerves. Thank you so much. If I ever get any money I'll pay ye back for sure, Lad."

Lange returned from his walk, and decided the only way he would have nerve to call Jean was if he called her right now. He did, and was almost hoping she was out. **"This is Lange, I think I am allergic to your lipstick. My whole cheek is blistering."**

"I just finished washing my hair and am about to put in the curlers. Otherwise, I could come over and try another brand."

"If I can't make it to work tomorrow will you explain it to Mr. Parks?"

"Oh, for sure. Of course I won't."

"Seriously, Jean, do you have any spare time this weekend? I'd be pleased to take you to a show, or whatever you like to do."

"A show would be grand. What day were you thinking of?"

"How about Saturday, unless that's not good for you."

"That would be wonderful, Lange. I would love it. Shall we not share the news with Mr. Parks?"

"I'd prefer it that way. Yes, let's keep it our secret."

"Great! I'll get back to my hair now, and I'm really looking forward to the show Saturday."

The rest of the evening, for both Jean and Lange, was partially spent in the universally used mental state of 'conjecture.' What do you do and say on the first date? Do you hug or kiss goodnight? On the cheek, or on the lips?

One question Jean did not ask herself, because she already knew the answer. **After the show she could not invite Lange into her Mother's small home.**

CHAPTER 43
THE RESCUE NEWS BREAKS.

The next morning, Wednesday the 26th, Lange turned on the early news when his alarm clock went off. The announcer was his usual cheerful self, as his listeners pondered the question, "How can anyone be so happy so early in the morning?"

"A pleasant good morning to all of my listeners this Wednesday morning, April 26. We are expecting the weather to be sunny and hope your dispositions will equal the weather.

We have just received a news flash as follows:

"IT IS RUMORED THAT AN AUSTRALIAN LIGHT CRUISER WAS IN A WEST COAST SOUTH AMERICAN PORT WHEN TWO AUSTRALIAN CIVILIANS WERE RESCUED FROM THE MILITARY JUNTA. WHY THEY WERE BEING HELD IS NOT KNOWN. THIS SUPPOSEDLY OCCURRED YESTERDAY, APRIL 25TH, WHICH IS ANZAC DAY FOR BOTH AUSTRALIAN AND NEW ZEALAND FORCES WHO PERFORMED HEROICALLY DURING WORLD WAR I.

THIS IS A REMARKABLE COINCIDENCE. IT IS ALSO RUMORED THAT SEVERAL BUILDINGS WERE DESTROYED INCLUDING THE MILITARY JUNTA HEADQUARTERS, THE MILITARY JAIL AND A BROTHEL. ATTEMPTS TO

CONTACT THE MILITARY JUNTA LEADERS HAVE FAILED
LEADING TO SPECULATION THEY HAVE DISAPPEARED."

With that news Lange's excitement could not be contained.
He almost yelled out loud, **"I'll bet those Aussies raised hell
with the military there. Another great day for the Aussies."**
It was just exactly that! When that news hit the Australian
Press you could hear Waltzing Matilda sung with even more
gusto, if that was possible, all over the nation. It was the greatest
Aussie news in years. People were glued to the radio and the
newspaper extras were flooding the streets. It was agreed by
everyone, **"What a bloody great way to celebrate ANZAC Day."**
The crew on the light cruiser had been so dedicated to
accomplishing their mission that they never took the time to
realize their actions would brand them as heroes the rest of
their lives. Newsmen and radio men were harassing Naval
Headquarters for more information.
The mission had not received any official sanction from
Military Headquarters so the spectacular news was downplayed.
Nevertheless the pride of the Aussie Navy shot upward. It was
a great day for pride and country. The New Zealand people and
press spoke of them as, "Comrades-in-arms."
On board the cruiser Reginald was receiving the second best
treatment the two medical men could conjure up. Della was the
best!
Wednesday morning he had still not shown much
improvement, but the intravenous feeding was doing it's
job and some special soups and broth were fed to him by his
daughter in the afternoon and he was able to contain them.
Occasionally he would seem to awake and open his eyes.
**Finally he said, "Della." Just one word. That was all his
broken body and mind could say.**
Most of the time he remained incoherent.
For a few short periods of time he seemed to improve and
then would lapse back into unconsciousness. Della's heart was
being torn in two as she tried to help bring her father back to
this world.

She was suffering terribly and the Doctor was having great difficulty in getting her to get any rest. She would not leave the room he was in. She tearfully said, "If he wakes and I'm gone, he might feel he was only dreaming."

The Doctor knew her fears were right and Reginald might give up and pass on. At least if he did die she would be with him at the time and would cherish those last moments with him for the rest of her life. "I cannot fail him now," she cried.

Word was received there were some American Medical Officers in Panama and the ship could also drop off the Rangers. If Reginald could be checked over by a larger medical staff they would be relieved. There was an American cruiser in the area and it was heading to Panama to also offer medical assistance.

The first order of business in Panama was to get additional medical attention for Reginald. This included visits from two American Physicians stationed in Panama as well as the Chief Medical Officer on board the American cruiser. The consensus was that Reginald should not have survived.

Just as in the Bataan Death march in the Philippines and the subsequent imprisonment, some made it, most didn't. **What was the elusive unknown factor that kept some men going?**

It was the imponderable question that left one's mortality in perpetual question. It was decided to not move Reginald from the ship and the vessel would sail to Southern California with the most knots per hour possible.

The Rangers were to leave the ship in Panama, but not before the Rangers that had returned on the C-47 came on board. When they arrived they had brought the Pilot, Co-pilot and radio operator with them and a load of fresh fruit and vegetables for the crew.

They had dinner on the cruiser and the best of everything was served including Melbourne Bitter Ale. The men cheered, names and addresses were swapped and the Captain concluded the dinner with, "It's an old adage that friendships formed in combat last forever!

"When you men find time to visit Australia try to do it on ANZAC Day. You'll find there won't be a hotel or a restaurant that will make a charge for their hospitality."

The Rangers were all permitted to look in on Reginald. Della was so profound in her thanks, as she had been continuously to the crew of the cruiser. The Rangers and the C-47 crew were truly disappointed to leave the Australians. The head Ranger spoke a final few words. **Then he shouted, "Long live the Australian Navy!"**

They he added, "Hip, hip, hooray!"

The Aussie crew that were on the deck with the Rangers shouted, "Hip,hip.hooray!"

The Rangers observed the special comradeship the crew shared. Their comments ranged from, "There's the kind of life a man needs, with buddies like that," to

"They are a bunch of Errol Flynns. I'm going to see every one of his movies again."

The women from the brothel were all returning to their own countries, but not until they had been interrogated and their testimony witnessed. All they would say was essentially, "There had been some confusion before and after the flight."

The Rangers didn't even admit to being on the flight. They claimed someone had stolen some Ranger uniforms two weeks before and they almost sounded like the Chinese when they said, "No one else to blame, always blame it on the Rangers."

CHAPTER 44
SCHANK AND HIS ATTORNEY LEXUS

The preliminary hearing for Schank was scheduled for the next Monday. The Captain had been informed that Della could be the critical witness. She was so important to the case the Los Angeles district attorney would endeavor to delay the preliminary hearing if Della could not reach Los Angeles by then, or if the continued deathbed condition of her father made it impossible for her to leave him.

Lexus was on his way to visit Schank that Wednesday and had his car radio on. He heard part of the news of the rescue. By the time he reached the Schank's jail he was very worried.

He whispered to Schank, "Cal, is it possible the Aussie gal that was rescued with her Father was your former companion? They haven't released any names yet."

"My goose would be cooked. Maybe your's too, Lexus."

The two men continued to whisper to each other. Schank asked, "What's this about the girl's Father?"

"Apparently the father was trying to rescue the girl and the Military Junta didn't take kindly to that. It would have been better if they had killed both of them."

"What's this about the General and his chief of staff being missing?"

Both men were feeding each other with worry as each recognized this placed the preliminary hearing in jeopardy. Lexus said, "I'll put out feelers, but you know how it is with military operations, especially a naval vessel at sea."

"First we're messing around with the Chinese and now the Australians. Come on, Lexus, what the hell's going on? Is this turning into international warfare?"

"You always were a big time operator. Now, maybe you're international."

"If you're trying to be funny, can it. You're outside. I'm inside. I should have been an attorney."

"That reminds me Schank, as your attorney I have another matter to discuss."

"Something else?"

"Yes, I received papers from your wife's attorney yesterday. They were delivered by special messenger."

"What does she want?"

"She has filed for divorce."

"How much is she asking for? Half of everything? She never earned it. I'll never agree to split with her!"

"Hold on, Schank. Just hold on. She surprised the hell out of me. She is not asking for anything."

"You must be joking Lexus! She is filing for divorce and not asking for a dime. Oh, come on, you must be crazy."

Lexus took a set of papers out of his brief case and handed them to Schank.

Then he continued with, "She is asking for an immediate divorce.

"With no estate to haggle over she'll get it fast."

"What's she going to live on. Isn't she even asking for the Montecito estate?"

"No, she only asks for her personal possessions and a few items of furniture, dishes and things she inherited from her Mother. The sum total is not expected to exceed $10,000.

Don't ask me. She's your wife. Maybe her folks left her something in trust. Do you want me to leave the papers with you?"

"No, they would just bug me. I would have given her a divorce years ago if I had any idea she wouldn't take me to the cleaners and demand half, plus monthly alimony, plus big time attorney fees. What's she asking for attorney's fees?"

"She is asking for absolutely nothing except the personal possessions and I doubt that you are interested in any of them."

"Should I sign it?"

"Sure, why not? I can notarize it. It might even help for you to in no way contest it. Go ahead and sign it."

Schank looked at Lexus with a grim face, "I just can't believe it. She'll give me a divorce and I'm in jail so I can't enjoy it. Now, what's the scoop on my son. What's being done for him?"

"I got another attorney for him. Would you believe The Shadow ratted on him and he's going to get a burglary conviction on that."

"That's my fault. He didn't want to do it. I forced him to."

"You asked a lot of people to do things that went beyond the law, **but like many a man it took a woman to bring you down."**

"What's the worst charge against him?"

"Accessory to counterfeiting. I told you not to stash that stuff with him. Why didn't you follow my instructions?"

"How did they find out?"

"Treasury Dept. and IRS have been going through your offices. Bob had it in his office safe. If he'd had any brains he would of stashed it someplace on your estate."

"You mean they are going through the L.A. office, too?"

"Probably with a fine tooth comb!"

"All our years of work! All our secrets! New charges on account of Della. They'll need a night shift just to write up the charges against me."

When Lexus left Schank sat on the edge of his bunk. He recalled how his oyster had been spread across the entire country. He merely snapped his fingers and his private rail car carried him in luxurious style. **Now his domain was less than 100 square feet.**

CHAPTER 45
BUSY WEEK SANTA BARBARA

After weighing the pros and cons, Lt. Merced called Bob
Schank into the prisoner's interviewing room. Bob's attorney
had been bugging the District Attorney, claiming the charges
were not clear, and his client was entitled to bail. Now that Lt.
Merced had viewed the forgery equipment, which was safely in
the hands of the Treasury Department, he was in the mood to
tell Bob they had the goods on him for sure.

"You are skum and filth, Schank. Just like your father.
Forging a poor old deceased English gardener's stock into your
own Dad's name. **Cheating a poor old housekeeper.**

"Stealing her inheritance, all the while you are set to
foreclose on her small duplex. **We intend to find out how many
other little old ladies you've been stealing from.**"

Bob hung his head for a time, then finally said, "Yes. I realize
you won't believe it, but I was against it. I could claim my father
turned me into a beast. For certain my mother did not. I guess I
made my own bed."

"What caused this change of heart?"

"My Mother came over to see me yesterday. She told me
something in confidence. I will tell you in confidence if you
promise not to tell."

"If it's illegal I can't promise, otherwise I promise."

"Rest assured it is not illegal. My Mother has filed for a divorce from Dad. She said she is going to give up everything that is connected to Dad. If I am going to hang in there and support Dad she is giving up me, too.

"If I will be honest for the first time in years she will stick by me."

"So when are you going to confess?"

"I would now, but I fear for my life."

That afternoon Lange called Lt. Merced. It took over an hour to reach him. "This is Lange. Are you real busy?"

"Why do people ask if you are busy and when you say you are they still want to talk your leg off? But go ahead, Lange."

"Let me run this by you over the phone. Maude's mortgage is due in a few months. She doesn't have a dime to pay against it. Now that Treasury and the IRS are in the ball game it may take years to get this mess straightened out."

"That's a fair guess as to time."

"I got this unofficially from one of the Treasury Agents. They told me to get a mortgage satisfaction made up and you get Bob Schank to sign it in return for you dropping the breaking and entering charge."

"Hey, I can't do that!"

"I know you can't, but the District Attorney could and keep in mind that the counterfeiting charge against him is major. The breaking and entering is peanuts."

"Well, it sounds a little goofy, but I'll take it to the D.A."

"Great, I'll get a Satisfaction of Mortgage filled out and at your office by noon."

"You know Lange, it would mean we wouldn't have to spend our time working that charge against him. By the way, you giving any more thought to taking over The Shadow's private eye business?"

"What have you got against me to try to turn me into a private eye?"

"We worked well with you when you came back from the South Pacific."

"Oh, you mean in the case of the Missing Fiance."

"You solved most of it yourself. You even helped the IRS."

"That involved some reversionary interests I learned about in law school."

"No matter where you learned it, you had the brain power."

"O.K. You win a little. For a puzzle that involves finances call me, but **I'm not going around shadowing people and packing a gun and getting in shoot outs.**"

"I see your point, Lange. I guess your judgment suits your life style best."

Lange had no sooner hung up the phone than his boss stepped into his office. "We need you to take a trip this afternoon to Ventura. A car dealer there wants an undercoating demonstration about 2:30. We just received a new spray nozzle from Grayco. They think it will work. I think the problem is in the material, not the nozzle.

"Grayco doesn't make the material. They are just trying to help."

Lange laughed and replied, "That is the messiest job I ever had. Reminds me of a story I once heard. I'll save it for later as I need to get a Satisfaction of Mortgage form filled out and over to the Police Department. I'll get one from the title company and the legal description at the same time."

"Thanks for not objecting. It is a messy job."

Lange thought to himself, "My good attitude is because when I'm through I'll stop at Sally's restaurant and see if she is there. If not, I'll still eat dinner and then I'll call her."

That added a bright note to the upcoming non-pleasurable demonstration. He said to himself, "Someday, someone is going to come up with the right nozzle and the right mix of fibers and material so it will all stick to the car and won't come out in blobs and slop back onto the guy that's trying to put it on.

"With the salt air causing rust why don't they undercoat the cars at the factory? That would make more sense. Wonder if they ever will?"[7]

CHAPTER 46
PAPUA, NEW GUINEA.

New Guinea is the second largest island in the entire world. It was there that the Allies finally stopped the relentless advance of the Japanese to the continent of Australia itself. It was the Battle of Buna. The battle was going badly and General MacArthur in desperation ordered his I Corp Commander, General Eichelberger, to take personal charge. **"Win that battle or don't come back alive,"** were his orders to Eichelberger. MacArthur's forces had lost the Philippines. The Japanese had advanced thousands of miles and there was talk of having to evacuate the northern part of Australia. This was MacArthur's first battle under his new command.

He committed 10,000 men of the 32nd Infantry Division. **Casualties were 9,965** and it was a miracle Eichelberger survived. He personally directed it from the front lines. Smaller island conquests under the Marines, like Iwo Jimo, some ten miles long received more publicity and had much more fire power and support. New Guinea was a terrifying and miserable experience. The battle to take it's over 1000 mile length went on for years. Papua was New Guinea's most populous province.

Reginald still had friends in Papua that went back to his days as a youth. His father had been an overseer on a plantation **and Reg had spent those formative years mostly getting in the way of the foremen asking a multitude of questions.** He had been repeatedly told not to fraternize with the fuzzy wuzzy natives.

Several native children were his own age. Finally his father realized that little Reg treated the native children as his equal and the native workers responded by being more reliable and working harder. The native children taught Reg their primitive skills and their elders did the same. **Reg learned their native language.**

The Papuans learned from him, too. It was a cultural step forward for both.

In later years, back on the mainland in the Northern part of Australia, he never forgot any of them. When he became a seaman he was thrilled to occasionally put in at Port Moresby, Milne Bay, Oro Bay and Finchhaven. Word would go by short wave that Reg was coming and as many as could would meet him.

Bo and Mo were his boyhood pals. They were the names he had come up with in those days when he was ten years old and less. Later Bo and Mo received training at the Buna Mission and became police boys wearing the white skirt uniform and carrying a spear.During the New Guinea campaign they worked carrying wounded as well as performing dangerous missions as scouts for the Australians and Americans. **The English they had learned from Reg opened even more doors for them.** They received some formal training in Australia after the war and returned to Papua where they served in middle status government jobs.

As the years progressed Reg had advanced from just a seaman on one of the thousands of Dutch boats that plied those seas to second officer on a large merchant marine vessel. Those larger ships visited only the larger harbors such as Port Moresby and Milne Bay. Particularly when his ship was in Milne Bay he would hop a small craft and go up the coast to Buna and Oro Bay where Bo and Mo were employed.

They had learned Reg had lost track of his daughter. In time hundreds of natives knew she was missing and **in their** own spirit world they were continually asking their Gods to deliver her safely back to Reg and his wife.

Bo and Mo were in daily contact, via short wave radio with Port Moresby and Milne Bay, who in turn were in daily contact with the Australian mainland. They were electrified when they heard the good news Reginald and his daughter Della had been rescued.

Then came the bad news Reginald might not survive. Suddenly the two were overcome with the desire to see Reginald. Perhaps they could bring enough of his youth with them to help him survive. They took a bush plane from Doboduro near Oro Bay to Port Moresby. From there they took one of the C-47's the military had not taken back.

That got them to Townsville. From there they flew to Brisbane and then to Sydney. All of Australia were praying for Reginald's survival. A wealthy businessman offered to pay the expenses for Reg's wife, and Bo and Mo after Pan Am agreed to fly them at half fare.

The two natives and Reg's wife, Joyce, arrived in San Francisco by Pan-American clipper. Thence to Los Angeles arriving at virtually the same time as Reginald and his daughter did. Reginald was too sick to go to the Chinese Tong.

He was placed in a military hospital for security purposes as well.

When they arrived Lt. Alex Brown personally escorted them to the hospital room. Reg's wife put her arms around her husband and each native took one of his hands.

They spoke softly to him. He said later, **"I thought I was about to finally die.** I felt my mind returning to my childhood and Bo and Mo were taking me by the hand and escorting me personally over that great divide. With my wife and daughter beside me.

"I lost all fear."

What was happening was the shock of the arrival of his wife and the two natives took some of the lethargy out of his system as well as giving his body a further shot of adrenaline. He opened his eyes and spoke, "Joyce, my beloved, and Bo and Mo. Have I gone to heaven? **And Della is here, too, isn't she?"**

"Here I am Dad, right beside you. Isn't it wonderful. We're all here together!"

The tears began to roll down Reg's eyes and soon everyone was crying. **Even Lt. Brown was seen to take his handkerchief out of his pocket.**

The Doctor standing by said, "Love supersedes all medicine."

Della wiped the tears from her Dad's eyes and said, "Mom and Bo and Mo flew here to help you get better."

"I had hoped Mom would come, but how were Bo and Mo able to make it?"

The two natives spoke and Reginald replied in Papuan. Everyone was amazed. Reg was acting like a human being again. **He was returning from almost eternity!**

Lt. Alex Brown realized Della might be able to testify at the Preliminary Hearing. He expressed his delight at the improvement in Reg's health and his regret he must return to other duties.

As he strode from the room his shoulders were erect, a slight smile on his face and a bit of a song in his heart. **Then he realized he was humming Waltzing Matilda.**

THE PRELIMINARY HEARING APPROACHES.

CHAPTER 47
BEFORE THE HEARING.

Every national news gathering organization, not the least of which were Associated Press and United Press, were having a field week batting out news releases on the ANZAC Day rescue. That was big enough and could easily have carried the press for several more weeks.

Reporters and photographers flew to South America, including Panama, for on-the-scene stories. It made fantastic headlines and the press blew it into a raging four alarm.

Then a wind blew in that stank, news that fanned the fire into a blazing inferno. It was rumored the rescued mystery woman was the former companion of Cal Schank. The fact that she had ended up in a brothel South of the border, and her Dad had been brutally beaten attempting to rescue her brought citizens to their feet in protest.

The District Attorney's office was deluged calls from all kinds of people from everywhere. Calls were even coming in from people who had business and personal dealings with Schank. **These included other women he had been involved with.**

The D.A. carefully reviewed the ones his staff recommended he read. He was aghast at the charges. **"This is the break we needed.** The hearing will now just be a formality. "Schank will be bound over for certain and I'll ask for the trial to be held as soon as legally possible. We won't be wasting the taxpayer's money on this one. He broke the Lindbergh Kidnapping Law a hundred times, as well as dozens of other laws."

He continued to express caution to his staff. "Do your job as if this isn't a pushover. I won't tolerate sloppy work in this department. Screw up and your head will roll."

There was a political crisis in South America both over the treatment of women like Della and her Father who had attempted to rescue her.

The country that had perpetrated the crime was claiming they were invaded by the Australian Navy and adopted a belligerent threatening attitude.

When that news reached the Australian mainland the Aussie people and press threatened reprisals and demanded full reimbursement for the cost of the rescue.

They made it clear Australians would be protected even if the entire Aussie Army, Navy and Air Force were needed.

The depositions from the women taken to Panama were quoted in part all over the world. Magazines were competing for rights to their stories and every studio in Hollywood was evaluating their possible interest in producing a film based on this amazing story.

Reginald's body was responding to the first real food and medicine he had received in months. He was still too weak to walk even with the help of a cane, so he was wheelchair bound. **He had been so severely beaten it was doubtful he would ever fully recover.** The Doctor declared, "He is no longer fully mentally competent."

Meanwhile the Santa Barbara police had moved Martha Schank to what they hoped was a reasonably safe haven. This involved an assumed name and a 24 hour guard.

This in no way daunted the romance between her and Dr. Emery Smith. He spent every evening with her. Their frustrating years alone had not permitted their hearts and souls to grow. Now, suddenly, the sunshine of love permitted them to bloom. The intensity of their affection for each other shocked them. Martha would repeat, **"Our romance is so beautiful it is indescribable, Emery. I'm speechless."**

"I've had several patients that remarried in middle age and I could tell they were totally transformed persons. I recognized maturity brings a special depth to one's mind and heart."

"We're old enough to have experienced many tragedies that life passes out when one least expects. When love comes again we know it's so precious we want to give it our full devotion and energy."

"Martha, when I hear you talk like this I realize your mind is as beautiful as you are physically. It's hard to describe someone as thoughtful and genuine as you are. All I can do is say I recognize it and that's why I am in love with you."

"You've seen hundreds of patients in your life, Emery. I get a little frightened when I think of that. Why did you pick me?"

"None of them were you. None of them were lovely you!"

Martha put her arms around Emery and cried. They were tears of genuine joy and appreciation. Mixed in were tears of surprise that her days of desperation had changed so suddenly. They were finding it increasingly difficult to part each evening.

Lange's undercoat demonstration in Ventura went about as usual. At first the asbestos fibers seemed to go through the spray nozzle O.K. and the undercoat spray was adhering to the underneath part of the car. Then things began to clog up and some big globs came out instead of a heavy spray. Lange took the nozzle off several times and cleaned it.

That helped only temporarily! Finally the dealer said, **"Let's knock it off for now.** A car dealer has enough mechanical problems to solve without taking on another one."

It took Lange over an hour to get the equipment and himself cleaned up and loaded. Then he headed for the cafe where Sally Stevens worked. She was not on duty. The waitress taking her place took Lange's order and then tried to reach Sally at home, but she was out.

Lange finished his dinner and knew he would be thrilled again as he drove between Ventura and Carpinteria with the ocean only 200 feet away. (Travelers today take the divided freeway farther from the ocean.)

As he watched the sun dip into the horizon instead of thinking of his days on the other side of the Pacific his mind turned to Cabrillo, who had discovered Santa Barbara.

Then his mind began to compare. Cabrillo had found many underground deposits of tar. The area became a haven to caulk their vessels with tar.

"Wouldn't Cabrillo have been amazed to see what he started. From tarring ships to tarring automobiles. Crazy world.

"And how about pioneer justice when many a confidence man was tarred and feathered. Boy, that was something!"

As he continued to think about tar he recalled those depression days. Kids in Portland would pick off a little of the asphalt paving and chew it like gum. Lange laughed again and said, "Yep, tar, you've come a long ways, baby."

The next morning Lange got a call from Lt. Merced. "Lange, it worked. Bob Schank signed the Mortgage Satisfaction and we have it notarized. **What a deal! Can you figure out a way to get me a Mortgage Satisfaction? I've got over 20 years left to pay and my wife already wants a new house."**

"So maybe I'll go into that business. Shows I'm not cut out to be a private eye. Lt. Merced, you should be congratulated. You got the signature."

"Well, yes and no. The District Attorney carried the ball. He made me promise to point out the government might claim prior right to all of Schank's assets."

"I know that– but I'd like to walk over now, pick up the papers and get them to the title company for recording. I don't want to lose a minute."

"I see you're on the ball, Lange. That's also what the D.A. said. I'm going out the door right now. I'll take them myself."

"Wonderful, you are a nice guy. That is most of the time," **and Lange laughed.**

As the day progressed Lange and Jean would keep looking at each other and realizing dating someone you work with has it's complications. Their first date would be tomorrow evening, and their prior easy business formality was being threatened. Just before quitting time Lange said to Jean, "I'm looking forward to tomorrow night."

"I sure am, too," was her quick reply.

"Can I call you Saturday morning and we can talk about the time? I plan to work much of Saturday bringing April right up to date financially. By the way, I am going to talk to Mr. Parks about getting off for one day for the Preliminary Hearing in Los Angeles."

"I'll be in all morning doing my weekly housework. Good luck Saturday at the office. You sure have been leading an interesting life since you've been down here. My life has been pretty dull. Except, of course meeting you and our date tomorrow."

"You kind of talked yourself into a corner. But thanks for the compliment, Jean. You are a very nice person."

Jean knew the best thing to say was, "Thank You."
Which she did with a nice smile and a little curtsy.

That evening Lange was finishing his usual non-exotic dinner. Mixed steamed vegetables, a boiled potato, some fresh ocean flounder, two cups of coffee and two oatmeal cookies, **he kept mulling over the question, "What do I tell Maude?"**

As he left his small stoop to move to her stairs all he had been able to think of was to play it by ear. After the usual greetings he sat down on her old bedraggled sofa and said,

"My rent money is due in a couple of days and I'm going to pay it early."

"Glory be. I've been praying for somethin' like that. **Would ye believe, Lad, I don't have a single farthin left in me bloomin' purse.**"

"I'm sorry, Maude. I know it's tough. I tried something in the last couple of days and it may have worked."

"What do ye mean, Lad?"

Lange began very slowly trying to keep it simple. As he progressed he said to himself, "This is just like the story of getting pregnant. Either you are or you aren't. I'm either going to tell her in full or not. Guess I'd better go for full disclosure and hope the mortgage satisfaction doesn't get shot down. She needs some hope now."

So Lange continued and Maude ran the gauntlet between surprise, amazement, disbelief and not understanding things like 'Mortgage Satisfaction,' and 'Maybe the Government may void it due to prior claim on Schank Investment Assets.'

Finally, in kind of desperation Lange said, "I'm kind of tired, Maude. I have an engagement tomorrow evening so may not come by, but look at it this way. You may no longer have a mortgage against your duplex. On the other hand you may."

"Lad, if ye got rid of me mortgage when I die I will leave anythin' I have left to you."

"Let's not go that far into the future. You are going to need money to live on. You might have to sell the duplex and rent, in order to have money to live on. Whatever happens if I'm around I'll try to help you with it. I promise you that."

Lange went back to his side of the duplex with his mind filled with the complexity of life. He said to himself, "One thing I do know for certain. I am not going to become a private eye. Those Charlie Chan mysteries are out of my world except for reading.

But I'm not as smart as Charlie Chan. I'm not even in the class with Alexander Botts in those great Earthworm Tractor stories. He always got the tractor that broke down to finally work and made the sale. **I can't even get a car undercoated.**"

Then he reassured himself by thinking of the smooth sailing he had with the Bank of America. Putting together the paperwork and the accounting was time consuming, but easy. "That's where I belong. I'm a businessman, not a mechanic or a private eye."

Lange went to bed in a cheerful mood, but nature choose to give him a nightmare as a sleeping companion. He dreamed that Lt. Merced had finally talked him into taking over The Shadow's business. He had rented a very small office in one of his favorite spots.

The El Paseo, sometimes called the Street of Spain, and located off State Street about in the center of town.

There were several small Spanish two story buildings. One he particularly liked had a stairway leading up to a balcony overlooking the courtyard. There were four doors and four small offices on the second floor.[8]

All entered from the balcony. They faced toward the ocean, but there was no ocean view. He rented the rear one. It had an old desk with a chair that squeaked. Also a battered filing cabinet, a coat and hat tree and straight backed wood chairs.

The landlord smiled and said, "It's the best I have to loan you. If you make your office too comfortable you and your clients will just want to lounge around and you won't get any work done."

It wasn't until the third day he received his first call. Some prior client of The Shadow called and made an appointment. He was in a hurry and wanted to come down right away. Lange, having waited three days for a client, laughed to himself and said, "Come on down. I can see you now."

"Thank you, Mr. Lange. I'll be there in 15 minutes or less."

Lange timed him. It was 17 minutes and 28 seconds. Not bad. A prompt guy.

He was a man of medium build, maybe 50 years old, hair still brown, his face was tanned with a few wrinkles. He was wearing an obviously expensive gray suit set off with a plaid tie. He didn't mention the business he was in as he looked Lange over.

Finally he took an envelope from the inside pocket of his coat and extracted a picture from it. He handed the picture to Lange. **It was of a beautiful lady, of perhaps his age.**

He wanted Lange to follow her for the next week. He put his hand in the right outside pocket of his coat and extracted a small wad of bills. "How much?"

So far all Lange had done was pay advance payments such as rent and telephone. It was kind of exciting with a guy sitting in front of him asking him, "How much?"

"$50.00 a day plus expenses."

"Here's $500.00. I expect a good job. Call me each day at least once and give me a report. Here's her address, and now I'll give you a list of some of the places she goes and you can pick her up and follow her from there."

It turned out to be rather simple. She went to the El Paseo Restaurant that evening and he hung around until she left and followed her. He hoped she was returning to her car as he had a parking place in the same block.

Lange was excited. His first job and things seemed to be going easily. She turned left walking to De la Guerra St. She crossed the street staying on the East side of State St. Then turned left on De la Guerra. As he followed her she didn't seem to be in any hurry.

What he didn't realize was she knew she would be tailed and she had a muscle man waiting in one of the building entranceways.

As Lange was abreast of the entranceway two strong arms grasped him and pulled him into the doorway, whereupon the grasper began pummeling him. Lange was fighting back and realized this guy had him by several inches in height and many pounds.

Lange held his left elbow and arm up high to ward off the blows.

Then Lange knew he must get away. He ducked low and put the full force of his body into his right fist driving it just below his opponents ribs. Then he pushed ferociously with both arms, intending to break from this one-sided match.

LANGE WOKE UP AS HE FELL OUT OF BED.

"Oh, my God. I thought I was going to cash out on my first assignment."

His head began throbbing. He had hit his forehead on the wood, non-carpeted floor. He felt it, then he laughed and said, **"When I have my normal nightmares I am back in the jungle. I seldom fall out of bed.**

"Even my subconscious is warning me. 'Don't become a private eye.' Wait until I talk to Lt. Merced. Think I'll doctor up the dream a little and make it into a real story."

As Lange ate breakfast that morning he pondered the age old question about **why the mind does not let a guy rest at night.** Instead it takes a person's worst fears and magnifies them into a nightmare. "The human body is a marvel, but that is one glitch in the system."

As Lange analyzed the dream he came up with a memory of his college days. "My dream last night had a memory tail on it. I remember when I was overseas we would talk about our life in the States. Incidents in school always were a good basis for stories.

"I thought about my boxing coach. His main coaching job was assistant varsity coach for the Oregon Duck Varsity Basketball team. When the boxing match finals were posted I was to box Calkins who was bigger and taller than I was. I told the coach a mistake was made. I was no match for Calkins."

He just laughed, "The only mistake is in your mind. You are fighting Calkins."

It was a three round fight and for three rounds I moved at the virtual speed of lightening. Calkins never laid a serious glove on me. **I survived. Calkins was really angry.** And now in the spring of 1950, Lange's realistic accounting mind knew he was no match for a 225 pound gorilla. "I went into the jungle at 175 pounds. I was a strong third year college student. I came out at 110 pounds, extremely weak and sick.

Now I'm up to 140 pounds. I'm not the right size to be a Private Eye!"

Lange called Jean Saturday morning and she had a suggestion. "Might it be nicer to talk and get better acquainted rather than just sit in a theater? I can fix some sandwiches and a potato salad and we can sit on the grass between the sidewalk and the sand, just off Cabrillo Boulevard, and eat a light dinner.

"Then maybe we could walk around. There's going to be a dance at the old hall on Cabrillo. I haven't danced for a year. We could change at your place for the dance."

"That sounds like a great idea. I only live a few blocks from it."

His first date, since he had returned to Santa Barbara, was coming up at 6 P.M. Lange's concentration on his work at the office was less than perfect. Many thoughts and questions came across his mind. Such as, "I wonder when her last date was? How do you act on a date with a Southern California working girl?"

Before he got too panicky he realized she was maybe asking herself the same questions. He forced himself to concentrate on bringing up the books through Friday. He had to evaluate the work in progress and assign the proper amount of overhead to it.

No easy task when there was a Service Station under construction. "I have a barrel of work I can do, but at 3:30 I am going to knock it off, go home and take a shower, and relax for a half hour. Maybe I shouldn't have gotten a date with the office secretary.

"Too late to come to that conclusion."

Lange arrived for his date promptly at 6 P.M. Jean had been looking for him and he had hardly gotten out of his car before she was bounding down her stairs holding a picnic basket with one arm, and what looked like a dress and her purse in the other. **"I'm excited, Lange, and hope you are, too."**

"You're my first Santa Barbara date."

"You sure know how to put a girl on the spot. I'm nervous, too. We'll do our best won't we? If I concentrate too hard I'll be out of step at the dance."

"We'll be all right at the dance. I've taken some dance lessons and have a little musical background so even though I don't know the steps real well, I can keep time."

As the blue coupe moved toward Cabrillo Blvd. the conversation continued on dancing. **"What dances do you like best?" asked Jean.**

"The waltz and fox trot are easiest. I never learned to jitterbug in high school or college so I'm only part way on that. As to the Latin dances, cha-cha, rumba and tango I understand the rhythm, but don't know enough steps for each dance to feel comfortable."

"I can help you on the jitterbug. You'll have to help me on the Latins. I'm not even to first base on them. Maybe half way between home plate and first base."

They found a pleasant spot to place a blanket and sit. Both were nervous as they ate the ham sandwiches and potato salad Jean had prepared. **There were many boats sailing and the splendid view of them and the ocean made talking easy.**

In much less than an hour they were through eating. They returned the basket and blanket to Lange's car and then walked to the end of Stearns Wharf paying attention to the way folks were dressed. Soon they reached the Harbor Restaurant.

Jean said, "Maybe we'll see a movie star."

Lange, being the practical not so wealthy young man with the excellent accounting background added, "Dinner for two doesn't come cheap at The Harbor."

After their tour of the wharf they drove to Lange's place and Jean used the bathroom to change from slacks into the dress she had brought. Lange used his bedroom to put on a dress shirt, tie and better slacks.

She sat on the small sofa and he joined her there. Lange asked, "How about a glass of wine?"

"I'd like that," was her pleasant response.

They sat there, side by side, talking and sipping the wine. Jean said, "The dance starts at eight. We can be a little late, however."

Their empty glasses were sitting on the small end table at one end of the sofa. She turned her face toward Lange wondering if she should lead the way and kiss him. Finally she took the step. She moved her head to his and their lips came together.

Lange had been sitting there wondering. With Jean so close he could not resist. Then they kissed again and this time the kiss was longer. Both realized they were very nervous.

"Maybe it's time to go to the dance," they said at the same time.

As they danced they found each had a natural love for music. Jean said, "Shall we pretend this five piece band is Glenn Miller and we are Fred Astaire and Ginger Rogers?"

"Sure, why not?"

They snuggled pretty close on the last couple of dances, both realizing they enjoyed each other and not wanting the evening to end. Then the dance was over.

As Lange started his car's engine Jean thought, I've really had a wonderful time, but I'm worried about getting too well acquainted on the first date.

They parked in front of her Mother's home. There was not much light. Lange moved around in his seat a little and Jean moved close to him. Lange put his arm around Jean. After a few minutes of silence they turned their heads to face each other and kissed.

One kiss led to another, each increasing a little in passion. **Finally Lange broke the silence with, "Maybe I'd better walk you to your door."**

Jean was very pleased he had taken the initiative as she didn't want to be the one calling all the shots. She pleasantly replied, "I'd like to see you again. For sure!"

Lange was able to honestly respond with, "I feel the same way!"

As Jean was inside her Mother's house preparing for bed and Lange was doing the same in his small duplex they were both wondering. **"Where do we go from here?"** Lange to himself, "Please, no private eye dreams tonight. Let me dream of Jean with the blond hair. And let's not dream of how we stumbled on the tango."

CHAPTER 48
THE PRELIMINARY HEARING ARRIVES.

The news had been leaked that the two star witnesses Lorie Owens and Della Robertson were under heavy security at two locations. Lorie at the New Chinatown Tong Headquarters and Della at a military hospital.

The obvious question was how were they to be brought to the Los Angeles County Courthouse safely? How was the courtroom going to be secure and how were the two women going to be returned safely? **Suffice it to say they would travel in heavily armored vehicles, in two separate convoys.**

As it turned out only a Presidential arrival at the Courthouse would have received equal security. The armored cars had police inside. Additional police vehicles traveled alongside and in front and back of the two armored vehicles.

They arrived without incident and the only reason the Los Angeles citizens did not turn out en mass equal to a Macy's parade in New York was the routes were kept secret. Taking no chances six alternate routes were worked out.

At the courthouse spectators were limited to known individuals. Only a few of the top news services, such as Associated and United Press and Life Magazine, were permitted. Their cameras were delivered to the police 24 hours earlier, where they were carefully checked, and then returned to the newsmen in the Courthouse.

Security personnel seemed to be everywhere. The hallways were clear except for police. Traffic was virtually prohibited.

Finally the proceedings were about to begin. Schank was brought in under guard and was seated next to his attorney, Lexus Taylor. This preliminary hearing was solely for Schank. His Los Angeles Manager, Ruppert Snyder, would be brought up for arraignment later. Snyder was there, under guard, as a witness for the defense.

The Prosecutor, Jack Adams, had maximum staff with him. **Delores, Lorie and Della were seated at the defense table and drew the most concentration of eyes.**

This rare public appearance of Delores, along with the fame of the stories written about the alleged genuine Dragon Lady was an event in itself.

In the front row nearest the defense table were Reginald Robertson in a wheel chair, his wife Joyce, the Papuan natives and a number of Chinese.

In the next row were Ah Wing, Lange, Wang Sing and several other Chinese. **The press were taken by surprise for they were without a dossier on Lange, someone obviously close to the Chinese.**

Schank was very nervous as he awaited the entrance of the judge. It was the day he had been dreading. He complained to his attorney, "The cards are stacked against me. I'm about to see what kind of a defense you have been telling me you've worked so hard on."

Lexus looked him in the eye saying, "Remember the ball game is changed. With Della in the picture you're going to get bound over for trial. I'm not going to reveal all our defense as I don't want to tip off the prosecution. On the other hand I'm going to work hard. You watch and see. You'll be satisfied!"

The bailiff announced that everyone should rise. Judge Nathan Hollister entered the courtroom. He walked with dignity and self assurance to his bench. He was well respected for his personal intelligence, honesty and tremendous knowledge of the law.

Hollister was six feet tall, weighed in at 175 pounds and his hair was turning from gray to white. He smoked a pipe, but not in court. His face bore many wrinkles perhaps in part because he had grown up on a cattle ranch in the middle west. He was the first in his family to go to college, then on to law school.

Normal legal procedure is the preliminary hearing is held before a judge, who decides if there is sufficient evidence to bind the defendant over for a jury trial. (In the famous Perry Mason mysteries, Mason the defense attorney, invariably came up with last minute evidence at the preliminary hearing and his client is freed.)

It was expected that unless Los Angeles had a sudden major earthquake, which was not impossible, Schank would be bound over for trial.

The charges were read by the bailiff and District Attorney Adams made his statement. Defense Attorney Taylor concluded with, "The defense will show that these charges were made up during the furor created by a kidnapping.

"While Ruppert Snyder may have been temporarily kidnapped we know for certain it was not by Schank. As to the alleged kidnapping of Lorie Owens the defense will have no problem at all showing she was never kidnapped.

"She merely met Schank for dinner at the Pagoda. Both charges have been trumped up by the Police and the Office of the District Attorney as a means of publicity so that they can get more funds allotted to the LAPD."

"Objection, Your Honor, the LAPD is being impugned by the defense."

"Objection sustained. The defense will stick to facts that are material to this case. The court reporter will omit any sentence that implies political activity by the LAPD."

"I understand, Your Honor," replied Lexus. "Now let me restate the sentence the court has objected to. Let me simplify it by saying the defendant has not committed any crime and therefore I request that the charges of kidnapping and interstate prostitution against my client be dropped, Your Honor."

"Your motion cannot be moved on at this time as we have not heard any of the prosecution witnesses. Let us proceed with the case. Call your first witness, Mr. Adams."

The first witness called was Choy, the Chinese cook on the Schankrila, Schank's private rail car. He was sworn in and Adams asked Choy to describe what he observed as cook on the Schankrila. Many times during the testimony Lexus objected to the statements, but Prosecutor Adams was successful in getting in most of Choy's testimony.

Lexus Taylor did want to cross examine Choy. His first question was, "Choy, did you not connive to come on board the Schankrila because you had been misinformed by the two Chinese who formerly worked on the private car?"

"I object to the question," Adams said rather loudly.

"The question may be out of order, but there is possibly some logic in the question. The objection is overruled."

"Thank you, Your Honor. Choy, please answer the question as you have been directed by the judge."

Choy had been cautioned and coached by the prosecutor. Speak slowly. Do not elaborate. Say as few words as possible. Take your time before you even say the first word. Try to ask a question instead of answering the question. This may put the defense attorney on the spot."

Choy took his time and finally said, "Chinese language over one thousand years old. **Do you speak Chinese, Mr. Taylor?"**

"That has nothing to do with this case. You have been asked a question. Please answer it. Operating this court costs the taxpayers money. Please proceed."

"Expecting to proceed, Mr. Taylor. To answer your question Choy must know answer to his question."

Judge Hollister intervened with, "The question may be out of order, but, Counsel, why don't you go ahead and answer it. Do you speak Chinese or not?"

"All right, of course I do not speak Chinese, " he said with disdain in his voice.

The Judge tried not to smile as he was admiring the small polite Choy and hoped Choy would not be overwhelmed by the articulate and polished defense attorney.

"Thank you, Mr. Taylor. Chinese language is impossible to explain in few minutes to people who do not speak it. **Likewise, my use of English language is very little.** It would be most difficult for Chinese with poor English to explain what other Chinese say in Chinese to you who do not understand Chinese. Maybe not fair for either of us."

Many in the audience chuckled and one newsman made the mistake of laughing out loud. The judge was delighted and wanted to laugh himself, but knew that he must pound his gavel and exclaim, "Order in the court!

"The newsmen will refrain from their gallery antics or there will not be any newsmen in the gallery. And the audience is to keep their silence unless requested to speak. Is that clear to everyone?"

Judge Hollister then pounded his gavel again as he said to himself, "I must act the part of the tough judge. I must be like Harry Truman and 'give them hell.'"

"Yes, Your Honor," was heard particularly from the newsmen who under no circumstances could afford to miss this top story.

Lexus Taylor recognized the ball had just been thrown back to him by the diminutive Choy. He realized beneath the calm demeanor of this slight reverent Chinese was a mind that had grasped legal tactics very well. The District Attorney had obviously trained him. In poor grace Lexus then said, "Your comment reminds me of what is found in a fortune cookie."

"Begging your pardon, Mr. Taylor. Fortune cookies are made up by you Americans. Chinese do not write those sayings."

"Be that as it may, is it correct that you were planted on the Schankrila as an employee? You were paid standard wages and instead you came on board as a spy."

"I object, Your Honor. The defense is making up statements and trying to trap Mr. Choy into accidentally agreeing with them. Particularly in that Mr. Choy is Chinese and not a student of the English language."

"Objection sustained. Mr. Taylor, unless you can understand Chinese, which I don't understand either, we must take particular care in asking questions of Mr. Choy.

"Make your questions simple and easy to understand. Let's be fair. If this were a Chinese courtroom instead of American, the shoe would be on the other foot. "

"Yes, Your Honor. I have no further questions of Mr. Choy, but I retain the right to call him back in the event I have further need."

Choy was followed by the steward and house boy, Wan, as the two Chinese had served as a team on the Schankrila. D.A. Adams said, "In the interest of time, Mr. Wan, do you disagree with any of the answers given by Mr. Choy?"

"Oh no, Honorable Choy very wise man. Speak much better English than I do. We discuss matter in Chinese. I agree 100% with Mr. Choy."

"That is fine and to be expected. Is there perhaps something Mr. Choy has not mentioned that has come to your mind while he was speaking?"

"Oh no, nothing else come to Wan's mind."

"Thank you, Wan."

Judge Hollister said loudly, "The defense may now question the witness."

Lexus Taylor realized he could take the rest of the day and not get another word out of Wan. It would look better on the court records for him to say, which he did, "I have no questions of this witness."

It was obvious to everyone the judge was relieved. He was in no mood to let the defense prolong the preliminary hearing with a lot of delaying tactics. The judge doubted there was any way he could dismiss the charges. He did, however, have to permit the defense their day in court.

As Wan left the stand the D.A. said, "My next witness is Lorie Owens. Please take the stand. "

The judge pounded his gavel and said, "I have noted and appreciate the need to move ahead rapidly, but I am afraid we are too near the lunch hour to start new testimony.

"The Chinese have in the interests of expediency volunteered to serve lunch in the courtroom for everyone. It is only 11:30. Let's take a 30 minute recess. Lunch will be served at 12 noon sharp and the court will reconvene at 12:45 sharp. Do I hear any objections from the defense or the prosecution?"

Both attorneys rose and in unison said, "No objection, Your Honor."

With that the judge moved quickly from the bench and headed for his chamber.

Schank turned to Lexus and said, "Those damn Chinese are too smart for you."

"Look who's on trial!"

"Don't be so smart. I could get you hung, too, by telling the police who arranged for the hit on Lorie."

"You could, but you wouldn't because then you would be admitting you instigated the attempted assassination."

Lexus continued with, "You can count yourself lucky that Sammy, your bodyguard, is dead. He would have broken down on the witness stand. His testimony would have been dynamite. The trial won't be for another sixty days. Maybe we'll get a break."

By then the Chinese were scurrying around with a selection of food in the traditional little cardboard take home containers. The containers were also in widespread use by grocers for everything from cottage cheese to pickles.

There was shrimp, egg roll, chow mein and fried rice with assorted additional ingredients. The quantities were small. **There was no time for the usual Chinese feast.**

It was expected to be a long afternoon and most everyone in the courtroom made a trip to the rest rooms to wash up or whatever.

Again the bailiff called for everyone to rise. Judge Hollister made his entrance. He was tempted to make a crack about the lack of fortune cookies, but decided this would be an unnecessary frivolity on his part. Beneath his calm demeanor was a finely toned sense of humor. Many a judge had said, "This was almost as important as one's legal ability."

Now it was time for Lorie Owens to take the stand. Up until a week ago Lexus Taylor had felt all he needed to do was to break down her testimony. This had been his singular wall to climb. His defense strategy was now in shambles with the unexpected appearance of Della.

He had suggested Schank attempt to plea bargain on some lessor charge, but Schank was adamant that they go through with the preliminary hearing. Schank had been right only to the extent the prosecution might fire some of their big guns letting the defense know where their firepower was coming from.

Lorie was a fearful, reluctant witness. She was still deathly afraid of Schank. She had never been told of the second attempt on her life.

She was near a state of complete collapse, torn between the need to testify against Schank and her fear to leave the safety of the Tong.

She had even said to Delores, "You saved my life. Is there any way the Chinese can adopt me? I would be satisfied just to be a housekeeper without pay working at the Tong."

Those words had told the Chinese how scared she really was. That was why they had never told her about the second attempt on her life.

Lorie had to be helped to the stand. After she was sworn in and seated the District Attorney, in a soft gentle voice, began the questions she had been carefully coached to answer correctly. His staff had spent untold hours going over and over her projected testimony.

Additionally, Lorie and Delores had studied the questions repeatedly at the Tong. The big question was if she could maintain her composure.

She told how the romance was short and Schank became arbitrary, short-tempered and then hostile. As she was forced to recall and expand on his mean spirited actions she started to

292

break down. The judge was very sympathetic and said to the prosecutor, "I will excuse her from the stand if you request it."

The prosecutor looked at Lorie and said, "Did you hear the judge?"

"Yes, I did. Thank you for not forcing me to continue. Give me just a few moments. Those kind words will help me. I will try to continue."

Those words from the judge seemed to give Lorie Owens a second wind. The judge smiled to himself as Lorie's testimony seemed to increase in vigor. Then she said, "I overheard Schank discussing getting rid of me."

"Who was he talking to," asked the prosecutor.

"To Ruppert Snyder."

"I object. She cannot bring into her testimony a discussion between Schank and Ruppert. The defense has not put Ruppert or Schank on the stand."

"You are touching on too many elements of the law, Mr. Taylor. You know only too well the purpose of this hearing is to see if there is sufficient evidence to bind the defendant over for trial. **Let's not grasp for straws."**

Then the judge turned to Prosecutor Adams, saying, "Objection overruled. Let the witness continue with her testimony."

The prosecutor snickered to himself as he said, "Take your time Lorie, you were discussing the conversation you overheard. Tell us about it."

All I heard Schank say was, "I've got to get rid of her."

"What did Ruppert say to that?"

He said, "Do you want her sent to the same place as the last gal?"

Did you hear Schank's reply to that question?"

"Yes, I did, I heard it very clearly. He said, 'Don't be a fool. Not the same place. Some other country.'"

"Are you certain that is what you heard?"

"Clearly enough to frighten the life out of me."

"Did you question Schank about that later?"

"No, absolutely not. I had become so terrified of him that I didn't dare let him know I had overheard."

"Did that prompt you to do anything?"

"Yes, it certainly did! I knew I had to reach someone quick! I decided to risk all and talk to the Chinese steward and tell him I needed to be rescued."

"What was his reaction?"

"He said, 'I understand, Missy Owens. I do what I can.'"

"Did you discuss it further with the steward?"

"Maybe a week later there was a couple of moments when he was picking up the dishes and the guard, Sammy, seemed to be asleep. Schank was out of the car."

"What did the steward say?"

"He said, I remember it so clearly, I will remember it to my dying day, which I hope isn't too soon, **'Missy Owen, Cook send message for help.** May not be easy. Be very careful. Say nothing to provoke Schank.'"

"What was your reply to that?"

"I told him how grateful I was and that I would follow his advice."

"Then what happened?"

"Not long after that the two Chinese were gone and Choy and Wan took their place. Once in awhile I would get a brief message of encouragement from Choy. Then I was told to insist I go to the dinner with Schank. He said Delores, whom I had once met by accident, had insisted I come. Schank was very unhappy the Chinese were insisting, but I guess Schank was involved in some deal with the Chinese."

"Objection, Your Honor. This testimony is to stick to the facts, not a guessing game."

"I will agree to striking out the last sentence. The fact does exist that Schank did have a business deal going with the Chinese and that is why he went to the Pagoda that evening. My witness is accurate."

The judge pounded his gavel and said, "Strike the last sentence. I have read the police report and Schank had a meeting scheduled with the Chinese. Let's move ahead."

"I ask that the police report be admitted as part of the evidence."

"Does the attorney for the defense object to that?" asked the judge.

"I object."

"Objection overruled."

Prosecutor Adams looked at Lorie and then the Judge. He said, "Your Honor, I have no further questions for the witness at this time."

Then he moved his eyes back to Lorie and said, "Thank you, Lorie."

Then he turned to Lexus saying, "You may question the witness if you desire to."

Lexus moved slowly from his chair next to Schank to the witness stand. He paused, looked at Lorie, and said, "You were living with a married man weren't you? He did not force you to live with him. Isn't that correct?"

"Only the first part is correct. I met him at a club in Atlanta. He called me repeatedly and begged me to take a trip with him in his private car to Los Angeles. I asked him if he was married. He told me he was legally separated, that it was against his wife's religion to get divorced. That he would never live with her again. He told me I would have my own private bedroom on the train."

"That's enough. You have already testified to that. I wanted to emphasize the fact that you traveled with a married man. Now you falsely claim he would not let you go."

"I object, Your Honor. The witness has testified to the facts. Now all the defense attorney is trying to promote is a claim she was free to go. She has testified to the contrary."

"Objection sustained. If you wish to challenge any particular sentence or point you may do that, but to generalize and try to get her to throw her entire case out the window is wasting the time of the court."

"Yes, Your Honor. Miss Owens, while you were living with another woman's husband, taking trips all over the U.S. while she stayed at home by herself, didn't you feel remorse for your actions?"

"Yes, I have testified earlier that I did."

"You could have left couldn't you?"

"**That is not correct.** When I realized I should leave I was not permitted to leave. I agonized many nights as I lay locked in my room as to when I should have left and when I still could have."

With each sentence from Lorie, Lexus was realizing more and more the witness was not just a pretty lady with a pretty figure. She had let romance cloud her reason. Now her true intelligence was showing. **As he looked at Lorie he could see in her eyes the depth of her anguish.** He said to himself, "This woman isn't forgetting a thing.

"Her suffering has etched this into her mind so strongly I could badger her for the next hour and achieve nothing. I could easily get her to break down on the witness stand, but this isn't going to win me any points with Judge Hollister.

"More important it is not going to get the Judge to release Schank. He is going to be bound over. I have Lorie's story. We have achieved that."

Then out loud he said, "**The defense has no further questions for the witness.**"

A flood of relief crossed the face of Lorie. She found it hard to believe she was going to be excused from the witness stand. She bowed her head for a moment and said a silent prayer. She said to herself, "I brought this on myself. I consorted with a married man. If I ever get the chance to live a normal life again I'll do what I can to discourage anyone from making the same mistake."

She was numb as she rose from the stand and she started to stumble. The bailiff took her hand, steadied her and led her to her seat. **The Judge looked at Schank.**

Many thoughts coursed through the judge's mind. Most important were two things. First, it would be an easy decision to bind Schank over for trial. The second was that while justice was for everyone supposedly, here was a ruthless character who deserved the justice of the prairie — **a quick hanging at minimum expense to the taxpayer.**

Now the time had come for Della Robertson to be called to the witness stand. She had been as terrified as Lorie. Now that Lorie had finished she realized the sky would not fall on her either, but it would be rough.

Della said to herself, "I am not going to let Lorie down nor my Father. I am not going to let myself down. I have been through hell in that brothel. Nothing can equal that. Now I'm going to be the best darn witness who ever got into the witness box."

The bailiff offered his arm to her, but she declined. She took the oath and sat down. The prosecutor noticed the assurance on her face as did Lexus Taylor. Schank said to Lexus, "That gal is going to crucify us."

"Della, will you start out by telling how you met Schank?"

"At the same lounge in Atlanta that Lorie did."

"A remarkable coincidence. I could have the witness go into greater detail, but we are trying to conclude this matter today. Please tell the court what occurred after that."

"I could almost copy the first part of Lorie's testimony. I was pressured to take a trip on Schank's private rail car. Finally the glamour of traveling across the country in a private car was too much for me although I had refused at least a dozen times.

"**I also was promised it would just be a friendly trip.** No romance would be involved. I hardly got on the private car before he was making forceful passes at me."

Della continued in detail. At times the prosecutor had to get her back on track as she got too detailed. She concluded that part of her testimony by saying, "He went out of control in his actions with me. He forced me to submit to him. He swore, yelled and threatened me. **I began sassing him back and one day I woke up on a private plane.** I do not recall leaving the Schankrila. I presume I was drugged. I barely recall being forced on the plane. I was fed something and then felt myself passing out again.

"I faintly recall getting off the plane and being held firmly by men on either side of me. I soon found myself in a brothel and I was horrified. I was overtaken by terror."

Publicly describing it brought the terror back. Now it suddenly seemed Della was in a trance. As if she were hypnotized.

"I screamed. I cried. I tried to bribe them. I begged them to please turn me loose."

Now Della broke down. She cried and cried. "Oh it was awful! It was so awful! I wouldn't want any person to have to go through it! It was so degrading!"

Suddenly Della seemed to collapse. Off balance her body quickly rolled from the chair and fell to the floor. The bailiff rushed to her and the judge pounded his gavel saying, "Court will recess temporarily. Get first aid and a Doctor for the witness."

The attention of everyone in the courtroom was riveted on the fallen witness. Being forced to testify before the entire courtroom about those terrible days was too much for her. **Everyone hoped she had only fainted and not suddenly died from a heart attack.**

The drama of the scene was overwhelming everyone! The cameramen and reporters moved swiftly to the witness stand. People were standing in the courtroom to get a better view. Security rushed to the witness stand to cordon it off. **Bedlam was overtaking the courtroom.**

Above it all Judge Hollister was pounding his gavel and shouting, "Order in the courtroom, order in the courtroom. Just because I declared a recess doesn't permit the spectators to turn this into a circus. Everyone will quiet down or I will clear the courtroom."

The noise and bedlam seemed to simmer only slightly for just a few moments. Then it was as if the entire courtroom went out of control again.

The shocking drama could not have been more overwhelming and dramatic if it had been a movie. But this was for real. The prosecutor and his staff realized her testimony was as forceful as they might only have dreamed of.

Then above the noise of the courtroom came strange sounds. They started slowly and rose in crescendo as they became louder. They were weird, bizarre and almost ear drum breaking in intensity. For a brief moment they seemed to fall and then rose more forcefully, sharper and higher than before.

They were an eerie and alarming mixture of voices and screaming from the jungles of Papua, New Guinea. They became so great they were echoing off the walls of the small courtroom. Even the judge seemed to be transfixed.

The judge's gavel had not previously quieted the spectators, but these voices did. **Everyone in the courtroom was spellbound. Many spectators were afraid!**

Everyone was listening to these strange jungle- like sounds. One second they seemed to be proclaiming danger or challenge–a few seconds later they were mournful. Their pitch changed with such suddenness. The spectators were overcome with awe!

Only Lange and the Robertsons understood. The two Papuan natives were standing facing the witness stand where Della had just fallen.

The Papuan jungle was a place of quick reaction to danger and distress. More so during the war. The sounds coming from their lungs now were a combination of sorrow coupled with native ferocity as their boyhood pal's daughter had fallen to the floor. **In their own way they were proclaiming things had gone to hell and they didn't like it.**

Lange recognized the alert they had sounded. In seconds his mind transported him back to the dozens of narrow beaches that adjoined the dense jungle on the thousand mile long island of New Guinea.

He was a dogface again with the 41st Infantry Division. He had learned many of those native sounds and had often called to the Papuans during the War.

All the king's horses, nor the judge, the bailiff nor security could not hold him back now. Lange had risen, as if in a trance, and his voice joined the two natives. He raised both arms giving familiar signals of not all that many years ago.

Lange became grim, tense and alert. Terror and danger were everywhere. Now Lange could hear the Robertsons voices as well. **One Papuans turned for a second, to make certain it was Lange.**

Then came their sound of welcome. He recognized it instantly. It was their special words for friendship which he had exchanged with many Papuans when they were so far apart he could hardly see them. The voices were becoming virtually deafening in intensity.

Suddenly there was a shot. Then a second, a third, a fourth and a fifth in rapid succession. Then there was a sixth sound Lange could barely hear. It sounded like something metallic had hit the floor. The Native voices continued for awhile — then began to wane.

**Everyone froze for a few seconds
and then tried to hit the deck.**

There wasn't room for all the spectators to lay flat on the floor, so many crouched in terror. The guards drew their revolvers worrying that any gunfire would put the spectators in a crossfire. Many spectators were screaming and yelling. Some were crying in terror! **"We're all going to be killed!"**

Lt. Brown had left the courtroom to get a Doctor for Della and he was just re-entering. Brown yelled at the Doctor, "Get back out of the courtroom until I find out what's happening."

The scene Lt. Brown observed was strange. He saw Reginald being moved by his wife and a Chinese toward the witness box. The Papuans were standing and so was Lange.

The Chinese were talking and gesturing, but didn't appear to be panicking. Virtually everyone else was crouched on the floor.

Several guards had their handguns ready to fire. Only now were the cameramen turning their attention to the main body of the courtroom.

Then Lt. Brown saw beyond the spectators a scene he had never observed in a courtroom before. Two men were lying immediately adjacent to the defense table. Blood was streaming from them onto the floor. Lt. Brown was afraid to move toward them.

He knew there was a mad gunman in the room. But where was he-or she-or them?

Were they crouched on the floor among all the spectators ready to fire again?

Then a guard near the front of the courtroom shouted, "There's a gun near the bodies. Cover me and I'll go for it."

For a moment Lt. Brown wondered–was it a murder and suicide? Had Schank perhaps killed Lexus Taylor and then killed himself?

Brown watched the guard move to where the gun was lying. He picked it up police style and carefully opened the cylinder. It took him only one second to glance at the primers and see all the cartridges were spent.

"Lt. Brown, I counted five shots-this weapon has just fired five."

Lt. Brown turned to the rear door of the courtroom where the Doctor was slightly visible. "O.K. Dr. Blake–it's up to you- do you want to risk going forward now?"

Doc Blake had interned in the field during World War II. His big one was the Battle of the Bulge where he was under constant enemy fire as he operated.

"I'm coming, Lieutenant," he yelled as he grabbed his medical bag and dashed to Lt. Brown. Another officer joined them as they dashed to where Schank and Taylor were lying.

Dr. Blake quickly checked if either man still had a pulse. **"They are both alive!** Get an ambulance. Meanwhile get me the courtroom emergency medical supplies."

Lt. Brown started to say something and the Doctor snapped, "Just shut up and follow my instructions. These guys took more than one shot. **They are bleeding like hell.**"

It was a grim Doctor as he and Lt. Brown worked feverishly to stop the blood flowing from both men. In minutes he and Brown were virtually covered with blood from the blood gushing from the victims.

Two ambulances arrived. Dr. Blake yelled to the attendants, "No diagnostics now, just try to stop the blood flow and let's move them fast to the hospital. **Sorry, I can only go with one of the ambulances. They both need help real bad!**"

.

CHAPTER 49
THE PRELIMINARY HEARING IS OVER.

Right after the shots were fired Lt. Brown had observed a Chinese lady, Mrs. Robertson and Reginald in his wheelchair headed toward Della. Brown's quick mind only had time to conclude that was going to get them away from the spectators and perhaps out of the center of a further gun battle.

As she neared her fallen daughter she noticed the first aid man had resuscitated Della. Mrs. Robertson began coughing violently and clutching her abdomen. She appeared almost incoherent as she neared the first aid man, "I hope I can make it to the rest room."

"Right this way, ma'am," as he and the Chinese lady helped Mrs. Robertson.

Inside Mrs. Robertson moved to toilet stall, closed the door and shortly thereafter the toilet flushed. Then it was flushed several more times as she continued coughing.

The first aid man sent a matron to the ladies room. She found Mrs. Robertson very shaken. She appeared very weak as she exclaimed, "I think I can make it. I must see my daughter now."

"Yes ma'am, we'll help you. Do you need a Doctor?"

"Let's wait a few minutes. I'm in shock. A Mother and wife can stand only so much! If Della had just stayed in Australia. "

"I understand how you feel, Mrs. Robertson. America isn't always the beautiful."

As the courtroom doors closed behind the stretcher Brown knew it was now his ball game. First, however, he looked at the Judge, both men knowing it was still Judge Hollister's courtroom.

Hollister strode back to his bench, grabbed his gavel, and pounded it several times. "Order in the court. Order in the court."

That command was hardly necessary. The spectators were some place between total shock and panic. The judge continued with, "This preliminary hearing is hereby canceled and courtroom proceedings for today are declared over.

"I am turning the courtroom over to Lt. Alex Brown who will give all orders for the rest of the day and from whom you must obtain permission before leaving. Do I make myself absolutely clear on that?"

With that he strode from the bench and walked over to Della, Lorie and Delores. He tried to look reassuring. "Della and Lorie, you have my deepest sympathy. And I don't care if anyone quotes me. Best wishes and good luck."

"Thank you, Judge Hollister," they replied in unison.

The Judge gave them a bow and turned around as he headed for his chambers.

Lt. Brown thought to himself he's passing the buck to me, but I know from old Harry Truman the buck really stops with the Chief of the LAPD.

He commanded one of the officers, "Try to get the Chief down here and more detectives."

Then Brown went to work. "Everyone stay exactly where you are. No movement whatsoever. The officers here will keep you covered."

Brown continued, "Did anyone here see anyone actually fire a gun?"

There was no answer to that question.

Immediately Brown said in a loud voice, "Who observed anything of value?"

There were several hands raised and Brown moved toward them.

It didn't take Brown long to conclude there was a strong possibility the shots came from the vicinity of the Robertsons and the Chinese in the front side rows. No one admitted they actually saw anyone do any shooting.

Brown's mind was racing. It would have been virtually impossible for someone to have done the shooting from one of the back rows. Could the shooting have come from the sidelines? Maybe someone had slipped a gun to Ruppert Snyder and he did it?

Had Lexus been carrying a gun and Schank had taken it away from him during the Papuan's war cries, and done the shooting?

He realized the wounded men had been moved, so establishing a line of fire right off the bat was impossible. Did any of the bullets penetrate through the bodies and lodge someplace solid so a line of fire could be established?

He called to the Sergeant that had the revolver. When he reached Brown he whispered, "Check it for fingerprints. Right now. I have to know the answer."

It was obvious to him he must interrogate the Robertsons, the Papuans and the Chinese. First his eyes sought out the Robertsons and he moved to them.

"Can you step aside, please, while I ask you a few questions?"

Mrs. Robertson, in her fast, Aussie accent filled with Aussie slang that Lt. Brown didn't fully understand said, "I'm afraid my husband and daughter come first. Right now you're more worried over who tried to kill Schank and his attorney than you are about my daughter and my husband who were almost killed by Schank."

Those words hit Lt. Brown squarely on his chin. He could feel those facts reach his heart and soul. He looked at Della's Mother not knowing how to answer those challenging words. He tried to maintain his outward composure.

"He went to the bailiff and whispered, "Has Mrs. Robertson been here all the time since she and her husband left their seats?"

"No, sir, she was coughing and clutching her stomach and crying to go to the ladies room. A Chinese lady and myself helped her. Then I sent a matron to check on her."

Lt. Brown had a sudden sinking feeling. He knew any search of the Robertsons and the Chinese lady would reveal nothing. Any evidence against them would be down the toilet and into the vast Los Angeles sewer system.

Then instead of being extremely angry at the bailiff he thought to himself that Justice should have it's day at least occasionally. <u>Otherwise criminals would run amuck, which they were almost doing anyway.</u>

He was headed back to where the Chinese were standing. He did an about face and walked back to the Robertsons.

"Mrs. Robertson, I don't expect to find anything, but routine police procedure makes it necessary for both you and the Chinese lady to submit to a search. Please wait for our instructions."

Mrs. Robertson snapped back, <u>"Perhaps the Ghost of the Jolly Swag man did it."</u>Look him up in Waltzing Matilta, soon to be our National Anthem."

Lt. Brown did not reply. He did another about face heading back to the Chinese.

Was Mrs. Robertson part of a plot and she was taunting him now?

<u>Brown tried to engage the Chinese in a meaningful discussion,</u> but it was obvious they were not going to be cooperative. <u>One would say something–then another would take the direct opposite view and argue.</u> He thought, **"Are they playing games with me, too?"**

Half the time they were talking Chinese and when they were speaking English it was obvious they were pretending they could hardly pronounce the words.

Finally Brown said, "I am going to risk my newly acquired gold bar and not have Ah Wing and Wang Sing searched, but the rest of you including Lange are going to be searched. "

Ah Wing replied, "Thank you, Lt. Brown, for your intended courtesy, but we do not want favoritism."

Wang Sing, who had a fine sense of humor jumped in with, "Hope we all had good sense to wear clean underwear today. I had bad vibes this morning and wore my very best with gold Chinese Dragons on them."

Lange laughed, "You know I wore my best too, but may not come back to this town again. Have you checked the rest rooms, Lt. Brown? The gunman may be hidden there."

Lt. Brown looked at Lange – and broke into serious laughter. Then he suddenly stopped laughing as he thought of how Mrs. Robertson and the Chinese lady may have already snookered him.

Lange thought everyone was laughing as they remembered how several weeks ago he had first suspected the phony doctors in the Los Angeles General Hospital rest room.

That wasn't the case at all. The Chinese were still laughing– but Lt. Brown wasn't.

The interrogations of the spectators continued and Ruppert Snyder, the Chinese, the Robertsons and Lange were searched- in private, of course.

Tests indicated one Chinese had fired a gun recently and an elated officer brought the news immediately to Lt. Brown and the Chief who had arrived with several other officers including the Chief of detectives.

His enthusiasm was short lived as tests indicated several others had telltale residue. Least surprising was the same results were found on the hands of Mrs. Robertson. **The officers were beginning to smell a very devious plot.**

No other evidence was found on anyone.

A most serious session was held involving the Chief, Lt. Brown, the head of the Detective Bureau and the inspecting officers.

The officer in charge of the revolver stated positively, "There are no fingerprints on the weapon. The serial number on the weapon has been carefully obliterated.

"We haven't submitted any fired shells to tie them in with the gun, but it has to be the same gun. <u>Obviously whoever fired this weapon was wearing some kind of a glove."</u>

Lt. Brown countered with, "Or else was a gun expert. There are several possibilities."

The chief said, "Go back and do the palm tests again."

When the tests had been run again the evidence was inconclusive. Every detective was given the opportunity to vent his suggestions and suspicions.

The Chief reluctantly concluded, "Release everyone."

Wang Sing sought out Lange and informed him they would welcome him for dinner at the Pagoda. "I'm very tempted, but I think I'll drive to Ventura, have dinner there and then it's only an hour more to Santa Barbara. I really need to be at work tomorrow morning."

"I understand and we are all very tired. The events of today have taken a great mental toll from all of us."

Lange went over and said good-bye to Delores Lee and said he had turned down an invitation from Wang.

"Lorie and Della have been pressed beyond the human endurance level. We are going to take Della to the Tong with Lorie. Perhaps the two ladies staying together can rehabilitate each other. I suspect each will be medicine for the other."

"I know you're right. They've been through the war with Schank. Just like two Army veterans who fought in the same battle. They are comrades-in-arms."

"That is our thinking, Lange. I hope it works. They do need more help–right now."

Lt. Brown had called the hospital and announced Schank and Lexus were still alive, both in extremely critical condition. Their vital organs had been severely damaged. Schank had been hit three times and Lexus twice. If either survived they could be badly crippled for life. The duty officer complained, "The press is driving us nuts."

CHAPTER 50
BACK TO SANTA BARBARA.

Lange in his blue coupe was soon on Hiway 101 headed west to the beautiful Pacific and the town of Ventura where he hoped Sally Stevens was on duty as a waitress. Again he struck out. She was not on duty. He went for the cook's famous chicken dinner and decided he was so tired he would not try to reach Sally at home.

News of the shooting of Schank and Lexus spread like wildfire. Associated Press and United Press teletype machines clattered in hundreds of cities across the country. The Santa Barbara police were being called by media all over the U.S. The local News-Press and local radio stations exerted all the pressure they could.

The local stations interrupted their programs to bring their listeners up to date.

Dr. Smith got the news before Martha did. He called her immediately. "Martha, have you been listening to the radio or had any calls ?"

"No, Dr. Smith," she said in the formal tone he had suggested she use as unknown others might pick up the phone in his office.

"I'd like to see you right now, but I can't. It will take me at least an hour before I can break away."

311

"What's happened, Dr. Smith, you don't sound like anything bad has occurred. In fact you sound a little elated."

"You can't fool a beautiful, intelligent lady. Can any man?
News has come in that Cal Schank and his attorney were shot at the Preliminary Hearing in Los Angeles."

"I'm speechless, Emery. Were they hurt badly?"

"Apparently they are still alive, but in critical condition. One theory is that Schank shot Lexus and then shot himself. The police are not talking.

"Martha, I can be free in not much over an hour. I can be with you by about 5:30. Why don't you not answer your phone, or turn on any radio news. Just wait until I get there. Then we'll turn on the news together. In the long haul I have medical friends in Los Angeles."

"Oh Emery, it is so shocking. Thank you for calling. I'll just wait for you."

As soon as he hung up Dr. Emery Smith said to himself, "The wheels of justice seem to be grinding Schank more and more. I sure am curious about his condition, but it will be wise for me to wait another couple of hours. Give the medics time for a firmer conclusion."

After they hung up Dr. Smith called his nurse, "Don't take any more appointments for me, emergency or not. I'm leaving in an hour."

His nurse, who had been with him for years, knew something major had come up. She could tell by the tone of his voice it was not a disaster. She was very curious.

"What's happened, Dr. Smith ?"

"Cal Schank and his attorney have been shot and seriously wounded at the Preliminary Hearing in Los Angeles this afternoon. The Santa Barbara police must have been psychic when they requested Martha go into hiding. It was a wise move."

In another part of Santa Barbara, in the beautiful Montecito area with it's hundreds of huge estates another scene was taking place. Tony G. was listening to the news and let out a whoop and a string of profanity. His wife who was in the next room hurried to where her husband was. "Good news, dear?"

"Yeh, good news. I feel like going out and celebrating."

He thought to himself, "I sure hope they croak. I'll be off the hook for my men botching the attempt to assassinate Lorie."

Then suddenly he remembered, "Damn it, I still have the Chinese to square with!"

"Tell me about it," asked his wife.

"You know our deal. I never discuss business with you."

"Are you going out for a drink with some of your friends ?"

"Yeh, I'm going to make me a call or two. I'll have dinner with you first. Then I'll be going out."

"Are you going to be gone for a long time?"

"No, just a couple hours."

"I'll read in bed until you get back."

Tony G. made two calls and then called one of his bodyguards to say after dinner he wanted to go out for a couple of hours. At dinner that evening Tony could not help but gloat over the shooting at the trial.

Finally after the cook had served his favorite roast beef and potatoes and had left the dining room, Tony said to his wife, "Babe, you're going to hear the news anyhow. Cal Schank and his attorney were shot at the Preliminary Hearing for Schank. They're in bad shape."

His wife knew only Tony had the right to an opinion in their house. She asked, "Tony, dear, is that good or bad?"

"Well, you know I don't discuss business."

"You seem so happy."

"Maybe it's just my good day today."

Just after dark had set-in and a little fog was coming in from the nearby ocean he called one bodyguard and said he was ready.

Soon the big green Packard appeared in the circular driveway with two men in the front seat, both bodyguards. One bodyguard stepped out as they approached the gate, opened it, let the car through, locked it and re-entered the Packard.

All the large estates in Montecito were secluded by masses of tropical foliage, including tall eucalyptus and pepper trees, along winding streets and narrow lanes.

Tony G. was spirited and jovial and his bodyguards knew they should respond in kind. The Packard turned and twisted as it wound through Montecito often taking sharp turns.

As they were making the last sharp turn before the narrow road straightened **a non-descript vehicle with four men inside appeared from behind large foliage.** It didn't make any attempt to slow down or turn. It hit the Packard broadside like one of the small cars they rent at amusement parks that smash into each other for thrills.

The Packard went over the ridge, rolling end over end, bursting into flames as it hit the bottom of the canyon.

One man got out of the other car and watched. Then he glanced at the double bumper on his car and smiled. He quickly stepped inside and the car moved swiftly and almost noiselessly away. One man remarked, "If we hadn't gotten a bug planted in his pal's apartment we'd never have known."

Another man said, "How did the bumper hold up?"

"Just like we expected it to. Take it off and the car is like new. They ought to make them standard on all cars."

"That was a great idea we came up with. I still remember bumper cars I used to ride as a kid at Jantzen Beach in Portland."

The other two men in the car smiled, but said nothing. **The four horsemen drove to an estate a few miles away,** where they moved quickly through the iron gate, the only entrance into the high walled property.

They moved their car into a garage. They then walked to another garage and entered another car. It had been backed in so they did not need to back out. One man walked ahead to the gate and inserted his key.

They passed through the gate and waited until it closed automatically and the fourth man entered the car. Then the vehicle wound through the roads in Montecito passing hundreds of beautiful estates visible as ghosts through the night darkened further by light fog.

Then it turned onto highway 101 going south on it's way to Los Angeles. One man switched the radio to the police band. The news was coming through. The flames had alerted neighbors. **It was a Packard, maybe green. It was not known if there were any survivors.**

CHAPTER 51
RUPPERT SNYDER IN HIS LOS ANGELES CELL.

Ruppert Snyder thought he might be a witness for the defense at the Preliminary Hearing. Now back in his cell he pondered what would happen next.

The next day he had an unexpected visitor. **He agreed to see the Chinese man.**

When they were seated in the visitor's area the Chinese man reached in his pocket and took out a fortune cookie which had already been broken apart. Inside it had the usual small slip of paper. He handed the broken cookie and the tiny piece of paper to Ruppert.

Then he said, "I find this slip in this fortune cookie. My name is not Ruppert Snyder so I bring it to you thinking I am doing you big favor."

Ruppert took the offering and read, "Time for Ruppert Snyder to confess all."

"Who told you to come in and threaten me."

The small Chinese stood up and spoke to the Guard. "It is time for me to leave. I have delivered Mr. Snyder's message."

The Chinese man left, and Ruppert was ushered back to his cell by one of the guards. **As he sat in his cell,** he said to himself, "If Schank dies maybe I have a chance. I know where a lot of money is hidden. But what about that damn Tony G.?"

Each morning the guard came by Ruppert Snyder's cell with a copy of the LA Times morning edition. Ruppert demanded it each day, so the guard saved time this way. Ruppert extended his hand through the bars with the money. Ruppert first scanned the front page news. On page two there was a small headline. **"Three men killed in flaming car accident in Montecito.** He eagerly continued. "The burned vehicle was a Packard, very likely green."

"That might be Tony G's car, " was the thought that ignited his pulse, and caused it to begin racing. "With Tony G. out of the way, if I ever get out life will be simpler for me. I know damn well he was going to take over Schank's operation."

The article caused Ruppert's mind to do an overview type of mind scan. "Let's see, I don't know who kidnapped me in Santa Barbara. I was on the floor of the back compartment of the vehicle, but I kept counting the turns and I think they took me to Montecito. At least when we left I'm sure we came off the Montecito hills and headed South on the coast hiway.

"I've asked myself a hundred times if Tony G. had a hand in that. Now that Tony G. might have taken a hit that means for certain someone doesn't like him, and doesn't like me.

I keep thinking the Chinese are involved. Maybe they hired someone to do it. That Dr. Fu is a power to be reckoned with. Too bad I didn't realize this a few years ago."

Just then the guard appeared and opened Ruppert's cell and Lt. Alex Brown walked in and the guard locked the metal bars that served as a door.

Lt. Brown looked at Snyder and said, "Are you having fun? I see you're concentrating on page two of the Times. Nice story, isn't it?"

"I don't know what you're talking about. I just turned to page two."

Lt. Brown snatched the paper from Ruppert, looked him in the eye, "You liar. I've been watching you read it. You were concentrating so hard I asked the guard to slow down so we could watch you. Tell me what were you reading on page two?"

"O.K. so you win. I was reading about the green Packard."

"And your buddies that took the hit?"

"No buddies of mine. I never heard of them before."

"You scum. You know who they were and so do I. They were the big honchos that engineered the hits on Lorie. That cost them four dead and one injured and captured. He has confessed all."

"You're lying to me. He would never confess."

Lt. Brown took his foot and skillfully put his toe under the bottom rung of Ruppert's chair. Then he yanked his foot, and the chair turned over backwards, sending Ruppert sprawling.

"Don't ever accuse me of lying again," said Brown as he stood over Ruppert with clenched firsts.

"You can't hit a man that's down, Lieutenant."

"Let's go back to Tony G. The flameout of the Packard took out Tony and two more of his men. That's seven out of eight dead, and one in jail. Not bad for our side."

"So what do you want from me?"

"It's very simple. I understand you got a fortune cookie yesterday."

"So that was a setup?"

"LAPD had nothing to do with that. Merely Chinese having cute way of saying, 'Either you confess now, or your future is over.' Do you get it?

"I want a complete confession from you and agreement you will answer all our future questions as well. You've got the Chinese and the Aussies against you. And I hate your guts."

"Gimme a little more time to think it over."

Lt. Brown stood up and moved toward Snyder with both of his fists clenched.

Ruppert quickly sat down. "You can't hit a man sitting down."

This time Lt. Brown gave the chair a shove with his foot sending Snyder sprawling across the floor again. Lt. Brown stood above him with his fists clenched.

"O.K., you guys win. I was just stalling. I was going to confess."

Lt. Brown had Ruppert move into what was at times called 'the confession room.' The furnishings were not so austere. Lt. Brown knew this confession was going to be so far-reaching he must personally guide Ruppert through it.

"I'll start by asking the most important questions. **Where is the money hidden."**

"Bank of America, Security Pacific, Wells-Fargo and a dozen other banks."

"Where is the big box with the real records?"

"North Hollywood Branch of Bank of America."

"Under what name ?"

"Under my name. I don't trust no one, but myself."

"We can get a court order, but instead we'll just have you sign a release. **Now who was Schank's contact when he sent Della to South America ?"**

"The guy that owned the Packard."

"You and Schank had such nice friends! Now start at the beginning and describe your operation. I'll interrupt when I want more information."

"Hey, that's going to take a long time."

"That's only because your outfit messed into so many lives. You've got the time now."

"I promise you I wanted to get out."

"Like the song, you stinking rat, 'We got the time and you got the money.'"

It was a long tedious session and sandwiches and coffee were brought in. As Ruppert got well into the first hour Brown was shocked at the virtually unlimited scope of Schank's activities. Brown complimented Ruppert on his ability to go in so many directions.

Fisherman Brown smiled to himself as Ruppert's ego took the bait and Ruppert went into even more detail. Neither man knew Schank was on the verge of replacing Ruppert because the irons he had in the fire were beyond Ruppert's ability to stay on top of them.

When all the papers were signed and initialed Lt. Brown went directly to the Chief. "I know who I need to call and I should do it now."

As the chief started to read Brown interrupted with, "Just give me your O.K. to go ahead. This is too hot to delay."

Reluctantly the chief agreed. "This is big time stuff. Schank's death won't clear up this dynamite. It's your baby, Brown, and I don't need to tell you how top secret this is. You report to me only. I'll clear it with the chief of detectives. He won't like to be left out."

Lt. Brown immediately went to a private line and began calling the various agencies that must be alerted. Each in one way or another had Schank Investment Co on their list.

Now they could close in. This was the break they needed. They would begin setting up the scaffolds and **this time make certain the hanging took place.**

CHAPTER 52
THE NEWS MEDIA.

The news media continued their relentless barrage of questions as to the condition of Schank and Lexus. The hospital staff and the police told them to stuff it, but that suggestion fell on deaf ears.

Even the Chinese were losing their cool. Ah Wing felt like he had loosed a giant dragon that was relentlessly swinging it's tail, as it breathed fire in all directions. They were all feeling the dragon's heat.

In this case the beast was the press, who often played that role to perfection. It was obvious that neither schools of journalism, nor newspapers, could force all reporters to take the time to be reasonable and ask intelligent questions.

Their brilliance was illustrated by questions such as, "What will happen to Schank and Lexus if they recover?" "Will they recover?" "What will happen to Ruppert Snyder?"

The press often had concluded that the first order of business for law and order was to listen to their idle chatter and harassment. They would demand conclusions when none had been arrived at. Their lives were dedicated to chasing the 'Big S.' **The more Scandal the better!**

Bulletins were demanded from the hospital at all hours of the day and night even though there were no new developments.

"We should do like the politicians do and give them some statement that doesn't make any sense. They wouldn't know the difference."

So a couple of the Doctors sat down and came up with one. They wrote, "The intensity of the wounds have caused violent reactions on the two men. That means they are very sick men. Immediate conjecture would be only temporary."

The reporters dashed to the nearest telephones. Sure enough both the news services and the newspaper headlines acclaimed, "Men very sick."

The doctors laughed and laughed. They said, "Maybe we could turn this ridiculous situation into some fun. After all the politicians have gotten very skilled at saying nothing."

A second Doctor laughed and said, "Hey, don't forget about the lawyers."

A third replied, "Most of the big time politicians are lawyers."

Three more reports came from the hospital that day. Each time they were handed out by a solemn faced Doctor, with an equally solemn faced nurse standing attentively by his side.

After the third devious report that day, Dr. Adolph said to the nurse who suddenly started to giggle, " Annette, we're going to have to replace you. Don't you have a serious bone in your body?"

"Don't be so mean, Dr. Adolph, aren't we having fun?"

On the other side of the coin were the truly professional journalists and reporters who took to the media and airways with constructive analysis and suggestions.

The subject of: WHO DID IT? provided a field day for sleuths ranging from reporters to mystery story writers to the common citizen who loved mystery stories and novels.

The courtroom scene was being discussed and cussed and of course the LAPD was placed under great pressure to let the public know what did happen. They wanted Perry Mason, M. Piorot and Charlie Chan on the scene immediately.

The LAPD was looking pretty good, however. All the assassination attempts had been foiled and the assailants had all been killed except the one captured.

The Chief and Lt. Brown had decided to keep secret the fact that Ruppert had confessed. They were buying time by not alerting anyone.

Several journalists expounded on the trial funds Los Angeles County would save by the likely death of Schank and Lexus, giving more money for things like schools.

However, the big news the public wanted was about the Robertsons and Lorie Owens. What connection did the Chinese have to all of this?

There was a great public clamor that the Robertsons should not be questioned further and should be given free passage back to Australia. Also, first claim on any of Schank's assets go to them as well as to Lorie.

It was even suggested that if any charges were placed against them this time the entire Australian Navy should go to their rescue.

Polls were taken of former Army Infantrymen, Marines, Navy, Air Force and Merchant Mariners and the results were unanimous, "Let the Robertsons go. They have suffered enough. **Give a Silver Star to whoever shot Schank.**"

CHAPTER 53
MARTHA, DR. SMITH AND BOB SCHANK

That evening, which was the second evening after Schank and Lexus were shot, Martha and Dr. Smith again were having dinner at Martha's hideaway.

In the middle of dinner his answering service called. "You have a call from LA, but the man said just to tell you Bert called."

"Thanks, I'll return it right away."

"Martha, I have a call from LA. Maybe a little more news."

When he reached his Physician buddy the conversation was short, **"Lexus has expired.** The two shots did too much damage for him to survive. One was too close to his heart. "

"What's the latest on Schank?"

"He's hanging in there, but not for long. Could go anytime. Might last a couple of days more. We've had him in surgery three times, but it's no use. His body indicates as a youth he was very muscular and strong. He obviously led a soft life of recent years and those three bullets hit him in the wrong places.

Whoever fired them was a mighty good shot. All three hit his chest. Same thing with the two that hit Lexus. Those slugs were at least police grade ammunition."

When Dr. Smith hung up he repeated the story to Martha.

"I don't want to see him. Does that sound heartless to you?"

"If you asked my advice I wouldn't want you to go near him."

"Emery, I've been spending some time thinking about whatever accumulation of wealth Schank has. I suppose I could claim half of it."

"I'm sure you can, Martha."

Dr. Smith said no more as he knew Martha had come to some conclusion.

"I don't want to ever live in the estate again. **I don't want to lay claim to anything.** After any funds are used to correct what injustices are correctable, **I would like to assign the entire balance to various crippled children's hospitals.**

"As to the Schankrila, many years ago I enjoyed its luxury for a half dozen trips. It is such a beautiful private rail way car. But I could never set foot in it again.

"Perhaps I could donate it to someone that will maintain it and provide six months free use per year for crippled children, who would benefit by a ride on a train.

"Doctors and nurses could also volunteer to take care of the children and the special facilities, including the small kitchen, would make this more feasible. I don't want any of Schank's ill gotten gains."

Dr. Smith looked at Martha. "I see you have thought it out well. It makes good sense, but what about Bob, your son ?"

"It's time for him to grow up. If he has any assets left after he gets out of prison he can live off of them. It's terrible for me, too. I raised a criminal."

"Your husband overpowered him."

"Thank you, but I must bear part of the blame."

"Let's go to something good we can do. It appears Cal will be dead in a few days. **We could get married next week!"**

"Could we, Emery? We could spend our nights together–all our time! Oh Emery, let's do it as soon as we can."

Martha wrapped her arms around his neck and kissed him.

In his cell in the Santa Barbara jail Bob Schank kept asking for the latest newspapers. No only the local Santa Barbara News-Press, but the Los Angeles Times as well. He mind would return to the night Ruppert became missing.

When he was found, Ruppert, his Dad and he had been arrested.

His Dad had been so worried over Tony G. muscling in and now the article in the paper about the flaming crash in Montecito involving a green Packard and the death of it's three occupants. So Tony G. didn't turn out to be his Dad's nemesis.

His Dad has been shot. By whom? The police weren't issuing reports on that. There were insinuations that his Dad had shot Lexus and then himself. Would his Dad do that?

Bob turned to thoughts about his Mother. There was something about a Mother most men wanted to protect. But did I? No, I didn't protect my Mother. I have disgraced her. Just then the guard said, **"Bob, your Mother is here to see you."**

As Bob entered the small room his Mother was seated in he could tell she was a little happier than on her last visit. "You're looking better, Mother."

"Thanks, Bob. You do notice! How are you doing?"

"Same old regrets, but if I had the chance to do it over I'd likely do the same thing. I took easy street–it was a bum street."

"It was, Son! Why don't you confess and throw yourself on the mercy of the court?"

"I can't, Mother. Until I met Tony G. and realized the power he had on Dad I really didn't understand Dad was only part of a giant web. I'm safer right here, Mother.

"Mother, tell me how you are doing without me."

"The bad news is it seems your Dad is only going to last a few more days at the most."

Bob looked crestfallen. "I didn't know that for certain."

"And, Dr. Smith and I plan to be married as soon as I am free of your Father."

Bob just sat there.

Finally Martha said, "Son, are you objecting?"

"No, of course not, Mother. I am very pleased. Your turn for happiness has been delayed too long. I can't look after you now."

Then he spoke loudly, **"THE EVIL EMPIRE OF CAL SCHANK"**

He paused, looked at his Mother. <u>"Assisted by his no damn good son, Bob Schank."</u>

Martha was sitting across a small table from Bob. **She buried her head in her hands.**

CHAPTER 54
LANGE AND MAUDE MAYBERRY.

The very next day Lange received a phone call from the Title Company. "We are calling you to advise you the mortgage is off and clear title is now in Maude Mayberry's name. "Would you be so kind as to check with her if she wants a title policy? When her Dad received title only an Abstract of Title was used to check the title."

Lange responded with, "Please go ahead and order the policy and I'll sign it. I have her Power of Attorney."

Lange sat there stunned with the good news. He asked himself, "Was it a slip up on the part of the government, or the Title Company?"

In the midst of his surprise Jean, the office secretary, buzzed him. He picked up his phone. A man introduced himself as Daniel from the West Coast Regional Office of A.T. & T.

"I understand from Hank, one of the Treasury Agents, you are managing the affairs of Maude Mayberry. Is that correct?"

"Yes, I'm the one."

"The Treasury Department and our office have spent a lot of time on this as we understand Maude is penniless."

"She is in desperate need of funds."

"Not any longer! We have gone way back into missing stockholder records. Her Father's name is of record. I understand he is deceased, as well as her Mother."

"That is correct. The title company researched this when she received title."

"Here is the news. Hold onto your hat, Lange. Her Dad's stock is worth around $75,000.00"

"How wonderful!"

"That's not all the good news. There is about $25,000.00 additional in dividends due her. They have been accumulating interest, which brought it to that total. We can send her that money anytime she requests it."

"You are telling me that Maude has $75,000.00 worth of A.T. & T. stock plus $25,000 in accrued dividends due her?"

"Exactly correct, Mr. Lange. We would recommend that you set up some kind of a trust account for her at one of the major banks."

"Could you maybe send her a check for a few bucks, like tonight? Could you send it Air Mail? By the way, one of my long term family friends is Richard Lawrence, in your actuarial department. Say hello for me."

"I know Richard well. He's been with us for years. I'll get a check for $500.00 out tonight via Special Delivery Air Mail. It should be in Maude's hands tomorrow. Nice to talk to you and bring good news!"

Lange got up from his chair and walked to the office where Jean was seated. **"Jean, would you pinch me?** Am I just dreaming? Surely, I misunderstood."

"The boss is out. **If you'll lean over my desk I'll give you a little kiss."**

"Then I'll know for sure I'm dreaming."

"Come on, Lange. Don't keep me in suspense. Tell me what's happened."

"It's not about me. It wonderful news for someone else. I must wait until tomorrow when the letter of confirmation comes in. Oh Jean, it makes me so happy I could hug you."

"Say, buddy, since when does it take good news for someone else to get you to want to hug me."

"Oh, oh! Sorry, Jean, if I blew it. Give me 24 hours and you'll understand."

"That's all you're getting. Just 24 hours."
Then she winked at him, and went back to her work.

After work Lange went directly to Maude's apartment.
First he asked her if she had any sherry left. She did and she
poured a small glass for each of them. "Take a good sip of it,
Maude. I have some very good news for you!"

"In the last couple of days, Lad, I haven't been seeing much
of you, but I have been having very pleasant dreams. **I wake
during the night and I've been with Mum and Dad.** They tell
me me worries are over.

"I'm going to move into a nicer place and I'm going to travel
in style to England. I'll be able to take two of me housekeeping
friends with me for company. Do ye ever dream such strange
dreams, Lad?"

"The ones I hate are the bad ones. Like I'm back in the
Infantry in New Guinea. Maude, tell me a little more about the
dreams you have been having."

**As Maude related more details Lange had an eerie feeling
come over him.** It was as if they were not alone. He was drawn
to the picture of Maude's Mother and Dad on the wall.

He'd read of experiences folks had attending a seance. The
picture of Maude's parents seemed to glow. **Apprehension
gripped him** as he realized there was a light shining on it.

Then her parents seemed to look directly at him. Their lips
parted and they said,

"Thanks for looking after Maude. You're in Santa Barbara
for many reasons, but Maude is one of the most important. **She
is all we really had in this world.**"

He felt their presence so strongly. As if they actually were in
the room.

He heard himself reply, "You sent for me to look after your
daughter, Maude? **Yes, I promise I will.**"

The light faded. "Son, did you see a light over my Mum and
Dad's picture?"

"Did you see one, too, Maude?"

"Just for a moment, Lad. Did I hear you say something to me just as the light faded? I must have been so busy looking I did not pay attention to what ye was sayin'. Maybe even one glass of sherry is too much for me."

Maude and Lange continued discussing what each had observed. Finally Lange said, "I know you don't read much, but for the last ten years of his life Sir Arthur Conan Doyle, writer of the Sherlock Holmes stories, traveled the world lecturing on matters like this. I had an identical experience to one Doyle experienced."

"Ye did, Lad?"

"Maude, what you dreamed of is coming true."

Then Lange discussed the calls from the title company and from A.T. & T.

Maude cried between her confusion and unbelief. The thought of having money seemed beyond her comprehension, for she never had any.

She still couldn't comprehend good fortune, but she was so thrilled her folks had come back to her in her dreams—-to tell her the good news first.

"I've missed Mum and Dad so much. Now I know they are still with me."

CHAPTER 55
NEWS HEADLINES.

CAL SCHANK DIES.

Cal Schank, who was shot at his preliminary hearing in the Los Angeles County courtroom, is dead. He never recovered from the three shots that entered his body. He was charged with kidnapping and interstate prostitution. Lexus Taylor, his defense attorney, who was also shot at the same hearing died a week ago.

Both were shot while sitting at the defense table. The District Attorney has not charged anyone with the crime which has turned into a double murder. Or was it murder and suicide?

Australian Mrs. Reginald Robertson is considered by some to be a suspect. Her husband was virtually beaten to death in an attempt to rescue their daughter, Della.

Della testified at the hearing it was Schank who had her drugged and shipped to South America. Both were rescued by the Australian Navy on ANZAC Day.

This news seemed to only increase the tempo of public interest in the case such as:

WERE MILITARY LEADERS DUMPED FROM PLANE ?

Where are the two Military Junta leaders that reportedly left their small port city for Panama? It is alleged there was a scuffle on the plane and in the resulting melee the door of the plane was opened and the leaders fell out. The Australian Naval command states they know nothing of the incident.

**Several days later. A newspaper article that took
the public by surprise.**

Prominent Santa Barbara physician, Emery Smith, and newly widowed Martha Schank were wed in Monterey, California where they are spending their honeymoon. When asked about being the sole heir to her husband's vast resources she replied, "I have moved out of the estate. Whatever is not needed to satisfy people that have been wronged is going to crippled children's hospitals. I am not taking a dime of his ill gotten gains."

The Papuans were restive and wanted to return home. Lorie and Della had become close friends. Each was getting some psychiatric counseling, but they found a special comfort in confiding to each other.

Lorie's parents were both deceased and Lorie asked Della if she could return to Australia with them, where she would feel much safer from any mob reprisals..

Mrs. Robertson hounded the District Attorney's office with phone calls, after the Doctor said, "I believe Reginald has recovered sufficiently to return to Australia by boat."

She said, "He has spent his life at sea, and a comfortable trip in a ship like the Monterey might do him good, but we've spent all our savings trying to rescue Della."

When that word reached the Australian and American Press everyone wanted to contribute. Contributors ranged from newsboys to wealthy residents of Montecito. The later offered to pay for the entire trip. The men from the Australian Light Cruiser wanted to help.

American, New Zealand and British Military who had served with the Aussies all wanted to assist the Robertsons.

With that outpouring of public support the District Attorney called the Governor's office and asked for a meeting. Both men had greater political ambitions and both were worried this unsolved case could become a political football.

The meeting was held and one day later a special news release was made.

NO CHARGES WILL BE MADE AGAINST
THE ROBERTSONS

The District Attorney of Los Angeles County in consultation with the Governor have decided there is insufficient evidence to make any charges against the Robertsons. Both her husband who vainly attempted to rescue their daughter, Della, and Della have not recovered, but are anxious to return to Australia..

"After the inhuman treatment suffered by Della and her Father at the hands of Schank and his vicious associates it would be cruel and inhuman to torture them further. Taxpayers money and police time can be put to much better use."

With that good news their departure was expedited for fear some reversal of the good news might occur. Lorie Owens was to accompany them.

At the sailing The Robertsons, Lorie Owens and the Papuans were confronted by dozens of photographers and newsmen. The Papuans, small in stature, with fuzzy hair, pipes in their mouths and broad grins on their face were in stark contrast to the others.

Bo and Mo were very attentive to Lange with Reg helping interpret. Bo and Mo concluded, "We were police boys after battle of Buna. We think we remember you at Doboduro, maybe Finschaven."

Lange responded with, "I will never forget the fuzzy wuzzies, as we called you. Too many memories to ever forget."

"You come visit us. We much like to see you again."

"I would like to see you again, but too many bad times in the jungle for me to return. Very hard on me. Still not recovered from malaria and other jungle diseases."

Soon the Monterey was moving away from the dock. The passengers had flung their confetti overboard as fond farewells and Bon Voyages resounded.

The Chinese had not attended the departure as they preferred to stay in the background. However, they had invited Lange to dinner at the Tong immediately after the ship departed.

At the meal he sat between Ah Wing and Delores. Ah Wing said, "Lange, the Chinese must not be mentioned in connection with the Australian Navy rescue. Therefore your vital role in the rescue of Reginald and Della will never be known to the public.

."**However, in the strictest confidence I give you this information.** If ever in your lifetime you are in desperate need of something that can be solved by the Australian Navy contact fleet headquarters and say you are 'Earnest ANZAC50 Lange.'

"It is very simple. It means you participated on an exceptionally high level with their Navy on ANZAC Day 1950. Don't be surprised if some day you get a call and the man asks for Earnest ANZAC50 Lange. He may have an assignment for you."

Lange felt his stomach churn as he realized the complexity of life. He said to Ah Wing, "Thank you for the information. I'm out of the Army, but I guess I'm in a new war now."

Ah Wing reflected for almost a minute before he replied, "Wise Chinese Philosopher was facing many problems. He said, 'Problems must be considered as opportunities to participate in life.' You are lucky young man. You have many unusual opportunities."

Lange smiled as he thought, **He just told me, "Don't bitch, just go out and do it."**

Delores knew it was time to change the subject. She said, "We are going to remain in Los Angeles for another two weeks. Everyone is so tired and there are other matters to handle that were pushed aside due to this emergency.

"Chinese friends in Santa Barbara have invited us to visit them. We were going to take the early Southern Pacific 'Daylight' to San Francisco. We may stop in your city."

"Wonderful. Do you have a Tong there?"

"We have an association. Perhaps you should meet some of them."

Lange thought to himself, **"This world is made up of powerful groups of people."**

To Delores he answered, "I would like that."

There were many questions Lange wanted to ask, but he knew it was not the time. Instead the talk was about places to visit in Santa Barbara. The dinner hour was short and soon Lange sensed it was time for him to leave.

He thanked them for dinner and for their company, and once again pointed his blue coupe in the direction of Santa Barbara.

CHAPTER 56
THINGS END SURPRISINGLY WELL.

It had been a long day for Lange. He was keyed up enough that when he reached Ventura he decided not to stop at the cafe to see if Sally Stevens was working.

Seeing the Papuans again brought the war back to him. Driving the next 30 miles to Carpinteria on Hiway 101, with the Pacific Ocean virtually alongside made it so real again. He wondered if his service nightmares would ever cease?

He turned his mind to Maude. He had Maude's funds transferred to a trust account at the Bank of America, and would also act as a co-signer, as she had never previously written a check in her life. **"I almost feel like I'm her guardian angel."**

She had moved into the security of the apartment Martha had occupied, as the bank agreed she could be the subject of all kinds of problems by unscrupulous individuals. The apartment had a phone, but it was to remain unlisted, just as it had been for Martha.

Lange felt a great satisfaction as he thought of the small notation a few days ago in the local papers.

British Society Tea
Maude Mayberry, retired Montecito housekeeper, is planning to return to England for an extended visit to her birthplace. She will be accompanied by two of her friends. She

will host a British Tea May 15th at the Society Headquarters. Time will be 2 P.M. She invites any of her friends she has worked with over the past 50 years.

Lange had taken the paper to Maude that evening **and she smiled so broadly.** "I never had me enough money to buy a newspaper, much less be in society."

Lange and Jean found time once a week in the evening to meet at Stearns Wharf and walk beautiful Cabrillo Boulevard. They had another dancing date and again Jean did not invite him into the home she shared with her Mother.

They took a cautious approach to the second dancing date, but they sat in Lange's car for an hour after the date. It wasn't all spent in conversation.

THEN ONE DAY A BLOCKBUSTER HIT THE PRESS.

BUSINESS AND POLITICAL SCANDAL
It has been discovered Schank Investment Company had been accumulating pictures of various business and political leaders engaging in indiscreet liaisons with beautiful women. The potential for blackmail was enormous!

Most of the pictures were taken at various conventions, but some of the action may have taken place in their place of business or political office.

It is not known who has possession of these files, but it is rumored that Hoover, Head of the FBI, is demanding the files be turned over to him.

That article let loose a torrent of arguments and protests.

WHO DOES AN UNAUTHORIZED PHOTO BELONG TO ?
Powerful business men and politicians are demanding that any such blackmail material be immediately destroyed with criminal and civil liability against any leaks.

It was additionally revealed that the blackmail scheme covered about 150 men and wails of anguish can be heard from many who use conventions as a means of playing rover boy. This news seems to destroy any remaining urgency to prosecute the killer of Schank.

It did not do away with requests from many, particularly attorneys, that Lexus Taylor's killer be brought to justice.

The newspapers were full of juicy discussions, and spicy quotes as to the pictures.

Some small events were taking place in Lange's life.
He received three phone calls several days apart. All offered to make his life more complex. The first from Lt. Merced, of SBPD, asked him again if he would consider becoming a private eye and taking over The Shadows business.

The second phone call was from Treasury Agent Hank asking him if he would meet with him and seriously consider being a Treasury Agent.

The third call was from Mr. Stanford Potter. He met with Potter at his estate and the gist of the matter was that Potter had a special assignment he wanted Lange to take on. Potter claimed it was right down Lange's alley. It would give him a serious opportunity to further evaluate a possible part or full time relationship with Treasury.

The debate over the custody of the incriminating pictures was heating up.

PRESIDENT TRUMAN URGED TO TAKE CUSTODY
There is a fairly authentic rumor that certain business men and politicians are so worried their transgressions may have been recorded on film they are trying to get the President into the act. President Truman declines to discuss the matter.

After days of pleas, threats and political slandering

TREASURY ANNOUNCES ALL PHOTOS DESTROYED

It is reported that notwithstanding a subpoena by Edgar Hoover the Treasury Depart-ment has destroyed all the incriminating photos. Unsubstantiated is the report that the buck did pass to President Truman.

One morning on the 7 A.M. news, and in the morning News-Press, came the wrap-up.

TREASURY DEPARTMENT TOPPLES
ANOTHER MOB FAMILY.

Ruppert Snyder was the Los Angeles area General Manager of Schank Investment Company. His complete confession was obtained by Lt. Alex Brown of the Los Angeles Police Dept. This news was never made public for fear many guilty parties would flee the country. Cal Schank had been arrested for kidnapping and interstate prostitution.

His offices were closed. His defense attorney was Lexus Taylor, long known as a successful mob defense attorney. It was thought Cal Schank headed his own operation. Schank and Taylor were both seriously wounded at the preliminary hearing. They have both died.

With the confession of Ruppert Snyder along with a thorough investigation of Schank's files it was realized that Schank did not make the big decisions such as the photo blackmail operation that had been building for years.

The final break came when it was proven beyond question

THE REAL HEAD OF THE MOB WAS
ATTORNEY LEXUS TAYLOR

------THE END-----WELL – NOT QUITE-------.

CHAPTER 57
BRISBANE, AUSTRALIA AND SANTA BARBARA

The Robertsons were unable to return to their home in Rockhampton, Queensland. This was because Reginald needed major medical facilities for continued treatment. They were available in Brisbane, much closer to Rockhampton than Sydney would be.

International News Services were tossing the news ball between the U.S. and Australia.

It was reported that Lorie Owens would apply for Australian citizenship and she and Della were like twins. One never going anyplace without the other.

They were living with Reginald and his wife, Joyce, as he needed 24 hour care.

Back in the States the discovery that **it was really THE EVIL EMPIRE OF LEXUS TAYLOR** removed any support from the public to find who fired the fatal shots.

When the news was verified that Mrs. Robertson was a crack shot there was increased speculation she did it. The press was on her back for her comments.

Finally one day she answered, "The day of the shooting I told Lt. Brown they were shot by the Ghost of the Jolly Swag Man, like in Waltzing Matilda".

Back in the States the Chinese were harassed by reporters and various allegations and insinuations were made. The Chinese refused to issue a statement, or talk to reporters.

There was continued speculation among the public, amateur sleuths and the news media as to what actually happened. Not the least of these were Lange who even subscribed to one of the big Los Angeles papers so he would not miss any juicy tidbit.

Many journalists and cartoonists played up the discomfiture that thousands of wayward husbands were going through wondering if a trial developed would their picture show up? **Were they one of the 150 'in the nude?' They were not 'in the mood' to find out.**

Additionally journalists and cartoonists were having a field day on the subject of 'The Jolly Swag Man.' Sales of Waltzing Matilda skyrocketed moving it to number one.

Neither the Chief, Lt. Brown or any other LAPD officer would comment on the case. However, it was concluded by several retired detectives that Mrs. Robertson could easily have done the job. **They said, "She got to the rest room before being searched.**

"This permitted her to tear up the glove and flush it down the toilet into the Los Angeles sewer system. The glove kept her palms clean and her fingerprints off the weapon."

Lt. Brown came to Santa Barbara on a Friday to consult with the SBPD. Saturday morning he and Lange went fishing off Stearns Wharf. At lunch Lt. Brown looked at Lange saying, **"O.K. Lange, lets hear your opinion."**

Lange smiled and replied, "I thought you would never ask."

Then he became serious and said, "I figure Mrs. Robertson vented her hatred for Schank in front of her daughter and Delores Lee and told the Chinese of her plans to kill Schank. **"She felt certain no jury would ever convict her.**

"By this time Dr. Fu had ascertained the hits on Lorie and Della, which could have easily killed Delores as well, must have come from Lexus Taylor. Additionally, Dr. Fu must have concluded Lexus was really the big gun. He confided all that to Mrs. Robertson. To involve Delores was where the mob crossed the Chinese line in the sand."

Lange looked at Lt. Brown and asked, "Am I too far out?"

"No, you're batting 100% in my league. Keep going."

"The Chinese do things well! If Schank had declined to bring Lorie to the dinner at the Pagoda you had another search warrant in your pocket and you would have rescued Lorie."

"Yes, we would have broken into the Schankrila that same night and rescued her."

"Now to return to Mrs. Robertson several plots were concocted. They knew that if Mrs. Robertson was caught she would never be convicted. She could claim insanity. That clinched the deal. Della was to faint, the Papuans were to create the noise and confusion. Mrs. Robertson, a crack shot, was to shoot Schank and Lexus. **She did a great job!**

"She got a real break by getting to the rest room before being searched. **The glove and maybe some extra shells all went into the Los Angeles sewer system,** where Schank and Lexus also belonged — well, I'm sure they are in hell now where they belong. I don't doubt she threw up in the rest room. **I'll bet she was nervous!"**

"Lange, you figured it out 100%. You have an excellent mind, but what about her comments to me about the about the Ghost of the Jolly Swag Man?"

"I wouldn't be surprised if she believed he was helping her–actually with her!"

A Los Angeles reporter flew to Brisbane and came back with the following.

One of the top Admirals in the Australian Navy visited the Robertsons. Afterwards he said, "We regret to learn that Merchant Mariner Reginald Robertson has suffered such severe injuries he will never again be able to serve as a sea going officer.

"As there is a strong rumor the Aussie Navy rescued him and his daughter Della from certain death on ANZAC Day, perhaps we should be partly responsible for him. If he ever sails on any ship of mine I would consider it an honor to give up my cabin for him."

And all over Australia you could hear. "Hip, hip, hooray, and good-o-mates."

And Waltzing Matilda being sung with even more gusto!

[1]Part of the plot in the Author's mystery, The Case Of The Missing Gambler.

[2]The Author actually took this job on State Street. Time period was approximately two years earlier.

[3] At the time this mystery is being written $476,000 would not even buy one of the cottages.

[4]Now in 1995 that former small hotel is an absolutely gorgeous residence.

[5]*The author knows firsthand how it was to be caught by a Japanese Zero while in an unarmed C-47 in the pass in the Owen Stanley Range in New Guinea where you can't turn or land or do any evasive action. You don't pray, you just say good-bye world. Then 50 years later you can't believe you made it. The jungle was so dense they wouldn't have looked for the plane or your body. There was NO survival percentage. You wouldn't have even gotten one of those little white crosses in a clearing in the tall Kunai Grass in the Jungle.*

[6]. In the 3rd through the 5th grades the Author stood outside the main entrance of Jantzen selling the Saturday Evening Post. Less than 20 years later he designed systems for Jantzen, as an employee of the Standard Register Corporation. That is America at it's best.

[7] So now the Car Manufacturers do undercoat the cars at the factory.

[8] The Author has two pictures of that building. In case he ever weakens and becomes a Private Eye.

www.ingramcontent.com/pod-product-compliance
Lightning Source LLC
Chambersburg PA
CBHW030013180626
46810CB00001B/13